HEALING RYKO

I groped for a hold on the energy world, the thread of the song slipping from my clumsy grasp. I knew only one dragon command; the call of union. I screamed it out—*Eona.* Within the roar of my despair, I heard her song sharpen and hook my flailing focus, drawing me back into the golden melding of our *Hua.*

Even as our joy rang out once more, an influx of sour energy buffeted our union. The ten dragons. We braced against their heavy pressure, caught between Ryko's desperate need and their hammering power.

If the song broke again, Ryko would die.

We sang his healing, barely withstanding the savage energy that clawed at our connection. Around us, the ten bereft dragons shimmered into pale, howling outlines.

The Rat Dragon suddenly reared from his corner, his tense pain replaced by sinuous speed. He rammed the opaque Ox Dragon beside him, then launched above us, sweeping in a circle that drove back the other advancing dragons. Deep inside we felt another voice, screaming with effort.

Lord Ido.

FIREBIRD
WHERE FANTASY TAKES FLIGHT™

The Blue Sword	Robin McKinley
Chalice	Robin McKinley
Eon	Alison Goodman
Factotum: The Foundling's Tale, Part III	D. M. Cornish
Fire	Kristin Cashore
Fire and Hemlock	Diana Wynne Jones
Firebirds Rising: An Anthology of Original Science Fiction and Fantasy	Sharyn November, ed.
Foundling: The Foundling's Tale, Part I	D. M. Cornish
The Harp of the Grey Rose	Charles de Lint
I Am Mordred	Nancy Springer
Incarceron	Catherine Fisher
Lamplighter: The Foundling's Tale, Part II	D. M. Cornish
The Riddle of the Wren	Charles de Lint
Sapphique	Catherine Fisher
Singing the Dogstar Blues	Alison Goodman

EONA
THE LAST DRAGONEYE

ALISON GOODMAN

FIREBIRD
AN IMPRINT OF PENGUIN GROUP (USA) INC.

FIREBIRD
Published by the Penguin Group
Penguin Group (USA) Inc., 345 Hudson Street, New York, New York 10014, U.S.A.
Penguin Group (Canada), 90 Eglinton Avenue East, Suite 700, Toronto, Ontario, Canada M4P 2Y3
(a division of Pearson Penguin Canada Inc.)
Penguin Books Ltd, 80 Strand, London WC2R 0RL, England
Penguin Ireland, 25 St Stephen's Green, Dublin 2, Ireland (a division of Penguin Books Ltd)
Penguin Group (Australia), 250 Camberwell Road, Camberwell, Victoria 3124, Australia
(a division of Pearson Australia Group Pty Ltd)
Penguin Books India Pvt Ltd, 11 Community Centre, Panchsheel Park, New Delhi – 110 017, India
Penguin Group (NZ), 67 Apollo Drive, Rosedale, Auckland 0632, New Zealand
(a division of Pearson New Zealand Ltd.)
Penguin Books (South Africa) (Pty) Ltd, 24 Sturdee Avenue, Rosebank, Johannesburg 2196, South Africa

Registered Offices: Penguin Books Ltd, 80 Strand, London WC2R 0RL, England

First published in the United States of America by Viking,
a member of Penguin Group (USA) Inc., 2011
Published by Firebird, an imprint of Penguin Group (USA) Inc., 2012

1 3 5 7 9 10 8 6 4 2

LIBRARY OF CONGRESS CATALOGING-IN-PUBLICATION DATA IS AVAILABLE
ISBN: 978-0-670-06311-6 (hc)

Firebird ISBN 978-0-14-242093-5

Printed in the United States of America

Set in Goudy Old Style

For Ron

EONA

Ox Dragon
N
Tiger Dragon
NNE
Rabbit Dragon
ENE
Dragon Dragon
(Mirror Dragon)
E
Snake Dragon
ESE
Horse Dragon
SSE
Goat Dragon
S
Monkey Dragon
SSW
Rooster Dragon
WSW
Dog Dragon
W
Pig Dragon
WNW
Rat Dragon
NNW
壽

Ox Dragon
Compass: NORTH
Color: Purple
Dragoneye: Lord Tyron (deceased)
Keeper of Determination

Tiger Dragon
Compass: NORTH-NORTHEAST
Color: Green
Dragoneye: Lord Elgon (deceased)
Keeper of Courage

Rabbit Dragon
Compass: EAST-NORTHEAST
Color: Pink
Dragoneye: Lord Silvo (deceased)
Keeper of Peace

Dragon Dragon (Mirror Dragon)
Compass: EAST
Color: Red
Dragoneye: Eona (Before Eona, the Mirror Dragon had been missing for over 500 years.)
Keeper of Truth

Snake Dragon
Compass: EAST-SOUTHEAST
Color: Copper
Dragoneye: Lord Chion (deceased)
Keeper of Insight

Horse Dragon
Compass: SOUTH-SOUTHEAST
Color: Orange
Dragoneye: Lord Dram (deceased)
Keeper of Passion

Goat Dragon
Compass: SOUTH
Color: Silver
Dragoneye: Lord Tiro (deceased)
Keeper of Kindness

Monkey Dragon
Compass: SOUTH-SOUTHWEST
Color: Ebony
Dragoneye: Lord Jessam (deceased)
Keeper of Resourcefulness

Rooster Dragon
Compass: WEST-SOUTHWEST
Color: Brown
Dragoneye: Lord Bano (deceased)
Keeper of Confidence

Dog Dragon
Compass: WEST
Color: Ivory
Dragoneye: Lord Garon (deceased)
Keeper of Honesty

Pig Dragon
Compass: WEST-NORTHWEST
Color: Dove Gray
Dragoneye: Lord Meram (deceased)
Keeper of Generosity

Rat Dragon
Compass: NORTH-NORTHWEST
Color: Blue
Dragoneye: Lord Ido
Keeper of Ambition

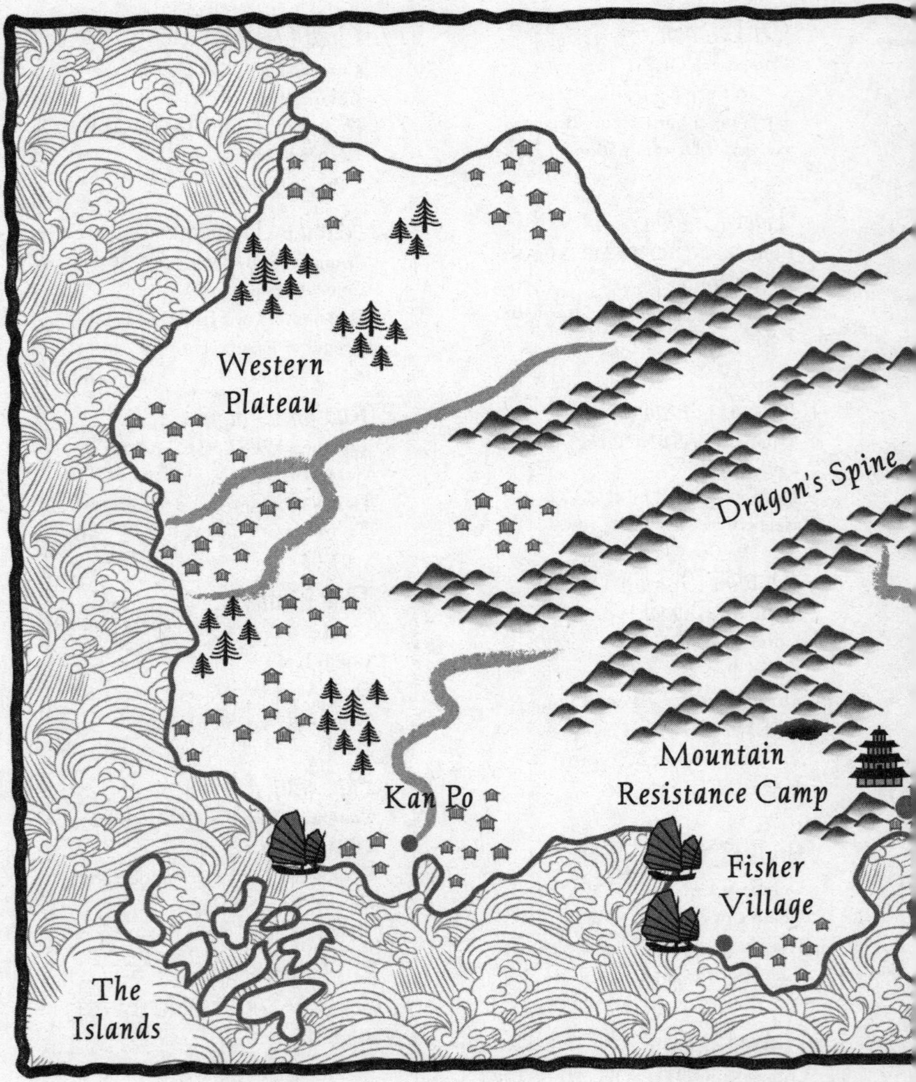

THE EMPIRE OF THE

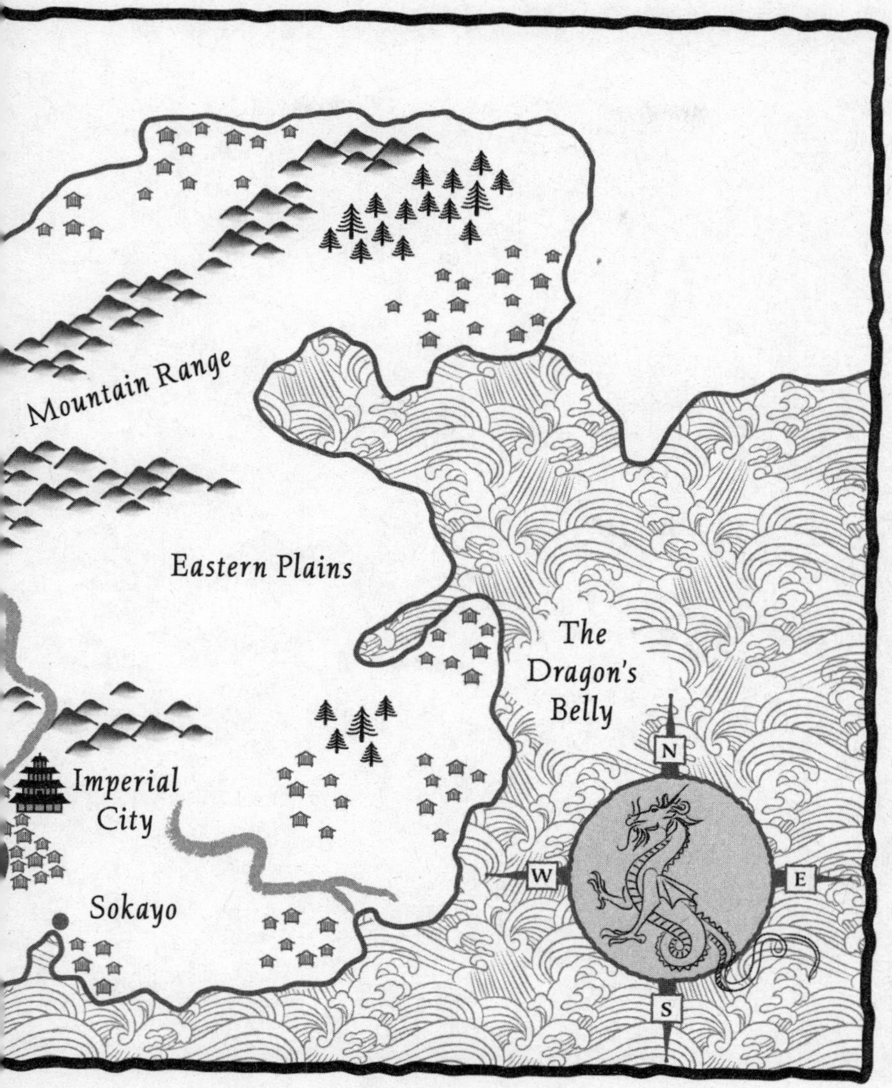

CELESTIAL DRAGONS

PREFACE

From the hand of Teacher Prahn, Imperial librarian and tutor of His Majesty, Kygo, rightful heir to the Imperial throne.

A WISE MAN once wrote: *In war, truth is the first casualty.* It is for this reason that I write a true account of the seizure of the Imperial palace and throne by High Lord Sethon, a day after the death of his brother, our revered Emperor of Peace and Harmony.

I was present during the army's brutal attack on the palace and saw many of my eunuch brethren slaughtered, although they held no weapons. I saw the harem invaded, the Imperial Guard cut down, and the royal household assaulted. To my eternal grief, I also saw the infant second heir to the throne and his mother murdered by High Lord Sethon himself. It has been officially reported that Prince Kygo—the first heir, who was anointed Pearl Emperor before his uncle's savage coup—was killed in the battle. However, no body has been found, and I have heard that he escaped with the remnants of his guard; may this be a truth from the gods' lips.

I can confirm a report that Lord Ido—the Rat Dragoneye—was instrumental in killing almost all of his fellow Dragoneyes and their apprentices in the quest for their power. I saw the bodies, and we have all felt the tremors in the earth and the thunder across the sky that is no doubt the sorrow of their ten dragons. Now the only Dragoneye Lords alive are the treacherous Lord Ido and the new Mirror Dragoneye, Lord Eon, who was seen escaping the Palace. Lord Ido's apprentice—Dillon—is also believed to have escaped. It is not known if Dillon shares his master's lust for power, but if he is indeed alive, he may become the Rat Dragoneye very soon. Lord Ido tried to double-cross High Lord Sethon and is now in the Imperial cells. It is said he cannot call his power and is at the mercy of the High Lord's rage.

No one knows the whereabouts of Lord Eon. I pray that he is hidden far from the City. I know that he was under the protection of Ryko, one of the elite Shadow Men guards, and Lady Dela, a twin soul with a man's body and a woman's spirit, whose resourcefulness is legendary among the courtiers. It can only be hoped that their combined skills will keep the young Dragoneye safe. Amid all the fear and lies circulating the Palace, a foul whisper has arisen that Lord Eon, a brother eunuch, is in a fact a girl. I have been in the presence of the new lord, and his delicate features and frame are usual in one of our kind who has made the sacrifice so young. I mention this rumor only to stop the profane idea of a female dragoneye from spreading through our wounded land and creating more panic.

I do not know how our Empire can survive with only two Dragoneyes and their beasts to control the elements, especially when one Dragoneye is an imprisoned traitor and the other an untrained boy. Although Lord Eon is quick and clever, he cannot control the earth energies by himself. For as long as can be remembered, it has taken the combined power of eleven Dragoneyes and their beasts to nurture the land. When the missing twelfth dragon—the Mirror Dragon—returned from exile and chose Lord Eon as the first Mirror Dragoneye in five hundred years, it was seen as an omen of renewed strength and good fortune. I pray that this is so, and that the return of the Mirror Dragon to the Circle of Twelve spirit beasts is not an omen of annihilation. A resistance force has long been gathering against High Lord Sethon's brutal war-mongering, but now they will have to stand against the entire army, and such a struggle will tear our land apart.

I will endeavour to get this account out of the palace. If you are reading this, I beg you to spread its truth as far as you can. I also ask that you offer a prayer to the goddess of death for my spirit. One of my eunuch brothers has betrayed me to High Lord Sethon and told the false emperor of my close association with his nephew. I am cornered in my library, and although I know nothing, I will soon be just another tortured body among the many in the High Lord's search for the Pearl Emperor and Lord Eon.

—Written by Prahn, son of Mikor,
on this twentieth day of the new Rat Dragon year

CHAPTER ONE

THE DRAGONS WERE CRYING.

I stared across the choppy, gray sea and concentrated on the soft sound within me. For three daybreaks, ever since we had fled the conquered palace, I had stood on this same rock and felt the keening of the ten bereft dragons. Usually it was only a faint wail beneath the golden song of my own Mirror Dragon. This morning it was stronger. Harsher.

Perhaps the ten spirit beasts had rallied from their grief and returned to the Circle of Twelve. I took a deep breath and eased into the unnerving sensation of mind-sight. The sea before me blurred into surging silver as my focus moved beyond the earthly plane, into the pulsing colors of the parallel energy world. Above me, only two of the twelve dragons were in their celestial domains: Lord Ido's blue Rat Dragon in the north-northwest, the beast's massive body arched in pain, and my own red dragon in the east. The Mirror Dragon. The queen. The other ten dragons had still not returned from wherever spirit beasts fled to grieve.

The Mirror Dragon turned her huge head toward me, the gold pearl under her chin glowing against her crimson scales. Tentatively, I formed our shared name in my mind—*Eona*—and called her power. Her answer was immediate: a rush of golden energy that cascaded through my body. I rode the rising joy, reveling in the union. My sight split between earth and heaven: around me were rocks and sea and sky, and at the same time, through her great dragon eyes, the beach surged below in timeless rhythms of growth and decay. Silvery pinpoints of *Hua*—the energy of life—were scurrying, swimming, burrowing across a swirling rainbow landscape. Deep within me, a sweet greeting unfurled—the wordless touch of her dragon spirit against mine—leaving the warm spice of cinnamon on my tongue.

Suddenly, the rich taste soured. We both sensed a wall of wild energy at the same time, a rushing, shrieking force that was coming straight for us. Never before had we felt such driven pain. Crushing pressure punched through our golden bond and loosened my earthly grip. I staggered across uneven rock that seemed to fall away from me. The Mirror Dragon screamed, rearing to meet the boiling wave of need. I could feel no ground, no wind, no earthly plane. There was only the whirling, savage clash of energies.

"Eona!"

A voice, distant and alarmed.

The crashing sorrow tore at my hold on earth and heaven. I was spinning, the bonds of mind and body stretched and splitting. I had to get out or I would be destroyed.

"Eona! Are you all right?"

It was Dela's voice—an anchor from the physical world. I grabbed at it and wrenched myself free of the roaring power. The world snapped back into sand and sea and sunlight. I doubled over, gagging on a bitter vinegar that was cut with grief—the taste of the ten bereft dragons.

They were back. Attacking us. Even as I thought it, a deeper part of me knew I was wrong—they would not attack their queen. Yet I had felt their *Hua* pressing upon us. Another kind of terror seized me. Perhaps this was the start of the String of Pearls, the weapon that brought together the power of all twelve dragons—a weapon born from the death of every Dragoneye except one.

But that was just a story, and I was not the last Dragoneye standing. The Rat Dragon was still in the celestial circle, and that meant at least one Rat Dragoneye was still alive, whether it be Lord Ido, or his apprentice, Dillon. I shivered—somehow I knew Lord Ido was not dead, although I could not explain my certainty. It was as if the man was watching me, waiting for his chance to seize my power again. He believed another story about the String of Pearls—that the union of his power and body with mine would create the weapon. He had nearly succeeded in forcing that union, too. Sometimes I could still feel his iron grip around my wrists.

"Are you all right?" Dela called again.

She was at the top of the steep path, and although she was unable to see or sense the dragons, she knew something was wrong. I held up my trembling hand, hoping she could not see the afterwash of fear. "I'm fine."

Yet I had left my dragon to face that bitter wave of need. There was little I could do to help, but I could not leave her alone. Gathering courage with my next breath, I focused my mind-sight and plunged back into the energy world.

The crashing, rolling chaos was gone; the celestial plane was once more a smooth ebb and flow of jewel colors. The Mirror Dragon looked calmly at me, her attention brushing across my spirit. I longed to feel her warmth again, but I let her presence pass by. If our communion had somehow called the grieving dragons from their exile, I could not risk their return. I could barely direct my own dragon's power, let alone manage the force of ten spirit-beasts reeling from the brutal slaughter of their Dragoneyes. And if these sorrowing creatures were now lying in wait for our every union, I had to find a way to fend off their desolation or I would never learn the dragon arts that controlled the elements and nurtured the land.

In his place in the north-northwest, the blue dragon was still curled in agony. Yesterday I had tried to call his power, as I had in the palace, but this time he did not respond. No doubt the beast's pain was caused by Lord Ido. As was all our pain.

With a sigh, I once again released my hold on the energy plane. The pulsing colors shifted back into the solid shapes and constant light of the beach, clearing to reveal Dela's approaching figure. Even dressed as a fisherman, and with her arm in a sling, she walked like a court lady, a graceful sway at odds with the rough tunic and trousers. Since she was a Contraire—a man who chose to live as a woman—her return to manly clothes and habits had seemed like an easy disguise. Not so. But then, who was I to talk? After four years of pretending to be a boy, I found my return to womanhood just as awkward. I eyed Dela's small hurried steps and elegant bearing as she crossed the sand; she was more woman than I would ever be.

I picked my way across the rocks to meet her, finding my footing with a smooth ease that made my heart sing. My union with the Mirror Dragon had healed my lame hip. I could walk and run without pain or limp. There had not been much time or occasion to celebrate the wondrous gift: one dawn sprint along the beach, each slapping step a shout of exaltation; and tiny moments like this—swift, guilty pleasures among all the fear and grief.

Dela closed the short space between us, her poise breaking into a stumbling run. I caught her outstretched hand.

"Is he worse?" I asked.

The answer was in Dela's dull, red-rimmed eyes. Our friend Ryko was dying.

"Master Tozay says his bowels have leaked into his body and poisoned him."

I knew Ryko's injuries were terrible, but I had never believed he would succumb to them. He was always so strong. As one of the Shadow Men, the elite eunuch guards who protected the royal family, he usually fortified his strength and male energy by a daily dose of Sun Drug. Perhaps three days without it had weakened his body beyond healing. Before the coup, I had also taken a few doses of the Sun Drug in the mistaken belief it would help me unite with my dragon. In fact, it had done the opposite, by quelling my female energy. It had also helped suppress my moon days; as soon as I stopped taking it three days ago, I bled. The loss of such a strong drug would surely take a heavy toll on Ryko's injured body. I looked out at a heavy bank of clouds on the horizon—no doubt caused by the dragons' turmoil—and shivered as the warm dawn breeze sharpened into a cold wind. There would be more rain soon, more floods, more devastating earthshakes. And because Lord Ido had murdered the other Dragoneyes, it would all be unchecked by dragon power.

"Tozay insists we leave Ryko and move on," Dela added softly, "before Sethon's men arrive."

Her throat convulsed against a sob. She had removed the large black pearl that had hung from a gold pin threaded through the skin over her windpipe—the symbol of her status as a Contraire. The piercing was too obvious to wear, but I knew it would have pained Dela to lose such an emblem of her true twin soul identity. Although that pain would be nothing compared to her anguish if we were forced to abandon Ryko.

"We can't leave him," I said.

The big islander had fought so hard to stop Lord Ido from seizing my dragon power. Even after he was so badly wounded, he had led us out of the captured palace to the safety of the resistance. No, we could not leave Ryko. But we could not move him, either.

Dela wrapped her arms around her thin body, cradling her despair. Without the formal court makeup, her angular features tipped more to the masculine, although her dark eyes held a woman's pain—a woman forced to choose between love and duty. I had never loved with such devotion. From what I had seen, it brought only suffering.

"We have to go," she finally said. "You can't stay here, it's too dangerous. And we must find the Pearl Emperor. Without your power, he will not defeat Sethon."

My power—inherited through the female bloodline, the only hereditary Dragoneye power in the circle of twelve. So much was expected of it, and yet I still had no training. No control. I stroked the small red folio bound against my arm by its living rope of black pearls. The gems stirred at my touch, clicking softly into a tighter embrace. At least I had the journal of my Dragoneye ancestress, Kinra, to study. Every night, Dela tried to decipher some of its Woman Script, the secret written language of women. So far, progress had been slow—not only was the journal written in an ancient form of the script, but most of it was also in code. I hoped Dela would soon find the key and read about Kinra's union with the Mirror Dragon. I needed a Dragoneye's guidance and experience, even if it was only through an ancient journal. I also needed some counsel; if I put my power in the service of Kygo to help him take back his rightful throne, then wasn't I breaking the Covenant of Service? The ancient agreement prohibited the use of dragon power for war.

Putting aside my misgivings, I said, "Did you see the imperial edict? Sethon is already calling himself Dragon Emperor, even though there are still nine days of Rightful Claim left."

Dela nodded. "He has declared that both the old emperor's sons are dead." I heard the rise of doubt in her voice. "What if it is true?"

"It's not," I said quickly.

We had both seen High Lord Sethon murder his infant nephew as well as the child's mother. But his other nephew, eighteen years old and true heir to the throne, had escaped. I had watched him ride away to safety with his Imperial Guard.

Dela chewed on her lip. "How can you be so sure the Pearl Emperor is still alive?"

I *wasn't* sure, but the possibility that Sethon had found and killed Kygo was too terrible to contemplate. "We would have heard otherwise. Tozay's spy network is extensive."

"Even so," Dela said, "they have not found his whereabouts. And Ryko . . ." She turned her head as if it was the wind that brought tears to her eyes.

Only Ryko knew where his fellow Imperial Guards had hidden the Pearl Emperor. Ever cautious, he had not shared the information. Now the blood fever had taken his mind.

"We could ask him again," I said. "He may recognize us. I have heard that there is often a brief lucid time before . . ."

"Before death?" she ground out.

I met her grief with my own. "Yes."

For a moment she stared at me, savage at my denial of hope, then bowed her head.

"We should go to him," she said. "Tozay says it will not be long now."

With one last look at the heavy clouds, I gathered up the front of my cumbersome skirt and climbed the path behind Dela, snatching a few moments of muted joy as I stretched into each strong, surefooted step.

The sturdy, weather-bleached fisher house had been our sanctuary for the past few days, its isolation and high vantage giving a clear view of any approach by sea or land. I paused to catch my breath at the top of the path and focused on the distant village. Small fishing boats were already heading out to sea, every one of them crewed by resistance with eyes sharp for Sethon's warships.

"Prepare yourself," Dela said as we reached the house. "His deterioration has been swift."

Last night I had sat with Ryko until midnight, and I had thought the islander was holding his own. But everyone knew that the predawn ghost hours were the most dangerous for the sick—the cold, gray loneliness eased the way of demons eager to drain an unguarded life force. Dela had taken the early watch, but it seemed that even her loving vigilance had been unable to ward off the dark ones.

She hung back as I pushed aside the red luck flags that

protected the doorway and entered the room. The village Beseecher still knelt in the far corner, but he was no longer chanting prayers for the ill. He was calling to Shola, Goddess of Death, and had covered his robes with a rough white cloak to honor the Otherworld Queen. A paper lantern swung on a red cord between his clasped hands, sending light seesawing across the drawn faces around Ryko's pallet: Master Tozay; his eldest daughter, Vida; and faithful, ugly Solly. I coughed, my throat catching with the thick clove incense that overlaid the stench of vomit and loose bowels.

In the eerie, swinging lamplight, I strained to see the figure lying on the low straw mattress. *Not yet*, I prayed, *not yet*. I had to say good-bye.

I heard Ryko's panting before I saw the over-quick rise and fall of his chest. He was stripped down to just a loincloth, his dark skin bleached to a gray waxiness, his once muscular frame wasted and frail.

The tight linen bandaging had been removed, exposing the festering wounds. His hand, resting on his chest, was black and bloated: the result of Ido's torture. More shocking was the long gash that sliced him from armpit to waist. Swollen sections of flesh had torn free from the rough stitching, showing pale bone and vivid red tissue.

The herbalist shuffled through the inner doorway. He carried a large bowl that trailed an astringent steam, his deep voice murmuring prayers over the slopping liquid. He had sat with me for some of my vigil last night, a kind, perpetually exhausted man who knew his skill was not up to his patient's injuries. But he had tried. And he was still trying, although it was clear that Ryko was walking the golden path to his ancestors.

Behind me, I heard Dela's breath catch into a sob. The sound brought Master Tozay's head up. He motioned us closer.

"Lady Dragoneye," he said softly, ushering me into his place by the pallet.

We had agreed not to use my title for safety's sake, but I let it pass without comment. The breach was Tozay's way of honoring Ryko's dutiful life.

Vida swiftly followed her father's example and shifted aside for Dela. The girl was not much older than my own sixteen years, but she carried herself with quiet dignity, an inheritance from her father. From her mother came her ready smile and a practical nature that did not recoil from oozing wounds or soiled bedclothes.

Dela knelt and covered Ryko's uninjured hand with her own. He did not stir. Nor did he move when the herbalist gently picked up his other, mutilated hand and lowered it into the bowl of hot water. The steam smelled of garlic and rosemary—good blood cleaners—although the whole arm looked beyond help.

I signaled to the Beseecher to stop his calls to Shola. There was no need to bring Ryko to the attention of the death goddess. She would arrive soon enough.

"Has he roused again? Has he spoken?" I asked.

"Nothing intelligible," Tozay said. He glanced at Dela. "I am sorry, but it is time you both left. My spies have Sethon heading this way. We will continue to care for Ryko and look for the Pearl Emperor, but you must go east and seek safety with Lady Dela's tribe. We will rendezvous with you once we have found His Highness."

Tozay was right. Although the thought of leaving Ryko was a hundredweight of stone in my spirit, we could delay no longer. The east was our best chance. It was also my dragon's domain, her stronghold of power. Perhaps my presence in her energy heartland would strengthen our bond and help me control this wild magic. It might also help the Mirror Dragon hold off the ten bereft dragons if they returned.

Dela shot a hard look at the resistance leader. "Surely this discussion can wait until—"

"I am afraid it cannot, lady." Tozay's voice was gentle but unyielding. "This must be your good-bye, and it must be swift."

She bowed her head, struggling against his blunt practicality. "My people will hide us beyond Sethon's reach," she finally said, "but the problem will be getting to them."

Tozay nodded. "Solly and Vida will travel with you."

Behind Dela, I saw Vida square her shoulders. At least one of us was ready for the challenge.

"They know how to contact the other resistance groups," Tozay added, "and they can act the part of your servants. You'll be just another merchant husband and wife on a pilgrimage to the mountains."

Dela's focus was back on Ryko. She lifted his inert fingers to her cheek, the swinging lamplight catching the shine of grief in her eyes.

"That may be," I said looking away from the tender moment, "but our descriptions are on the lips of every news-walker, and tacked to every tree trunk."

"So far you are still described as *Lord* Eon," Tozay said. His eyes flicked over my straight, strong body. "And crippled. The description for Lady Dela cautions everyone to look for a man or a woman, making it just as useless."

I was still described as Lord Eon? I was sure Ido would have told Sethon I was a girl, either under duress or as a bargaining tool. It did not make sense for him to protect me. Perhaps the Mirror Dragon and I had truly changed Ido's nature when we healed his stunted heart-point and forced compassion into his spirit. After all, that first union with my dragon had also mended my hip, and I was still healed. I pressed my hand against the waist pouch where I kept the family death plaques of my ancestors Kinra and Charra: a wordless prayer for the change to be permanent. Not only Lord Ido's change, but my own wondrous healing. I could not bear to lose my freedom again.

"Sethon will not only be looking for you, Lady Dragoneye," Master Tozay murmured, a touch to my sleeve drawing me a few steps away. "He will be seeking anyone close to you that he can use as a hostage. Give me the names of those who you think are in danger. We will do our best to find them."

"Rilla, my maid, and her son Chart," I said quickly. "They fled before the palace was taken." I thought of Chart; his badly twisted body would always attract attention, if only to drive others away before his ill fortune tainted them. I felt a small leap in my spirit: never again would I be spat on as a cripple or driven away. "Rilla would seek somewhere isolated."

Tozay nodded. "We will start in the mid-provinces."

"And Dillon—Ido's apprentice—but you are already searching for him. Be careful with Dillon; he is not in his right mind, and Sethon will be hunting him for the black folio, too."

I remembered the madness in Dillon's eyes when he had wrenched the black folio from me. He'd known the book was vital to Ido's plans for power and thought he could use it to trade with his Dragoneye master for his life. Instead, he had brought Sethon and the entire army upon himself. Poor Dillon. He did not truly understand what was in the small book he carried. He knew it held the secret to the String of Pearls. But its pages held another secret, one that terrified even Lord Ido: the way for royal blood to bind any Dragoneye's will and power.

"Is that all who may be at risk, my lady?" Tozay asked.

"Perhaps . . ." I paused, hesitant to add the next names. "I have not seen my family since I was very young. I hardly remember them. Perhaps Sethon would not—"

Tozay shook his head. "Sethon will try everything. So tell me, if they were found and held, could Sethon coerce you with their lives?"

Dread curdled my stomach. I nodded, and tried to dredge up more than the few dim images I had of my family. "I remember my mother's name was Lillia, and my brother was called Peri, but I think it was a pet name. I can only remember my father as Papa." I looked up at Tozay. "I know it is not much. But we lived by the coast—I remember fishing gear and a beach—and when my master first found me, I was laboring in the Enalo Salt Farm."

Tozay grunted. "That's west. I'll send word."

Beside us, the herbalist lifted Ryko's dripping hand from the bowl and laid it back on the pallet. He leaned over and stroked Ryko's cheek, then pressed his fingertips under the islander's jaw.

"A sharp increase of heat," he said into the silence. "The death fever. Ryko will join his ancestors very soon. It is time to wish him a safe journey."

He bowed, then backed away.

My throat ached with sorrow. Across the pallet, Solly's face was rigid with grief. He raised a fist to his chest in a warrior's salute. Tozay sighed and began a soft prayer for the dying.

"Do something," Dela said.

It was part plea, part accusation. I thought she was talking to the herbalist, but when I looked up she was staring at me.

"Do something," she repeated.

"What can I do? There is nothing I can do."

"You healed yourself. You healed Ido. Now heal Ryko."

I glanced around the ring of tense faces, feeling the press of their hope. "But that was at the moment of union. I don't know if I can do it again."

"Try." Dela's hands clenched into fists. "Just try. Please. He's going to die."

She held my gaze, as though looking away would release me from her desperation.

Could I save Ryko? I had assumed that Ido and I were

healed by the extra power of first union between dragon and Dragoneye. Perhaps that was not true. Perhaps the Mirror Dragon and I could always heal. But I could not yet direct my dragon's power. If we joined and tried to heal Ryko, we could fail. Or we could be ripped apart by the sorrow of the ten bereft dragons.

"Eona!" Dela's anguish snapped me out of my turmoil. "Do something. Please!"

Each of Ryko's labored breaths held a rattling catch.

"I can't," I whispered.

Who was I to play with life and death like a god? I had no knowledge. No training. I was barely a Dragoneye.

Even so, I was Ryko's only chance.

"He is dying because of you," Dela said. "You owe him your life and your power. *Don't fail him again.*"

Hard words, but they were true. Although I had lied to Ryko and betrayed his trust, he had still guarded my back. He had fought and suffered for the hope of my power. Yet what was the good of protecting such power if I did not have the courage to use it?

I gathered my skirt and kneeled beside the pallet, instinctively seeking more contact with the earth and the energy within it.

"I don't know what will happen," I said. "Everyone must stand back."

The herbalist hurriedly joined the Beseecher in the far corner of the room. Tozay ushered his daughter and Solly away from the bed, then turned back for Dela, but she ignored his outstretched hand.

"I'm staying." She saw the argument in my eyes and shook her head. "I will not leave him."

"Then don't touch him while I am calling my dragon." The first time I had called the Mirror Dragon, the wild surge of power had ripped through Lord Ido as his body locked mine against the harem wall.

Dela released Ryko's hand and sat back.

Perhaps the key to this healing magic was to touch Ryko, just as Ido had been touching me when the dragon and I had forced compassion into his stunted spirit. Gingerly, I placed my palm on the wasted muscle of Ryko's chest, above his heart. His skin was hot, and his heartbeat as fast and light as a captured bird's.

Taking a deep breath, I drew on my *Hua*, using the pulsing life force to focus my mind-sight into the energy world. There was a sudden shift in my vision, as though I had lurched forward. The room shimmered into the landscape of power that only a Dragoneye could see, swirling in intricate patterns of rainbow colors. Silvery *Hua* pumped through the transparent energy bodies of my friends and around the room, the flow irresistibly drawn east to the huge power presence of the red Mirror Dragon, and returning in abundance from the great beast. Over my left shoulder I caught sight of the coiled form of the Rat Dragon in the north-northwest. His energy was sluggish and thin.

There were still no other dragons in the celestial circle. Were they waiting for another chance to rush to their queen?

Grimly, I pushed away that fear and opened my inner pathways to the Mirror Dragon, calling out our shared name. She answered with a flood of energy, and the sweet spice of her greeting filled my senses until I could no longer contain my delight. A joyous laugh broke from me.

Across the bed, the transparent figure of Dela straightened. The power center at the base of her spine flared red with anger, the emotion igniting the other six centers that lay in line from sacrum to crown. I could see it as though she was made of glass; each spinning colored ball of energy stoking the next, bright with misunderstanding.

Although I stifled my joy, I did not stop to reassure Dela; the ten bereft dragons could return at any moment. I gave myself over to the Mirror Dragon's power, and was swept into a dizzying gold spiral. For a moment, all was bright, rhythmic color and a single pure note—the song of my dragon—then my vision split between earth and heaven.

Through dragon eyes high above, I saw the fading life force of Ryko, the light within each power center guttering like a spent candle. From my earthbound body, I saw my own transparent hand, flowing with golden *Hua*, touching Ryko's chest above his pale green heart point. Just like I had touched Ido. I focused all of my being into one thought: *Heal.*

Then I was more than a dragon conduit.

We were *Hua*.

As one, we understood the massive physical injuries that were too heavy for the weakened life force. There was not much time; Ryko was near the spirit world. Our power sought the delicate pattern of life that repeated in tiny twists of complexity. We sang to them, a silent harmony of healing that wove golden threads of energy into each intricate braid, quickening the cycle of repair. We drew power from the earth, from the air, channeling it all into his body, knitting together damaged flesh and sinew, broken bone and spirit.

"Holy gods," the herbalist gasped from the corner of the room. "Look, his wounds are closing."

His words penetrated the song, breaking my concentration. The lapse shivered through my connection with the Mirror Dragon. I felt my mind-sight waver, my vision narrowing back into the limits of my earthly body. The flow of *Hua* faltered.

Ryko wasn't healed yet; there was still so much to do.

I groped for a hold on the energy world, the thread of the song slipping from my clumsy grasp. I knew only one dragon command; the call of union. I screamed it out—*Eona.* Within the roar of my despair, I heard her song sharpen and hook my flailing focus, drawing me back into the golden melding of our *Hua.*

Even as our joy rang out once more, an influx of sour energy buffeted our union. The ten dragons. We braced against their heavy pressure, caught between Ryko's desperate need and their hammering power.

If the song broke again, Ryko would die.

We sang his healing, barely withstanding the savage energy that clawed at our connection. Around us, the ten bereft dragons shimmered into pale, howling outlines.

The Rat Dragon suddenly reared from his corner, his tense pain replaced by sinuous speed. He rammed the opaque Ox Dragon beside him, then launched above us, sweeping in a circle that drove back the other advancing dragons. Deep inside we felt another voice, screaming with effort.

Lord Ido.

We recoiled from the acrid orange taste of his power, but this time he was not seeking control. He was defending us.

The Rat Dragon reared again and met the wild energy of the ten bereft dragons. The roof of the fisher house exploded, raining wooden shingles and dust into the room. A beam plunged to the floor, crushing the Beseecher. The silvery flow of his *Hua* flickered and was gone.

"Get out," Tozay bellowed, dragging Vida toward the door. The herbalist scrambled up from the dead holy man and ran after them.

Dela threw herself over Ryko, shielding him from the falling wreckage. Chunks of wood showered my earthly body, but there was no pain. Tozay pushed Vida into Solly's arms.

"Get away from the buildings," he yelled, then turned back to Dela.

With the roof gone, we were suddenly beyond the room in a dizzying embrace of dark sky. Through dragon eyes we saw the bright figures of Vida, Solly, and the herbalist clear the house and run for the village road. We rolled through the black thundering clouds, feeling brutal power slamming into us. Our claws connected, ripping and throwing dragon bodies. Beside us, the Rat Dragon blocked the Snake Dragon, the clash of *Hua* shearing off the edge of a cliff far below.

Focus. It was Lord Ido's mind-voice, piercing the frenzy. *Block!*

How? I didn't know how!

My mind-sight plunged into the earthbound room—Tozay hauling Ryko upright—then lurched back into dragon-sight and the rolling battle across the sky. Below us, the sea was a boiling mass of energy, ramming tiny boats against the rocks and sweeping away a line of waterfront cottages. A dozen or so bright dots of *Hua* ran from the village buildings, the wall of water crashing over them, extinguishing their light.

"Eona." It was Dela, pulling at my earthly body.

For a moment, I came to myself and met her wild eyes. The walls were collapsing, creaking under the pounding power of a searing wind.

"Move," she yelled, pulling me toward the doorway as Tozay carried Ryko out into the courtyard.

Eona! Ido's mind-scream wrenched me back into the Mirror Dragon. We swirled, claws flailing against the agile pink Rabbit Dragon. Above, the Rat Dragon collided with the Tiger Dragon, the impact resonating through Ido's mind into our union.

For a bewildering second, we were in another room—a stone room—wrists and ankles shackled, pain pulsing through our flogged and broken body. Ido's body. Another shock wave as

Ido's dragon slammed into the other beast again, and suddenly we were small, crouched under a bush, black book open, dark words burning our mind—Dillon, screaming, *Find Eona, find Eona, find Eona.* Then he was gone, and we were back in the sky above the crumbling fisher house, claws slashing, shrieking our defiance. Around us the ten bereft dragons were closing the circle.

They must not close the circle, Ido's mind-voice rasped with pain and alarm. *Give me your power.*

No!

Below, Dela staggered out into the courtyard, half carrying my earthly body.

They will tear you apart. You will die. Give me your power!

No!

The combined power of the ten dragons battered us. We could not hold out much longer, but we could not give our power to Ido. Not after his brutal grab for it at the palace.

Help me stop them! Fear sharpened Ido's mind-voice.

Ten stark songs of mourning pounded against us, searching for the relief of union.

There was nowhere else to go. We did not have enough power, enough knowledge. With a howl of despair, we opened our pathways to Ido.

His desperate power burst through us, drawing up all our golden energy. We were emptied, defenseless. As one, the ten bereft dragons rushed at us, their need circling like a vise. With iron control, Ido and the Rat Dragon gathered our energies, binding them with the shrieking wind and crashing water.

Prepare! Ido's mind voice yelled.

He threw the massive weight of power outward, the strain searing through his mind into us. The booming explosion ripped through the circle of dragons, knocking them backward. Below us, the remains of the fisher house spun into the dark sky, the rest of the cliff collapsing into the sea.

Block now! Ido roared.

But we did not know how. The shockwave of power hit us like a hammer, slamming me back into my own body. For a moment, I saw Dela's face above mine, her strong arms cradling my head. I screamed, pain pulsing through every part of my being. But the agony was not all mine.

Help me, Ido's mind-voice gasped. *I can't—*

Then swirling blackness dragged me away from his tortured scream.

CHAPTER TWO

MY WHOLE BODY JERKED, forcing my eyes open. A white blur sharpened into the arch of a cotton canopy, sunshine flaring through its tied-down edges. I squinted against the light and the nagging pain in my temple. Another jolt rocked me and intensified the midsummer smell of straw. I was lying on a pallet, in an enclosed traveling cart. Gingerly, I raised my head and peered through an ill-fitting wood joint at the moving landscape. Terraced rice fields, the yellowing harvest flattened under high water.

"My lady?"

Ryko rose from somewhere near my feet, swaying as the cart hit a rut. For a moment, I was still in the fisher house, my hand on his laboring heart, then the memory shifted and I was back in the cart with Ryko before me. Alive and smiling. Awe caught my breath: we had saved him, the Mirror Dragon and I. But was he fully healed? Even as I opened my mouth to ask, a dizzying barrage of images swamped me: the golden song, the ten bereft dragons, the battle.

Lord Ido.

"He was in my mind again!" My voice was a dry croak. I struggled up on my elbows. "Ido was in my mind!"

And Dillon, too, for a moment. I was sure of it, although the image of him was not clear. I could still feel his terror.

Ryko moved toward me. He was favoring his right side. "What do you mean, my lady?"

"Ido drove back the other dragons." An echo of our mind union shuddered through me, doubling the pain in my head. So much power.

"Lord Ido was not in the village, my lady."

"No, he was in my mind again." Ryko winced as I clutched his arm. "He was in my mind. I had to let him. Do you see? I had to let him or we would have died or—"

"What do you mean, in your mind?" Ryko pulled away, the sudden distrust in his voice silencing me. "Surely Ido is dead."

"No." I closed my eyes, once again feeling the weight of iron shackles and the raw agony of flogged skin. "Sethon holds him prisoner. I saw through his eyes. I think he's dying." I felt a small surge of pity.

Ryko grunted. "A just end."

"Only if he could die twenty times over," I said quickly. Ido did not deserve my pity.

I sat up into a wave of dizziness and flung out a hand, finding an anchor against the wooden side-panel.

"Ryko, is she awake? Is she all right?" It was Dela's voice, calling from outside the cart.

A large front hatch slid open to show the laboring rumps of two harnessed oxen. A familiar figure was walking alongside, guiding the beasts: Solly, his bulbous features made even more grotesque by scabbed cuts and grazes. He smiled and bowed, then Dela leaned in and blocked my view. She was no longer disguised as a fisherman. Instead, she wore the black cap and blue high-collared robe of a successful merchant.

"Are you all right, Eona?" She scanned my face. "We thought you would never come back to your senses. How do you feel?"

I licked my lips, suddenly aware of the dry need in my body. "Thirsty. And sick," I said. "My head hurts. How long has it been?"

She glanced at Ryko, the moment heavy with warning. "Two days," she said.

"Two days?" I searched their faces. "Truly?"

They both nodded, but neither volunteered more, their uneasy silence broken only by the creaking cart and Solly's voice urging the oxen onward. Ryko held out a ceramic water flask, his face set into harsh lines.

I unplugged the vessel and sipped. The cool water soothed my throat, but my stomach churned at the tiny amount of liquid. I had not felt this ill since the imperial banquet, a lifetime ago.

I handed back the flask, fighting the urge to vomit. "Someone is going to have to tell me what happened."

"Do you not remember?" Dela eyed me anxiously. "You were

healing Ryko—and then everything exploded. Huge rains and winds ripped apart the whole house. The whole cliff."

"And the village," Ryko said tightly.

Dela glared at him.

"She has to know," he said.

Foreboding settled in my chest. "Know what? Tell me, now!"

Ryko straightened, meeting my order. "Thirty-six villagers were killed. Nearly eighty were hurt." He bowed his head. "To save me."

My throat was dry again. "Thirty-six?"

So many people dead because I could not control my power. Because I had recklessly called my dragon, although I knew I did not have the skill.

"May the gods forgive me," I whispered. Yet even if they did, how could I forgive myself?

Ryko made an awkward bow, lurching with the cart's motion. "My lady, do not be uneasy. It is true you healed me at great cost, but the fault is not yours. The gods will know those lives were not taken by you." He turned to Dela. "It was Ido. He invaded my lady's mind while she was healing me."

Dela gasped. "Ido caused all that destruction? Was he after your power again?"

I hesitated. How easy it would be to blame all those deaths on Ido and slip out from under the heavy yoke of guilt. But I could not lie to my friends again, or to myself. If there was one thing I had learned from the last few weeks, it was that such lies could be deadly.

"No," I said. "Ido saved us all. When I tried to heal Ryko, I was nearly torn apart by the ten bereft dragons."

They both looked at me blankly.

"It is what I call the beasts of the slain Dragoneyes. I think they are trying to unite with their queen, although I do not know why. Lord Ido and his dragon forced them back."

Ryko's eyes narrowed. "That does not sound like Ido. His every breath is governed by self-interest. If what you say is true, he must have some dark reason for helping you."

I let the jibe at my truthfulness pass—Ryko had every right to mistrust me. He had been the most devastated by my lies. Although in my defense, the biggest lie—my male masquerade—had been forced upon me by my master. Perhaps one day Ryko would forgive me. For now, I would shoulder his disillusion.

"All I know is that he drove away the ten dragons, and without him we would not have survived."

"Where is Ido?" Dela asked. "I don't understand. How could he drive away—"

"Begging your pardon." It was Solly's gruff voice.

The cart bounced—another weight climbing aboard—then the resistance fighter peered in beside Lady Dela.

"Ryko, there's a troop of soldiers coming up behind," he said with urgency. "Looks like a mountain patrol. They've seen us, too. You haven't got time to get out." He gave a quick bow to me, then retreated from view.

Ryko frowned. "A troop so high up in the mountains? I

hope His Majesty is secure." He glanced across at me. "We go to retrieve the Pearl Emperor."

For a moment, relief stole my breath. "He is alive, then?"

"As far as we know," Dela said. "Ryko says there is a safe place just past the next village. If all has gone well, he should be there."

She ducked away from the hatch. A worried nod on her return corroborated Solly's report. "They are coming up very fast, Ryko," she added. "You need to get into the box." She grasped my shoulder. "You and I are husband and wife. I am taking you to the Moon Lady Waters for healing. Understand?"

"Does the army know we are in this area?" I asked.

"No, it's probably just a regular scout party. We've got through all the checkpoints so far. Just remember you are my sick wife." She shut the hatch.

Ryko had already lifted the edge of my straw pallet and was pulling up the planks of the floor.

"What are you doing?"

"Hiding." He lifted another plank and exposed a hidden compartment. "Sethon is looking for a boy lord, a Contraire, and an islander. You two can switch your identities, but I can't get any smaller or change my skin."

"Are you really going to fit in there?" It was a very small space with a carpet of straw dust and a long cloth bundle wedged to one side.

"Here, hold this," he said, handing me the bundle.

As soon as I touched the rough cotton, I knew it held Kinra's swords; their familiar jolt of anger seared through me, intensifying the pain in my head. The black pearls around my arm clicked, as if greeting the blades that had also once belonged to my Dragoneye ancestress. I burrowed my hand into the folds of the bundle, exposing the moonstone and jade studded hilts, and the top of a familiar leather pouch; my Dragoneye compass. Beside me, Ryko slid into the cart recess, contorting his big body to fit the shallow space. He held out his hands for the swords. I rewrapped the cloth and returned them, feeling the tug of their power. At least some of the Mirror Dragon treasures were safe. I felt for my waist pouch; the long, thin shapes within reassured me that my ancestors' death plaques were also safe.

"Help me put these planks back," Ryko said. "And then the pallet over the top."

"Will you be able to breathe?"

"Plenty of air." With a tight smile, he patted my arm. "It will be all right."

I fitted the planks over his tense face, my fingers clumsy with a sudden rush of fear. A twitch of the straw mattress had it back in place. As I eased myself on to it and rearranged my long white tunic into modest folds, it finally dawned on me what I was wearing—the mourning robe of an almost-mother, the tragedy compounded by the orange sash of an unborn son. I cupped either side of my head, feeling the twisted cloth of the headdress that hid my hair and proclaimed my grief as recent. Not many men would want to come close to such ill luck, let alone search its sickbed. A clever ruse. It also gave a good reason for traveling at such a dangerous time; it was said that a woman could wash away such bad fortune if she bathed before her next cycle in the Moon Lady Waters, a mountain lake special to the gods. Still, it made me uneasy to wear such sad clothing. I touched the red folio in my sleeve for luck, and was comforted by the gentle squeeze of the black pearls.

The cloth flap at the back of the cart lifted. I closed my eyes and tried to soften my quick breaths into the deeper rhythm of sleep.

"It's me," a familiar voice said.

I raised my head to see Vida hoisting herself up onto the slow-moving cart. Her usual tunic and loose trousers had been replaced by a housemaid's gown. For all its modest coverage, the drape of the brown cloth and the artful binding of the sash served to emphasize her generous curves. She lowered the canvas flap and crawled toward me, her skirt snagging on one of the three large traveling baskets strapped against the side panel. She jerked at the garment, cursing under her breath.

"Let me help." I struggled up onto my elbows. My vision clouded, the cart swirling around me. I fell back on to the pallet.

"Just leave it," she snapped. Finally freeing the cloth, she closed the distance between us. "You look terrible, although I suppose it fits your disguise." She took my hand, but there was no comfort in the gesture. "We've been stopped before and got through. All you need to do is keep your head. And if you can't do that, just shut up and play dumb." Although her words were harsh and tough, her hand was clammy and her grasp too tight.

I looked up at the girl—so closely connected to those who had died—and forced myself to ask the question: "Is your father all right?"

Vida nodded, but her face was cold. "He was not hurt."

Relief made me smile; Master Tozay was alive. At least I had not killed or injured the leader of the resistance. "I'm so glad."

Vida did not return my smile. "My father is well," she continued softly, "but I lost my—I lost good friends among those who died." Her grip tightened until I gasped. "I have seen your power, lady, and my father insists you are the key to our success. Even so, part of me did not want you to wake up."

I tried to pull my hand away, but she did not let go. Over the sound of our cart's progress came the jangling of armor and a harsh call for our halt.

Vida leaned closer. "So far you have done more harm than good. I hope you are worth all this pain." She released my hand as the cart jerked to a stop.

"In the name of Emperor Sethon, show your pass," a clipped voice commanded.

"I have it here," Dela's voice answered. Her usual light tone had deepened into masculinity.

Beside me, a soldier's silhouette appeared on the cotton canopy like a stick-puppet in a shadow play. Dela's angular profile dipped into sight and out again as she passed him a large octagonal token. A Blessed Pilgrim pass—hard to obtain and almost impossible to forge. For a few long seconds, the man studied it. Finally, he looked up and asked, "Where do you travel, merchant?"

"To the Moon Lady Waters. For my—"

"It is a bad time to be traveling. The roads are flooding and an earthshake has destroyed one pass across the mountain."

"We trust in the gods—"

"How many in your party?"

"Myself, my wife, and our two bondservants."

"No guards?"

"No, sir. We have a Blessed Pass and fly the official pilgrim banner. Surely we are safe."

"There have been reports of bandits along this road attacking pilgrims." The soldier handed back the token. "Have you seen any other travelers? A big islander, a boy, and a woman, perhaps? Or two men and a boy?"

It was as if all of the air had been sucked from the cart. They were searching for us; I had known it as reports and warnings carried to the fisher village, but now it was real. Now it was soldiers around us with orders to capture or kill. I clenched my shaking hands.

"No, sir," Dela answered.

"Check the cart," he ordered his men with a jerk of his head.

I pressed myself deeper into the straw and tried to relax my limbs into a listless sprawl. Beside me, Vida rearranged her fierce intensity into meek servitude. We glanced at one another, momentarily bonded by the threat.

The flap at the end of the cart lifted, and two men peered

in with swords drawn. They scanned the cart, both of them skimming across my white clad figure to pause for a moment on Vida's body.

"A woman and her maid, sir," the older of the two reported.

Their officer appeared, and they both made way for him. He was younger than I expected, with a good-humored face dragged down by weary responsibility. Hanging from a length of leather around his throat was a red jade blood amulet. I had seen them before on ranked soldiers: a carved plea to Bross, God of War, for protection in battle. A blood amulet only worked if it was received as a gift, and one carved from red jade instead of the usual ox-stone would have cost a lot of money; someone wanted to keep this soldier alive.

He was staring at my white robe, a stricken look on his face.

"Sir?" one of his men prompted.

The officer's eyes flickered, then focused on me.

"My apologies for intruding, madam," he said gently. "Now I see why you journey at this time. I am Haddo, Lieutenant of the East Mountain Patrol." He bowed. "You will understand that I must ask you to step down while we search your cart."

Vida straightened. "Please, sir, my mistress is not well." Her voice had taken on the soft lilt of service.

Haddo ignored her protest. "If you will step down, madam."

"Of course." I busied myself with gathering up my gown, trying to hide my trembling hands. Below me, I felt Ryko's desperate presence like another pounding heart.

Vida hurriedly took my arm and pulled me upright. "Lean on me, mistress." Her body was tense against mine.

Hunched under the canopy, we moved toward the lieutenant, our progress slow and awkward. It was not all an act—after two days of lying in the cart, I could hardly move. With every shaking step, my nausea increased.

Vida helped me down on to the roadside, softly fussing with the hem of my gown as we stepped around a puddle. When I turned to face the lieutenant, I finally saw the true extent of the threat. A troop of twenty men surrounded us: mainly foot soldiers with swords, but also a small number carrying deadly mechanical bows. There was no way we could we fight our way out. Vida's grip tightened.

"Is my wife all right?" Dela called.

"Stay where you are!" Haddo ordered. He nodded to the two waiting soldiers. "Search it."

They climbed into the cart. I could not watch—surely my face would be a map that led straight to Ryko—but I could not look away. The older man flipped open the traveling baskets, one after another, and dug through them, scattering food, clothing, and bedding. The other soldier lifted the thick straw mattress, sending up a swirl of dust. He speared it with his sword, once, twice. Then his attention turned to the floor. Beside me, Vida sucked in a tense breath. My stomach tightened into a rush of intent.

"I am going to be ill," I said.

As I turned toward the flooded ditch, Vida's iron grip pulled me around to face the lieutenant. There was no time to object. Doubling over, I retched out a thin stream of water and foul bile at his feet.

Haddo jumped back with disgust. I retched again, bringing up more of the bitter liquid.

"Please, sir, my mistress needs to lie down," Vida said, the weight of her body edging me toward the man. In reflex, I pushed back. She dug her fingernails into my arm until pain and a sharp pinch bent me over again.

The lieutenant retreated another step, then looked up at his men in the cart. They were both smirking at his discomfort. "Well? Is it clear?"

The man holding the mattress let it drop. "Yes, sir."

"Then get out of there and let this poor lady rest."

The men climbed down and, with a salute, returned to the waiting troop.

As they walked out of earshot, Haddo said softly, "Do not be distressed, madam. My own wife had the same kind of sickness . . . afterward." He gestured at my white robe. "We found good fortune at the Moon Lady Waters. I'm sure the gods will return your health, too, and favor you with another son."

I summoned a weak smile.

"Since we are set in the same direction," he continued, "you and your husband can travel with us to the next village. It will be safer and quicker."

"That is very generous of you, Lieutenant Haddo," I said, forcing gratitude into my voice. "But we would not wish to keep you from your duties."

"My troop is crossing the mountain, anyway," he said. "And I am sure the gods would want me to assist your pilgrimage. We should reach Laosang village before nightfall." He bowed and walked away, no doubt to tell my husband of our good fortune.

Vida eyed me as I spat out the last of the bile.

"Next time, don't fight me," she murmured, guiding me to the cart.

I longed to shake off her hands, but I was too weak to climb back inside alone. And I had to admit her quick wits had saved the day, if not my dignity. Without missing a beat, she bent to one knee at the back of the cart, the other knee raised—a good maid offering her sick mistress a mounting-step. Although it was tempting, I did not take the opportunity to tread heavily. I crawled onto the pallet and heard Dela trying to reject Haddo's offer. Every attempt was courteously turned aside; the man was intent on helping us. It seemed our clever ruse had become our trap.

"Well, I am very grateful, sir," Dela finally said. We had no choice but to accept—blunt refusal would make the lieutenant suspicious. "It will be a relief to have your protection."

Vida pulled down the back flap, the strain in her face a mirror of my own; every moment we spent in the company of these soldiers could mean discovery. And now we were traveling alongside them.

"Forward, then," the lieutenant called.

Silhouettes moved along the canopy as the cart jerked into motion. The front hatch slid open and Dela leaned into the cart.

"Are you all right back there, wife?" Her voice was all

consideration, but her eyes were fixed on Ryko's hiding place.

"I will be glad to stop for the night, husband," I answered.

Dela nodded. We all knew there was nothing we could do for the moment or, indeed, for as long as we were surrounded by Sethon's men. Ryko would have to stay where he was until darkness gave us some cover to extract him.

Dela cast one more anxious look at the floor, then withdrew.

I rolled onto my side and carefully lifted the edge of the straw pallet, ignoring Vida's soft hiss of protest. Pressing my cheek against the floor planks, I whispered, "Tonight," just in case Ryko could hear me over the rumbling of the cart. It was unlikely, but I could not bear to think of him in that tiny space with no idea of what was happening or when he would be able to escape.

I fell onto my back as another rise of nausea soured my throat. Near my feet, Vida was stuffing the mess of food boxes and bedding back into the traveling baskets.

"Here," she whispered, passing me a fresh flask of water. "You need to rest. Drink a little, but take it slowly or you'll vomit again. It is like you have been hit hard on the head, and there is no remedy for that, except rest."

"You knew I'd be sick out there?"

She shrugged.

No sympathy, but what did I expect? A tentative sip of water made my stomach churn. I replugged the flask and nodded my thanks, but Vida had already turned away. I was still the killer of her friends. I stared up at the cloth canopy, searching for thoughts that would not bring guilt or fear. It was a futile effort.

At first, I could only think of the soldiers around us, and Ryko trapped beneath me. Then came the ghosts of those I had killed. I tried to push away the stark image of the Beseecher crushed under the fisher house roof, but his lifeless face became every face in my mind: men swept away by roiling seas, women buried in their houses, children torn and bloodied.

I took a shuddering breath, hoping to clear my mind of such grim imaginings. Instead, I saw my dying master convulsing in my arms, Lord Tyron beheaded on the road like a traitor, and the terrifying moment when I knew Lord Ido had slaughtered the other ten Dragoneyes and their young apprentices. So much death, and most of it in the name of Ido's ambition. Even the villagers had been killed by his power as much as mine.

Why did Ido save me? Ryko was right; Ido did nothing without some gain for himself. If he was still after my power, he could have had it at the fisher house; I had been defenseless. I shuddered, remembering the first time he had forced his way into my mind, during the King Monsoon test. He had not only taken over my power, but my body, too. Yet this time he did not try to take either. Perhaps Ido was truly a changed man. Still, I would not gamble on his transformation: darkness was woven too tight into his nature. It was more likely he was trying to force an obligation upon me—to save him from Sethon. Did he really think I would risk my life to rescue the man who had killed my master and the other Dragoneyes?

"Laon, take your team and fan out to the south." It was Haddo's voice, near the front of the cart. "Sen, your team goes north. Remember, there is no bonus if the young Dragoneye lord is hurt in any way. The emperor is not fussy about the others. Corpses will do."

I heard Vida's soft intake of breath. When I looked across, she was staring at the canopy, face drained of all color. Her eyes flicked to mine—a fleeting admission of fear—then she straightened her shoulders and continued stacking our belongings in the traveling baskets.

Beneath my sleeve, I stroked the folio with its rope of guardian pearls and sent a prayer to Kinra: *Keep us safe.* The gems shivered and clicked, but this time I found no comfort in their tight embrace.

CHAPTER THREE

IT WAS DARK by the time our cart lurched to a standstill in the courtyard of the Laosang village inn. The sudden lack of noise sharpened the sounds around us: Haddo ordering his men to their billeting duties, the low of our hungry oxen, and the clang of kitchen pots. Soft yellow light edged the canopy and brought more detail into the cart. Vida had wedged herself upright between two of the larger traveling baskets. Her pale face was hollow from exhaustion. Throughout the long day, I had been lulled into uneasy naps by our slow swaying progress and the patter of intermittent rain on the canopy. Vida, however, had made a point of staying awake the whole time. I scrubbed at my eyes, strangely irritated by her stoicism.

The front hatch slid open and Dela peered in at us.

"I will arrange for a room, wife." Every crease on her face was marked with dark dirt, like the painted lines of an opera mask. "You, Vida, see to your mistress and then come and help Solly clean the cart and prepare it for tomorrow."

A good plan, especially as most of Haddo's men would be busy with their own needs for an hour or so. We met one another's eyes, silently acknowledging the risk.

"Here is your cloak, mistress," Vida said, forcing brightness into her voice. She handed me the garment. "You must wrap up against the night air."

Dela was waiting for me as I clambered out of the cart. She offered her hand, in her role as husband, and frowned with concern as I sagged against her body.

"Are you all right?" she whispered in my ear, bracing me.

"It's just travel cricks," I said. Then I caught the aroma of meat and rich gravy. My empty stomach clenched into a growl. All nausea gone. "By the gods, I'm hungry."

The magnificent smell was coming from the inn's tavern across the courtyard. The two-story building formed one side of the large cobbled compound, a space that could easily take eight of our carts side by side, and just as many lengthwise. Out in front of the tavern were three rows of wet eating benches, all empty. Red paper lamps were strung under the eaves, and the ground floor shutters were open to catch the cooler night air, showing a few patrons eating at long tables inside.

I pulled toward the promise of food, but Dela stood firm.

"We cannot eat in there," she said.

Of course: a rich merchant couple would take a private room, especially if they were on pilgrimage. I slumped back against Dela.

A thickset man—the innkeeper, by his striped outer robe—had emerged from the tavern and was making his way toward us. He paused every now and again to brusquely direct soldiers to the two low-set buildings on either side of the gateway. From the blessing flags that hung across the windows, I could tell the buildings were normally used as pilgrim dormitories. Now they were barracks.

"We need to move the cart," I murmured to Dela.

She grunted assent, then nudged me back a step. I winced at such a basic mistake—a good wife always stood behind her husband. The innkeeper approached and bowed, his eyes registering Dela's heavy waist pouch and my fine linen robe.

"Greetings, good sir, and welcome," he said. "It is a relief to see at least one paying customer." A wry smile softened his words. "Are you seeking rooms? I can offer you as many as you want for an excellent price." He lowered his voice. "This trouble in the city is dreadful for business. And coupled with these bad floods and earthshakes, no one is traveling if they can help it." His eyes found my white robe again. Realizing his blunder, he quickly added, "Your wife's devotion to her duty, even in such dangerous times, does you great honor."

Dela nodded at the tacit apology. "One room will be enough, thank you."

The innkeeper bowed again. "And dinner? My own wife makes an excellent pilgrim meal. We can serve it in your room." He tilted his head at the passing soldiers. "You'll not want to venture downstairs once they get into the rice wine."

"Yes, we'll take dinner," Dela said. "My servants can have

whatever is being served in your tavern." She looked around the compound, then motioned the innkeeper closer. "I mean no offense, my good man, but is there somewhere safer I can put my cart? My servants will stay with it, of course, but I would prefer to have it out of this main thoroughfare."

"Out of harm's way," the innkeeper agreed. "I have a stable around the back with room enough for your oxen and cart. For a small fee I can feed the beasts, too."

"Accepted," Dela said, touching forehead and heart to seal the bargain.

The innkeeper repeated the gesture, then nodded at Vida standing quietly behind us, a traveling basket in her arms. "A word of warning: I wouldn't make your girl sleep in the cart, even if your man does." He rubbed his forehead. "I can put a pallet in your room for her."

"For a small cost?" Dela asked blandly.

The innkeeper laughed. "No cost, good sir, no cost. I would not have any female at risk in my establishment. She can eat in the kitchen, too."

"That is very kind," Dela said, bowing.

"You," the innkeeper called to Solly. "Take the cart around the back to the first stable." Then he motioned for us to follow him to the lodging house.

I stayed one step behind Dela and kept my head down. Even so, I managed to see Solly lead the oxen and cart along a narrow alley between the main house and the compound wall. It seemed our luck had finally changed; with the cart hidden in a back stable, Solly would have plenty of time to help Ryko slip away to find the Pearl Emperor.

Yet a small voice inside me whispered that it was too easy. My disquiet doubled at the sight of Lieutenant Haddo watching us from across the courtyard, a still figure among the industry of his men. If he discovered Ryko, I had no doubt he would put the puzzle together and realize we were his quarry. There was a keen mind behind that youthful façade. And if he did unmask us, then it would come down to a fight. Five against twenty. His eyes met mine, a sweet concern in his face. I looked away—the modest goodwife—my heartbeat hard in my chest.

The innkeeper held aside the red door flags of the lodging house and ushered us inside. I hurriedly followed Dela over the raised threshold into a foyer that was little more than a corridor and stairwell. Gone was the rich enticement of stewed meat and gravy. Instead, the smell of rancid matting soured the air, the burn of fish oil from two dirty wall lamps adding to the stench. At the end of the passage, a back doorway opened to an outside area—judging from the tang of manure on the slight night breeze, it led to the stable yard. Somewhere out there Solly was stabling the oxen, waiting for a chance to free Ryko.

Vida and the innkeeper entered the narrow space, and I was forced back against the edge of a steep staircase, its handrail patched with mismatched wood. I caught Dela's eye; she had covered her nose and mouth with her hand, trying to hide her disgust. Beside the luxury of her palace home, this place was a hovel. Still, it was good compared to some of the inns my master and I had endured five years ago.

The unwelcome memory cut through me like acid. Even though my master was dead, his betrayal was still raw. That long-ago journey was before he had deliberately had me crippled; I was newly delivered from the slavery of the salt farm, learning to act like a boy, and reveling in the freedom to move without the bite of a whip or the weight of a salt bag. Then my master secretly arranged to have my hip broken to hide my sex and make me untouchable. All in the pursuit of the power and money he craved. In the end, he regretted causing me such pain—he told Chart as much—and even came to love me in his own way. Perhaps now that I was healed and had the power of a dragon, I should forgive him. Yet my rage was as hollowing and hot as ever.

The innkeeper unhooked one of the oil lamps and climbed the stairs. We filed up behind him, me struggling with my long gown, Vida straining under the weight of the traveling basket.

The air was no better on the second floor; the day's damp warmth had carried the fishy stink throughout the house. The innkeeper led us along a short passageway that ran between the sleeping chambers, each divided from its neighbor by paper walls. There would be no unguarded talk tonight.

"My best room," he said, sliding open a flimsy screen. "Since there are no other guests, I've put you at the back of the house, so you won't get the tavern noise."

It was surprisingly spacious. Two bedrolls rested against the far wall, ready to be laid out, and a low eating table stood in the center. There was no rancid straw matting—a godsend—although the large gaps in the bare planked floor let in weak lamplight from the foyer below. A stained screen in the corner shielded a night bowl from the sleeping area, and a shuttered window promised fresh air.

The innkeeper hung the lamp on a hook just inside the doorway and bowed us into our accommodation.

"I'll have your dinner and the extra pallet brought up by next bell," he said.

Another pleased bow took him from the room. We waited in silence until his footsteps descended the stairs and were lost in the lower level of the house.

Finally judging it to be safe, Dela murmured, "Vida and I will go and help Solly."

"What about me? What can I do?"

"You'll have to stay here. No merchant woman would enter a stable, let alone wander an inn by herself." She saw the rebellion in my eyes. "I know it is frustrating, but only a whore or a servant girl would venture downstairs, especially with these soldiers about. You must stay in character."

"I know, Respectable Woman Overcome with Grief," I said sourly. "Maybe I can keep watch for you." I crossed to the window and pushed open the shutters, but the view was of a ramshackle building beyond the compound wall, lit ghostly by the three-quarter moon. The room did not overlook the stable yard.

Dela patted my shoulder. "Don't worry. We'll be back soon."

Reluctantly, I nodded. "Tell him 'good fortune,' then."

With one last squeeze of my shoulder, Dela headed into the corridor. Vida dumped her basket on the ground and, without a backward glance, followed. Their two shadows moved along the paper wall and disappeared.

For a mad moment, I wanted to run after Dela and tell her she should wait until the inn was asleep to free Ryko. Then again, perhaps this was the right time, when Haddo and his men were setting up their camp, and a bondservant cleaning out a cart would blend into the background.

I slid shut the screen door and surveyed the room again. The place suddenly felt like a prison. I counted my paces across the room: eighteen. Twelve took me its length. For almost five years I had lived as a boy, and even as a lowly candidate I'd had more freedom than this role as a woman. I should be downstairs, helping Ryko, not measuring a room with my feet. I grabbed a handful of my long gown; even the clothes were designed to hinder movement. With the hem tucked into the sash, it made walking easier, but I still had nowhere to go.

I pulled off the mourning headdress and dug my fingertips into the tight coronet of braids; either Dela or Vida had taken care to weave my hair into the style of a grieving mother. At the salt farm, I had seen my friend Dolana do the same for a woman whose son had died from the Weeping Sickness. Although we had tried to comfort the poor woman and observe the death rituals, her grief had grown into madness until she had torn out her own hair and blinded herself with salt.

My thoughts returned to Lieutenant Haddo. A kind man, obviously touched by a son's death himself, but still a soldier with orders to capture me and kill my friends. I tossed the headdress onto a bedroll and crossed the room again. Our pilgrim masquerade seemed like a flimsy shield against such ruthlessness. One mistake, one tiny moment of inattention, could destroy us all. Still, I was practiced in pretense; lying for my life was second nature.

My restless pacing was interrupted by the arrival of a serving girl. She hauled in the promised pallet and murmured a timid reassurance that our food was on its way.

When she was gone, I squatted under the lamp and unwound the pliant black pearls from my arm to release Kinra's journal. There was no use dwelling on the threat of Haddo and his men. It merely stoked my fear. Instead, I forced myself to study a page of the precious folio, recognizing only one of the faded characters: *Duty*.

In the few days of recuperation at the fisher house, Dela had started to teach me Woman Script. It was usually passed down from mother to daughter, but I had been sold into bond service before I was taught its secrets. My progress with it was painfully slow, the task of reading the uncoded parts of the journal complicated by the ancient form of the script. Even Dela was having trouble translating it, and I still knew only ten or so characters, not enough to discover what I desperately needed to know: how to control my power and ward off the ten bereft dragons.

The soft sibilance of voices broke my concentration. Were

Dela and Vida back already? I strained to hear who was talking—two men, in the foyer below. Not my friends, then. I pushed the folio back under my sleeve. The pearls slithered up behind it and held the small book tightly against my forearm.

On hands and knees, I pressed my eye to a generous gap in the planking. Below me, all I could see was the dimly lit foyer wall and floor. Whoever was talking was out of my sightline, and too far away for their words to be distinguished. Did I dare creep to the stairwell and listen? Dela would be furious if she found out I had left the room. But there was no real danger—I could run back to safety if anyone mounted the stairs. And maybe I would hear something useful rather than just waiting for the others to return.

Gathering my skirt, I stood and carefully slid the screen door open. The corridor was clear. As I edged closer to the top of the staircase, one of the muffled voices sharpened into Haddo's crisp authority.

". . . and I'll need to restock with rice and some of that salted fish. Same as before."

"I haven't been paid for the last lot." It was the innkeeper, his tone rising into peevish complaint.

"You'll get it on our next pass over the mountain," Haddo said. "Right now, my problem is hungry men, so have the supplies ready. We're moving out at the dawn bell." There was a pause and then Haddo asked, "Tell me, do you know the whereabouts of the merchant who arrived with us?"

"I think he's out back overseeing the stabling of his animals.

Why, is something amiss? They don't bring more misfortune with them, do they? I gave them my best room, too."

"Don't worry, I'm sure the lady's misfortune will not taint you or your inn." The lieutenant's voice was wry. "I just want to offer them an escort tomorrow. That door leads to the stable yard, doesn't it? Or must I go round?"

My heartbeat quickened. If Haddo went outside now, there was a chance he would see Ryko. I tried to estimate how much time had passed since Dela and Vida had left the room; not even a quarter bell. It was possible that Ryko was still being freed. We could not risk it; just a glimpse of the islander would give us all away. I had to stop Haddo. A few short steps took me to the top of the staircase, Dela's warning loud in my head. She was right. I could not go downstairs; no respectable woman would approach two men by herself. I had to stay in character.

"All I'm saying is she's got the markings of a lost one," the innkeeper said. "I've seen a lot of them on their way to and from the Moon Lady Waters, and some of them never come right. He'd be better to return her to her parents and move on to one who can produce a living son."

I clutched the handrail, his harsh words bringing a sudden, desperate idea.

"Keep your voice down, man," Haddo said, lowering his own. I strained to hear his next words. ". . . to the Moon Lady Waters as fast as possible. It worked for my wife."

"I meant no disrespect," the innkeeper said hurriedly. "Your wife was one of the blessed. Maybe this girl will be, too. Go straight through, it takes you into the yard. The merchant is in the far stable."

If ever there was a time for skillful pretense, this was it. I yanked a few of my braids loose and, with a mute prayer to the gods, pushed myself forward, bundling my tucked skirt even higher above my ankles.

"Is that you, husband?" I called, running down the stairs. "I have seen him, husband. I have seen our son!"

As I rounded the tight landing, I saw the startled, upturned faces of Haddo and the innkeeper. I smiled and directed my quavering words at the lieutenant. "He is in our room, husband. You must come now."

I took the last of the stairs and grabbed Haddo by the arm, trying to tug him up the first step. The man was immovable. "He is crying, poor little man, and wants his father."

A silent, horrified exchange crossed between Haddo and the innkeeper; *She is mad*, it said. *What do we do?* I tugged at him again. Men were always quick to believe in the madness of women.

Haddo peeled my hand off his arm. "Madam, I am not your husband. I am Lieutenant Haddo. Do you remember me?"

"Of course I remember you, husband." I smiled into his pity. "What a strange thing to ask. Come now, before our boy returns to his sleep."

"I'll get her upstairs, sir," the innkeeper said. "You go get her husband."

They had to be kept from the stable yard. I pictured the

wretched ravings of the bereft mother at the salt farm. "Look, he runs out to play," I said, hoping they could not hear the desperation in my voice. "Come back, son." Praying that both men would follow, I pushed past Haddo, batting my way through the door flags into the main courtyard.

"Wait, son. Wait for Mother." I aimed my words at a trio of soldiers walking close by. They turned, eyeing me with surprise.

"It is too dark to play outside," I added loudly, focusing on the young man in the center. "Come inside."

I felt his attention sharpen. "All right, let's go inside and play."

On either side, his companions sniggered, their approval sending him across the few lengths that separated us.

"What do you charge, girl?" He caught my wrist and jerked me against his body. One hand found my waist, the other brushed across my breast. I froze, his touch bringing another stark memory from the salt farm: the grabbing hands of the whipmaster, and Dolana kicking him away.

"Let her go."

It was Haddo. The clipped command sent the soldier into a tense salute. Suddenly free of his restraint, I stumbled. Haddo's iron grip caught my arm and held me up from the cobbled paving.

"Sorry, sir," the soldier said. His friends edged back into the shadows. "I thought she was one of the local—"

"Use your eyes, Laon, not your prick. She's wearing a mourning robe."

"Yes, sir."

"Practice your observation skills on guard duty. *Now!*"

The soldier saluted again and was gone. Haddo, his grip still tight around my arm, peered into my face.

"Madam? Are you all right?"

There was no doubt he could see the sanity in my eyes; I could not keep conjuring madness under such scrutiny.

"Lieutenant Haddo," I said, frowning. "What am I doing outside? Why do you hold me?"

He let go of my arm. "You were"—he paused—"*indisposed.* But I see that you have now come back to yourself."

I studied the ground, avoiding his keen eyes. "I do not remember."

"It is sometimes like that," he said, and awkwardly patted my shoulder. "My wife thought she could feel the breath of our boy on her cheek. It will get better."

"Where is she?" It was Dela's voice, coming from the lodging house.

The innkeeper's bulk pushed the door flags apart. "This way, in the courtyard," he said, leading Dela through the doorway. "You should not have left her without her maid. I can't have madwomen running around my inn."

"She is not mad," Dela said, reaching into the pouch tied at her waist. "It is just grief and the rigors of the journey. Here, a small sum to ease your inconvenience." She passed a coin to the innkeeper, then saw me beside Haddo. "Lieutenant, I believe you have also been of assistance to my wife. I thank you, and am sorry for your trouble." She bowed, the courtesy stiff with anger. I had a feeling it was not part of her act.

Haddo returned the bow. "No trouble, sir. And no harm has come to her, although I suggest you do not leave her alone at this time."

Dela gripped my arm tightly. "Come, wife. Let me take you back to the comfort of our room." She pulled me toward the doorway, nodding once to the lieutenant. "Again, my thanks."

Vida was waiting inside the lodging house foyer, holding the bundle that held my swords and compass.

"Do you think only of yourself?" she hissed, thrusting the bundle into my hands. "You put us all at risk."

For a moment I closed my eyes, absorbing the familiar jolt of Kinra's angry energy through the cloth. I knew Vida's tongue was sharpened by grief and fear, but the unfair charge still stung. She had not heard Haddo's intentions. Who was she to judge my every action? I clenched my fist, transfixed by an image of driving it into her face. Abruptly I turned and followed Dela upstairs, startled by the violence of my resentment.

At the landing, Dela turned to Vida. "Stay here," she whispered. "Let me know if anyone comes into the house, front or back."

Vida gave a sharp nod and pressed herself against the wall. "*I* know how to follow orders."

I trailed behind Dela and braced myself as she slid the screen door closed behind us. Dressed as a man, her sharp features and spare frame lent her a stern handsomeness that had hardened into fury.

Two strides and she was upon me. "That was beyond foolhardy," she said against my ear, each word like a slap. "I thought you had some sense. And yet you put yourself—you put us all—in danger!"

I hugged Kinra's swords, my own fury rising. "Haddo was going to the stables in search of you. I had to do something. Or would you rather I sit by and let him find—" Caution made me stop, my abrupt silence also checking Dela. Our voices had become too intense.

She took a deep breath, then whispered, "In search of me? Why?"

"He wants to offer us an escort to the next village."

Dela shook her head. "That's bad news."

I nodded. "At least our friend has gone, hasn't he?"

"Yes."

"And he is all right?"

"He has not been 'all right' since the village." Her low voice was harsh. She pressed her palms against her eyes. "Forgive me, I am tired. He is well enough. And on his way." With an effort, she rallied her authority. "You must promise you will not put yourself in danger again. We cannot afford to lose you."

"I had to do something."

"No, Eona, we had it in hand." Her eyes held mine until I looked away. "At least your feigned madness will be a good excuse to stay here while Haddo and his men move on. If all goes well, we'll know by tomorrow afternoon if our journey has been worthwhile."

"Master," Vida called from the passage, "the serving girl is here with your dinner. May she enter?"

Before long, the girl had set out our repast on the low table and left with Vida to show her the way to the kitchens and her own meal. I knelt on the dusty cushion opposite Dela and eyed the meager array of vegetables, rice, and pickles accompanied by a small bowl of tea to wash it down. Good pilgrim fare. It was a silent meal—with Vida in the kitchens and Solly guarding the cart, we had no lookout and could not risk a real conversation. I sensed that Dela did not want to talk, anyway. Her worry for Ryko was like another guest at the table.

After the serving girl cleared away the remains, Vida returned to the room, yawning, her fatigue so great that it blunted her hostility into clipped sentences and sidelong glances. All of us were tired and irritable with fear, but I was the only one not completely bowed by exhaustion, so I took first watch.

Both Dela and Vida were asleep as soon as they stretched out, fully clothed, on their bedrolls. I unwrapped Kinra's swords and laid them carefully on the floor, ignoring their flare of anger. The compass had been bundled with them. I picked up the leather pouch and slid the heavy gold disc out onto my palm. It was divided into twenty-four concentric rings, the center point housing a huge round ruby and the outermost ring studded with smaller red gems at the cardinal points. The other rings were etched with pictures of the celestial animals and elegant Woman Script. The compass was meant to focus the Mirror Dragon's energy and draw on the earth's ley lines, but until I could use my power and read the ancient characters, it was little more than a beautiful decoration. I returned it to its cover and placed it next to the swords.

My waist pouch was next, quickly untied and laid beside the compass. Then I struggled out of my over-robe, glad to be free of it, and sat in my thin shift, listening to the faint sounds of the soldiers singing and laughing across the courtyard.

As my watch hours passed, I examined my decision to stop Haddo from entering the stable yard. Dela had called it foolhardy. Admittedly, there had been some risk, but the threat of discovery had been real. I could not have sat by while Ryko was in danger—it was not in my nature. There was a saying that the strength of a man's steel was only known under the hammer of circumstance. If anyone had asked me a few hours ago, I would have said that nearly five years of boyhood had hammered me into constant fear and excessive caution. But now I realized it had done the opposite. It had shaped me into someone who stepped forward and reached for what she wanted. It was too late for me to tuck my hands behind my back and wait like a good woman.

Finally, at the toll of a distant midnight bell, I leaned over and shook Dela awake. She sat up immediately, groping for her knife.

"Your watch," I whispered. "Nothing to report."

She flashed a tired smile. "Didn't I just lie down two minutes ago?"

"Four." I returned her smile, glad that sleep had softened her anger and worry.

I settled back on my bed as Dela headed for the night bowl. Slowly, my focus drifted, dipping in and out of sleep, over and over again, as the inn eased into silence around us.

It was the unmistakable clash of blade against blade that brought me up on to my knees, still half asleep. The room was gray with predawn light. I struggled to my feet, listening for the direction of the threat.

Below, in the courtyard.

The sound of footsteps running along the corridor swept away my confusion. Vida was already crouched with a knife in her hand. Dela rolled off her pallet, tense and ready. I fumbled for my swords, their ancient energy burning into me.

The screen snapped open.

We all froze, gaping at the figure in the doorway.

Ryko.

The faint light from the window caught a thick wet shine across his face and chest. Blood. A lot of it.

CHAPTER FOUR

THE BIG MAN staggered into the room, his chest heaving in ragged gasps. He dropped his sword and doubled over.

Dela ran forward. "You're hurt."

"No." Ryko caught Dela's outstretched hand and held her at arm's length. "It doesn't matter." He took a shuddering breath. "The Pearl Emperor is below."

"Here?" Vida was aghast. "Why?"

Ryko's face was stark in the moonlight. "When I found His Majesty, I told him Sethon killed his mother and brother. He went mad. Some kind of blood rage. He killed two of his own guard—and then he came down here, looking for Sethon's men. He's cutting down everyone in sight. Everyone."

"If he is killed, everything is lost," Vida said.

I stared down at the moonstone and jade hilts in my hands.

Their pale glow blurred into a vision of the Imperial Pearl sewn into the base of Kygo's throat. I shook my head, trying to clear the image from my mind. It shifted, but a soft hum settled into the base of my skull.

"We must stop him," Vida said. "Disarm him. Get him out of here."

"Disarm him?" Ryko said. "We cannot raise a weapon against the emperor." He wiped blood out of his eyes "Dela, get Lady Eona to safety. Go, while the fighting is confined to the courtyard."

"I'm not going anywhere," I said. "We have to stop the emperor." The hum was louder now.

"We can't stop him," Ryko said. "We can't touch him."

I tightened my grip on Kinra's swords. "I can."

I had already hit the Pearl Emperor once. It was less than a week since I had rammed the heel of my hand into Kygo's throat to stop him from strangling me. He had thought I was Lord Eon, his powerful ally. When I had confessed I was just a girl, his rage had been terrifying.

I turned to Vida. "Find Solly and get us some horses."

"From where?" she protested.

"I don't know. Just do it!"

I headed for the door, but Dela blocked my way.

"Let me pass," I said.

"No. You must not endanger yourself. Not again."

"Get out of my way, Dela." I tried to move around her, but she matched my step.

"If you die, Lady Dragoneye," she said, "the emperor has no chance of reclaiming his throne."

A rush of energy—not my own—exploded through me. I slammed my elbow into Dela's chest, punching out her air. She dropped to the floor.

For a long moment no one moved, then Dela took a rasping breath, her eyes wide with shock. My own astonishment pressed me back a step. The violent energy had come from the swords. From Kinra.

"Stop her, Ryko!" Dela finally gasped.

He backed away. "I cannot." He looked wildly at me as if I was the one stopping him. Fear bleached his face. "I cannot."

"What?" Dela's voice shrilled into disbelief. She lunged for me as I pushed past Ryko into the dim passageway. I ran to the staircase and took the steps two at a time. As I rounded the landing, the muffled struggle in the courtyard separated into loud screams and cries above the ring of clashing swords.

"What's wrong with you, Ryko?" I heard Dela demand. They were following me. "Why didn't you stop her?"

"I don't know! I—I couldn't move!"

I jumped the last few steps and landed heavily, still unused to the mobility of my healed body. Kinra's determination was thrumming in my mind, driving me toward the battle. Ryko and Dela clattered down the steps behind me.

"Eona, wait," Dela pleaded.

I ducked away, fighting a wild urge to raise my swords against them.

"Don't go out there!" It was the innkeeper at the back door, his face a pale blur of fear. "Come this way, sir. Quick, I have a place to hide." He grabbed Dela's arm and pulled her toward the stable yard.

The red flags across the front doorway hung limp in the heavy predawn air, obscuring my view of the battle. Although the sounds of combat were close by, Kinra's experience told me the heart of the struggle was farther across the courtyard. With a deep breath, I slashed through the flags into the first brightening of dawn.

For a moment, all I saw was mayhem: shadowy bodies strewn on the cobblestones, horses rearing, knots of men fighting. Around me, the clang of steel on steel and groans of effort were punctuated with the screams of frightened horses and injured men. The stench of blood and piss made me step back. Then Kinra's knowledge surged through the swords and made sense of the melee. Kygo was on a horse in the center. He was not wearing armor, only the white mourning robe I had last seen on him at the palace, the heavy silk streaked with dirt and ominous sprays of dark blood. He did not even have a helmet—his long braid, glinting with jewels, swung from the back of his shaven head as he hacked at anything that moved. Scattered around him, four imperial guards were fighting off soldiers, forcing them away from the young emperor. For all of the uneven numbers, the guards were holding their own.

My eyes were drawn to the pale luminescence at the base of Kygo's throat—the Imperial Pearl, as big as a duck egg. Along with the hum in my head came a flash of sensual memory: my fingers stroking a man's throat, stroking the pearl, its smooth beauty sewn into the hollow between his collarbones. I heard him moan with pleasure. Any minute now I would have my chance to rip the pearl from its moorings of skin and flesh. To rend its power from him.

I gasped, breaking the thrall. They were not my fingers stroking the pearl, and not my emperor. Whose memory was this? Whose treason?

There could be only one answer: Kinra. My ancestress.

She had tried to steal the Imperial Pearl. The shock loosened my grip on the swords. For a moment, I considered dropping them—the weapons of a traitor!—but the impulse was lost in the hum of their power, and the certainty that I could not disarm Kygo without them.

Behind me, Dela and Ryko burst from the lodging house. Their arrival caught the attention of the nearest guard, who was fighting off three soldiers. I remembered the man's lean, deeply lined face from the palace: Ryko's friend, the Captain of the Imperial Guard. He parried a vicious slice with one sword, swinging the other to meet a low sweep from his right. He outclassed his opponents, but he was tiring fast.

"Ryko!" he yelled. A sword connected with his metal breastplate. He staggered backward.

Ryko charged at the closest attacker and swung his heavy blade down like an ax on the soldier's helmet. The man buckled to the ground, his sword skittering across the cobblestones toward us. With frightening speed, Ryko jumped over the slumped body and slammed his hilt into the face of the next fighter.

Dela cursed under her breath and grabbed the fallen soldier's sword.

"Eona, get back inside," she ordered, and ran after Ryko.

But I did not move; Kinra's ancient energy was pounding through me. My eyes found Kygo again and tracked the pearl at his throat as he ducked and swung at the men on the ground. Kinra wanted the pearl. It was her calling. Her destiny. Her right.

We had to take the pearl.

We? I gritted my teeth, fighting for control. I was here to disarm Kygo and save him, not steal the Imperial Pearl! I was no traitor, nor would I be an ancient traitor's slave. My will had been wrested from me once by Ido. It would never happen again.

I flung the swords away. They hit the cobblestones, the clang breaking Kinra's battle cry in my head. But the sharp sound stopped a soldier running toward Dela. He turned and saw an easier target. Raising his blade, he came at me.

Better to have treasonous thoughts than dying ones. I launched myself at the discarded swords, landing heavily on hands and knees. My fingers closed around one hilt; the other was too far away. Still on my knees, I twisted around to face the soldier. In three steps, he'd be on top of me.

First step—he swung his sword.

Second—his blade sliced the air.

Third—I was ready, weapon raised, thighs braced. As steel met steel, the hum of my sword rose through me.

Drop your shoulder and roll.

The instruction was like a half-heard whisper, but I obeyed. The soldier's blade clanged against the stones where I had knelt just a moment before. His surprise held him over his sword. Through Kinra's eyes I saw the opportunity and swung at his knees, connecting in a messy crunch of bone and blood. Screaming, he crashed to the ground.

I scrabbled across the blood-spattered stones and snatched the second sword. Again, the hum intensified, burning Kinra's mission into my mind. It was clear I could not survive without her knowledge—but I had to find a way to resist her hunger for the pearl.

I backed up against the lodging house wall. Before me, the battle shifted and twirled like a court dance, counted to the beat of shrieks and cries. My eyes found the white-robed emperor again, still on his horse, still hacking wildly. Kinra's energy quickened, her warrior knowledge reading the patterns of combat. We both wanted to reach Kygo, but only she had the skill to carve a passage through the fray. I had to let Kinra lead me through the battle. It was a dangerous gamble: I just hoped that when we reached Kygo, he would be facing Eona, his ally, not an ancient traitor intent on slashing the pearl from his throat.

Kinra found the entry point. It was on the emperor's right flank: a young imperial guard had cut down three attackers, and a wary space had opened up around him. Still, we needed someone to protect our back. I clamped down on the thought; *I* needed someone to protect *my* back.

"Ryko!" I yelled. "With me!"

At my call, he broke away from the clumsy thrust of the soldier in front of him.

"Go," Dela shouted at him. "I've got this covered." She feinted at Ryko's opponent, drawing his attack. Nearby, the captain had forced a soldier against the lodging house wall, his blade opening up the man's belly. Hurriedly, I looked away from the spill of entrails.

"My lady, get back inside," Ryko yelled, running to me. "I'll help the emperor."

"No! Disarm him!" Another image—my hand closing around a man's throat, around the pearl—broke through my defenses. Gathering my will, I focused on Ryko and resisted the humming treachery of the swords.

"My lady," he pleaded. "I cannot engage the emperor."

"Then help me stop him."

Our eyes locked. I felt Ryko's massive energy like a second pulse through my body—then it melded with the beat of my own heart as though we were one.

"What is that?" he gasped. "Are you doing it?"

"I don't know."

An animal scream cut through the cries and clash of metal. The emperor's horse reared, its forelegs barely touching the cobblestones before it bucked and staggered. The emperor jumped from the animal and landed awkwardly, folding into a tangled heap of white silk.

"Now!" I yelled.

I ran, propelled by Kinra's exhilaration. From the corner of my eye I saw Ryko stoop and grab a second sword from the ground. The emperor was already clambering to his feet. His terrified horse kicked at dodging men and flickering shadows. I felt Kinra focus on the Imperial Pearl at the emperor's throat.

A soldier in unfastened body armor turned to meet me, his swords raised in a classic block. Even before I saw his face, I knew it was Lieutenant Haddo. His startled gaze took in my shape under the thin robe. Then his eyes found mine and I saw shock flare into anger. He lowered his blades.

"Put those swords down, woman," he shouted. "Get back inside. You'll be hurt."

I faltered; the man still thought I was defenseless. In my head, I heard a command: *Strike him now.*

"Stay close to me," he added. "I'll get you to the house."

Before I could collect myself, Ryko ran past me, swords swinging at the lieutenant's head. Haddo raised a hasty block, but the force of the attack drove him back toward the horse. The animal reared at the sudden movement, its plunging hooves grazing the lieutenant's shoulder. Ryko leaped away as Haddo stumbled and fell, tucking into a roll to escape the horse's stamping frenzy. The maneuver twisted off the man's unsecured armor and sent it sliding across the stones. Nearby, a soldier saw his lieutenant go down and lunged at Ryko. The islander whirled around and deflected the strike.

I tightened my grip on Kinra's swords and felt her battle experience flow into me. *Give no quarter,* her voice whispered. *Take Haddo now.* I readied my blades. But the man was still on his hands and knees.

"Haddo," I yelled. "Get up."

He raised his head at my call, his eyes suddenly widening. "Behind you! Stop! I order you to stop!"

I turned. One of his men was coming at me. Either he didn't hear the order or didn't care because he kept coming, sword swinging at my neck.

With Kinra's reflexes, I angled my blades into a desperate parry. His steel hit mine, the force sending a cascade of pain through my arms. He lifted his weapon for another strike.

"Stop!" Haddo roared.

The man pulled back, startled.

"The islander. Get the islander," Haddo ordered. The man ran at Ryko.

Across the courtyard, I saw a soldier heading toward Vida. The girl had caught the emperor's horse and was doggedly holding on to its bridle, all her attention on the plunging animal. As I opened my mouth to scream a warning, Solly ran out of the laneway and clubbed the man with a yoke.

Haddo turned to me with the beginnings of enlightenment. "Who are you?"

My answer was a punishing set of Tiger cuts aimed at his

chest. He blocked reflexively, his face sharpening at my borrowed skill. Ahead, the emperor was holding off two soldiers with rage-fueled savagery. Again, I felt my focus drawn to the base of his throat. To the pearl. With grim determination I turned my attention back to Haddo.

The lieutenant had already recovered from his surprise; he met my next barrage of cuts with efficient blocks. I changed tactics, swinging into the circular upper and lower body attacks of the Goat. Our swords connected in a sudden stop, our faces a finger-length apart.

"Are you resistance?" he gasped.

I could not brace against his weight much longer—he would have me off balance. Kinra whispered: *Rabbit feints and kicks.* Summoning courage, I relaxed my trembling hold. The sudden lack of opposition made him lurch forward. Throwing all my strength into a downward disengage, I jumped free of our grapple. My landing buckled into a fall; once again, I had forgotten the new strength in my healed leg. I scrambled upright.

A few lengths away, Ryko and Dela were holding off three soldiers who had advanced on the unhorsed emperor. Although I was facing Haddo with swords ready, he seemed transfixed by the islander and the graceful man fighting beside him. Then I saw him make the connection.

"By the gods, you're *them*." He rounded on me. "You're not a woman. You're the Dragoneye!" As he took another breath to shout the alarm, I lunged.

My sudden thrust stopped him, but his return was quick

and strong. He launched into a volley of savage cuts, his anger driving me backward. Suddenly, a devious flick of his left blade sliced across the back of my hand, close to the folio bound above my wrist. The pearls around it snapped up like a striking snake. I cried out, but it was the show of blood that tempered Haddo's rage; he had to take me alive, unhurt. He withdrew, allowing both of us a moment to recover. The pearls tightened around my arm, securing the folio and stopping the blood. Was it their mandate to steal the Imperial Pearl, too? I could no longer trust any of Kinra's treasures. Taking a shaking breath, I readied myself for Haddo's next attack.

This time his pass was more subdued; a cautious hunt to disarm.

"You must know you will be caught," he said, disengaging from my low block. "The whole army is looking for you."

"You serve a traitor," I said.

"He has the blood, and the right." He thrust at me, but I turned away the blade, catching his second sword in a last-minute slide.

"Prince Kygo has the true right," I said, retreating a few steps. "Sethon claims that Kygo is dead. But he is not—there he is, right in front of you."

Haddo glanced across at the young emperor, who was beating back a soldier with frenzied blows. The Imperial Pearl shone at his throat, a beacon of the truth. Kinra's ambition flared again. I concentrated through her humming fervor.

Haddo lowered his swords. Cautiously, I matched him. We

faced each other, still and watchful, our weapons at the ready in case this strange truce broke.

"Why do you think Sethon wants me alive?" I asked.

"You are a lord."

"No. He wants to use my dragon power for war."

Haddo eyed me. "That is forbidden. You're lying."

"It is Sethon who is lying."

Haddo glanced at the emperor again: living proof of Sethon's lies. Then I saw him focus on something behind me.

"Eona!" It was Dela's voice.

I risked a glance over my shoulder. Dela was circling the emperor and Ryko. "Eona, stop him! He'll kill Ryko."

Kygo's frenzy had turned on the islander. Although Ryko was valiantly blocking the emperor's blows, he was not engaging. Neither Ryko nor Dela would raise their swords against their master. Dead and wounded men lay on the ground around them. A quick scan of the courtyard showed only Ryko's captain and another guard still fighting a handful of soldiers. Almost all of Haddo's men were down.

"Eona?" Haddo repeated. "You really are a woman? A woman Dragoneye?" I could see the shock in his widened eyes. He touched the blood amulet around his neck.

"Dela, take over here," I ordered, and backed away from the lieutenant. He stared at me, bewildered, until Dela rushed him, whooping a battle cry.

I spun around and felt Kinra gauge the scene. Ryko was retreating from the emperor with every strike against his swords. At each step, the islander shouted his allegiance, but Kygo kept advancing. The young emperor's face was dark with rage and effort, his wild swords only finding their mark from years of relentless training. Kinra's focus dropped to the pearl. *He does not deserve it.* I ignored her treacherous thought.

"Ryko, get out of the way," I yelled.

He ducked under the emperor's slashing blades.

"He does not know who we are," he gasped. "I cannot rouse him."

"Your Majesty," I called. "It is Eona." The emperor's gaze traveled across to me. There was no recognition, only the fever of madness. He raised his swords. I was a fool—he had never known my true name.

I tried again. "Your Majesty. I am Lord Eon. Your ally."

Kinra's reflexes saved me from the slice at my face and the cunning lower cut. I leaped back, landing on the soft give of a fallen body. It spasmed; the man underfoot was not dead. He shrieked his agony, clawing at my legs. Cold horror propelled me off his bloodied torso. The shock weakened my hold on Kinra. Her purpose surged through me like water smashing through a dam, my terror and pity obliterated by angry ambition.

She swung the swords and I felt them sing Kygo's death, not his deliverance. Desperately, I tried to wrest back control, but Kinra held true, aiming for the emperor's chest. The wicked thrusts slammed against Kygo's blades. Steel slid along steel in screeching protest. I gritted my teeth and wrenched the swords free, fighting Kinra's desire to drive them into his heart.

Something flickered across Kygo's glazed eyes. Fear? Or was it recognition?

"Your Majesty!" I groped for something that might bring him back. "Kygo! We have a pact. Mutual survival." But the humming in my head screamed his destruction.

He lunged, swords circling in a high Goat attack. Kinra's experience blocked his heavy charge, her sliding parry forcing the emperor off balance. Before I could pull away, she flicked up the grip. The vicious punch caught Kygo in the forehead. He reeled backward and staggered over the legs of a splayed body.

Take the pearl!

The command drove me over the corpses to the emperor. All I could see was the pearl stitched to his throat, only a sword thrust away. Kygo was dazed, swaying on his feet, blood welling from the burst skin above his eye. He would not see me coming. One sharp stab. I raised my blades.

"My lady, now's your chance. Disarm him!" Ryko's voice broke through the triumphant humming in my head. Something within me—deep and dragon-forged—reached out to the islander's massive energy. Once again, his strength pulsed through my body, his heartbeat melding with mine. Instinctively, I grabbed at his solid presence and silently chanted, *Disarm, disarm, disarm*, to drown out the building shriek of the swords.

"Disarm, disarm!" Ryko ran at Kygo, horror twisting his face as he bore down on his king. My chant was overriding his actions. Somehow, I had a hold on his will.

I stopped chanting, but it was too late. Ryko rammed the slighter man. They staggered and fell. Ryko rolled away as the emperor landed on his hands and knees, both swords jarring from his hold. Kinra saw the opportunity. In my mind, I saw her lift her blades and bring them down. Cleaving spine from skull. Slicing out the pearl.

Screaming, I raised Kinra's swords. Their arc downward felt like a thousand years of breathless terror.

And in every second of those thousand years, I fought Kinra for control. I fought her for my mind. I fought her for Kygo's life.

The blades smashed into the stones a fingertip from the emperor's face. The force vibrated through my hands, howling Kinra's disappointment. As the emperor recoiled, I saw fear pierce the madness in his eyes, slamming him back into his mind.

I gasped as relief twisted into my chest. "Kygo!"

He slumped, the fierce rage draining away.

"Your Majesty, are you all right?"

Slowly, he looked up, his breathing ragged and pained. "Lord Eon?"

I let go of Kinra's swords. The sudden absence of her fury was like my backbone had been yanked from my body. I collapsed onto my knees.

"I am here, Your Majesty."

He reached out and touched my shoulder, checking that I was truly in front of him. "They are dead, Lord Eon." His voice broke as he fought back his sorrow. "My brother. My mother. Dead."

"I know."

He looked at the carnage surrounding us. "What is this?"

He closed his eyes. "I remember Ryko coming to the camp, telling me about the coup. And the soldiers . . . He pressed his fists to his eyes. "By the gods, *I* did this, didn't I? Killed my own men? And those people, in the village—"

Gagging, he bent double. The tension in his body gave way to shivering. He did not seek comfort; he was both man and king. Yet something within me knew I had to reach out and breach his lonely despair. It was a risk. His royal body was sacred, inviolate. And I had just fought a desperate battle to stop Kinra from killing him.

It was the guilt and pain in his bloodied face that made me take the chance. I understood guilt and pain. I touched his shoulder, the hard muscle flinching under my fingers. His head snapped up, a lifetime of learned distance swamped by sudden need—something else we had in common. Awkwardly, I drew him closer, as much to escape the horror in his eyes as to comfort him, and murmured sounds of solace against his sweat-slick skin. His ghosts would come soon—as mine had—but the least I could do was hold them back for a while with my touch and a voice that was not screaming for mercy.

Nearby, Ryko hauled himself to his feet, using a sword for leverage. At the corner of my eye, a flicker resolved into Haddo, still trading blows with Dela. He was very close to breaking the Contraire; her blocks were slipping, and there was no strength left in her thrusts. Ryko saw it, too. He gathered himself and ran at the combatants.

"Dela, fall back," he yelled.

With a desperate burst of strength, she disengaged. Ryko caught one of Haddo's swords in a sweeping cut that sent it spinning into the air. It crashed to the cobblestones, loud in the sudden, eerie calm.

I realized there was no clashing swords or cries of effort; the battle was over. The sounds now were of pain and prayer. Only two other men were standing: the captain and another guard. Both of them saw Ryko's struggle and ran to help.

Haddo turned to face the islander, his sword weaving with exhaustion. Every movement was a beat too slow; he would not last long, especially now that the captain and the other guard were on their way. Although I knew Haddo was the enemy, I could not see him slaughtered this way. There had already been too much death.

"Your Majesty," I said, grabbing the emperor's shoulder.

He lifted his head.

"Order Ryko to stop! Please."

Even as I said it, Ryko lunged. One blade flicked away Haddo's remaining weapon; the other sliced across his shoulder, opening up a shallow gash. The lieutenant stumbled and fell, landing heavily on his back. Desperately, he rolled and clambered to his knees. But it was too late; Ryko swung his sword for the kill. Haddo's fingers closed around the blood amulet at his throat; a final plea to Bross.

"No!" I screamed, flinging out my hand at the islander.

Energy leaped between us. Deep within me, our pulses thundered together, our heartbeats drumming into one.

Ryko froze, the sword suspended in its deadly arc above Haddo's head. The islander's massive shoulders strained to finish the blow, the fruitless effort drawing his lips into a snarl. He could not bring the sword down. Through our link, I felt his confusion explode into searing fury.

"What are you doing?" he bellowed at me.

Haddo saw his chance and threw himself to one side, twisting away from the hanging sword—straight into the path of the captain.

The emperor rose to his knees. "Take him alive!"

But the captain's blade was already punching through Haddo's chest, severing flesh from spirit in a gasping rush of death.

CHAPTER FIVE

AS HADDO'S *HUA* drained away, Ryko roared his freedom, his sword finally finishing its futile journey. I knew I should turn to the islander—swear that the control was not deliberate—but I could not take my eyes off Haddo as he slumped into death, impaled on the captain's sword. His senseless slaughter pierced me like a barbed arrow.

"You were supposed to take him alive!" I shouted. "You should have taken him alive! You failed your emperor."

I launched myself at the captain, but a brutal grip on my shoulder brought me up short.

"No! It was I who failed!" The emperor jerked me back against his body. "My command was too slow."

I turned on him. "He could have stopped. He had time."

The emperor shook his head. "It was too late."

"The Lady Dragoneye is correct, Your Majesty," the captain cut in, his voice cold. "I did not follow your order."

The emperor abruptly released his hold on me, putting space between our bodies.

"Of course," he murmured, flushing. "*Lady* Dragoneye."

I pulled farther away from him, only to see the captain wrench his sword out of Haddo's chest. The action dropped the lieutenant onto the stones like a discarded puppet. The man had been our enemy, but he had also been kind, and a caring husband to a wife now bereft. I closed my eyes, but found no respite; instead of Haddo, I saw the lifeless eyes of the soldier in the conquered palace. My first kill, but probably not my last. I had no business judging the captain.

"Your Majesty, the failure was mine," the captain said. "I offer you my sword and my immediate death."

He knelt before us. Touching his forehead to the ground, he held up his weapon to his emperor. Although he had wiped down the blade, the steel was still smeared with Haddo's blood. I looked away.

The emperor drew himself up. The effort of pushing through his fatigue and horror showed in his clenched jaw. "Captain Yuso, I decline the offer. Your death is useful to me elsewhere."

I could hear the ritual within the words: both men taking refuge in the ceremonies of honor.

Yuso bowed. "My life is yours, Heavenly Master." He sat back on his heels. "Still, it would be pointless suicide to stay here much longer, Your Highness," he added with a grim smile. "My men tried to contain the patrol, but if any of them got past us, it will not be long before they bring reinforcements. I suggest we clean up and move out."

The emperor surveyed the courtyard. "Good advice."

Yuso's expression shifted into careful neutrality. "Your Highness, we cannot afford to take any prisoners"—he glanced at the fallen figure of one of his guards—"nor care for any injured who cannot ride."

I saw Ryko straighten, as if in protest. The other imperial guard who had survived the skirmish glanced uncertainly at the islander, then back at the captain.

Beside me, the emperor sucked in a breath. "Is that necessary, Yuso?"

The captain gave one short nod.

"I disagree," Ryko said, dropping to his knees. "Forgive my outspokenness, Your Majesty, but I think—"

The emperor raised a hand, silencing the islander. The sunlight caught the gold of a heavy ring on his finger as he considered Yuso. "Your reasons, captain?"

"The less information High Lord Sethon gets, the better," Yuso said. "We hold only a few advantages—our number and direction are not known, and the Lady Dragoneye is still thought to be Lord Eon—all of which will be passed on to the High Lord, either from loyalty or torture, if we leave *anyone* behind."

Until that moment, I had not fully understood what they were discussing. Now it became sickeningly clear. Yuso wanted to kill everyone left alive on the field. Friend or foe. I could not even find voice for the brutality of it.

"Ryko?" the emperor prompted. There was a faint plea in his voice.

"What Captain Yuso says is true," Ryko said reluctantly. "But it is not what your—it does not feel honorable, Majesty."

"Perhaps you have been in the harem too long, Ryko," Captain Yuso said.

The emperor's face stiffened. Kygo had once confessed to me that he feared his harem childhood had made him too tender. Too womanly. If Yuso knew this, then he was a man who played a deep game, for his barb at Ryko had found its true home.

As if nothing had happened, the emperor motioned to someone behind me. "Is that you, Lady Dela?" I turned to see Dela bow deeply. "Escort the Lady Dragoneye from the battlefield and prepare for our evacuation." The emperor looked up at the pink-streaked dawn sky. "We leave in a quarter bell."

"No!" I said. "Your Majesty, you cannot be thinking—"

"Lady Dragoneye!" His voice was harsh. Exhaustion had pared the last roundings of youth from his features. His was now a man's face, weary and heartsick. "Go." He nodded dismissal to Lady Dela.

She took my hand and pulled me upright. I met her eyes, trying to enlist support, but she gave a slight shake of her head.

"Where are your swords?"

My swords: for a mad moment, I wanted to pick them up and feel Kinra's strength slide under my skin and into my heart. She would stop the emperor. I shook my head free of the impulse—no, she would kill him.

"I will bring them with me," Ryko said curtly.

Dela tightened her grip and led me to the edge of the courtyard. On the ground ahead, a sprawled body shuddered. I heard a faint groan.

"Are they really going to . . . ?" I could not finish the sentence.

Dela ushered me past the groaning soldier. "I don't know. We are fighting for our lives now, Eona."

"I could try and heal them."

"Have you found a way to control your power?" Dela asked.

"No."

"Then you can't help."

"But it is wrong." I pulled against her hand.

She yanked me closer, forcing me to keep up with her quick steps. "They do not want women here to remind them of life—of mercy—when they must embrace war and brutality."

I thought of Kinra: not all women were about life and mercy. And what of myself? I barely knew how to be a woman and, after the carnage at the village, I was hardly a symbol of life. Even so, Yuso was urging murder. And the emperor was allowing it. I clenched my fists.

Dela bundled me through the red door flags of the lodging house. The single wall lamp had guttered, leaving the foyer in shadowy half-light. I strained to hear what was happening in the courtyard. Part of me dreaded the sounds that might reach us in the stuffy cloister, but another part knew I had to listen. So far, nothing penetrated the walls beyond the awakening birdcalls and lows of our oxen.

"Are you injured?" Dela propelled me toward the staircase.

"Only my hand." I held it up for inspection.

The pearls around my forearm shifted, securing the folio against my skin. For the first time, their clicking embrace frightened me. If Kinra's swords were tuned to the emperor's death, then what was her journal's purpose? Maybe it, too, had *Gan Hua* worked into it—negative energy distilled from *Hua* and aimed at the emperor. *Gan Hua* could be a very deadly force without the balance of its positive energy opposite, *Lin Hua*. I fought back a rise of panic. I had placed all of my hope in a traitor's journal. Even if it did hold the secrets of my dragon power, it was useless; the words of a woman who had tried to kill her emperor and sent her hatred across five centuries could not be trusted.

I could not risk carrying a book whose power might snake into my mind and take it over, like the power of the swords.

"My lady?"

We both turned. Vida was at the back doorway.

"Solly and I have caught some of the guards' horses," she said. "I've packed as much as I can into the saddlebags."

"Good," Dela said. "Where are our clothes? Lady Eona has to dress. And she needs doctoring."

I also needed to remove the folio from my arm—and my presence. The decision thickened my throat with loss. The folio had been a constant companion over the last few weeks—a symbol of hope and power. I felt as if a loyal friend had suddenly betrayed me.

Vida beckoned us through to the stable yard. Outside, the air smelled of frightened animals, grain feed, and dung, a relief from the stench of blood and spilled entrails in the courtyard. I drew in a shaking breath, hoping to break through the despair that threatened to overwhelm me. If I could not trust the journal, how could I learn to control my power?

Four horses were tethered along the stable rail. Solly moved between them, calming each with gentle strokes and soft words. He saw us coming and stopped our progress with a raised hand.

"My ladies." He ducked his head into a quick bow, his usual broken-toothed grin reduced to a thin line. "Stay back from the horses. They're all battle-trained and will kick anything near their hindquarters."

Dela ushered me toward the stable. "Go with Vida. Get your arm bound," she said. "And get dressed. Not the mourning robe, though. Something less conspicuous."

Giving the horses a wide berth, I followed Vida into the shed. The oxen lowed as we passed their stalls. They were probably hungry. I realized that I was, too, and couldn't help a wry smile; my body did not care about treachery or despair, only food and rest.

Vida looked over her shoulder. "How bad is your wound?"

The tight embrace of the pearls had deadened the pain. Now, as I focused on the cut, it stung with every flex of my fingers. I showed her the shallow slash across the back of my hand. "It is not too bad," I said. "It's not bleeding anymore."

"I saw what you did for His Majesty. How you stopped him," Vida said. "It was bravely done."

I eyed her warily, unaccustomed to such warmth from the girl.

She hurried behind our cart. "All the bandaging has been packed in the saddlebags. I'll find some when you are dressed." She flipped back the canvas canopy flap, opened the nearest basket, and dug her hands into the contents. "Here, take these."

She passed me a pair of woven rush sandals—thin-soled, meant for the paved roads of a town—and went back to rummaging. Finally, she pulled out two packets of neatly folded cloth, one the color of rust; the other, olive green. With a flick of her wrists she shook out the rust cloth into a long, full skirt. The green was an over-tunic: the day wear of a merchant woman. The resistance had supplied us well.

She squatted down, holding open the skirt. "Quick, my lady."

I stepped into the middle of the pooled linen. Vida pulled it up over my blood-streaked shift, then deftly fastened the ties around my waist. Although it was just past dawn, the air was already hot and close. By midday, I would be stifling under all this cloth.

"Arms, please."

Obediently, I raised them. The familiar action brought the bittersweet memory of Rilla dressing me at the palace. Were she and Chart safe? Although I had freed both of them from their service bonds when I came into our master's inheritance, and made Chart heir to his estate, it was no guarantee of protection. Especially if High Lord Sethon had them marked as a possible ransom for my surrender.

Vida worked the tunic over my head, pulling it down over my chest and hips. Another dip into the basket brought out a red sash—silk, by the rich sheen. It made me wonder whose clothes I wore; the skirt and tunic were not new, and no merchant woman would easily surrender the one length of silk she was allowed by law. A terrible thought came to me: were these the clothes of a woman I had killed? I shook off the morbid idea. No—the cloth was too fine for a villager.

Vida wrapped the long sash around my waist three times and tied it at the front. She stepped back, scrutinized me, then adjusted the tunic's high collar. "Your hair is wrong," she said. "I suppose it doesn't matter; we won't be traveling on the roads for anyone to see."

I forced my fingers under the sash; it was very tight.

"I found these in the room." Vida withdrew two worn leather pouches from the deep pocket in her gown. "They're important, aren't they?"

My Dragoneye compass and the death plaques. I reached for them, then stopped. The compass had belonged to Kinra, too. It was probably anchored to her power even more than her journal.

"Pack them," I said. Vida started to return them to her pocket. "No, wait."

I grabbed the pouch with the death plaques and pushed it between the layers of my sash. When there was a quiet, solitary moment, I would pray to Kinra—beg her to leave me alone.

To cover my abruptness, I bent to work my feet into the

sandals, but the voluminous skirt got in my way. "All this cloth is impossible," I said, gathering the hem into one hand. "I would rather be in a man's tunic and trousers."

"Wouldn't we all," Vida said.

I looked up from my task; was she softening toward me?

"Not everyone. Not Lady Dela," I said, trying a quick smile.

She gave a sharp laugh. "That's true."

"What's true about Lady Dela?" the Contraire asked, her passage past the oxen triggering their plaintive cries.

Vida flushed and stepped back, but I said, "We want to get back into trousers while you want to get back into a skirt."

Dela smiled grimly. "More than anything." She held up a loop of string threaded with dried fruit—army travel rations, no doubt salvaged from Haddo's supplies. "Eat something before we move out. And get that hand bound."

"Dela," I said, stopping her retreat. "Will you do something for me?" I unwound the pearls, ignoring their stiff resistance and the small piercing of my heart. "Will you take care of the folio?"

"You want me to carry it?"

I held out the book, the pearls wrapping themselves tightly around it again. "Only you can decipher the script," I said. "This way you can work on it at any time."

She studied me for a moment, her hand hovering over mine. Did she sense I was holding something back? Yet I could not tell her that my ancestress, on whom all our hopes rested, had been a traitor. I could not tell anyone. No wonder Kinra's name had been expunged from the records, and her dragon had fled the circle for five hundred years. This was the tainted blood that flowed in my veins. This was the unforgivable legacy I had to make right with the gods.

Dela finally picked up the folio. "I am at your service, Lady Dragoneye," she said, and tucked the journal and its rope of guardian pearls inside her tunic.

Vida was tying the bandage around my hand when the emperor emerged from the side lane. His walk was stiff and quick. Ryko, Yuso, and the one unscathed imperial guard followed him at a prudent distance. Even from where we sat outside the stable door, I could see the strain between the men.

"Are the horses ready?" the emperor snapped at Solly. "Have they had water?"

The resistance man dropped to his knees, his forehead touching the ground. "Yes, Your Majesty."

Vida followed Solly's example and kowtowed into the dirt. I knelt into the bow of the crescent moon. It was not until Dela hissed, her flattened hand motioning me further down, that I realized my mistake; I had made the obeisance of a lord, not a lady.

"Rise," the emperor said curtly.

We climbed to our feet. His eyes swept over the horses.

"Only four?" he said. "What is our number?"

"Eight, Your Majesty," Dela said.

"We double up, then. We must put as much distance as we can between us and this miserable inn, as quickly as possible."

Ryko stepped forward. As promised, he held Kinra's swords. The blades were wiped clean. They had come so close to drawing the emperor's blood; I could not risk touching them in his presence.

"Your Majesty," Ryko said, "may I suggest you allow Lady Eona to ride with you? Your horse is in no condition to carry two men."

It was sound reasoning, but I knew he had suggested it to stay as far from me as possible. There had been no opportunity to speak to him about my strange hold on his will during the battle. I tried to shake off a sense of foreboding. I did not want to control anyone's will—and I certainly did not want the control to come between us. Ryko's trust in me was already clouded by suspicion.

"No, Ryko." Yuso shook his head, the strength of his opposition drawing him level with the islander. "It is not good strategy to have His Highness and the Lady Dragoneye on one horse."

The islander raised his chin. "It is in this case, captain. We can surround and protect both while still maintaining speed."

Yuso studied his subordinate. "And if we are pursued and engaged, we could lose both. No, better to split up our treasures than have them in one place for the taking."

"Enough," the emperor said wearily. "We do not have time for this. Lady Eona will ride with me. Ju-Long has a strong heart, but he is almost spent, and a lighter load will make the difference."

The two soldiers bowed.

The emperor looked down at his blood-streaked mourning robe. "Lady Dela, find me something to wear. This robe no longer honors my father. The rest of you, pair off with an eye to saving the horses."

"This way, Your Majesty." Dela ushered him past us and into the stable.

"You should eat more of that fruit," Vida said, motioning to the travel rations tied to my sash. "It is going to be a hard day."

"Vida," Solly called. "Bring those feed bags over here."

She nodded again at my rations, then slung the long, bulging bags over her shoulder. I turned my attention to Ryko and his fellow guard as they checked saddles and stirrups. Heavy silence weighted the air. What had happened in the courtyard to cause such tension? An image of Haddo, sword through his chest, leaped into my mind.

Hurriedly, I untied the fruit string from my sash, focusing fiercely on the task to stop the terrible image. The string finally came free and I tore off a large chunk of dried plum. The whole piece went in to my mouth—a boy's habit that would have to change—but this time, no one was watching. I closed my eyes and chewed into a sudden flood of dusty sweetness. As though the sugary fruit had been a trigger, I felt deep fatigue wash over me. All I wanted was to sleep—to find some respite from the blood and horror—but a day of hard riding was ahead. I sent up a small prayer to the gods: *Help me stay on the emperor's horse. And help me find a way to live with these insistent ghosts.*

"Lady Eona."

I opened my eyes. The emperor stood before me dressed in a plain brown tunic and trousers. A high collar covered the Imperial Pearl, although I could see the top of the rough stitches that secured the gem to his skin. I quickly swallowed the remains of the plum.

"Your Majesty," I said, and started to bow. Halfway down, he caught my arm, guiding me up again.

"This is not the time or place for court etiquette." He let go. "I see that you are no longer lame. Surely a gift from the gods for your courage."

I opened my mouth to answer, but did not get the chance.

"You have my gratitude," he continued. "For pulling me out of the killing rage. I know . . ." He paused, his dark eyes suddenly bleak. "I know everything that happened. Your courage and loyalty . . ."

"Everything?" I echoed. Did he know Kinra's swords had tried to kill him?

He stared through me. "I can see every one of them. Every face."

Ah. I was not the only one struggling with ghosts. Although I knew I should not ask about the soldiers in the courtyard, the shared horror of the morning and his pained gratitude made me bold again. I touched his arm.

"Did you kill those injured men, too?"

He stiffened, the vast chasm of rank once again between us. "That was a military decision, Lady Eona. Do not overstep your station."

"Your father would not have done such a thing," I said.

"You do not know what my father would or would not have done."

From the corner of my eye, I saw Ryko and the other guard turn from their preparations. But I could not leave it be; I wanted Kygo to be his father's son.

"Did you kill them?" I asked again. "Tell me you did not."

"Who are you to speak to your emperor like that? You are not my *Naiso*; I do not take advice or criticism from you," he said coldly. "You are not even a true lord. Know your place, woman."

For a moment, his dismissal robbed me of my voice. Then something seared through the bindings of duty and fear. Was it my own anger, or was it the last embers of Kinra's ancient rage? I did not know and, suddenly, I did not care. All I knew was that it was strong and it was mine.

"I am the Ascendant Dragoneye," I said through my teeth. "Whether I am lord or lady or neither, I am your only link to the dragons. *Remember that.*"

The truth of my words registered in the dark flare of his eyes.

He moved closer, using his height to crowd me. "I hope you can back up that claim," he said. "There are many men and women depending on your power. Yet Ryko tells me you still cannot control it. That you destroyed a village and killed thirty-six people. Innocent people who could not fight back."

"At least I did not do it deliberately," I said, holding my ground. "At least I knew it was wrong."

"I could not control it! You saw me. I did not know what I was doing."

"I'm not talking about your killing rage," I said doggedly. "I'm talking about those men left alive in the courtyard."

I thought that he was going to strike me. Instead he stepped back, fists clenched by his sides. "I do not need another conscience, Lady Eona. Look to your own morality and stay out of mine."

He strode across the yard to Ju-Long, the big dappled gray still tied to the stable rail. I watched as he ran his hand over the animal's sweat-stained shoulder, his head bowed. Although anger still roared through me, something dank and sour joined it.

Disappointment.

"Lady Eona," Ryko said.

I turned, stopping his approach. I could not face his anger, too.

He held out Kinra's swords. "There is no place for another saddle-sheath on his Majesty's horse," he said belligerently. "Do you wish to carry your swords in a back-sheath?"

"No!" It was almost a shout. I took a deep breath, forcing moderation into my voice. "Carry them for me. Please."

He gave a quick bow, his face shutting down. It was a servant's face. "As you wish."

The emperor led his horse out into the center of the stable yard and swung himself neatly into the saddle. He summoned the other guard.

"Tiron, assist Lady Eona on to Ju-Long. She does not have any saddle skills."

My face burned. The last time he had seen me on a horse was the night of the palace coup—the same night he had found out I was not Lord Eon, but a girl. For a shamed moment, I remembered his scathing glance up and down my body, and his fury.

The emperor motioned me closer. "You will ride behind me. Use your knees to hold on, but try not to hinder Ju-Long's movement." A flick of his hand sent Tiron down on his knees beside the horse. The young guard blushed as I gathered up the full skirt. He politely looked away as I placed my foot into his waiting hands.

"Ready," I said.

Suddenly, I was rising through the air. I twisted around, awkwardly flinging my healed leg over the animal's flank and grabbing for the back of the saddle. My landing was heavy, the reflexive dig of my knees sending the animal sidewise across the cobbles in a clacking crab-walk. As the emperor pulled the horse around, I desperately tried to keep my seat as the huge, bony joints and muscles shifted under me.

"You have permission to touch me, Lady Eona," the emperor said curtly as he brought the horse to a fidgeting standstill. "Otherwise you'll end up on the ground."

Tentatively I let go of the saddle and held the emperor's waist. Through the cloth of his tunic, I could feel the warmth of his body and the tension in his muscles as he controlled the horse.

"I said, 'Hold on.'" He pulled my arms more tightly around

his waist and pressed my hands against the flat of his stomach.

I inched forward, coming up hard against the back of the saddle.

"You may mount," he ordered the rest of our troop.

I did not dare look over my shoulder in case the movement made me slide off the horse. From behind us came the clatter of hooves and a sharp curse from Dela as she missed her first attempt into the saddle. I focused on the tiny red jewels woven into the emperor's long braid, and slowly adjusted the pressure of my knees against the horse. Already the strain was cutting into my thighs, and my neck was aching. The only logical place for my head was against the flat of the emperor's shoulder blade, but the position was too intimate. I could not take such a liberty.

"Move out," he called.

We lurched into a walk that, in a few steps, quickened into a trot. Instinctively, my arms tightened even further around his waist as I tried to find a rhythm that did not slam my rump bones against the horse or grind me into the raised back of the saddle.

"Do not fight it," the emperor said, glancing back with a frown. "Relax and lean into me or you'll pull us both onto the ground."

It was then I realized where we were heading. "Are we going out the front gate?"

"Yuso wants us to ride through the village before we head into the forest."

I felt him tighten his hold on the reins as we rounded the corner into the courtyard. The stench brought the horse's head up, a loud snort registering its protest. Before us, bodies lay on cobblestones that were wet with blood and excrement. Black carrion birds were already picking and pulling, our arrival sending them skyward in a heavy beat of wings. The emperor pulled the horse to the edge of the compound, then urged it past the corpses. I wanted to close my eyes, turn my head, but something caught my attention.

Movement.

A soldier dragging himself to his knees. And another rocking and groaning, propped up against the lodging-house wall.

"They're not dead," I said. "You didn't kill them."

"They'd be better off if we did." The emperor's voice was harsh. "Most of them will die, even with the local physician's care. And those that don't will betray us."

"I'm glad you didn't."

He looked back at me. "Will you be glad when my uncle uncovers your disguise? When he learns of our whereabouts?" He steered the horse through the inn's gateway. "There is nothing to be glad about here."

But he was wrong. As he kicked Ju-Long into a bone-jarring canter, I placed my head against his shoulder and leaned into the solid anchor of his back.

CHAPTER SIX

YUSO CALLED A HALT at dusk. We gathered in a small, natural clearing in the forest, the deafening chitter of birds heralding the end of daylight. Through the ferns and undergrowth, I caught sight of a bloated stream, fed by the recent monsoon rains. The downpours had been heavier than usual, untamed by the Dragoneyes and their beasts. With only two of us left in the circle—one dying and the other useless—it would not be long before some grave disaster tore at the land and the cries for help would go unanswered.

I slid off Ju-Long's sweaty back, the sudden contact with the ground sending spikes of pain through my legs. For more than twelve full bells we had alternated between short bursts of speed on the horses and long, hot slogs on foot, leading the tired animals. My thighs, unused to the rigors of riding, were a solid ache of overtaxed muscles and chafed skin.

It was almost unbearable to lower myself into a crouch and drop backward onto the damp forest floor amid the heavy, hot folds of my skirt. I cursed, and pushed away a fallen branch caught under my hip. The bandage around my hand was filthy, but the wound no longer stung, even when I flexed my fingers. Across the clearing, Solly unsaddled the horse he had shared with Tiron, while the young guard attended to Ju-Long. Ryko handed his reins to Vida and started toward me, our postponed discussion in his eyes. I readied myself, but the emperor sat down beside me, cutting off the islander's approach. Relief made me sag; I had no answers for Ryko.

"Here, take some water," the emperor said, passing a lacquered flask. "A few more days on Ju-Long and you'll get used to riding."

"A few more days and I'll be dead from arse pain." I clapped my hand over my mouth; the profanity had just slipped out.

He gave a low snort of laughter.

Hesitantly, I smiled back. I had only ever seen him laugh once before, at one of his father's jokes. Admittedly, there had not been much to laugh about in the imperial court. His smile reminded me of his dead mother. Lady Jila's delicate symmetry of cheekbones and chin were, in her son, bolder and more masculine, but I could see her sensuous beauty in his dark eyes and full mouth.

Poor Lady Jila; may she find peace in the garden of the gods. Although it was only weeks ago, it seemed like years since we had sat together in the harem and I had promised her I'd protect her son and be his friend. So far, I had done little to keep either promise.

"I have never heard a lady say 'arse,'" the emperor said mildly.

"I haven't been a lady for long," I reminded him. A little demon—made of exhaustion and the emperor's smile—pushed me into adding, "For five years I've been saying 'arse.' It's hard to stop saying 'arse' after that many years. I suppose I should stop saying 'arse,' since ladies don't say—"

"'Arse,'" he finished for me.

I met his grin.

Yuso kneeled on the ground before us. "Your Highness."

The emperor straightened, the ease gone from his face. "What is it?"

"I estimate we are at least a day ahead of any search, even one on horse. Still, I advise we do not light a fire for cooking and make do with rations. The girl will bring them to you." He tilted his head at Vida, who was fitting a nosebag on one of the horses. "She says there is a resistance group less than a day away. We should make for them. They'll have current news of Sethon's movements."

The emperor nodded. "Good. I want to muster as many men as we can and march on the palace."

Yuso sucked in a breath, his careful control shifting into something hard and intense. It lasted less than a second, then smoothed back into his usual dourness. "We do not head for the eastern tribes, then, Your Majesty?" he asked. "Ryko says the resistance will be gathering there."

"No. By the time we go east and return, the twelve days of Rightful Claim will be long over. It must be now."

I chewed on my lip; to march on the palace without a full army would be suicide.

"As you wish, Your Majesty," Yuso said.

He knew it was suicide, too; I could see it in his eyes. Why didn't he say something? But he merely bowed: the dutiful, loyal soldier.

"Your Majesty," I said hesitantly. "The resistance is expecting us to meet with them in the east. That is where you can be assured of strong support." I glanced at Yuso. "Is that not so, captain?"

He would not look at me. No doubt he did not want to be pulled into the arrow's path. "His Majesty wishes to march on the palace," he said woodenly.

I glared at him. Someone had to tell the truth, but I was not going to fall alone. "I'm sure you will agree, captain, that it is unlikely there will be enough men between here and the palace to make an effective army," I said carefully. "At present, High Lord Sethon has the greater force."

The emperor eyed me impassively. I had seen his honored father wear the same stony mask when dealing with unwelcome news. I tried not to shift under the relentless stare. The old emperor had been a shrewd politician, willing to listen to opposing views without reprisal. I hoped his son had the same restraint.

"You may go, captain." The emperor waved his dismissal. Yuso bowed and backed away.

The emperor waited until he was out of earshot, then said, "My uncle may have the greater military force, Lady Eona, but he does not have the Imperial Pearl, nor your power behind him."

"My power, Your Majesty?" I dug my fingernail into the gold peony etched on the flask. "Are you asking me to use my dragon for war?"

"War?" He shook his head. "There will be no war. That is why we have the days of Rightful Claim; to prevent such a disaster. I have the ancient symbol of sovereignty"—he touched the pearl at his throat—"and I have the support of the Mirror Dragoneye, the symbol of renewed power. My uncle will see that his claim cannot stand against mine."

I knew I was untutored in the ways of statecraft, but I was sure I had not mistaken Sethon's ambition. Nor his ruthlessness.

"Your uncle is not dealing in symbols, Your Majesty. He is dealing in force. He has already decreed himself emperor, pearl or no pearl."

His hand went to his throat again. "You don't understand. Without this pearl, my uncle *cannot* hold the throne. It is what keeps the dragons with us—the seal of our celestial bargain."

"Then he will kill you and take it." For a moment, all I felt was the pearl's soft fire under my fingers, and the burn of Kinra's purpose. I clenched my hands, fighting off the memory.

"If he takes it, he will not have to kill me," the emperor said dryly. "It is now part of my *Hua*, joined to me through blood. I die if it is removed."

"Part of you? I don't understand."

"It is said the pearl is a living link to the dragons. Once it is sewn into an emperor's throat, the two are joined forever through the blood. It is why it must be transferred from a dead emperor's body to the living heir in less than twelve breaths. Otherwise the pearl will die and the seal of our bargain will be gone."

I studied the gold setting that circled the pearl and counted twelve stitches in gold thread radiating from it. The three at the top were neatly placed but the rest were a mess, the flesh around them still bruised and scabbed. "Twelve breaths does not sound very long for such delicate work," I said.

He gave a rough laugh. "Less than a minute and a half for twelve stitches in the throat. As you can see, my physician was both nervous and pressed for time."

"It must have hurt."

For a moment, he hesitated intent on some inner debate. Finally he looked me square in the eye. "It was the most painful thing I have ever endured," he said, and I knew it was no small thing for him to make such an admission. Or for me to receive it. "The setting around the pearl has twelve barbs that first pierce the skin and hold the pearl against the throat," he added. "Each barb also has an eyelet so it can be stitched into the flesh too." His finger circled the edge of the damage. "And there is something else; a burning that enters into the blood and feels like acid flowing through the body for hours afterward."

I found myself swallowing in sympathy. "Does your uncle know about the pearl dying?"

"Of course. Twelve-breaths-twelve-stitches is taught to all royal males in line for the throne."

"Then he must take you alive so that he can transfer the pearl to his own throat safely."

He shook his head. "You seem very sure my uncle will ignore Rightful Claim."

I steeled myself for what I was about to say. "Your uncle has slaughtered your mother and brother, and poisoned your father. Why would he stop at you?"

Had I gone too far? I knew my words had struck their target—it was in the widening of his eyes—but I refused to flinch. The emperor may have felt blood rage at the news of his family's death, but he had not seen Sethon's sword impale his infant brother. Nor had he seen the bloody corpses of the palace household, nor his uncle spurring his troops into baying savagery. Someone had to tell him how things stood.

Still, it took all of my will not to drop into a kowtow.

Nearby, Vida dug through a saddlebag; Tiron conferred with Solly; and Dela wearily loosened her hair from its tight binding—none of them aware that their emperor thought he could just walk into the palace and take back his throne.

"You are very blunt, Lady Eona," he finally said. He pressed his hands against his eyes. "I'm a fool. My father stubbornly trusted his brother, and now here I am, doing exactly the same thing." His long sigh relinquished the hope of a bloodless claim. "Of course you are right. He will try and take the pearl. He certainly will not be the first to think he can steal its power."

The emperor knew the history of the pearl; perhaps he knew about Kinra. Here was my chance to discover if the memories that came with her swords were true, if my blood was truly tainted. In the space of a quickened heartbeat, I fought a battle between risk and opportunity.

"Like Kinra," I said, and the two words took all of my breath.

He lowered his hands, startled. "How did you hear of Kinra?"

I scrabbled for a plausible story. "I—I saw her name in one of Lord Brannon's record scrolls." His surprise faded. "It only said she tried to steal the pearl. Was she an assassin, Your Majesty?"

"No, just a Blossom Woman. She nearly bewitched the pearl from Emperor Dao. He had her executed as a traitor by the Twelve Days of Torture." He leaned closer. "I've heard the executioners can keep someone alive for days even after they have cut out the main organs. Something to keep in mind for my uncle."

I turned away, hoping my face did not betray me. The stories were not the same—somehow my ancestress had become prostitute rather than Dragoneye—but in my vision, I had been Kinra, caressing an emperor's throat, stroking the pearl. Perhaps the stories were not so far apart. Was this how she was erased from history, reduced from Dragoneye Queen to treacherous whore?

The emperor touched my arm. "My apologies, Lady Eona, I did not mean to frighten you."

I rallied a weak smile. "I think I am just tired, Your Majesty."

A gesture brought Vida to his side. "Bring Lady Eona some food. And a rug." He stood. "I will leave you to rest."

In a few strides he was beside Tiron, advising the guard on Ju-Long's rubdown. I prayed he would rethink his strategy and return to our goal of the east. Although he had inherited his father's misguided loyalties and sense of tradition, it also seemed he had inherited his mother's flexible mind and quick insight.

"I will take that to Lady Eona," I heard Ryko say.

Before I could prepare myself, the big islander was standing before me. He held out a piece of hard-bread and a gnarled strip of dried meat.

"Thank you." I took the bread, avoiding his eyes.

His free hand clenched into a fist. "How did you control me?"

"I don't know." I looked up at him. His mouth was tight with disbelief. "Ryko, I truly don't know!"

"Why, then?"

"There had been enough death."

"Can you do it whenever you want to?" His stern expression could not mask the fear in his voice.

Dela crossed over to us. "What is this about, Ryko?" She laid her hand on his arm. "You are towering over *Lady* Eona." She emphasized my rank.

He shrugged off her hold. "*Lady* Eona has some kind of power over my will. She stopped me from fighting."

"Power over your will?" Dela repeated, but her eyes questioned me.

"It's true," I said, lowering my voice, "but I don't know how. It's as if a link opens between us when things are desperate."

"Is it only Ryko? Do you have power over anyone else?" she asked.

"No, only Ry—" I stopped, overwhelmed by a sudden, unwelcome truth. "Yes. Lord Ido, too. It is not completely the same, but they both have some kind of link."

"Ryko and Lord Ido," Dela said slowly, thoughtfully. "What is the connection?"

"Nothing connects us," Ryko said coldly. "I have nothing in common with that whoreson."

"Not true," Dela said. Dawning comprehension paled her face. She shot an anxious glance at me. "Both of you have been healed by Lady Eona."

We looked at one another, the logic undeniable.

"The exchange of *Hua*," I said. "My power flowed through you, Ryko. And it flowed through Ido, at the palace."

He caught his breath. "So this is the price for life? To have my free will ripped from me? To be forced into action that is contrary to my nature?"

"I didn't know!"

Dela broke in. "It was I who begged Lady Eona to heal you."

"Then you have done me a disservice, lady," Ryko said harshly. "Have I not already given enough for this cause? Now I don't even have my own will."

"But I could not let you die," Dela said tightly. Again, she reached out to him, but he stepped back.

I caught Dela's hand. This was not the time for her to declare her feelings. "Perhaps there is a way to break the link," I said. "In the folio."

"I will search," she promised.

Ryko glared at me. "And if there is no way, am I your creature forever?"

"I will not use it again," I said. "I swear."

"All well and good. But you are a proven liar, and I cannot stop you."

"Ryko!" Dela protested.

He shot her a savage look, and walked to the other side of the clearing.

"He does not mean it," Dela said, her eyes following him. She squeezed my hand, then let it go. "I will start searching now."

She pulled the journal from her tunic, and headed over to a shrinking patch of late sunlight.

Slowly, I opened my other hand; the rough hard-bread had left a deep ridge in my palm. I could not blame Ryko for his rage; I had been just as angry when Lord Ido wrested away my own will. And now, if Dela was correct, I had some kind of lasting link with Ido, born from healing his stunted heart-point.

I shuddered. I did not want power over Ido. I did not want anything to do with him. Yet his final cry still stretched between us like the anchoring thread of a spider web.

"My lady," Vida said, interrupting my dark thoughts. She was holding a worn rug. "Something for you to sleep on."

Murmuring my thanks, I took the roll of thin cloth and spread it out behind me. Each shift of my rump made my hips ache. Fatigue dragged at my every move. It was even too much effort to chew the tough hard-bread. I made do with another piece of fruit from the waist-string, then gingerly lowered myself onto the rug. For a moment, I was aware of the unforgiving ground and the smell of old leaves and earth, and then sleep claimed me.

I was woken by the insistent need to relieve myself. The half-moon was high, silvering the outline of the tree canopy. The roosting birds had given way to the screech of night hunters and the deafening shrill of insects. Through half-open eyes, I saw the shadowy shapes of huddled, sleeping bodies and the watchful figure of someone on guard. By my reckoning, it was close to midnight—I could have at least another four or five hours of precious sleep. Maybe if I stayed completely still, I would just slide back into oblivion.

It was not to be. I struggled to my knees, wincing with pain. Every muscle had locked into stiff protest. With a soft grunt, I hauled myself upright. The guard looked around as I hobbled to the tree line. It was Yuso, moonlight carving his face into bold-lined relief like a woodcut. Beyond him, another figure sat staring up at the night sky. From the set of the straight shoulders and pale, shaved head, I knew it was the emperor. Perhaps his ghosts had returned.

Stiff muscles, skirts, and passing water do not mix well. I took so long behind my tree, I was sure Yuso would come looking for me. As it was, both he and the emperor were hovering nearby when I stepped back into the clearing.

"I thought you had got lost, Lady Eona," Yuso said.

"No. I was only a length or two away."

"Go back to your post, captain," the emperor ordered softly.

Yuso bowed and made his way around the edge of the camp. Only when he was in position again, did the emperor say, "Sit with me."

I blinked at the sudden command. Something was pressing urgency into his voice. Was he angry with me, after all?

"Of course, Your Majesty."

He led me along the tree line, a good distance past the sleeping forms of Vida and Solly.

"This will do."

He sat on the ground, and painfully, I lowered myself beside him, tucking my skirt and undershift around my legs. The cloth was sour with horse sweat and dried blood. I should have taken the time to wash before I slept.

"Do you know what my father said about you?" His voice had dropped into the mix of whisper and murmur used for private conversations at court. If I had not been leaning close, I would not have heard him beneath the constant chirr of insects and the rush of water.

Holding my astonishment close, I matched his low tone. "No, Your Majesty."

"He was most impressed with you in the Pavilion of Earthly Enlightenment. He said you had the ability to see both sides of an argument—that, although you were unschooled, you were a natural strategist."

I flushed. A natural strategist? I turned the compliment over in my mind, studying it like a precious stone. If worrying out the motivations of others could be called strategy, then perhaps the Heavenly Master had been right.

"He did not know the half of it, did he?" the emperor added dryly. "I wonder what he would have said of a female Dragoneye."

I flushed again. "He did say that a hidden nature is not necessarily an evil nature."

"Yes, I remember," the emperor said. "From the teachings of Xsu-Ree, the Master of War. 'All generals have a hidden nature. Whether that nature be strong or weak, good or evil, it must be studied if victory is to be yours.'"

"Know your enemy," I murmured.

He started. "How do you know the teachings of Xsu-Ree? Only kings and generals are permitted to study his treatise."

"Even the lowest servant knows that maxim," I said. "How else would he predict the mood of his master, or outwit the servant above him?"

"Then tell me, what do you know about our enemy?" the emperor asked after a moment. "What do you know about my uncle?"

I'd seen High Lord Sethon only once, at the victory procession held in his honor—the same procession where my poor master had died, poisoned by Lord Ido. I pushed away the gruesome image of my master's convulsing body, and concentrated on picturing Sethon. He had looked very much like his half-brother, the old emperor. They'd both had the same broad forehead and chin and mouth. Sethon, however, had been marked by battle—his nose broken and set flat, and his cheek puckered by a heavy crescent scar. Yet it was his voice that made the sharpest memory: a cold monotone that held no emotion.

"Not much," I said. "A High Lord and successful general. The leader of all the armies."

"And the first son of a concubine, like me," the emperor said. "We have the same birth rank."

"But he was not adopted by the empress as true first son, as you were," I pointed out. "You are an acknowledged first son whereas Sethon has always only been a second harem son."

"My father was borne by an empress. I was not. There are those who would argue that Sethon has as much claim to the throne as I have."

"One of those being Sethon." I tried to imagine what it was like to be Sethon; always second harem son, and now second to a nephew who had, more or less, the same birth rank. "You think Sethon truly believes his claim is equal to yours? That it is not only ambition that fuels his ruthlessness, but a sense of entitlement?"

"My father was right, you are sharp-witted," the emperor said. "Xsu-Ree says that we must find the key to our enemy. His weakness. I think this arrogance is the key to my uncle. What do you think?"

"'When a man lifts his chin in pride, he cannot see the chasm at his feet,'" I said, quoting the great poet Cho. I frowned, teasing out the idea of Sethon as a man weakened by arrogance. It did not feel right. "High Lord Sethon has waged many battles and not been tripped up by pride," I said. "It might even be the core of his success."

The emperor smiled. "You have not disappointed me, Lady Eona."

I sat back, wary at his amused tone. He touched my arm and drew me close again.

"Lady, you have punched me, crossed swords with me, abused my decisions, and disagreed with my judgments." The warmth in his voice held me still. "It is not often that an emperor finds someone who will do all of this in the name of friendship. I need someone who is not afraid to stand up to me. Who will tell me when I am failing my father's legacy or speaking from inexperience." He took a deep breath. "I am asking you to be my *Naiso*, Lady Eona."

The night sounds around me dropped away into the sudden roar of my heartbeat. The *Naiso* was the emperor's most important advisor—the only appointment in the court that could be refused with impunity. In the ancient language it was the word for "bringer of truth," but it meant more than that—it meant brother, protector, and perhaps most dangerously, the king's conscience. It was the responsibility of the *Naiso* to challenge the sovereign's decisions, criticize his logic, and tell him the truth, however hard and unpalatable.

It was often a very short-lived position.

I stared out into the darkness, fighting through the tumult in my mind. The *Naiso* was always an older man. A wise man. Never a woman. A female *Naiso* was almost as unthinkable as a female Dragoneye. A small, mad laugh caught in my throat. I was already unthinkable—maybe I could be twice unthinkable. Yet I had no business advising a king. I had no experience in the deadly politics of an empire. I had no knowledge of warfare or battle.

"Your Majesty, I am only a girl. I am no one. I cannot advise you."

"As you so rightly reminded me, you are the Ascendant Dragoneye."

"Yuso would be a better choice," I said, glancing back at the silent figure walking the perimeter. "He is a career soldier. Or Ryko."

"No, both of them have trained me," the emperor said. "They are good men, but there must be no memory of the student when challenging the king."

"Lady Dela?" I ventured.

"She is a courtier and a Contraire. I am not asking you because you are the only one available in our small troop. No emperor is compelled to appoint a *Naiso.* I am asking you because I believe you will tell me the truth when others would lie and pander." His voice hardened. "And betray."

"But I lied to you about who I was," I said. "I lied to everyone."

"You came to my father's ghost watch and told me the truth when you could have been halfway to the islands. Even when it has put you in mortal danger, you have never worked against me. I trust that."

Trust: the word pierced me. I had given up the right to be trusted, and yet here was my emperor willing to place his life in my hands.

If I said yes, I would step into a quicksand of influence and responsibility.

If I said no, I would lose that trust and his good opinion. I would lose the way he leaned toward me as if what I said was worth an emperor's attention.

Could I be what he wanted me to be? A king's conscience.

I took a deep breath and within in it was a prayer to any god who listened: *Help me be his truth. And help me know my own truth.*

"I am honored to be your *Naiso*, Majesty," I said, and bowed.

"As I am honored by your acceptance," he said, a grin overtaking the formality. "You may call me Kygo; the emperor and the *Naiso* meet as equals."

I tensed. No doubt he believed what he said, but I had seen his idea of equality weeks ago, in the Pavilion of Earthly Enlightenment. The pavilion was supposedly a place where minds of all rank could meet, but when his teacher had crossed his will, suddenly equality had been forced into a groveling bow. There seemed to be many levels of equality; I had to find which one he meant for me.

"There is another part to that old maxim *know your enemy*, Kygo," I said, stumbling over his name. "'Know yourself.' What is your weakness? What will High Lord Sethon use against you?"

"Inexperience," he said promptly.

"Perhaps." I narrowed my eyes and tried to see this young man as his uncle would see him. Inexperienced, by his own admission. Untried in war, but courageous and well trained. Progressive and merciful, like his sire, and upholding the same ideals—the very ideals that Sethon hated. "I think your weakness is that you seek to emulate your father."

He drew back. "I do not consider that a weakness."

"Nor do I," I said quickly, "but I think High Lord Sethon will. He has already defeated your father once."

He flinched at my blunt appraisal. I dared not move—dared not breathe—in case his idea of our equality did not match mine.

"My heart does not want to believe you, *Naiso*," he said. "But my gut says you are right. Thank you."

And then he bowed.

It was no more than a dip of his head, but it sent a chill through me.

It was too much equality. Too much trust. I had done nothing to deserve an emperor's bow. I had not even fulfilled my first duty as *Naiso*: to bring him the truth, however difficult and dangerous. And the truth that I still kept hidden was very dangerous, indeed.

He had offered me his trust. If I was to be his *Naiso*, I had to be worthy of such trust.

"I cannot call my dragon." Even as the words left my mouth, I wanted to claw them back.

His head snapped up. "What?"

"I cannot use my power."

He stared at me. "At all?"

"If I try, the ten beasts who have lost their Dragoneyes rush us. Everything around me is destroyed."

"Holy gods!" He rubbed at his forehead as if the pressure would force the bad news into his head. "When did you find this out?"

"At the fishing village. When I healed Ryko."

"Tell me," he said sternly. "Everything."

With a tight hold on my emotions, I described calling the Mirror Dragon, healing Ryko, and the destructive force of the other beasts as they sought union with us. Finally, I told him about Lord Ido's return.

"Are you saying you cannot use your power without Ido?"

"No! I am saying that he knows how to stop the other dragons, and I don't. I've had no training. I was beginning to learn, but then—" I shrugged. He knew only too well the events that had stopped my training.

"What about the red journal? You told me it had the secrets of your power."

"I'm *hoping* it has the secrets," I said. "It is written in an old form of Woman Script, and in code. Dela is deciphering it as fast as she can, but even if she could read the whole book to me now, it would be of no use. If I called my dragon to practice its secrets, the other beasts would overwhelm me before I could do anything."

"So you need Ido," he said acidly. "You need him to train you and hold back the dragons."

I wrapped my arms around my legs and dug my chin into my kneecap.

"Do you, or do you not need Ido?" Kygo's voice sharpened into command.

"He's probably dead, anyway."

"We need to know if he is or not. You saw through his eyes once. Can you do it again?

"No!" I looked over my shoulder, afraid my vehemence had woken the rest of the camp. Yuso half drew his sword, but no one else stirred.

Kygo raised his hand, forestalling the guard's approach. "Eona, we need to know if he is still alive. However much I despise the man, Ido is the only trained Dragoneye left."

He had used my name without title. The small, sweet honor was overwhelmed by the danger of his request.

"I cannot risk calling my dragon," I whispered. "People die."

This time I could not hold back the memories: the fisher house crumbling around me; the pressure of wild power deep in my core; the hammering need of the sorrowing beasts; and the Rat Dragon, launching himself at them with savage speed.

The Rat Dragon! If he was in the circle, then there was a Rat Dragoneye still alive. And if it was Ido, then maybe I would feel his presence again through the dragon.

I clutched Kygo's arm. "I can just look into the energy world. If Ido lives, I'm sure I will feel his *Hua*!"

"You just said the other dragons would rip you apart."

"No, not if I don't *call* my power. I'll just go in, look, and get out again as fast as possible."

"And that will be safe?"

"It will be safer than calling my dragon."

"Do it," he said. "But be careful."

I hesitated. Was it safer? "If anything starts to change"—I pointed up at the night sky—"like the wind or the clouds, pull me back. *Immediately*."

"How?"

"Shake me. Yell in my ear. Punch me if you have to. Just don't let me stay in the energy world."

With an uneasy glance skyward, he nodded.

Ignoring my fear, I sat back and focused on my breathing, slowly deepening each inhalation until I eased into mind-sight. The shadowy forest buckled and shivered into a cascade of colors and flowing light. As I concentrated on the movement of *Hua*, the energy world coalesced. Above, the faded outline of the Rat Dragon was still in the north-northwest. And I still felt Ido's presence as if he watched me. He was alive, although the pallor and languor of his beast did not bode well. In the east, my beautiful Mirror Dragon glowed red. She stirred, her presence sliding around me, questioning. She had never done that before. I longed to answer her and feel the swell of power within me, but I could not risk the rush of the ten bereft dragons. I forced my attention away from the red beast. Yet the taste of her cinnamon still spiced my tongue.

Beside me, the figure of Kygo had faded into transparency. Silvery *Hua* pumped through the twelve pathways of his body, and his seven points of power—spaced evenly from sacrum to crown—spun with vitality.

My eyes were drawn to a pale glow in the line of bright whirling spheres. Unlike the others, it did not move but throbbed with silver energy at the base of his throat. The Imperial Pearl. Its power drew me, its soft fire caressing my skin as I reached across and brushed my fingers over its luminous beauty. The warm cinnamon in my mouth echoed the heat from the pearl. It was so close; I could tear it from its mooring. My palm cupped its weight, my fingertips resting on Kygo's throat, his pulse quickening under my touch.

"What are you doing?" His hand closed around my wrist, a heavy gold ring biting into my flesh.

The pain wrenched me from the energy world in a blur of streaming colors. I blinked, the forest once again shadows and moonlight. Kygo stared at me, his eyes wide and intense. My fingers were still pressed against his racing pulse. I snatched my hand away.

"I don't know."

It was my first lie as *Naiso*.

CHAPTER SEVEN

DAWN FINALLY BRIGHTENED the sky. Wearily, I propped myself on my elbows, the thin rug beneath me bunched into a map of my restlessness. Surely daybreak would end the dark unease that had kept me awake for hours, reliving the caress of the pearl. I hauled myself to my knees and tried to shake off the lingering sensations that still whispered in my blood.

I knew that Kygo had also been disturbed by what had happened between us. After I came to my senses, I was barely able to whisper, "Ido lives," before he had ordered me away from him, his voice hoarse as if with anger. Perhaps he had felt Kinra's presence, too.

And with that thought, a new dread surfaced. I had not been holding Kinra's swords last night, yet I had still been driven to reach for the pearl in the same way she had reached for it hundreds of years ago. This time it had felt different; there was no rage, only single-minded desire. Maybe her will had merged with mine—and I was so much in her thrall that I could not tell the difference. The possibility was like an icy hand gripping my innards.

I rolled my shoulders, working tension out of the stiff joints. Kygo still sat where I had left him hours ago, beyond Vida and Solly. Although he had not said as much, I was sure he was planning to rescue Ido. Did he not realize it would be like catching a snake by the tail? I used all of my will to keep from looking at his face, but some part of me knew he was watching my every move. It was as though his *Hua* pressed against mine.

Nearby, Yuso stood over Tiron and nudged the young guard awake with a booted foot. Would they follow their emperor into such a dangerous and repugnant enterprise? They were Imperial Guards, but I could not even guess at the depth of their loyalty. At the very least, Yuso doubted his young overlord's judgment. There were, however, no doubts in Vida and Solly. They were resistance; placing Kygo on the throne was their cause.

Lady Dela would follow, too, although her loyalty was forged by necessity. Unlike his brother and nephew, Sethon was not tolerant of difference. Particularly Dela's difference. She sat on her blanket with the red folio already open and propped against her knees, her face set into fierce concentration. Now and again she glanced across at Ryko, who patrolled the perimeter of the clearing, but his attention was fixed on the surrounding forest. Ryko was loyal to the emperor, but he would balk at any plan that involved Ido. Except, perhaps, assassination.

"Lady Eona." Vida bowed by my side. "His Majesty has sent me to assist you."

Kygo stood with his back to us, talking to Yuso. Perhaps I had been mistaken about him watching me. Then again, he had known when to send Vida to my side.

"Here." She offered her hand.

I stifled a groan as she pulled me upright; I did not want to sound like an old, rheumy villager. I already stank like a stable hand.

"I need to wash."

"It will have to be quick, my lady. His Majesty wants us to assemble."

Quick was not going to be possible, but I nodded and hobbled after her into the undergrowth. We wove through the dense stand of mountain ash, the early sunlight barely breaking through its canopy to the thick layer of leaf litter underfoot. It was a short walk, but by the time we came to the stream, the dawn breeze had already shifted into the stronger wind that brought the monsoon rains.

"Be careful," Vida warned. "The flooding has made the edges soft."

The grass along each bank was lying flat, a sure sign of receded water. A few lengths downstream, a large area of churned mud showed footprints and the deep cut of hooves.

"I am not looking forward to another day on that horse," I

said, hoping to create some ease between us. "I feel like I have been twisted and tied into an eternity knot."

Vida smiled. "It will pass."

"So I've been told." A careful press of my foot found soft but supportive ground. Gingerly, I crouched and dipped my hand into the cold water, letting it flow through my fingers. "You seem unaffected," I added. "Have you done a lot of riding?"

The silence was too long for the question. I turned.

Vida stood with her arms wrapped around her body, her face swollen with unshed tears. "My betrothed taught me."

For a long moment, we were caught in each other's pain—her loss and my dawning guilt. Her betrothed had been one of the villagers.

"I didn't know. I'm sorry," I whispered. Such inadequate words.

"Lady Dela said you couldn't control it."

"No."

Vida nodded, accepting my answer. *"You have to."*

I turned back to the fast-flowing water, away from her sadness. My fingers were numb with cold. I rubbed them on my skirt, forcing warmth into them. I knew I should say something else—a reassurance, or another apology—but by the time I looked back over my shoulder, she was already retreating into the undergrowth.

She would be back; Vida would not disobey her emperor's command. Still, she deserved a few moments to grieve. Although I could not offer any worthwhile consolation, I could at least use the time alone to honor her demand and try to control my power. Even if it was only to ask Kinra to stop aiming her ghostly rage at Kygo and her ancient greed for the pearl into my heart. If I were lucky, she would answer my prayer.

The death plaque pouch was bound tightly under my sash. I pulled it free and loosened the drawstring, then upended it. The two black lacquered finger-lengths of wood slid onto my palm. I picked up the plainer memorial: a thinly etched line bordered the edge, and workmanlike carved characters spelled out "Charra." My unknown ancestress. I pushed it back into the pouch and returned it for safekeeping under my sash. I had no quarrel with Charra.

The other plaque was far more worn, but the remains of elaborate decoration were still visible. I ran my thumb over the elegantly carved "Kinra"—faintly inlaid with gold—and traced the tiny dragon that snaked under her name like a flourish.

I settled on to my knees. The sodden earth squelched under me, pushing cold water through the layers of skirt and shift. I held out the plaque and closed my hand until I felt its edges through the layers of my bandage.

Kinra, Mirror Dragoneye, I prayed, and channeled all of my fear and frustration into my tight grip. *Leave me be. Please stop bringing your anger and desire into my heart. Please stop trying to hurt Kygo and take the pearl.*

It was not an elaborate prayer, but I was not a Beseecher. I opened my hand and stared at the relic, overtaken by the memory of a holy man who had preached to us at the salt farm, years ago. He had not only believed that our ancestors resided in the local shrines, but he had insisted that their spirits also inhabited their death plaques. My friend Dolana had dismissed the teaching as a zealot's frenzy. Now I wondered if the holy man had been right. Perhaps that was how Kinra had visited me last night.

At the thought, I jerked my hand back and lost my grip on the plaque. My reflex grab missed. The plaque dropped into the stream and spun into a drift of silt. I launched myself at it, but was pulled up short, my knees anchored in the soggy folds of my skirt. Even as I grabbed for the plaque again, the quick water pulled it from its mooring, out of reach.

I struggled to my feet, slipping on the waterlogged grass along the bank. The plaque was forced up against a tiny dam of twigs and mud, the water dragging it through the disintegrating mound.

I stopped.

Maybe I should let it go. Let the water carry Kinra's treachery away from me. I could close one of her doorways to this earthly plane forever.

Yet, she was my history. My legacy. A link to my family.

The plaque slid into a widening breach.

I wrenched off both sandals, then ripped at the drawstring around my skirt and kicked it off. I plunged into the water, the slap of cold against my shins, knees, thighs forcing my breath out in high gasps. My shift and tunic wrapped around me in a wet weight, the ends of my silk sash flicking and darting from my waist like red carp. The plaque slipped, then caught against the collapsing dam. I waded toward it, the current pressing against my legs. Rocks below shifted under my weight, jarring my ankle bones and scraping at my skin.

The remnants of the tiny dam loosened into a swirling mess of twigs and sediment. The plaque disappeared, then bobbed up. I clutched at it, but only scooped water, the force sending the plaque down again. Had I lost it? Hands ready, I focused fiercely on the dizzying surface. The plaque shot up an arm's length away. I pounced. As my fingers closed around the memorial, my feet slipped and both knees slammed against the rocky bed. Another shock of water soaked me up to my chest. But I was holding the plaque.

Shakily, I found my footing. My pursuit had brought me level with the horses' watering place. I clambered onto the bank, my shift and tunic dripping water down my bruised legs. Cold mud oozed between my toes.

I wiped a smear of silt from the plaque. Kinra was a part of me; casting aside her death plaque would not change my heritage. Nor would it change the burden of her treachery. I ran my hand over my drenched sash and found the pouch—Charra's plaque was safe, too. Sighing my relief, I pulled the dripping bag free, shook off the water, and slotted Kinra's memorial back inside.

"Eona?"

I spun around. Dela stood at the tree line.

"Are you all right?"

"Fine." I softened the curtness with a quick wave and limped over to my abandoned skirt and sandals.

"His Majesty wants us to assemble. We will be leaving soon." Dela made her way across the damp ground, picking up her feet as though she wore silk slippers instead of sturdy merchant sandals. She clicked her tongue. "You're soaked."

We both turned at the sounds of approach. Vida emerged from the forest a few lengths away, pausing as she met our scrutiny. Even from where we stood, I could see her eyes were red from crying.

"Vida," Dela said. "Do we have dry clothes for Lady Eona?"

"We only have what we're wearing," Vida said.

"Swap with her then, until hers are dry."

Vida's jaw shifted.

"No," I cut in. "We don't have to do that. They'll dry soon enough." It was not true—nothing dried quickly in these humid monsoon days—but I did not want to add to Vida's resentment.

Dela waved aside my protest. "You can't ride behind the emperor in wet clothes. He may get damp."

There was no counter to that argument. I soon stood in Vida's gown while she struggled to pull on the waterlogged layers of my skirt, undershift and tunic.

"I'm sorry," I muttered.

She shot me a dark look.

I tugged at the gaping neckline of the maid's dress. On Vida, it had sat modestly over her curves. On me, it plunged too low, and the wide cut emphasized the jut of my collarbones. I yanked it up again, bunching the loose cloth at the waist in my other hand.

"Here, let me help." Dela wrapped the rough-spun sash around me. "This will keep it up."

She tucked and tied until everything was covered, although the neckline was still too low. I pressed my hands over the pale skin of my chest; it was not only my collarbones that were emphasized.

Vida bent and picked up the pouch from the ground. "My lady, do not forget this," she said, handing it to me.

I was fairly sure that Kinra's death plaque was not as dangerous as her swords, but I still did not want to carry it. "Lady Dela, will you keep this for me?" I held out the pouch. "With the journal?"

Dela eyed the offered bag. "Vida, return to the others," she said, the dismissal firm. "Tell His Majesty that we are soon behind you."

Vida cast her a curious glance, but headed back toward the forest. As soon as she was gone from sight, Dela reached across, but her hand grasped my wrist instead of the pouch. "What is going on, Eona?"

I pulled back, but she held fast.

"You will not carry the journal, your swords, or your compass," she said, "and now you want me to take your ancestors' death plaques. Something is wrong."

I bit down on my lip. I should have remembered Dela's keen eyes; after all, she had survived the imperial court through quick wits and insight. I had no doubt she wanted to help me—Dela always wanted to help. Yet telling her about Kinra would be just the same as telling Ryko, and he would go straight to the emperor.

"I don't know what you mean," I said. "Nothing is wrong." Another jerk of my wrist freed me from her grasp. "His Majesty awaits us."

I pushed the pouch into the deep pocket of Vida's gown. I would be rid of the ill-fitting dress soon, and with it, Kinra's plaque.

I arrived at the clearing ahead of Dela. She had dropped a few lengths behind me—the distance, no doubt, a silent rebuke for refusing her help. While we had been gone, the camp had been packed away and the horses saddled. The only signs of our occupation were tamped-down grass and a patch of soft muddy ground around the trees where the horses were tied.

The emperor was waiting. He stood with his arms crossed, the rest of our troop kneeling in a loose semicircle before him.

"Lady Eona." Kygo waved me to his side.

Had he already told them I was his *Naiso*? They all watched as I made my way across the grass, but I saw no shock or disapproval.

They did not know yet.

Kygo's eyes flicked over my body. "You are unhurt?"

"Yes." I crossed my arms over my chest. "Thank you," I added awkwardly.

Dela's arrival turned his attention from me. The Contraire

sank into a low court bow, murmuring apologies. She dropped to her knees beside Ryko as I joined the emperor. With a small nod, he indicated that I should stand behind him, at his left shoulder.

"Traditional position," he murmured close to my ear. "You guard my weakest side." The warmth of his breath raised an answering flush in my cheeks.

None of the six tired faces before me seemed to have registered the symbolism of where I stood. But then, why should they? The old emperor had never appointed a *Naiso*, and a female advisor was unthinkable.

Ryko's gaze was still squarely on me, his jaw set. No forgiveness there. Solly was expectant, his ugly face red and shiny from the heat. Vida was smoothing the wet tunic over her thighs, her attention on Kygo. Captain Yuso was his usual watchful self. Next to him, Tiron was excited, but doing his best to copy his superior's calm confidence. I caught Dela's quick sideways glance at Ryko; she was worried about the islander. But then, so was I.

"Ever since the palace was taken," Kygo said, "we have been reacting to my uncle's strategies. Now it is time for us to act."

Yuso nodded approvingly.

"You will have noticed the change in the rains and winds," Kygo continued. "Without the full circle of dragons and their Dragoneyes, our land is not protected from the whims of the weather demons or the angers of the earth." He glanced back at me. "Nor can Lady Eona control any earth forces by herself. She has no training and, at present, cannot use her power."

Although his voice was dispassionate, the stark announcement of my failure sent shame through me. I dared not look around the circle; I could feel their disillusion like a thousand pin pricks on my skin.

"Cannot use it at *all*, Your Majesty?" Yuso asked. I winced at the dismay in the man's voice.

"Lady Eona needs training," Kygo said firmly. "This is why we now go to the palace to free Lord Ido."

No one moved. All I could hear was the hammering of my heart.

"Free Ido?" Ryko finally said. He sat back on his heels. "You want to free that murdering bastard?"

"Yes, we must free *Lord* Ido." The emperor's soft emphasis was a warning.

Ryko ducked his head, but his eyes searched the silent semicircle for support. He found it.

"Your Majesty," Solly said, bowing, "forgive my blunt speech, but we cannot go near the palace. It is too dangerous. We must rendezvous with the Eastern Resistance, not be sidetracked into a worthless enterprise."

"It is far from worthless," Kygo said coldly. "There is more to war than the number of soldiers on each side. A war is won or lost by five fundamentals, and the first and foremost is the *Hua-do* of the people. If the people's will is not at one with their ruler, then he will lose the war."

"Highness," Tiron said hesitantly. "I am truly stupid, for I cannot see how freeing Lord Ido will win the *Hua-do* of the people. He is feared, not loved."

Kygo frowned. "This is the decision I have made. There will be no more discussion."

"Your Majesty," I said, "may I speak to you in private?"

I turned away from the startled faces before us and walked a few steps, the emperor matching my pace.

"You may want to explain your reasoning to them," I said softly.

He shot me a sharp look. "Explain? They should just follow my orders. Discipline is the second fundamental."

"They will always follow your orders," I said. "But it will be easier if they are—as you say—at one with you. If they understand your strategy."

He gave a wry smile. "You use my own words to counsel me, *Naiso*, yet bring greater wisdom." He gripped my shoulder. "Win their *Hua-do*, win the war. Thank you."

We both looked at his hand resting on the exposed curve of my collarbone. I felt the heat rise to my face again. His other hand found the pearl at his throat, his own color rising around it.

Abruptly he walked back to the troop. I waited a moment longer—until the flush had receded from my face—then followed him. This time, my position by his side was noticed; Dela sucked in a sharp breath, her eyes finding mine. I could not wholly fathom her expression. There was shock, of course, but also something else. Something akin to wonderment.

"There are only two Dragoneyes left alive," Kygo said. "One is here," he nodded at me, "the other is held by my uncle. Around us, our land is being rocked by the loss of its Dragoneye protectors. We are already seeing the floods caused by the unchecked monsoon rains. Crops are being ruined, and with that will come starvation and disease. But it will not only be floods and crops. It will be mudslides, tsunamis, cyclones, earthshakes. There will be more destruction, more despair, more death."

He looked up at the sky. Inexorably, we all lifted our heads, too. A dark bank of low cloud spread from north to south, the warm wind carrying the sweet metallic tang of rain.

"The emperor who brings back the protection of the dragons will win the *Hua-do* of the people," Kygo said. "And the emperor who holds the *Hua-do* will hold the land." He paused, allowing that implacable truth to find its mark. "This is why we must rescue Lord Ido. We cannot allow my uncle to have a Dragoneye at his command, even one who is under duress. And we must have the two Ascendant Dragoneyes working together to calm the land and show the people that we can protect them."

"Your Majesty, there is no guarantee that Lord Ido will agree to help us, even if we do manage to get him out of the palace," Ryko said.

"That is true. There are no guarantees. There is, however, the certainty that without Lord Ido, Lady Eona will not be able to use her power. She must be trained, and he is the only Dragoneye left to do it."

There was also another certainty, known only to me. Ido would jump at the chance to mold my power. He thought I was the key to the String of Pearls and the throne. For a moment I considered offering the insight, but the idea of Ido with access to my power would not reassure anyone.

And there was always the chance that I had truly changed him.

Yuso bowed deeply, the others quickly following his lead. "Your wisdom is heaven-sent, Your Majesty," he said. Around the semicircle, murmurs of agreement sounded.

"I also have an excellent advisor," Kygo said. "Lady Eona has agreed to be my *Naiso*."

"What?" Ryko reared out of his bow.

Yuso was not far behind, astonishment shifting into disbelief. The others were just a blur as I lowered my head, bracing against their shock.

"Your Majesty, *no*!" Ryko's anger propelled him forward on his knees. "You don't know her." The venom in his voice struck at me. I clenched my fists.

"A girl, Your Majesty? How can a girl advise you?" Yuso demanded. "It is against nature."

"She is not just a girl," Dela said, "she is the Ascendant Dragoneye."

"She has no training," Yuso countered. "No military background. She knows nothing."

"It is not the first time a woman has been *Naiso*," Dela said.

I looked up; did I hear that right? Another woman?

"Lady Eona is the emperor's choice." Vida's voice was high-pitched with her audacity.

"Vida, know your place," Solly snapped.

"Enough!" The emperor's command dropped the troop back into crouched bows. "Lady Eona is my *Naiso*. That is the end of it."

Slowly, Ryko lifted his head. "Your Majesty, please allow me to speak. As a member of your trusted guard, and as your loyal subject."

Kygo hissed out a breath. "You are straining those bonds, Ryko."

"Please, Your Majesty. It is for your own safety." Ryko glanced at me, the hostility in his eyes like a blow to the chest.

Kygo nodded. "What is it?"

"Lady Eona cannot be trusted to bring you the truth."

"Ryko," Dela whispered beside him. "No."

Solly and Tiron raised their heads, tense and watchful. Vida stayed tightly tucked into her bow.

"Are you accusing Lady Eona of being a liar?" the emperor asked.

"Yes."

Kygo nodded. "It is a fair accusation."

I wove my fingers together, shunting all of my anguish into the painful pressure. Kygo did not trust me, after all. He must have realized I had lied to him last night.

"And one that Lady Eona has admitted herself," he added. "That is all in the past."

My tension eased. Kygo glanced back at me with a reassuring smile.

"But it is not just straight lies, Your Majesty."

Ryko straightened from his bow. I glared at the islander. He had been told it didn't matter. Yet he still pushed.

"It is more insidious than that," he said. "It is half-truths and omissions—"

I took a step forward. This was not duty; this was plain malice.

"Ryko," I said. "Stop it."

His face did not even register my words. "—and even if she does give some truth, you cannot—"

My rage rose like a savage creature howling its freedom. It reached across to Ryko, clawing at his life force. I felt his heartbeat meld into mine, the quick rhythm of his rancor overwhelmed by my pounding fury. I had control of his *Hua*. I had control of him. The rush of energy drove me another step past the emperor.

Ryko's eyes found mine. "No! You swore—"

It was happening again. Just like the battlefield. Ryko tried to haul himself upright—I felt the strain in his energy—but his limbs were frozen into hunched obedience. Sweat dripped down his face as he struggled against the weight of power. Against me. Why did he struggle? It was his place to obey. With just a thought, I forced him lower and lower, until his face was pressed into the dirt.

His eyes were still locked on mine, a silent scream in them. I could make him do whatever I wanted.

A clear thought forced its way through the blinding power: I was doing what Ido had once done to me. Cold shame doused my anger. What was I thinking? Ryko was my friend. I sucked in a desperate breath and focused inward, groping for the link. Whatever it was, I had to find it. Break it. I had given him my word.

It was deep within me—a single golden thread of his *Hua* woven into the intricate tapestry of my own life patterns. A conduit for his life force that I could tap at any time through my anger or fear. But once I had grabbed it, how was I supposed to stop it? His bright pounding energy pulsed through me, caught in the rush of my own thundering *Hua*. It was like trying to hold back a torrent of water with my hands.

"Ryko, I can't stop it!"

A figure rose from the ground. Straight for me. The impact knocked me sideways before the pain exploded through my jaw. I staggered and fell heavily to my bruised knees. The agony in my face and legs doubled me over as the link with Ryko snapped. I gasped into the sudden release. Through a blur of tears, I saw Dela standing over me, her hand still raised.

"Dela! No!" Yuso dragged her back a few steps. Nearby, Ryko was crumpled on the ground, gulping for air.

Kygo squatted beside me. "Lady Eona, are you all right?" His hand was on my back, the gentle weight steadying me.

My nod sent pain into my head. Cradling my jaw, I tentatively moved it from side to side. A man's strength had been behind Dela's blow.

"Lady Eona, forgive me." Dela shook off Yuso's hold and crouched before me.

I spat, tasting the copper warmth of blood. My tongue

found the soft ragged sting of bitten cheek. "Did you have to hit me so hard?"

Dela bowed her head. "I didn't know what else to do."

I nodded again and winced. "At least you stopped it."

"Was it the other dragons?" Kygo asked. "Did they come through the link you have with Ryko?" He saw my surprise. "I overheard you discuss it last night. Ryko was not over-quiet."

"I don't know what it was, Your Majesty." Hoping to avoid more questions, I motioned to Ryko. The islander was still hunched over, breathing heavily. "Ryko, I'm sorry. I couldn't stop it."

"Are you all right?" Dela asked him, crossing the short distance on her knees.

"Stay back."

I could not tell if the harsh words were aimed at Dela or me. Perhaps they were aimed at both of us. Dela stopped just short of him, stranded between her own need and his bristling rage. Ryko was a proud man, and he had just been felled by a woman and saved by a Contraire. He would not forgive either of us quickly.

Vida cautiously moved toward him. Ryko allowed the girl to help him straighten. His tight smile of gratitude pushed Dela up onto her feet and across the clearing, away from them.

Kygo stood and offered me his hand. "If you are able, we will move on. The sooner we free Lord Ido, the sooner you will get some control over these dragons."

I nodded and clasped his hand. Yet some horrified part of

me knew that it was not the dragons, or even Kinra, who had forced Ryko into the dirt.

It was me.

Once again, we set up a schedule of short rides and long walks. This time, however, we were heading back to the palace, Solly's well-honed forest skills keeping us at a safe distance from any road or track. The one exception was a bridge over a swollen river. We could not risk fording the rushing waters, so we chanced a slippery peasant crossing made of rough planks and rope. With the thundering deluge only an arm's length below, it took all of my nerve to edge over the slimy, moss-covered boards. The horses were not keen, either: each animal had to be coaxed across by a mix of Solly's croons and Ryko's iron grip.

As we moved downstream, heavy monsoon clouds tracked our progress. The thick gray expanse above us was like a smothering blanket of heat, but occasionally there was a current of cooler air that chilled sweat and promised rain and relief. The impending downpour added urgency to our search for the resistance group who, according to Vida, was entrenched in the area. They would give us a safe place to wait out the rains and mudslides, she said; more importantly, they would have news of Sethon's army.

Ryko was quick to volunteer for scout duties and spent most of the morning ahead of us, looping around at intervals to report to Yuso. Only once did Dela try to talk to him; his cold courtesy plunged her into grim silence.

As before, I rode behind Kygo, and on the long, slogging walks he taught me the wisdom of Xsu-Ree. His father had insisted he memorize the Twelve Songs of Warfare, and as we pushed our way through the undergrowth, he recited them to me in the low tone of secrets, his voice audible only if we walked side by side, our heads close together. Each song was a series of wisdoms about an element of warfare. I did not wholly understand any of them, but a few caught my imagination: the Song of Espionage with its five types of spies, and the Song of Flames that told of five ways to attack by fire. Within the rhythms of Kygo's deep voice, I heard the treacherous tread of double agents and the screams of men burning alive. With such skill, he could have been a Grand Poet.

"Do you recall the five fundamentals in the first song?" he asked at the end of his recitation.

It was near noon and we were walking parallel to the river, the water hidden by a thick stand of pine trees. For the time being, the steep mountainside had eased into a gentler slope, the scrubby woodland overrun by long-tailed pheasants. Bell crickets sang in the heat in a pulsing drone, and sprang out of the damp grass as we passed. A sign of good fortune, some would say. Kygo opened the collar of his tunic, a concession to the stifling humidity. I caught myself staring at the strong column of his throat, the smooth skin at the base marred by the rough, scabbed stitches that circled the gold setting of the pearl. I did not know if it was Kinra or the memory of the gem's caress that drew my eyes. Those boundaries had become blurred.

A few lengths ahead of us, Tiron was leading Ju-Long, the battle-trained horse unmoved by the birds that bolted out of the undergrowth in front of him. A good way behind, Solly, Yuso, and Vida were leading the other horses in a straggling line. Dela walked by herself, her attention shifting between the path we were forging through the bushes and grass, and the red folio open in her hands.

I searched my memory for the five fundamentals, determined not to disappoint my teacher. "They are *Hua-do*, Sun/ Moon, Earth, Command, and Discipline." My jaw ached when I spoke, but at least the swelling was beginning to recede.

"You learn faster than I do," he said, smiling.

"But you understand them." I shrugged against the damp cling of my borrowed gown. Sweat had gathered around the low neckline, but I did not want to wipe it away while he watched.

"You will understand, too."

Although his firm belief bolstered me, I was not so sure a few days would be enough to grasp even the rudiments of Xsu-Ree's wisdom. There was so much I did not know. All I had was the cunning of a salt slave and the reflexes of a liar.

He held back a branch as we pushed through a patch of spiny brushwood. "What is the Way of War?" he asked.

"The Way of War is the Way of Deception." I glanced sideways at him, the little demon of mischief coming back to prod me. "I understand that one. From experience."

He stopped, his smile deepening. "Indeed you do, *Lord Eon*."

We stood, grinning at each other, cocooned in the hot thicket. Then something changed, as if the air contracted between us. He stepped closer. "You are not a lord now."

I had to tilt back my head to meet his eyes. "No, I am—"

The rest of my words were lost in his intent gaze and the brush of his hand against my cheek.

For a moment, I smelled the green snap of tree gum on his fingers and the faint scent of smoky leather and horse. His skin was damp with sweat, the stark contours of his shaved head lost in a day's dark growth. From someplace deep came an urge to reach up and run my hand across the soft bristle.

But I had seen that same look in Ido's eyes. In the whipmaster's eyes. Even in my master's eyes. I stepped back.

"I am your *Naiso*," I said.

It was a flimsy shield. As my emperor, he had the right to take whatever he wanted. Yet his hand dropped from my face, the intensity pulled back on an indrawn breath.

"My truth bringer," he said.

I bowed my head. If our eyes met again, he would see the weakness in my armor. And my guilt.

"You are right," he said. "I should not emulate my father."

His words brought my head up, but he had already turned away. As he strode past the last of the overhanging trees, he ripped off a branch and flung it with such force that it startled a pheasant into whirring flight.

"You have a talent for irritating His Majesty," Dela said behind me.

"It is my duty, isn't it?" I said, not quite sure what had happened between us. "I'm his *Naiso*."

"That kind of irritation is not usually one of the *Naiso*'s duties," she said wryly. She touched my arm, urging me to walk by her side. "Then again," she added, "he is only following his father's example."

I caught her shoulder, pulling her around to face me. "He mentioned his father, too."

She nodded, as if she had overheard our conversation. "It was not common knowledge, but the old emperor did have a *Naiso*. She was his concubine and mother of his first-born son."

"Lady Jila was his *Naiso*?" My mind struggled to recast the elegant beauty into political advisor.

Dela's smile was sad. "And a most worthy one, although the old emperor did not listen to her warnings about his brother. She was a remarkable woman. No wonder the old emperor eschewed all others."

We both looked at the straight-backed figure of Kygo ahead. "I am not going to be his concubine," I said fiercely.

"You are missing the point," Dela said. "Lady Jila was not just a concubine. Certainly, she had the power of her body, but she also had much more."

"I don't understand."

"I know. It is something you must come to yourself." She held out the red folio, her face somber. "Your ancestress should have considered the dangers of such power."

"Have you found something?"

She stroked the red leather binding and the rope of pearls in her palm clicked in response. "This is not Kinra's journal of her union with the Mirror Dragon."

I closed my eyes, the disappointment like a bright pain in my head.

Dela took my hand and squeezed it gently. "I'm sorry," she said. "I know you were hoping for some guidance. I don't think there will be any clues to your link with Ryko, either."

I returned the pressure; Ryko would be even more unhappy at such news, and I knew it pained Dela to hurt him.

"What is the journal about, then?'

She lowered her voice. "It is not clear yet, but I think it tells of some kind of conspiracy. It must have been dangerous information, since Kinra felt it was necessary to write most of it in such a difficult code. And I have also discovered an entry that is not in Kinra's hand."

"Whose hand is it?"

She shook her head. "I don't know. It is not signed in any way. It is little more than a few lines right at the very back." She paused. "Eona, it notes Kinra's execution. For treason. I do not know what she did, but Emperor Dao had her killed for it."

Our eyes met. Within that glance was a whole conversation: my shame and fear of discovery, her grave acknowledgment, and the decision to keep the information between us.

"Is this why you will not touch her belongings?" she asked.

"She was a traitor," I whispered, knowing such dishonor

would be enough for Dela. She did not need to know about the Imperial Pearl or the pull of Kinra's energy.

"It is a burden I wish you did not have to bear." She touched the red leather again, delicately tracing the three long gouges in the cover. "Kinra was Emperor Dao's lover."

Was this what I felt through Kinra's swords? Love? Yet it was violent and angry and full of death.

"And she had another lover," Dela continued. "The unnamed man. It seems her downfall lies in the nexus of this triangle. As I decipher the text, I will bring it to you."

"Thank you."

But her attention was on the scrub wood ahead. Kygo had stopped walking, his hand on his sword hilt. Tiron was tugging on Ju-Long's bridle, pulling the big horse back around.

Then we saw what they had already seen—Ryko, running toward us, someone small slung over his shoulder.

The islander lifted his fist.

The sign for Sethon's army.

CHAPTER EIGHT

RYKO'S FIST PUNCHED three fast signals: *twenty-four, on foot, northbound.*

Crouching, I pulled Dela down into the grass and scanned the woodland behind the islander, every part of me focused on finding movement. My eyes caught on the quick flip of a pheasant tail, a branch bobbing in the hot wind, the shift of light between leaves.

"I can't see any soldiers," I whispered.

"What's Ryko carrying?" Lady Dela said. "Is that a child?"

"Lady Eona!" We both spun around at Yuso's low call. Beyond him, Vida and Solly were struggling to turn the horses.

"Make for those trees," the captain said, pointing to a thick copse at the steeper edge of the slope.

I knew I should move, but something about Ryko's small passenger held me still. His presence was almost like a taste in my mouth. Ryko had reached the emperor, and the two men were running side by side through the grass. The islander was losing momentum, his big chest heaving under the strain of his squirming burden. Whoever was slung over his shoulder did not come willingly. Behind them, Tiron had finally faced Ju-Long in the right direction. He dragged the horse into a reluctant trot.

"Lady Eona, you must go now!" Yuso ordered.

Ryko's head jerked to one side—a nasty punch in the face from his passenger. He stumbled and lost his grip on the child. They both hit the ground and rolled in the long grass, legs and arms flailing. Kygo slowed and turned back. With easy strength, he pulled the child upright, but jumped back from the frenzied kicks and punches. Free of the emperor's hold, the boy whipped around to face us, his hair half unraveled from a high-bound queue.

My heart tightened with sudden foreboding. I knew that tender curve of cheek and frail shoulder.

"That's Dillon." I stood up for a better view.

"Lord Ido's apprentice?" Dela said, rising to peer at the boy, too. "What is he doing here?"

But I had a more pressing question on my mind.

"Can you see the black folio? Does he still have it?"

The last time I had seen Dillon, he had attacked Ryko and me and wrenched the black folio from my keeping. He had thought he could trade the book to Ido in return for his life. The poor fool did not realize it held more than the secret of the String of Pearls—it held the way for royal blood to enslave us and our dragon power.

No one but Ido and I knew it, and I could still hear the Dragoneye's last, urgent words to me at the conquered palace. *Anyone with the blood can bind us. Find the black folio, before Sethon does.*

Merciful gods of heaven, I prayed, *let Dillon still have the folio.*

"I don't see it," Dela said, quick to understand. "It's not there!"

A glimpse of dark leather sent dizzy relief through me. "No, he's got it. Under his sleeve. See!"

My shrill triumph carried across to Dillon. His eyes fixed on me, his face widening into a scream. "Eona!" He ran a few steps, his hands beating the air. "See, see, I found her." He struck himself in the head. "See!" His fist slammed into his skull again. "It's Eona. See! It's Eona!" Both fists pounded into his forehead, over and over. Although we stood at least fifty lengths from him, we could hear the dull thud of each blow.

Beside me, Yuso curled three fingers into a ward-evil. "Is he possessed?"

"No, Sun Drug," I said, remembering the rage that had overtaken me with just a few doses. "Ido tried to kill him with it."

Dela's hand covered her mouth. "Poor child."

"If he doesn't shut up, he'll bring the whole army down on us," Yuso said, even as Kygo caught Dillon by the shoulder and clapped his hand over the boy's mouth, muffling his screams to muted shrieks. Yuso pushed me back a step. "Get to cover," he ordered, then ran to help his emperor.

Ryko had already crawled over to the struggle and was dodging Dillon's vicious kicks as he grabbed for the boy's legs. Tiron looped Ju-Long's reins over a nearby tree, obviously intending to join the fray.

"They're going to hurt him," I said.

Dela tugged my sleeve. "Come, we must get to safety."

"No." I broke free and ran toward the three men struggling to contain Dillon. My breath came in hard gasps, more from fear than from the desperate sprint. Dillon's ruined mind would push him past surrender; he would force them to hurt him.

I ducked around the knot of men, trying to find a way to Dillon. Across his writhing body, Ryko's eyes met mine in clear communication. *Still insane.* The moment of understanding was as brief as a heartbeat, but my spirit lifted. Perhaps all was not lost between us. And perhaps all was not lost for Dillon. I launched myself into a gap between Yuso and the emperor.

"Dillon, it's me," I yelled. My hand grazed the boy's shoulder. "It's Eona. Stop fighting."

"I told you to get back," Yuso snarled. "Tiron, get her to safety."

The guard ran up behind me. I dodged and searched for another opening in the shift of straining, sweaty bodies.

Yuso had one of Dillon's shins clasped to his chest, his other hand trying to catch the boy's wild punches. A pale flash flicked up from the boy's forearm—the rope of guardian pearls, its end curled back like a whip above the black folio. It lashed out at Kygo, but Yuso deflected it with his fist. With breathtaking speed, it flailed Yuso's hand, lifting skin and blood. The guard recoiled, cursing. Ryko clamped down Dillon's other leg and arm, and Kygo locked his arms around the boy's chest, his own head craned back to avoid the pearls and the boy's frenzied head-butts. With savage intensity, Dillon bucked against the brutal hold on his body.

I saw a chance and lunged across the tangle of arms and legs, grabbing the boy's ragged queue. "Dillon! Stop!" I roared against his ear.

Abruptly, he stilled. With a last click, the rope of pearls collapsed onto the black folio, then slithered around it, binding it back to his left forearm. Dillon's jaundiced eyes fixed on mine. "Eona, Eona, Eona," he chanted. "What happened to Eon?" He gave a shrill giggle.

"For Shola's sake, keep him quiet," Yuso snapped at me. "Ryko, what's coming?"

I stroked Dillon's clammy cheek, hoping to calm him as Ryko gave his report.

"Twenty-four men, fan formation, with a local upfront. They're tracking the boy. They were two arenas away at least when I picked him up, but they're moving fast."

Yuso stared down at Dillon. "Why are they after you, boy?"

Dillon giggled. "Why are they after you, boy?"

Yuso's lean face darkened.

"They want the black folio," I said quickly. "Sethon thinks it holds the key to a weapon made of all the dragon power." Between the tightly coiled pearls, I could make out the twelve interconnected circles embossed on the leather cover: the symbol of the String of Pearls. "Lord Ido thinks so, too."

"Black words," Dillon muttered. "Black words. Inside me."

"I remember this boy now," Kygo said. "Lord Ido's apprentice." His eyes found mine, but I could not read his expression. "Another Dragoneye. How does he come to be here?"

Dillon's eyes darted from me to the emperor. "My lord sent me," he said. "He's in my head. 'Find Eona, find Eona, find Eona.' Always in my head."

"What does he mean?" Kygo asked me.

But I could not speak, silenced by an obvious truth. If Ido died, the only thing that stood between the bereft dragons and me was Dillon—a mind-sick apprentice as untrained as myself. There was no chance he could hold back the beasts. We would both die, torn apart by their grief. I fought for air as if I was surfacing through oil.

We had to get Ido out of the palace, alive.

Yuso suddenly straightened, his dark eyes scanning the eerily quiet woodlands around us. "Your Majesty," he said quietly. "We don't have time to question this boy. We must move, now!"

"Not until we get the black book off him." Kygo's face held a new intensity. I had seen its like before, on Ido and my master: the burn of ambition.

Yuso's jaw clenched, but he gave a curt nod and reached for the folio. The last two pearls lifted, like a snake's head. He yanked back his hand. "Are they alive?"

"They have *Gan Hua* worked into them," I said. "They'll strike at anything that tries to move the folio."

Even now, the negative energy woven into the pearls was

nauseating me. No wonder Dillon was still so sick in mind and body; he did not have a chance between the book and the damage from the overdose of Sun Drug. Both Tiron and Ryko leaned away from Dillon's arm.

"Your Majesty, we must move," Yuso said.

Kygo's jaw tightened. "All right. Leave the book where it is. The boy comes with us. Just keep him and the book safe."

"Yes, Your Majesty." Yuso fixed me with a hard stare. "You seem to be able to control him, Lady Dragoneye. Keep him quiet."

At his nod, all the men loosened their grip on Dillon, allowing him on to his feet. He staggered, striking out weakly at their steadying hands until I hooked him into the circle of my arms. His thin body stank of fevered nights and driven days.

"You've got to stay with me and *be quiet*," I said, holding him upright. "Do you understand?"

"He's still in my mind," Dillon whispered. I grabbed his fist as it arced toward his forehead. It was not going to be easy to keep him quiet—or alive.

With one last look at the tree line, Yuso herded us forward. "Go!"

I pulled Dillon into a stumbling run. A downrush of cold air from the heavens cut through the heat, chilling the sour sweat on my face and neck. The monsoon was coming. Yuso overtook us, joining Kygo a length or so ahead.

"Your Majesty, take Ryko and the others southeast," the captain said, keeping pace beside the emperor. He looked up at the heavy mass of roiling clouds.

"Ride as long as you can, but don't take any risks in the mud. I'll lead the soldiers north, with Solly and Tiron."

"Understood," Kygo said.

He and Yuso drew away from us, intent on mobilizing the others. I squeezed Dillon's bony hand, urging more speed. Dela was only thirty or so lengths away, frantically waving us in. Further back, Solly and Vida waited with the horses.

"Is that Lady Dela?" Dillon asked in such a normal voice that I slowed to stare at him. "Why is she dressed as a man?" For a moment, I saw the gentle Dillon I had once known—bewildered and lost—then he was gone again, bright madness back in his eyes. "My lord said he'd get out of my head. Why isn't he out of my head?" His voice rose piteously. "*Find Eona. Find Eona. Find Eona.*"

I had heard Dillon call my name like that before. But when? The elusive memory hardened into an image: the dragon battle at the fisher village. Dillon screaming for me through the power of the Rat Dragon. Through Ido.

"Did Lord Ido send you to find me?"

"He's in my head."

Yuso and Kygo reached the thicket. I tugged Dillon into a sprint. A second gust of wind brought light pulsing across the dark clouds. For one heavy moment, time hung between hot earth and cold heaven, then the land shuddered under the sky's roar. Dillon screamed, dragging at my hand. I looked over my shoulder. He was bent, as if the gods pressed him to the ground. Close behind us, Ryko and Tiron led Ju-Long in a tight hold between them, the horse blowing hard with fear.

With grim effort, I pulled Dillon into a run beside me. "Does Lord Ido want you to give me the black book?" I eyed the folio bound to his arm.

Dillon's features sharpened. "It's my book," he panted. "It's mine. Lord Ido can't hold onto the dragon. They make him drink the black beast. All his power is draining away." He giggled in tight, painful gasps. "It will be mine soon, then I can make him hurt. Just like he makes me hurt."

Part of me hoped I was listening to the ravings of a ruined mind—yet I had seen my old friend in that moment of sanity. Although his words were feverish, they still rang with truth. Dillon knew that Lord Ido was losing hold of the Rat Dragon. And he knew he would soon have Ido's power. I shuddered, pushing my coursing fear into a final burst of speed. We were almost there.

"Dillon, how sick is Lord Ido?" I tightened my grip on his damp hand. "We can't let him die. Do you understand? We have to save him."

"Save him?" Dillon's glassy eyes narrowed. "No!" This time his fist was too quick. The crack of knuckles against his skull made me wince. "He hurts me."

"I know, I know," I soothed. "But we're going to save him, so he can train us."

"No!" Dillon shrieked. "I want him to die."

He twisted in my grip like a wild dog fighting a noose. I stumbled after him, towed by his savage fury. Another blast of cold wind slammed into us, bringing the smell of sweet, wet grass. The piercing cricket song stopped, the sudden silence pounding in my ears. I looked up in time to see a claw of light rake the sky, then a booming shock surged over us.

"Eona, behind you!"

Kygo's frantic voice swung me around to face the dense tree line at the far end of the slope.

A wide semicircle of soldiers had broken out of the woods, all carrying *Ji,* the hook-bladed pikes braced for attack. They were no more than one hundred lengths away and moving with wary speed. I heaved on Dillon's hand, but he had dropped to his knees, a shrieking anchor. I felt the gusty wind flex into the heavier muscle of the monsoon, its brutal strength knocking me back a step and stealing my breath. Before me, the grass flattened and the trees bowed in obeisance as the gale brought the first drumming drops of rain. A panic of starlings burst out of the trees and spiraled upward, turning in a sharp arrow ahead of the wind. I gasped as the sudden rush of cool water streamed against my hair and face, its weight stinging my skin and scalp.

A few lengths away, Ryko pushed Ju-Long and Tiron onward, then turned and drew his swords. The islander's lone figure blurred in the thick veil of pounding rain as the shapes of Tiron and the gray horse forged past us. I thought I heard the young guard call me though the teeming water, but Dillon pulled my hand again. He was back on his feet. My relief froze into realization; I was no longer holding Dillon. He was holding me.

Even as I tried to wrench free, he caught my other hand and with brutal strength swung me around in a splashing circle, as though we were children again, playing Dragon Spin.

"What are you doing?" I yelled. "Stop it!"

"Dragon day, dragon night, dragon spirit with the right," he sang. *"Call your name, bring your light—show us who will have the sight!"*

The wet hem of my gown wrapped around my legs. I tripped, collapsing onto one knee in the pooling water. The wind was gone, the rain now falling in a seamless gray curtain as if the gods were emptying a pitcher over our heads.

"Dillon, the soldiers are coming!" I blinked, trying to clear my stinging eyes of water. It ran in rivulets down my face and the front of my gown, soaking the rough cloth into a dead weight. "We have to run."

"Which dragon? Which dragon? Choose!" he singsonged. "Choose!"

He yanked at my hands, grinding the thin bones together as he hauled me upright. Such strength was not natural. I threw my weight backward in a bid to jerk free, but he held me locked in his game.

Just above our wrists, the rope of white pearls loosened its stranglehold. The last two perfect gems lifted again, this time like a snake tasting the sodden air. With clattering purpose they uncoiled, leaving only one loop binding the folio to Dillon's arm. The rest of the rope slithered around the edges of the book and settled a protective rank of pearls along each groove of exposed paper. Then, with a snap and lunge, the lead length wrapped around my right wrist, strapping my hand to Dillon's as if it was a wedding bind.

I strained against the shackle. Heat engulfed my arm and rolled through my body on a wave of thick nausea. Bitter power rose behind my eyes, whispering words that struck at my mind with acid. Ancient words. The book was calling me, folding me into its secrets. It was a book of blood, of death, of chaos. It was the book of *Gan Hua*.

If this was what burned in Dillon's mind, no wonder he screamed and pounded at his head.

Desperately, I pulled against the pearls; I did not want to follow Dillon into madness. Already, the words were searing their mark into me. Although I had beaten back the *Gan Hua* in Kinra's swords, that had been a mere flicker compared to this blazing bitterness. If I did not stop it now, it would consume me.

I pushed back against the scorching power as I had pushed back against Kinra's swords. It made no difference to the book's relentless, blistering force.

Perhaps Kinra could hold back this ancient power. I did not trust her influence, nor did I want to touch her treachery. Yet she'd had the strength and skill to shape *Hua* into a dark force and send it across five centuries—the swords were proof.

I still had her death plaque in my pocket, although I could not reach for it. Would its presence be enough? I sent out my plea: *Kinra, please stop the folio from burning its madness into me.* Then I sent another prayer to my ancestors who had brought her Dragoneye power to me: *Stop Kinra's own madness from burning me, too.*

As if in answer, a force rose through my blood. An aching cold flowed across the acid words like frost, extinguishing the burn of the book. Then the words and the chill were suddenly gone. But neither the pearls nor Dillon eased their brutal grip.

"Choose," Dillon cried again.

I shook my head, trying to clear away the aftershock of the searing words.

"Choose." His fingers tightened into a bone-crunching demand. "*Choose!*"

"I choose the Ox," I gasped. The second dragon; two spins in the game. If I could find Kygo, maybe I could drag us in his direction.

"I choose the Rooster," Dillon called. Ten spins.

I clenched my teeth and swung with him into the twirling count of twelve.

"One," he yelled. The landscape was a blur of gray and green, Dillon's pale, grinning face the only fixed point.

"Two." His weight pulled at the end of my hands, wrenching me into a splashing stagger.

"Three." His voice changed. No more playful singsong—just flat command. I closed my eyes against the relentless water and the whirling sickness in my head.

"Four."

Every spin dug us deeper into the mud, closer to the raw force of the earth. At the edge of my reeling senses, I heard him murmuring more words. Although their form and meaning were lost in the deafening tattoo of water, the Dragoneye in me knew they were the same ancient words that had attacked my mind.

Dillon was calling dark energy. It was embedded in the deep resonance of the numbers and in his fevered chant. Four was the number of death, and I could feel it coming with the pounding certainty of my own heartbeat.

"Eona!" Kygo's voice. I opened my eyes. His tall figure flashed past.

I dropped onto my knees in the watery mud, dragging all of my weight against Dillon's hold, but his savage strength jerked me back up into stumbling submission. Power prickled along our bound hands.

"Five," he yelled.

"Dillon, what are you doing?" I yelled.

"With you, I'm strong enough," he screamed.

Strong enough for what?

Around us the rain slanted, caught in the roaring gusts of a sudden wind from the northwest. Kygo flashed past again, bent into the brutal slam of air, his swords drawn. I tried to call his name, but water filled my eyes and mouth.

"Six."

I shook my head, fighting for sight and breath. A smear of dark figures coalesced into running soldiers, their battle cries broken into a staccato wail by the buffeting wind and the spine-snapping momentum of our spins.

"Dillon, the soldiers!" I screamed.

"Seven!"

His eyes were closed, head craned back. The drone of his chant rose into a shrill keen that matched the shriek of the wind. I tasted the ancient power within it. It dried my mouth like a sour plum, but something else lay within the bitterness. A familiar, sweet tang of cinnamon—the taste of the red dragon's power. Was he calling my dragon? Impossible, yet there were also the faint notes of vanilla and orange. Lord Ido's beast. Dillon's ravings sharpened into one clear moment of fury: *I want him to die*.

Merciful gods, he was using me to kill Ido.

"Dillon, no!" I slammed my body back, yanking at his hands, but I was still held fast.

"Eight."

From nearby came the clash of steel meeting steel. Swords! My heart contracted into a hard ball, then burst back into drumming fear. Had the soldiers attacked Kygo? A dark knot of struggling men flickered past. Ryko, beating back three soldiers.

"Nine."

There was nothing I could do to stop Dillon in the earthly plane; he was too strong. Focusing on his ecstatic face, I tried to shift into mind-sight. It was like forcing my way through a briar made of pelting water and panting terror. As he spun me around, I managed three deep breaths. On the fourth, the gray-green earthly plane yielded to the iridescence of the energy world.

"Ten."

I staggered into the next spin, disoriented by the sudden assault of bright color. Before me, Dillon's flesh and blood shifted into the streaming pathways of his energy body. I gasped, repulsed by the swollen network of dark power that flowed through him in a thick, oily slip. What had happened to his *Hua*? Even the seven points of power along his spine—usually pumping with the silvery life force—were black and bloated. And something else was wrong with them. I stared at the heartpoint in his chest, only a faint tinge of its green vigor left in the murky depths. It was spinning in the wrong direction.

He raised his head, the dark energy swarming through his eye sockets.

"Eleven," he said and smiled. "He's dying."

My head snapped back as he pulled me into the second-to-last pivot. I locked my eyes on the crimson dragon above, desperate for a fixed point of sanity. Her huge, sinuous body thrashed against an invisible enemy. Ruby claws raked the air in futile slashes. A channel of bright gold *Hua* stretched between her and Dillon—he was siphoning her power, with no return of vital energy. With no defense against the ten bereft dragons.

"Dillon, let her go. Before the others come. You can't control this!"

"I can do anything," he yelled.

Fury roared through me, bringing a new surge of strength. He was hurting my dragon. Using my power.

"*Eona!*" I screamed, calling our shared name, but there was no answering cascade of golden energy through me. It was all streaming into Dillon. Somehow, he was blocking us from union. Another channel, thin and stuttering, leached from the blue dragon. The beast was barely an outline, its small, pale body rolling in agony.

"Dillon, stop it! You're hurting them." A terrible thought seized me—could he kill the dragons?

He cannot. Ido's voice. It was barely a whisper in my mind, ragged with pain and effort.

Are the others coming, Ido? Can you hold them back?

They will not come near the Black Folio, he rasped. *Stop the boy from draining my dragon. Please, before—* His voice broke into a scream that ripped through me.

"How?" I yelled. "How do I stop him?"

Get the book, Ido panted. *Cut him from its power.*

I did not want to touch the book.

"Twelve!" Dillon shouted, triumphant.

He wrenched me into the final spin, breaking my hold on the energy world. Its jewel colors slid back into the dull, wet landscape of the mountainside. With a shrieking rush, the rain and wind disappeared, the flooded ground suddenly dry and hard under my stumbling feet. No more driving rain. My face, gown, hair: all dry. Ryko and the three soldiers flashed past again, but they were no longer fighting. All four men were staring up at the sky.

"Look at that!" Dillon shouted through a new roar of gushing water. He stopped spinning, the sudden halt jerking me into a gasping standstill. "Look at what I can do." He threw his head back, laughing.

Above, the rain was still streaming from the heavy clouds, but not downward. It was horizontal, sucked into a ring that circled the entire slope like an immense whirlpool suspended in the air. It spun around us, a thundering torrent four houses high that ripped up trees and bushes into its swirling sluice. All of us, friend and foe, were corralled in its center, our sanctuary already shrinking as the vortex churned across the pine trees, yanking them into its swelling depths.

"Dillon, push it back," I roared. "Push it back!"

A shrill animal scream cut through the booming rush. A horse broke out of a thicket near the churning wall, dragging Solly behind it by its reins.

"Solly, let go," Vida yelled. She and Dela pulled the other two horses clear. *"Let go!"*

The stocky man released his hold and tucked into a ball, barely escaping the slicing hooves. The horse galloped past us—eyes rolling white—toward Ryko and the soldiers. All four men still stood gaping at the expanding water and debris, the horse's pounding progress lost in the deafening rumble.

"Ryko, *move!*" Kygo yelled. But he was too far away.

The horse plowed into the middle of the group, stamping over Ryko and a screaming soldier. For a moment horror stole my breath; then the islander moved, rolling away from the frenzied beast. A few lengths away, the water swept up a chunk of mountainside in an explosion of cracking wood and earth.

Dillon looked up at his handiwork, his delight draining into sudden pallor. "It's too big." A fine spray of cool water wet my face and Dillon's hair. He dropped my unbound hand, digging his freed fingers into his forehead. "It hurts," he gasped. "Is it supposed to hurt?"

"Give me the book." I dug at our pearl shackle. "Let me help you."

"No!" He shoved me in the chest, pushing me back a step. "You want my power. Just like my lord." He bared his teeth in a vicious smile. "Can you hear him? He's screaming."

I grabbed him by the front of his tunic. "Dillon, you can't kill Ido. If he dies, we die." I shook him. "Do you understand? We have to save him!"

"Save him?" Dillon spat the words. "I'm going to kill him. Before he kills me."

His yellowed eyes bulged with hate. He would never save Ido. Never help me. I felt the roaring water around us falter, the fine mist gathering into drops that hit my face with ominous weight. Dillon was losing control.

I had one chance to get the book before he killed us all. But he was stronger than me in every way. What did I have left?

Sucking in a desperate breath, I slammed my forehead into his face. The impact jarred my head back in an explosion of bruising pain and streaming light. I heard Dillon howl as he recoiled, pulling me with him. Through a blur of tears, I lunged at the pale rope binding the folio to his forearm. My fingernails scraped the embossed cover and connected with the row of pearls. I rammed my fingers between gems and leather and pried open a gap, enough space to hook the rigid rope. My first yank loosened its straining resistance. On the second, half of the pearls lifted. Once more and I would have it.

I hauled, but instead of releasing, the pearls snapped back, clamping my hand against the leather binding. Dillon straightened, blood welling from a gash above his eye. Frantically, I tried to pull my fingers free, but there was no slack. Both my hands were bound to the folio, and the folio was bound to Dillon. His fist swung back, but I had nowhere to move. The savage undercut caught me in the delta of my ribs and slammed out my air. I doubled over, my breath locked in my chest.

I had lost my chance to get the book.

The pearls closed even more tightly around my fingers, sending burning pressure up my arm. Heat rose through me, unclenching my chest into gasping relief. Sour acid flooded my mouth as soft words seared my mind. The black book was calling me again, whispering ancient promises of perfect power—whispering a way to stop Dillon.

For a moment, the book's treachery held us still, each caught in our own desperation.

"No!" Dillon screamed. "It's mine!" His wild punches hammered my arms and chest.

All I could see in front of me was Dillon's flailing madness and the sickening memory of his black, bloated *Hua*. Was this the book's promise to me, too—the dark grip of *Gan Hua* and burning madness? There was no choice. I had to let the acid words score their power into my mind. I had to risk its madness. Everything else had failed.

Around us, the circling wall was shedding waves of rain laden with stinging stones and mud. The air rippled and streamed with collisions of water, as if huge bucketfuls were being thrown from all directions. An uprooted tree spun out of the torrent and crashed into the ground near Solly, reaming a hole in the mud. Only a few lengths away, Kygo ducked as a bush flew past his head and bounced across the flooding slope. It was all coming down.

I closed my hand around the pearls and prayed to Kinra again. But this time I asked her to call the black book and let it carve its dark *Hua* into my mind.

The heat slammed through me like a physical blow. I staggered and pulled Dillon off balance. The pearls coiled and squeezed our connected hands like a rattling constrictor, pulling the book across the bridge of our wrists. Bitter gall parched my mouth and throat, shriveling my howling pain into a whimper.

The book was coming to me, bringing its scorching power.

"No!" Dillon swung his body into mine. "No!"

His weight knocked me to my knees in the muddy water, the momentum bringing him splashing down beside me. Bracing his shoulder against mine, he tore at the shifting, contorting pearls. His nails gouged my flesh, his fingers sliding under the gems in the slip of my blood. I rammed my body against his, but it only added more leverage to his heave on the pearl rope. The book lifted. Dillon hauled on them again, murmuring words that sang their power through my head. In an explosion of unraveling pearls and shrieking *Hua*, he wrenched the book free.

I screamed as the ancient energy ripped out of me.

For a moment, I saw the stark triumph on his face. Then the swirling wall of water dropped with a roaring crash that sent up plumes of mud like a ring of explosions. Huge peaks of water collided around us in all directions, breaking into rolling, swelling waves black with dirt and debris. I saw Solly and Dela disappear under the roiling torrent that swept toward us. Near the tree line, a backrush caught a group of running soldiers, their leather armor dragging them under. A horse squealed, the sound suddenly cut off as the poor beast was swamped. I lunged for Dillon, hoping to grab him before the full force hit us, but my fingers only grazed his shirt. I heard Kygo scream my name. He was only an arm's length away from me. But so was Dillon. As I lunged for the boy again, the pearls coiled around his forearm, wrapping themselves around the exposed edges of the book. It knew the water was coming.

The wave hit me like a cold sledgehammer. It slammed me backward, then pulled me under its dark surface, flipping me into a straining tumble. I heard only the rush of water and my heartbeat pounding the sudden lack of air. Legs caught in heavy folds of cloth. Swirling stones and twigs pelting me. *No air. No air.* Was I up or down? Something hit my shoulder. I grabbed it—the buoyant length of a branch. *Up, please let it be up.* I kicked frantically, my feet tangled in the twists of my gown.

Chest searing with the end of my last breath. *Up, up.* Clinging to the wood, I broke the surface, gasping, my ears ringing with the relief of air, and the deafening crash of water.

Something snagged my sleeve.

"Grab the tree."

Yuso's blurred face. I reached for him. His cold hand locked into mine and pulled me over the solid round of a tree trunk.

"Hold on," he yelled and hooked his arm over my body.

We spun, caught in a violent eddy, then lurched back into the wild current rushing down the slope. Pale shapes under the roiling water bumped and tumbled past. Bodies, their flailing limbs brushing against me. For a few lengths a sobbing horse swam beside us, struggling to keep its head above the murky rapids. Then our tree trunk snagged on another and swung around. For a breathless moment, I saw Dillon clinging to a tree, the black folio swarming up his body like a rat finding higher ground. The pearls wrapped around a branch and pulled him to safety.

Then our makeshift raft broke loose and Yuso and I spun back into the deadly plummet downhill.

CHAPTER NINE

YUSO'S GRIP TIGHTENED, his body locking mine against the trunk, as we plowed relentlessly toward the ridge of the slope. The flood had leveled everything, churning the earth into a thick mud that gushed over the edge.

"We're going over!" Yuso yelled. *"Don't let go."*

We sheared the tops of scrubby bushes and a bank of foul debris. For a moment the drop hung before us, its base obscured by a cascade of muck—and then we plunged over, heavy mud raining down on us as we rode the sliding, falling earth into the gully below.

Screaming, I felt my hold slip on the slimy bark. All I could taste and smell was dirt. Yuso's body lifted from mine. I slid forward, groping frantically for a secure hold. Then his strong arms pulled me free and we were falling together, his yell loud in my ear.

We hit, the impact jarring us apart. Blindly, I rolled

and rolled, my gown wrapping my legs in a sticky weight. I slammed against something hard. The brutal stop sent a shock of bruising pain through my back. Around me was the sound of loud slapping, and my own hard breathing. I spat out dirt and wiped my eyes, blinking the world back into bleary focus.

A nearby mound of mud resolved into the shape of a dead horse. Next to it was a drowned soldier, still holding his *Ji* in a death-grip. I sat up—too fast, my head spinning—and backed away from their glassy stares. Cold mud oozed through my toes. I had lost both sandals.

"Lady Eona? Are you all right?"

Yuso's voice. I jerked around. He was only a few lengths away, buried up to his chest in a deep pocket of sludge. Only one arm was free, held awkwardly in the air. Behind him, mud rained down over the ridge: the source of the slapping sound. It was getting faster and heavier.

I started toward him. "Are you hurt?"

"Stop! I don't know the size of this hole."

"Are you hurt? Can you get out?"

He *had* to get out—I didn't want to be alone in the middle of all this destruction. For all I knew, Yuso was the only other survivor. I briefly wished it had been Ryko who had saved me. Was the islander even alive?

I fought back a rise of panic. Was Kygo alive? Dela? I did not even know if Ido had survived Dillon's drain of his power. Although he must have—otherwise, the ten bereft dragons would surely have torn me apart.

"I'm not hurt, but every time I move, I sink," Yuso said. "And there's nothing to pull myself out with."

I took another step.

"No, don't!" The force of his cry drove him farther into the sucking mud.

I tensed, holding my breath as the level settled under his armpits. "All right, I won't come any closer. But we've got to find a way to get you out. The ridge is going to come down"—I glanced up at the steady fall of mud—"on top of you."

Very slowly, he shifted his head back to look, then gave a low, desperate laugh. "Don't suppose you could hold it back with some of that power I just saw?"

"It wasn't mine," I said, scanning the devastated landscape for something to throw to him. Everything was camouflaged by a thick layer of brown slime. My eyes skipped over the dead horse and soldier, then flicked back. The *Ji*.

"You mean it was all the boy's power?" Yuso was talking softly but rapidly, holding back fear with words.

"No, it was the black book," I said. "It bound us together."

I felt an echo of the book's burning power in my mind. Without Kinra, I would not have survived its onslaught. My breath caught; did I still have her plaque? I plunged my hand into the slimy pocket of my gown. The pouch was there, still safe.

Gingerly, I edged across the mud to the dead soldier, testing each oozing foothold. What if he wasn't quite dead? What if he had become one of the *Halbo*, a demon spirit of the drowned? I lowered myself into a wary crouch beside the body, but it did not move or clack its teeth.

"So the binding is true, then." Yuso's voice abruptly stopped. I spun on my heel, terrified he had gone under, but his head and shoulders were still clear. "What are you doing?" he whispered.

"I'm getting this *Ji* to pull you out."

"No, it's too dangerous. Leave me. There's time for you to climb to safety."

I wrapped my hand around the handle and yanked it free from the soldier's grip. The man's hand lifted and slapped back down, as if he were blessing me. Shuddering, I whispered a quick call to Shola on his behalf, then carefully retraced my own safe footprints back to Yuso.

The captain was watching me, anguish written in deep creases of mud on his thin face. Hurriedly, I extended the pole across the mire until the handle hovered near him.

"Grab it. Quickly."

I glanced up at the slopping mud fall behind him. It was flowing into the hole, raising the level.

He caught the wavering wood. "I will be too heavy for you."

"I am strong," I assured him, although the same doubt had blown its cold breath on me. He was lean for a Shadow Man—the Sun Drug issued to the eunuch guards usually built more bulk—but he was still tall and well muscled. "Don't worry," I added. "I won't leave you."

He flinched as a heavy branch fell beside him, splattering his face with more mud. I tested the ground with my toes and found a section that was not too soft. Working my heels into it, I wiped a length of the pole clean.

"Ready?" I asked.

He nodded.

Taking a resolute breath, I hauled on his weight at the end of the long pole, careful to keep the hooked blade away from me. I felt a small shift. I heaved again, and again, inching backward through the stiff mud. Suddenly his other arm swung free, dripping with sludge. He grabbed the pole with both hands.

"Keep going," he urged.

I dug my heels into the mud again and pulled as he painstakingly lifted one hand and placed it above the other on the pole. Panting, Yuso smiled across at me. I smiled back—it was working. On his nod, I heaved again as he dragged himself along another hand-length. Every muscle in my arms and back burned with the strain of holding his weight, but his chest was almost out of the hole.

He lifted his hand again, but this time tried to reach too far. His grip slipped. The sudden loss of his weight on the pole yanked me to my knees. I saw him slide backward, groping wildly for purchase. Instinctively, I braced knees and toes in the mud and anchored the *Ji*. His hand connected and gripped.

"Got it?" I gasped.

"Yes." He pressed his forehead into the crook of his arm, gulping deep breaths. "How's that ridge holding?" he finally asked.

"Not that good," I said. "Ready?"

He lifted his head. "Lady Eona, I cannot—" He stopped, his eyes bleak. "I have a son. His name is Maylon. Find him, tell him—"

"Yuso." I caught his gaze, holding him steady, although my

own doubt pounded through me. "I'm not leaving until you're out of there."

With a nod, he clenched his teeth and once again started the laborious hand-by-hand crawl up the pole. I heaved back on his weight over and over, finding a rhythm in between each desperate handhold that gave him precious impetus. Gradually, his chest and waist emerged. When his hips finally breached the sucking mud, I dropped the *Ji* and slithered toward him on hands and knees. Grabbing his outstretched hands, I pulled him free. In a clumsy mix of sliding, dragging, and crawling, we made our way back to secure ground.

Yuso turned to study the ridge, then gave a soft grunt of relief. "It is still holding, but we should get out of here." He stood up and tested his right leg. A large tear in the thigh of his mud-soaked trousers was dark with blood.

"Is it bad?" I asked.

He dismissed it with a shake of his head. "I can walk." He offered me his hand and pulled me upright. My own legs were trembling with the afterwash of effort. And fear.

"Did you see what happened to the emperor?" I asked, as he ushered me forward. "Or any of the others?"

Yuso shook his head.

"What if . . . ?" I couldn't voice the possibility.

"If His Majesty is dead, then it is all over," Yuso said flatly. He picked up the *Ji*. "There is no reason for a resistance."

"But Sethon can't be emperor. He will destroy the thousand years of peace."

"Whatever way it goes, the thousand years of peace are over," Yuso said.

Using the blade at the end of the pike to test the ground, he limped toward the horse and soldier. I wanted to deny his bleak assessment, but the ache in my chest knew he was right. I followed his footprints across the firmer mud.

"Did you say you have a son, captain?" I asked, trying to focus on something other than our tortuously slow progress through the sludge.

He turned, his eyes narrowed. "It would be better for both of us if you forgot I said that."

"Why?"

"It is forbidden—on pain of death—for an Imperial Guard to have family ties." He held my gaze. "Do you understand? *No one else* must know of my son."

I nodded. "I swear on my dragon I will not tell anyone. But how did you become a father?" A foolish question, but I wanted him to keep talking. Any silence was too full of the relentless slap of falling mud and my own terrible imaginings.

Yuso turned back to navigating the treacherous ground. "I was not born a eunuch, my lady." He stopped in front of the dead soldier and peered into the man's slack face. "I sired my son before I was cut. I was very young."

A few limped steps took him to the horse. He bent and stroked the animal's mud-caked neck. "One of our mares, poor girl." He looked up at the ridge, gauging its stability again, then unbuckled the saddlebag and heaved it free. "His mother died when he was born—may she walk in heaven's glory—so he is my only family."

"He must be very precious to you."

"He is now a lieutenant in Sethon's army."

I looked down at the soldier, my spine prickling. "Is he stationed in this area?"

Yuso dug the *Ji* into the mud.

"I don't know where he is," he said. He slung the saddlebag over his shoulder. "That is what this war will be: father against son, brother against brother." He scanned the stark landscape, then pointed east and beckoned me onward. "It is our duty to restore peace as soon as possible at whatever cost—otherwise there will be no land to rule." He glanced back, his lean face grim. "You will come to know that, my lady, and I am sorry for it."

We were climbing the other side of the gully when the ridge came down.

It dropped in a crashing roar, the terrible sound bouncing off the rock faces around us in a rolling echo. We both stopped and watched the deadly churn of mud and debris slide across the valley below us. It smothered everything in its path and sent the stink of wet earth and decay into the air.

I felt Yuso's hand grip my shoulder in sympathy. "We can't go back and look," he said, answering my unspoken question. "It will be too dangerous—and whatever came down with that is already dead."

"We survived," I said mutinously.

"Let's keep doing so," he said, his grip shifting from compassion to command.

Just before nightfall, Yuso grabbed my shoulder again.

"Stop!" he whispered, the word barely audible under the screeching night calls of roosting birds.

My last reserves of energy coiled into tense readiness. I scanned the spindly trees and tall bushes around us—all threatening in the half-light—and hooked my hand more securely around the saddlebag. It was not much of a weapon, but it could catch the end of a soldier's *Ji*.

As if formed from dusk shadows, the shapes of six men stepped from the dark undergrowth. Silently, they circled us, a mix of swords and axes raised. Yuso's hand slid down the *Ji*, ready to thrust.

"Who are you?" he demanded.

A thin man with straggly, unbound hair shook his head. "Six against two." His voice had a soft mountain accent. "I think the question is: Who are *you*?"

"Captain Yuso, of the imperial guard."

His name sent a ripple of excitement around the circle of men. I felt their attention shift to me. I gripped the saddlebag even tighter.

"Are you Lady Eona?" the thin man asked.

"Yes."

"Thank the gods you are alive." His teeth showed in a quick, relieved smile. The weapons around us lowered. "We are from the Chikara Mountain Resistance. I am Caido. It is an honor to be the ones to find you, Lady Dragoneye."

He bowed, the other five following his lead in a ragged wave.

"Thank you," I said, swaying from the sudden release of tension. "Have you found the emperor?"

"Yes. He is alive, but deep in the shadow world. When we were last at our base, he had still not roused. We need to get you back there as fast as possible."

My gut clenched. At least he lived. "And the others, are they all right?"

"Ryko has minor injuries. As does the woman, Vida. The young guard has—"

"Tiron," Yuso interjected.

"Yes, sir, Tiron," Caido said. "He's broken a lot of bones and may not walk again. We have not found the other three of your party."

Dela, Dillon, Solly—missing.

"So the boy has not been found?" Yuso demanded. "The one they call Dillon?"

"No, sir. Not yet."

"He must be your priority now," Yuso said. "He holds something vital to His Majesty's cause."

"We can only search with the light, Captain." There was a note of defense in Caido's soft voice. "But we start again tomorrow at dawn. Are either of you hurt?"

"Nothing serious," Yuso said. "Did Ryko tell you about the troops in pursuit? Twenty-four. A full company."

Caido nodded. "We've accounted for nineteen, sir. Most of them drowned. Our best teams are hunting the last five."

Yuso nodded, satisfied.

Caido gave another small bow, then turned to his men. A quick series of hand signals sent them into a diamond formation around us, except for one very large man, who stood stolidly behind Caido.

"My lady, we need to move fast," Caido said. "Would you allow Shiri to carry you on his back?" The large man dipped his head.

Although my weariness was like a hundredweight hanging on each limb, I drew myself up. "I will not fall behind, Caido."

"No, my lady," he said, and bowed.

He waved us forward.

An hour later, I was perched on Shiri's back. The man smelled of old sweat, greasy hair, and sour spillings, but I did not care. His back was broad, his arms were hooked securely around me, and I could finally rest my exhausted body. I tried to stay awake as we climbed through the last of the scrubby terrain into a thicker growth of forest, but the rocking motion of Shiri's long stride lulled me. As I slipped into the shadows of uneasy sleep, I once again felt the intent hold of Kygo's eyes as he brushed my cheek, and the strange heat of the pearl beneath my fingers.

"My lady?" A firm shake on my arm woke me. I squinted. The half-moon night had reduced Caido's face to a series of sharp planes. "You must walk the last section," he said quietly. "Only one person can pass through this entrance at a time."

Shiri released his hold and lowered me gently to the

rocky ground. The forest was now well below us.

"Thank you," I murmured.

The big man dipped into a bow. "My honor, Lady Eona," he said, backing away. "My honor."

"He will tell his grandchildren about the time he carried the Mirror Dragoneye," Yuso said, close to my ear.

"How long did I sleep?" I stared up at an immense moon-silvered cliff that rose before us. Were we going to climb it? Even after my rest on Shiri's back, I doubted I would make it.

"We've been walking for about four bells," Yuso said, every step of them in his rough voice.

Caido pointed up to a dark crack in the rock face. "We are nearly there," he said. "That is the way into our camp."

As we drew nearer to the cliff, the dark crack became a fissure large enough for a man the size of Shiri. With a reassuring smile, Caido slipped into it. I followed him, the warm night air instantly cooling as I stepped into a narrow stone passage. A slit of sky was still visible above us, although very little moonlight made it to where we stood.

"My lady, please hold on to my shoulder," Caido said. "It will be safer and quicker."

We shuffled in a hand-to-shoulder line as Caido called the news of our rescue to watchmen stationed on high ledges. I caught sight of two guards craning over to catch a glimpse of us as we passed, the tips of their mechanical bows outlined in the dim light. It would be a deadly trap for an approaching enemy.

"This is one of four passages into the crater," Caido said. "Of course, it is not the most accessible, but it was the closest and will give you a good view of our camp." His voice was quick with pride.

Ahead, I could see the other end, gray with light. Kygo was somewhere in this camp, hurt. And Ryko and Vida. My toes clipped Caido's heels. I stumbled.

"I'm sorry, my lady," Caido said. "Are you all right?"

"I am just eager to see His Majesty," I said.

The end of the passage was twice the size of its entrance, the night sky visible through the wide opening. Two silhouetted figures moved into view, the moonlight catching a flash of silver hair on the taller of them. I hoped they were there to take us straight to the emperor.

"My lady, after you," Caido said.

As I stepped out onto a broad natural ledge of stone, the silver-haired man moved forward, but my attention was caught by the sight below me—a huge bowl of a crater, its floor studded with flickers of firelight that cast a glow on multitudes of tents and rough-builds. Along the steep sides, more campfires lit the shapes of caves. Gathered below the ledge were the shifting figures of hundreds and hundreds of people watching our arrival. I had not given much thought to what the resistance would look like, but I knew that I had not expected such a large camp.

"Lady Eona?" the silver-haired man said, in obviously a second or third attempt.

"I am sorry. It is so . . ." I finally looked at him and faltered. The gray in his hair was not from age; he could be no more than twenty-five. Perhaps it was from the burden of command or the effect of some great tragedy. There was certainly a hint of melancholy in his intelligent face.

He smiled. "Yes, it is breathtaking. A natural fortress." He bowed. "I am Viktor, leader of the Chikara Mountain Resistance." He gestured to his companion. "This is my lieutenant, Sanni. We are relieved to have found you, my lady. And you, Captain Yuso."

"Thank you," I said. "Where is His Majesty?"

"In our main cave, my lady. The Beseechers have been praying since he arrived, but we have been waiting for your arrival to physick him."

"Waiting for me?" Ryko must have told them about the fisher village. Guilt and shame prickled across my scalp. They were waiting for me, the mighty Dragoneye, to heal the emperor. But I could not risk it again; I did not want to kill any more innocent people. And I certainly did not want power over the emperor's will.

"I cannot heal him," I said. "You must understand; I cannot heal him."

"No, of course not, my lady. We do not expect you to have a physician's skill," Viktor said, frowning. "The girl Vida told us that you are now His Majesty's *Naiso*. Is that not true?"

"Yes, it is true."

"Then you are the only one who can touch his sacred body. Our physician must work through you."

I bit my lip. They only wanted me to help examine him. I could do that.

"Let us go to him, then," I said.

Viktor ushered me toward steps cut into the steep slope. "My men have already trespassed upon His Majesty's sanctity by carrying him back here. They are good, dutiful men, my lady, and their deaths would serve no purpose. I beg you to pardon them."

His words sent a twinge of unease through me. The rank of *Naiso* brought unexpected responsibilities. "They are pardoned," I said quickly.

He ducked his head. "Thank you, my lady."

Every part of me wanted to run to the cave and help Kygo, but the press of cheering people that lined the pathway around the crater limited us to a quick walk. At first I moved away from the excited, wondering faces and the hands that reached out to touch me. They had never seen a Dragoneye in the flesh, let alone a female Dragoneye. Yuso tried to insert his body between me and their reaching need, his rough warnings lost in the chant of my name. Then a deep voice rose above the others. "Let the gods protect Lady Eona. Let the gods protect His Majesty." I found the caller across the sea of heads—a middle-aged man with tears in his eyes—and I finally understood.

I was their symbol of hope, their guarantee that the gods had not abandoned them. Although I was not worthy of such reverence or faith, I had to be what they needed. "Stand back," I told Yuso. Reluctantly, he stepped behind me. I straightened my shoulders and walked on, brushing my fingers across the hands that strained to touch hope and salvation.

We finally reached the main cave. An altar had been built to one side, and two Beseechers kneeled before it, their swinging lanterns throwing patterns on the dark rock face. Two large brass incense burners stood like sentinels on either side of the entrance, their wisps of white smoke spreading the peppery cleanse of clove through the air. The cheers and calls quieted as we passed the altar. I caught sight of a circlet of bloodstones arranged in front of the prayer candles, and a ceremonial sword. The shrine was in honor of Bross, the god of battle. A good choice. As we entered the cave, I sent my own silent plea to the war god for Kygo's recovery.

I paused for a moment, trying to take in the size of the cavern. It was at least as big as a large hall, but the true dimensions were lost in the dim light, the high, shadowy ceiling, and the sheer number of people milling around. The murmur of anxious voices echoed around the stone walls. Only one area was clear—a far corner partitioned off by a large, five-paneled screen. It was painted in the beautiful Shoko style—Blossom Women on a rich gold background—but large sections had peeled away, and one panel was split. Its ruined opulence was out of place among the plain wooden benches and tables that lined the cave walls. Even without the two guards that stood before it, I would have known that the screen hid the emperor from view. It was a poor people's offering to their stricken king.

"My lady! Captain Yuso!" I turned to see Vida break away from a group of people clustered around a large brazier. She was clean and clothed in a fresh gown, the long scratches on her face the only outward sign of our ordeal. "Are you all right?" she asked me, bowing low. "I am so glad to see you."

I caught her hand, the warmth in her voice bringing a sting of tears to my eyes. Behind her, Ryko rose slowly from a bench along the wall. He was also clean and clothed, but he held his body as if nursing broken ribs. Our eyes met just before he bowed. His pain went much deeper than bones and blood.

Vida's grip tightened. "Have they told you?"

I nodded.

"His Majesty has still not woken?" Yuso asked.

"No," she said. "And Solly and Lady Dela have not been found. There was so much water, so much mud—"

"It's all right," I said, although it was not. "How is Tiron?"

A shadow passed across her face. "In much pain, but he is being well looked after."

"My lady, this way." Viktor gestured urgently toward the screen.

I squeezed Vida's hand. "Yuso is injured," I said, waving away the captain's protest. "Look to him. We will speak later."

I crossed the cave with the resistance leader. Groups of people shifted out of our way to create a pathway to the screen. Soft blessings followed us as we passed, but dread settled over me. I looked down at my hands, suddenly aware that I was grinding my fist into my palm.

The guards saluted as we paused at the edge of the first panel.

"The physician is waiting for you at His Majesty's bedside, Lady Eona," Viktor said. "He has been with him for over seven bells. I will stay here and await his report."

With both fists clenched, I rounded the screen.

An older man slumped on a stool beside a raised pallet immediately looked up. Under his flat physician's cap, his expression shifted from weariness to relief. "Lady Dragoneye?"

He bowed, but all of my attention was on the still shape beneath the blanket. Although Kygo's face was smeared with mud, I could see the stark pallor of his skin. His eyes were closed, but there were no flutterings of dream or nightmare. At some point he had bitten through his lower lip; the swelling was still high. The blanket was pulled up around his neck—I could not see any part of the Imperial Pearl or its stitching—but the edge of a dark bruise extended from his jaw line under the woven blanket edge. The rise and fall of his chest was smooth and regular, yet I could not look away from one breath to the next.

The sharp hiss of water on coals broke my stare.

The physician stood over a large brazier, swirling liquid in a pan. "Shall we proceed, my lady?" he said, fresh energy in his voice.

"How is he?"

"From observation, I would say his *Hua* is keeping him from returning from the shadow world until he has sufficient strength." He set the pan on the brazier and joined me beside the pallet. "I have never attended anyone of royal blood before, my lady. Nor have I ever examined a patient without touching him."

"And I have never been a physician's instrument before," I said, meeting his anxious smile with my own. "How should we start?'

"I am of the Meridian school, my lady." Seeing my obvious ignorance, he added, "My diagnosis is through the pulse and the energy lines. Do you know if His Majesty leads with the sun side or the moon side?"

I tried to picture Kygo fighting; in which hand did he hold his primary sword? Unbidden, the image turned into his right hand softly touching my face. "He is sun," I said abruptly.

"Of course," the physician murmured. "The Heavenly Master would naturally be allied with sun energy." He beckoned me along the side of the pallet. It was stacked on four rougher straw mattresses. "Now, my lady, take his wrist and find his pulse between the tendons."

I carefully lifted the blanket, exposing Kygo's muscular abdomen and the lean length of his thigh. Only a scrap of material lay in between. Heat rushed to my face. "He is only wearing undershorts," I said tightly, focusing fiercely on the cave ceiling. Yet the image of his strong body stayed clear in my vision.

"That is how he arrived," the physician said. "Either he discarded his clothes to avoid drowning, or the force of the water ripped them from him." He leaned closer. "Is that bruising? Please let me see his chest and ribs."

I pulled the blanket down and quickly dropped it over his lower body. Still, I caught sight of the deep line of muscle that distinguished flat belly from hipbone. Such strength. And such frailty.

The physician bent down, studying Kygo's ribs. The width of his chest was marred by a long gash, and deep blue-black bruising flowered across his right side. My gaze slid over the Imperial Pearl, its glowing beauty like a gentle pressure at the base of my skull.

"My lady, would you please—very gently—press through the swelling to the bones beneath the bruises and tell me what you feel?"

"Won't that hurt him?"

He looked up at me, surprised. "A good question. Does a patient in the shadow world register pain—or anything else for that matter? It is hotly debated across the schools. Let us say that, if he does feel it, he won't remember his pique when he awakens." He smiled, but there was steel beneath it. "My lady, I need to know if his ribs are broken and threaten his breathing."

Under the careful direction of the physician, I pressed the darkened swelling around Kygo's chest. His skin was reassuringly warm, the dried smears of mud dusting my fingers and leaving a powdery track of my progress. I found no shiftings or softenings of bone along his ribcage.

The physician nodded, pleased. "Only bruised." He noted something on Kygo's head and moved to study it. "This injury on his crown; I cannot see how deeply it penetrates. Pull it apart for me so I can see within, please."

We exchanged places. The wound sliced through the regrowth on Kygo's shaved head, alongside the mud-matted imperial queue. I positioned my fingers on either side and carefully shifted the thin flesh.

The physician peered closely at it, then sighed with relief.

"It is only a shallow cut. That is good news. The point of power in the crown is the seat of the spirit. If that is damaged, there is no way to heal it."

I nodded. In Dragoneye studies, the vivid purple point was also called the House of Truth. It was the center of insight and enlightenment—vital for an emperor.

The physician ushered me back along Kygo's body. "Now, his pulse. Sun side."

I picked up Kygo's right hand, cradling the long fingers and broad palm in my own. He wore a ring on his middle finger—I had not noted it closely before—a thick gold band studded with rounds of red jade. It was a blood amulet, like the one Lieutenant Haddo had worn around his neck, calling on Bross for protection in battle. I touched the ring, expecting cold metal, but it held Kygo's heat. Positioning my three mid fingers along the tendons in his wrist, I found the steady, strong rhythm of his life force. The last time my fingertips had pressed upon his pulse, the rhythm had been much faster. My gaze locked on the pearl at his throat.

"Now, feel the full movement within each beat."

I focused my senses on the tiny shifts beneath my fingertips as the physician led me through his art. It took all of my concentration to understand how to distinguish the three basic divisions of each beat and their projections. Finally, I mastered the fine differences, and the questions began. Was the tiny sign of life deep or superficial? Did it start boldly or hesitate? Was there any hold at the end, or did it rush forward into the next? How long was each peak and lull? The examination was endless. And then it was all repeated again with the emperor's moon pulse.

Finally, the physician sat back and rubbed his lined face. "Thank you, my lady. I have enough information." He bowed. "You have done very well. It usually takes years to develop such a finely tuned sense of touch."

"Will he be all right?" I asked.

"I must admit I am anxious. He has been a long time in the shadow world, and every bell he does not awaken makes it more dangerous."

I took a steadying breath. "But he will come back, won't he?"

The physician crossed to the brazier. "Sometimes the shadow world keeps its visitors. We must pray that his *Hua* is strong enough to resist its lures. To help him, I will prepare a ginseng wash. It will both cleanse his body of the ordeal and kindle his sun energy. Do you know of the twelve meridian lines in the body, my lady?"

I nodded. Every time I entered the energy world, I saw the twelve pathways in my own body and in the energy bodies of those around me. It had also been part of the basic training of a Dragoneye candidate; the flow of *Hua* was the basis of everything in the world. "I have studied them," I added.

The physician looked up, relieved. "You will need to wash him along those meridian lines." He struck a small gong, its rich resonance echoing through the waiting cave. Then he poured water into the pan set on the brazier.

I nodded my understanding, although the impending task

made me shift uneasily on the stool. I had never touched a man's body in such an intimate way.

The physician selected a small ceramic bottle from a wooden crate on the floor and pulled out the stopper with a small pop. The whole flask was emptied into the pan. Then another bottle was selected, its contents carefully sprinkled across the top.

A small boy appeared at the edge of the screen. "I am sorry I took so long, master," he said breathlessly. "There are so many people out there." His wide-eyed stare was fixed on me.

The physician looked around. "Ask Madina for more washing and drying towels and bring them back here." He cast a professional glance across at me. "Also ask her to make some soup for Lady Eona. She will know the one I mean. But tell her to leave out the toll herb."

The boy bowed and backed away.

The physician took a long, carved stick and stirred the contents of the pan. "For maximum benefit, His Majesty should be washed by a male." He looked across at me and smiled apologetically. "Your moon energy could nullify some of the efficiency of the ginseng. However, since only you can touch him, I have used all of my ginseng stock. Hopefully that will overcome the problem." He took the pan off the brazier and poured the steaming liquid into a large porcelain bowl. Halfway through he paused, pan still held high, as if struck by some thought.

"My lady, forgive my bluntness, but are you and His Majesty lovers? You touched him with such tenderness that I must ask. If you are, it will affect my preparations."

Bright heat rose through me, exploding into a choking laugh. "No," I said. "No, we are not." Involuntarily, my eyes flicked over to Kygo, the heat intensifying. "I am his *Naiso.* That is all."

He nodded and poured the last of the liquid into the bowl. "Then if there is no physical bond, the measurements should be correct."

I stared down at my muddied feet. Did a tender touch on the cheek count as a physical bond? Perhaps I should tell him. But how could I explain the pearl? Something had ignited within Kygo when I had caressed it. And, if I was truthful, something within me as well. I let the small acknowledgment settle into my spirit.

Dealing with Kygo had been much easier when I was Lord Eon. Admittedly, I had walked a deadly tightrope of disguise, but there had been none of this uneasy desire to touch and be touched. I knew about the physical act of love; once or twice on the salt farm I had accidentally come upon the hurried, furtive couplings of the other bond slaves. Did those acts arise from the same longing I felt in my blood when I touched Kygo? Yet at the same time we were barely friends. Allies, at best.

The physician carefully brought the filled bowl across to me. As he placed it on the low table, his apprentice slipped around the screen with a stack of cloth in his arms.

"Madina says the soup will be ready soon, master," he said, and bowed.

The physician took the bundle, dismissing the boy with a flick of his fingers.

"My lady, once you have washed His Majesty, you must eat and bathe in our thermal waters to restore your energy. You are as important to this resistance as His Majesty." He placed the cloths next to the bowl and bowed. "I must give my report to Viktor, but I will return soon. Do you have any questions?"

No questions, but I did have a confession. I forced myself to meet the man's kind eyes. "I have not lain with His Majesty," I said. "But he has touched me once with . . . gentleness." I pressed my fingers against my hot cheek, remembering the soft caress.

The physician smiled. "A gentle touch does not affect my measurements."

He bowed again, and backed around the edge of the screen.

I was alone with Kygo. I picked up a folded cloth and dipped it into the ginseng wash, keeping my eyes averted from his body. The fragrant water still held the soft sting of heat. I squeezed out the excess, juggling the cloth between my hands, and held it up for a moment to let it cool.

The anxious whispering in the main cave ebbed into silence. The physician must be consulting with Viktor. They had moved too far away to hear their conversation, but even from behind the screen I could feel the held breath of the waiting crowd.

Where to start the wash? My gaze skipped over the pearl and landed uncomfortably on the blanket across his hips. Perhaps I would start with his arms: they had strong meridian lines and did not have any intimate beginnings or endings.

I slid my hand under his right forearm, noting the strong flare of muscle from wrist to elbow, built from long hours with his sword, and the thick ridge of blue vein. From my studies, I knew the sun arm held three meridian lines: heart, lung, and vessel. The heart meridian, fed from the point of power in the chest, represented compassion and governed spirit. I glanced at Kygo's face—even though he was lost in the shadow world, his features held nobility and determination. No doubt his heart meridian, which stretched from shoulder to ring finger, was strong and clear of blockage. I rested his arm along mine, the muscled weight of it bringing a sharp memory of Ido's body pressing mine against the palace wall.

I paused, disturbed by the strange alignment of the two men in my mind. Both were tall and powerful, but Ido's physicality always held menace. With a shiver, I pushed away the image of the Dragoneye. If he was still alive, I could do nothing for him at present. And if he was dead, then let the gods help us all.

I swept the cloth from Kygo's shoulder to wrist, first following the meridian lines and then once again following the long, dense contours of muscle. Gently, I lowered his arm back on to the bed.

I soaked and squeezed out another cloth. For the sake of balance, I should wash his moon arm. Instead, I was drawn to his face. Had I looked so serene when I was senseless? I could not remember anything of the shadow world, although I had dwelled there for two days. Perhaps Kygo was living another life where he was just a man, and not the hope of an empire. Was that why he did not want to return? I could understand the relief of dropping such a burden. Delicately, I wiped his broad forehead and then under his eyes, following the meridian line across the high plane of his cheekbones. His face had strong, clean angles: if I'd still had my drawing ink and paper, I could have sketched him with a few bold lines. Yet I doubted my small skill would have done justice to the harmony of his features.

I paused, considering the problem of his split lower lip. If I wiped it clear of blood, it could start the flow again. Carefully, I touched the damp cloth to his mouth, trying not to pull at its tender fullness. The corners held a natural uplift, or maybe he was smiling at someone in the shadow world.

Two men had kissed me in my life—the salt farm whipmaster, before Dolana had stepped in and made a bargain of herself to spare me. And Ido. I pressed my lips together, remembering the sweet vanilla and orange. He had tasted like the essence of his dragon. Neither kiss had been welcome—but then, neither man had sought a welcome. They had both just taken what they wanted.

I bent closer to Kygo and felt the feather flow of his breath against my mouth. If I brushed his lips with mine, would he feel it in the shadow world? The earthy scent of ginseng rose from the warmth of his skin, settling deep inside me. The physician had said Kygo would not remember his pain when he returned. Was it the same with pleasure? The rhythm of his breathing became mine. I felt the colors around us blur, a soft, hypnotic slide toward the energy plane. For a moment I hung above him, our breaths intermingled. Could I take what I wanted?

I pulled back, ashamed of the impulse. Such an act would be dishonorable. I would be no better than the whipmaster or Ido. I shook my head, trying to clear the strange residue of power. I had not meant to shift into the energy world. What little control I had seemed to be slipping away.

I squeezed out a new cloth, my disquiet wringing it into tight folds. I needed help, soon, but this was not the time to dwell on my failures. With fierce concentration, I washed Kygo's bruised jaw, the soft material catching on the darkening of stubble. Another cloth took me down the strong column of his throat. I stopped just above the curve of the Imperial Pearl. Mud had encrusted its gold setting, and collected in the half-healed stitching that secured it in the hollow between his collarbones. The pearl itself was pristine, its presence still crouched at the base of my skull.

Slowly, I prepared another cloth, my eyes fixed on the glowing gem. I did not dare clean the mud from around it. My encounter with the black folio had taught me that Kinra's heritage was strong in my blood, and getting stronger. And Kinra wanted the pearl, at whatever price. I dug my hand into my gown pocket and pulled out the death plaque pouch, then placed it carefully beside the washbowl. Away from me, just in case.

I wiped the fresh cloth down Kygo's chest, trying to keep my focus on the vital central meridian along his breastbone. Yet the pearl's luminescence stayed within the periphery of my vision. Slowly, its glow drew my eyes up his body until I stared into its shimmering depths, and saw a silvery shift within it.

Heat rushed through me, bringing the memory of warm power beneath my fingertips and Kygo's racing pulse. I clenched my hand around the cloth, fighting the desire to reach across and bring that strange moonlit moment again. Certainty whispered within me: the pearl would call Kygo back. The pearl would kindle his sun energy, quicken his blood, and strengthen his *Hua.* All I had to do was place my hand on its pale beauty.

As my fingers touched the gem's velvety surface, Kygo's breath broke into a harsh rasp. He shuddered beneath me, his eyes opening wide and wild. He was still caught in the shadow world. With frightening speed, he gripped my wrist and wrenched me along his body. I sprawled across his chest, instinctively pulling away, but his other hand grabbed the back of my neck. He swung himself upright on the pallet, his legs locking around my waist.

"Kygo! It's me! Eona!"

His eyes finally focused, awareness breaking like a wave over their dark savagery. We stared at each other—shock stripping us both bare—and then he pulled me against him, our mouths meeting in hard recognition. Something within my spirit surged, matching his intensity in the brutal, searching connection. My free hand found the back of his head and guided him closer, deeper. I felt the press of his tongue against mine, the sudden union sending a jolt through my body. I gasped and pulled my head back, the taste of salty copper and ginseng on my lips.

"You're bleeding," I said and touched his mouth.

His tongue found my fingertip, his teeth grazing the skin as his lips closed into a kiss around it. I pulled my hand away, frightened by the answering rush through me. His eyes met mine, both of us poised in a moment I did not understand. Then with a shuddering sigh, he leaned his forehead against my shoulder.

"Eona," he whispered.

Hesitantly, I laid my hand on the nape of his neck.

"Your Majesty, you are awake!" It was the physician's voice. His loud relief echoed against the stone walls and ceiling.

We both tensed, Kygo's legs tightening around me. Behind us, the silent cave erupted into ragged cheers that grew louder and louder as the news of the emperor's return from the shadow world rippled back through the cavern. Kygo drew me closer as the joyous sound rolled over us, his breathing warm against my shoulder. I leaned into his solid chest. As the last cheer faded, he finally lifted his head, his eyes finding mine in a moment of regret. Then he unwound his legs from my body and released my wrist, his thumb stroking a parting promise across the tender skin.

"Approach," he said to the physician, and his voice was a command.

CHAPTER TEN

I WADED INTO the center of the thermal pool, the pungent heat sending a shiver across my shoulders. Around the stone edge, dozens of paper lanterns made the small cavern glow, silvering the ripples in the water and casting Madina's angular shadow onto the back wall. The physician's wife sat on the rough steps that led to the pool, guarding my privacy and waiting to attend me once I had bathed.

I stretched my arms along the surface of the water and luxuriated in the loosening of my muscles and the blessed quiet of the small chamber. Kygo's recovery had initiated a flurry of formal introductions and military reports that seemed set to continue for hours. Thankfully, Madina's husband had quickly stepped in and insisted that both the emperor and his *Naiso* be given the chance to eat and bathe before the strategizing began in earnest.

The thought of Kygo sent a shock of pleasure through me. I ducked lower in the water, as if the memory of our kiss was engraved upon my body for anyone to see. I closed my eyes and relived each moment of it, the hot bath masking the flush that crept across my skin. His need had been overwhelming, but the memory of my own brought an even deeper heat to my face.

Did he think me immodest? Dolana had once told me that men were frightened by female passion. I could understand why; my response had terrified me. I thought back to the lingering touch on my wrist as Kygo had released me, and the furtive glances between us as Viktor had formally welcomed him and reported on the rescue of our party. Every time our eyes met, it had felt as if his lips were once again on mine. And I had seen the echo of it in his eyes, too. How could such heat remain when we were not even touching?

I stood up, seeking the relief of cooler air. Perhaps our response to each other had not been wholly our own. Perhaps it had been guided by Kinra. I turned the idea over, unsure if the possibility was a relief or a bitter disappointment. I had removed the death plaque from my pocket before I touched the Imperial Pearl. Even so, I had been driven to touch it by some force, in much the same way I had been driven before.

According to Dela's reading of the red folio—now lost with her—Kinra had been a woman trading in passion, caught in a triangle between Emperor Dao and another man. Had the residue of such violent feeling affected Kygo and me? I stared into the dark water and tried to reconcile my feelings with my thoughts. It would be much easier if such passion could be blamed on my ancestress. Kygo and I could go on as before—just allies. Yet what I felt was not secondhand, nor five centuries old. And I had to admit that I did not want Kygo's ardor to be anything other than his own.

With a sigh, I ducked into the water again, away from the troubling thoughts. There were more important concerns: the harrowing loss of my friends and the two folios. And, of course, the biggest worry: was Ido still alive? There was an obvious way to answer that question. All I had to do was enter the energy world and see if I could feel the Dragoneye's presence through his beast, as I had before. Yet it had been a risk then, and it was an even greater risk now. If Ido was dead and his protection gone, simply entering the celestial plane could destroy me. Even if he was still alive, I did not wholly trust that I could surface from the energy world. The ancient forces within me seemed to be getting stronger.

Still, it had to be done. Our plans depended upon knowing whether the Dragoneye still lived. I knew it would be easier to slide into the energy world while I was in the pool. Baths always eased my journey between the earthly and celestial planes. It was the heat and the soft hold of the water that loosened mind and body from the physical world. Admittedly, there was the added risk of drowning if something went wrong or, like the time in the palace bath, being thrown against a wall. But this time I was not alone. With a prayer to the gods, I waded across the pool and found a secure handhold in the rocky edge.

"Madina," I called.

The woman half rose from the step. "Yes, my lady."

How was I to explain what I was about to do? She knew I was the Mirror Dragoneye, but that would only mean rank and power to her, not the possibility of destruction and death.

"I need to find my dragon in the energy world. Will you stand by me and, if I should go under or seem in trouble, pull me from the water?"

She eyed me for a moment. "Of course, my lady." Gathering her skirt, she walked around the edge of the pool and crouched beside me.

I looked up at her calm face. "It may be dangerous."

"Do what you must, my lady," she said earnestly, her hand resting on mine for a moment. "I will be here."

I lowered myself into the hot water until my shoulders were immersed, and turned my focus inward. For all my trepidation, it took only five deep breaths to ease open my mind's eye and shift between the worlds. The dim cave became a vibrant swirl of color and energy; above me, Madina's transparent figure raced with *Hua*, her outward calm belied by the fear that pumped quicksilver through her body. Hesitantly, I reached out into the energy world with my own *Hua*, as if prodding soft ground with a staff.

Was it safe?

There was no rush of grieving power or the sense of another force taking over. All I could feel was the rich, warm presence of the red dragon pressing against me, an irresistible invitation to unite. I eased fully into the energy world, transfixed by the red beast that filled the eastern corner of the chamber. Her power slid around me like a deep caress, drawing me toward the call. My mouth could taste the cinnamon roundings of our shared name. All I had to do was voice its warmth and we would be one. I clenched my teeth; I must not. Ten powerful reasons not to were waiting to tear us apart.

Gathering all my will, I turned from the bright presence of the Mirror Dragon toward the north-northwest corner. My breath caught; the smaller Rat Dragon was almost transparent, its crouching body rigid and withered.

Ido? I called silently. Could he still hear me through the blue dragon?

The beast slowly lifted his head. A set of pale opal talons reached toward me.

Eona. Ido's voice was a shiver in the warm air and was gone again.

I flinched from the suffering within it, my grip sliding from the rock. Madina caught my shoulder and pulled me back to the edge. The energy world buckled, shuddering back into the dim interior of the cave.

"Are you all right, my lady?" Madina asked.

I nodded, unable to speak through the ache in my throat. The Rat Dragon was so frail. If Ido was as debilitated as his beast, then he did not have much longer to live.

"Are you crying, my lady?"

"Everything is all right," I said. "Thank you." I turned away from her scrutiny and scooped up a handful of water, splashing its hot camouflage across my face. I had known the Rat Dragon's magnificent power; in fact, I had joined with it. To see the beast so diminished tore at me, even if he was the foundation of Ido's dark power. And I could not deny that the Dragoneye had risked himself twice to save me. It did not absolve him of his terrible crimes, but perhaps even he did not deserve this torment.

Another shadow appeared on the back wall of the cave; a serving woman bowing to Madina, the soft sibilance of her whisper rolling off the stone. By the time I had turned, she was already backing away, message delivered.

"My lady," Madina said, rising stiffly. "His Majesty wishes you to join him as soon as possible." She opened a wide drying cloth.

I held still in the water, a rush of exhilaration and dark unease searing me. *Kygo wanted to see me, as soon as possible.* Once again, I felt his legs around my waist and his muscular body against mine. I took a shuddering breath. How could I want something so much and yet wish to avoid it with just as much fervency? Thank the gods I had something to bring him—the news that Ido still survived.

After the moment passed, I waded over and caught Madina's steadying hand. With a strong pull, she had me up the steps and quickly wrapped in the rough cloth.

"His Majesty is not yet out of his own bath," she reassured me. "You have time to prepare yourself. Properly."

I caught her keen sideways glance. It was not unkind, but I felt myself flush. No doubt her husband had told her about discovering us. The man probably thought I had lied to him about my bond with Kygo.

"Viktor's wife is much your size and has supplied her best gown," she added, drying the length of my wet hair. "It is only cotton, my lady, but the weave is fine and it should fit well. The color will suit you, too."

I stopped wiping my arms. "You think it will suit me? What color is it?"

"Blue, my lady." She nodded at a gown hanging from a peg driven into the cave wall. It was indeed a rich indigo.

"Why will that suit me?" I had never given much thought to the color of my clothes. Then again, I had never been the one to choose them, even when I became Dragoneye.

"I am sure you look beautiful in all colors," she said, bowing.

"No," I said, stopping her obeisance with a hand on her arm. "No, I mean it. Why does blue suit me? I do not know about these things." I had spent too many years as a boy to know anything of female arts.

She searched my face. I had done the same myself when asked by a higher rank for an honest opinion; not all such requests were sincere, and the truth often brought a swift slap. "Because you have pale skin, my lady," she finally said. "The contrast will work well. And the shade will enhance the deep red in your lips and the brightness of your eyes."

I studied the gown again; all of that from just one color? I traced my top lip with my finger, the soft pressure conjuring the sensation of Kygo's mouth on mine. He had been surrounded by beautiful things all his life—clothes, art, women. He would understand the language of color and cloth.

"All right," I said slowly. "I'll wear it." Then I remembered the problem with Vida's gown. "Wait! Is it very low cut?"

"Only sufficiently so," Madina said, a smile at the edge of her eyes.

I did not have enough lightness in me to laugh, but I did manage a wry lift of my lips. "I am not very good with all of this," I said gesturing at the gown. "I have no knowledge of beauty or style." I looked down at my narrow chest. "Nor any pretensions of either."

"That is not true, my lady," she said. "It is said there are four seats of beauty." She touched her hair, her eyes, her mouth, and her throat. "All of us have at least one. Many of us have two. Some have three, and only a handful have all four in true harmony. You, my lady, are blessed with three."

Which three did she mean? My eyes, perhaps, and my mouth—I had all my teeth. But I could see no elegance of throat, and my hair was too thick and heavy.

I snorted. "I am no beauty."

She tilted her head, but did not voice what was behind her pursed lips.

"What? Speak your mind," I prompted.

"It is true that you do not have classic beauty, and yet you draw the eye. You have felt the power of it, yes?"

I felt my skin flush again, but this time with acknowledgment. I had seen Kygo's gaze follow me, and I had sensed my strange hold on him within it.

Madina patted her dark hair, the intricate braids and twists streaked with gray. "But I think what burns at your core is another kind of power, my lady."

I looked away. Could she see my desire for Kygo? No, it was impossible. Perhaps she referred to the red dragon. "What power is that?"

"Fearlessness."

I frowned. Fearlessness wasn't a power, was it? And I had certainly known fear.

She wrapped my hair in the towel again and squeezed water from its length.

"We could braid your hair into a low coil." She wound a thick tress around her finger and pressed it against my nape. "It will suit the neckline of the gown."

I was tempted to take advantage of Madina's arts, but I could not walk into a military meeting wearing both a gown and a maiden's braid. It was hard enough to be a female Dragoneye, let alone a female *Naiso*. In all truth, I knew I should reject the dress in favor of a tunic and trousers, but a smooth-tongued part of me insisted it would be churlish to refuse a gift from the wife of the camp leader.

"I will wear a Dragoneye double queue," I said, pleased with the compromise. I separated the heavy weight of my wet hair into two hanks. "I will show you how to club it."

Madina bowed. "As you wish, Lady Dragoneye."

The sky was streaked with pink dawn light as I climbed a set of shallow steps with two resistance escorts. According to the more talkative of the pair, the small cave ahead had been readied as a strategy room for the emperor. The word had gone out, he said, for the section leaders to gather there at daybreak. Below us, the camp was already stirring. Children carried buckets of water from the stream that crossed the floor of the crater, and women stoked cooking fires. A group of men headed toward the passage we had entered less than four bells ago, their ropes and packs marking them as a search party.

A familiar figure came out to meet us: Ryko, his big body hunched, arms cradling his ribcage. He watched our approach without expression, but I knew the islander well enough to see the tension within him.

"I will take Lady Eona to His Majesty," he said to my escort.

The two men quickly bowed and backed away. Ryko waited until they were out of earshot, then he bent close and said, "You must intercede on my behalf. Now."

I pulled away, startled by the fury in his voice.

"About what?"

"His Majesty has forbidden me to join the search parties."

"He must have a good reason."

"I do not care about his reasons," Ryko snapped. "I have to search for Lady Dela. Do you understand?"

"Ryko, you're injured. And you don't know the area. You'll just slow the local men down."

He glared at me. "Intercede. You owe me."

"*What* do I owe you?" I said, my own anger rising. How many times did I have to apologize? "Did you want to die? Should I have left you at the fisher village?"

"Yes," he hissed. "It would have had more honor than living like a dog, waiting for your next kick."

His truth hung between us, heavy and impassable..

He closed his eyes and took a deep, pained breath. "My lady, please." His touch on my shoulder was a plea. "I had her hand in mine and I let go. The water was too strong. She will think I abandoned her."

I looked away from the anguish in Ryko's face. I felt guilt every day, thirty-six times over. Perhaps I could spare him the guilt of failing Dela.

"All right," I said. "I will ask him."

I heard Kygo's voice before we reached the strategy chamber. The cave was made up of three small, linked caverns, and Ryko and I were passing through the second when the emperor's clear tones reached us.

"Is this a total of our numbers, Viktor? There are no others?"

My heartbeat quickened. For all of my reliving of our kiss and imaginings of his body against mine, I had not considered what might happen the next time I saw him. Would there still be the same heat in his eyes? Should I act as if nothing had happened? We were obviously not going to be alone. A blessing, perhaps, although something akin to disappointment settled deep within me as well.

I smoothed the front of the gown over my chest. As Madina had said, it was not as low-cut as Vida's dress. Still, its round neckline showed the curve of my breasts, and the clinging waist needed no sash to accentuate my shape. My hands found the tightly clubbed braids that swung from the topknot at my crown. I flicked the two thick braids to the left, but decided it would look contrived and pushed them to the back again. Madina had said the manly style looked well on me, but there had been no mirror, and the reflection in the cave pool was too dark for detail.

"My lady, please wait," Ryko whispered.

He stepped up to the natural archway that defined the entrance to the third chamber. The first two caverns had been extravagantly lit by oil lamps set only an arm's width apart—but their glow paled in comparison to what came from the strategy chamber. It was almost like daylight.

"Lady Eona—Imperial *Naiso* and Mirror Dragoneye—approaches," Ryko called.

For a moment, his formal announcement held me still. It belonged to the court, not here, in a cave. Ryko was pressing home my rank.

As I entered, five men turned from their examination of a scroll spread across a table—Yuso and Viktor among them—and dropped to their knees in low bows. The sixth man remained bent over the scroll: the emperor.

He had bathed and shaved, although he had left the dark stubble on his head. The long imperial queue had also been washed and re-clubbed, but without the jewels and gold thread strung through it. No doubt they would soon be our army's food and weapons. His only jewel now was the Imperial Pearl, framed by the open collar of his borrowed red tunic: a very visible symbol of his right to command.

His skin still held the pallor of the shadow world, and his body had the careful bearing of pain, but overall he had recovered well. Slowly, he looked up, and my breath locked in my chest. His dark eyes held no warmth, only wariness.

"Do you no longer bow to your emperor, Lady Eona?" he asked.

I dropped into my own obeisance, hiding my confusion. Had I done something wrong? I stared fiercely at the woven rug on the cave floor, willing back the sharp sting of tears. There could be only one reason for his coldness. My passion had disgusted him.

"Rise," he said to us all.

I climbed to my feet, hoping the flush had faded from my face. The bank of oil lamps around the walls made the room airless, or perhaps it was my own shame that choked my breath. I pressed my hand against my chest, covering the pale skin above the deep blue cloth.

Ryko edged into the periphery of my vision—a silent reminder. I did not want to step forward, but I had promised.

"Your Majesty," I said, trying to add some steel to my voice. "Ryko wishes to join a search party and be of use. May he have your leave to do so?"

I was not ready to meet the ice in Kygo's eyes again. I settled for watching his mouth. All of its tenderness had tightened into a hard line of command.

"No. I have use for him here."

I bowed, Ryko dropping into his own obeisance beside me, only his clenched hands giving away his frustration.

"Lady Eona, come forward," Kygo said.

Stiffly, I moved a step toward him.

"We are discussing the black folio," he said. "Yuso says you claim that Dillon used its power to create the ring of water."

I glanced around the circle of men. Every face held some recognition of the tension between the emperor and me. Yuso's eyes met mine, wary.

"Yes, Your Majesty. Dillon called on the folio's *Gan Hua*."

"How does he call it? He has as little training as you."

"I don't know."

"Can he do it again?"

I lowered my head at his clipped assault. "I don't think so." I swallowed, trying to find some moisture in my parched mouth. "I think he would need my power again to use it, but I am not sure, Your Majesty. The black folio is a mystery to me, too."

"So it was your power as well?"

"Dillon took it. I did not give it, Your Majesty."

"And this black folio has the secret to the String of Pearls?"

"It is what Lord Ido told me."

"Lord Ido." Kygo's snort of suspicion sent a chill through me. "You are very keen to rescue him."

I lifted my head, meeting his challenge. "You know why, Your Majesty."

His dark eyes held no concession. "My priority has changed.

We must find the black folio before my uncle does. Lord Ido can wait."

I stepped forward. "No, he cannot! He is barely hanging on to life."

Kygo stiffened. "What did you say?"

Panic had pushed me too far. "Forgive me, Your Majesty. It is true we must find the black folio," I said, recovering some control. "But getting Lord Ido away from your uncle is, in my humble opinion, more important. Dillon is not in his right mind and, even if we find him, he will not be of any help with the monsoon rains and floods. He has no control over his power or his actions. As you have already seen, he is dangerous." I glanced around the tense circle of men. "Ido helped me hold off Dillon and the black folio's power. We need him."

Kygo leaned on the table. "Ido helped you? Why?"

"He was trying to save his own life as much as help me," I said. "Dillon was trying to kill him."

"How did he help you?"

"It is through the same kind of link I have with Ryko. The one made from healing. You saw it in the clearing when I could not control the energy." Beside me, Ryko flinched as if I had touched him with a whip.

"Did Ido come to you, or did you make him?" There was something strange in Kygo's tone—anticipation. But reluctance, too.

I stared at him, puzzled. "He just came into my head." I paused, realizing I did not truly know how it happened. "Maybe

I called him," I added. "I don't know; it was all too fast. I don't know enough about the way it all works. It is why I need Lord Ido to train me."

Kygo turned his back. "I wish to speak to Lady Eona." He did not raise his voice, but I could feel the threat. "Ryko, Yuso, stay. The rest of you, leave us. Leave the cave."

The other men could not bow and back away fast enough. As the sounds of their exit receded into the distance, I looked across at Ryko, but the islander was staring at the ground, his body tense. Yuso stood stolidly at the table, his attention fixed on his emperor.

"Tell me, Ryko," Kygo finally said, his back still to us, "did you feel Lady Eona's link with Ido as they fought the black folio?"

Ryko shifted. "Yes." He looked away from my shock. "The link held no sway over my will, but I felt it. As I said before, Your Majesty."

"Yuso, draw your sword," Kygo said.

The hiss of steel sent a creeping shiver across my back as if it had been drawn against my skin. "Kygo, what is wrong?" I asked.

He finally turned to me, his face set. "Take Ryko's will."

I heard the islander suck in a breath. For a moment I could not form any sound.

"Why?" I finally managed.

"Because it is my command."

"You saw what happened last time. I could not control it."

"Do as I say. Now!"

"Kygo, it is too dangerous."

He slammed his hand on the table. "I said, take it!"

"I promised I would not. Please, I don't want to hurt Ryko."

At the corner of my eye I saw Yuso flex his hand around the sword's hilt.

"Take it!" Kygo repeated.

"Why are you doing this?"

"Obey me!"

"No. It is wrong!"

My shout echoed over and over in the small cavern—a rolling chorus of defiance.

Kygo gripped the edge of the table. "So stubborn. Why won't you just do as you're told?" He nodded at Yuso. "Break Ryko's shoulder."

"What?" I stepped back, as if the command had been a blow to my own body.

"Take Ryko's will, or Yuso will break his shoulder."

With a deft twist of his sword, Yuso lowered the blade and shifted his grip, changing the heavy hilt into a bludgeon. Ryko stiffened.

"Yuso, no!" I said.

"I serve His Majesty," Yuso warned.

He walked toward us. Ryko's eyes fixed on Yuso, but there was no plea in them. Just a hard, endless stare.

I spun around to Kygo. "He is your man. He is loyal to you."

Kygo shook his head. "He is your man, Eona. Take his will."

"Why?"

He looked across at Yuso. "Do it," he ordered.

The captain pulled back the hilt, lining up the blow. Beside me, Ryko braced, his breathing quick and hard through clenched teeth.

"Stop!" I pushed in between them.

The islander stumbled backward. "My lady, please. No."

"I'm sorry, Ryko." I reached out with my energy, seeking the pathways of his life force. "Forgive me."

Beneath the pounding of my heartbeat, I found the frantic rhythm of his fear and fury, and pulled it into my *Hua*. The sudden brutal link flared through his eyes. He gasped as his will melded to mine, the merciless connection driving him to his knees. I felt the rush of his energy building within me. All of his massive strength was at my command.

A brutal grip on my arm wrenched me around.

Kygo.

I staggered, still caught in the torrent of power. The emperor hauled me upright again and grabbed my jaw, holding me still.

"Did you heal me?" he demanded. He was so close, I could barely focus. *"Did you heal me?"*

The dark fear in his eyes penetrated the rush of power.

"No!" My connection with Ryko snapped. The brutal release dropped the islander to the floor as I sagged, suddenly drained of energy. "No. I didn't heal you. I didn't!"

Kygo caught me and pulled me against his chest. I felt his heart pounding beneath my cheek, the glow of the Imperial

Pearl only a finger's length away from my eyes. I stared at its pale beauty, the shock of the broken link too strong for the small stirring of desire to touch it.

Kygo stroked the nape of my neck. "It's all right," he murmured against my hair. He looked around at Yuso. "See, she had no hold on me. And I did not feel her control of Ryko," he said. "Are you satisfied?"

Yuso sheathed his sword. "As much as I can be, given our lack of knowledge about her power."

"Then get out," Kygo said. "Take Ryko with you. Have the physician attend him."

I lifted my head, the sense of Kygo's words finally penetrating my daze.

"You did that to see if I healed you?" Another kind of energy burned through me—rage. And it was all my own. I slammed my fist against his chest. "Let me go!"

He tightened his hold, stopping my escape. "I had to be certain."

"You could have asked me!" I punched him again, wanting to hurt him in some way. As he had hurt me. He caught my wrist. This time his touch held no tenderness.

"Yuso," he said through his teeth. "Get out. Now!"

The captain hauled Ryko up onto his feet and steered him out of the cavern. Kygo forced my hand down.

"Do not hit me again," he warned. "I am your emperor."

"I am your *Naiso*," I said. "Or does that mean nothing?"

"I had to prove that you did not heal me."

"How could I have healed you?" I demanded. "I would

have destroyed the whole crater, like the fisher village."

"I did not witness that, Eona. And all who did are your people," he said. "I had to prove that my will is still my own."

"Why didn't you just trust me? I would have told you the truth."

"It would not have been enough," he said flatly. "I had to prove it to Yuso."

"Why? What is so important about Yuso?"

"It is his duty to protect me. To protect the throne. He had to make sure I was not compromised." The somber appeal in his eyes held me still. "This was not just between you and me, Eona. Everything I do has an effect on the empire. It has been so all my life. And now everything you do affects it, too." He hesitated, then cupped my cheek, the full tenderness of his mouth so near my own. "I know you are new to your power and rank, but you must understand that the empire is more important than a man and a woman. Whatever we may feel or wish."

I pulled my face away, gathering my resentment before me like a shield. "That does not excuse cruelty and dishonor," I said.

He flinched, and something savage within me rejoiced.

"You think that was cruel?" He released my wrist and stepped back. "This war with my uncle has just begun, Eona. What I just did was *honorable* compared to what is coming."

"Is that the moral gauge you are going to use for all your actions?" I asked. "It will no doubt bend to your every purpose as easily as green bamboo."

He gave a bitter laugh. "Is that my *Naiso* speaking? Or is it just a woman's pique sharpening your tongue?"

"It is obvious that you do not trust me. Perhaps I should not be your *Naiso*." My voice cracked. We both knew I was not only speaking of that exalted position.

"Perhaps you are right," he said.

It was my turn to flinch. He walked slowly back to the desk. I watched the unyielding line of his shoulders and back. I had been a fool to let myself believe he valued me.

"On your honor, promise that you will never heal me," he finally said.

"I will do better than my honor, since you hold it in so little regard," I answered, unable to keep back the acid of my hurt. "I swear it on my life."

His hand found the Imperial Pearl at his throat.

"Eona, I have been trained from birth not to truly trust anyone." The words were so soft they were barely audible across the distance between us. Perhaps they held the note of apology, but I was not willing to hear it.

"I do not trust easily, either," I said. "Especially when I am betrayed."

I saw the word bite deep. For a long moment, he did not move.

"It is a good thing, then, that obedience does not require trust," he finally said. He leaned over the map, his clenched fist pressed against the parchment. "Tell Viktor and his men to return."

I bowed and backed away, holding tight to my anger to stop the tears that stung my eyes.

CHAPTER ELEVEN

I STOOD FOR a few moments just inside the entrance of the cave, the soft sleeve of my dress pressed against my wet face, and listened for any sign of pursuit. There was none, of course—an emperor would never follow anyone, let alone a woman. All I could hear was the conversation of the men outside, waiting to be summoned again. I did not want to step out among them, but there was no choice. I straightened my dress, wiped the blur from my eyes with my forefinger, then strode out into the new daylight.

"His Majesty commands your return," I said, moving swiftly past their bowing forms. There was nowhere for me to go, but I did not pause, taking the steps with the pretense of purpose.

"My lady, please wait."

I glanced back. Vida stood on the top step.

"What is it?" I continued walking.

She ran up, her overlong gown bunched in her hands. I saw her note my swollen eyes. "Captain Yuso said you needed assistance."

That stopped me. "Did he, now?" I looked back at the cave entrance, but all the men had gone inside. "Did he tell you why I needed assistance?"

"No, my lady."

"Because he is a whoreson," I said, finding some release in the forceful obscenity. Nearby, a woman walking with a child holding each hand stiffened. "He is a whoreson, and his master is a—"

"Madina has prepared a sleeping chamber for you," Vida said quickly. "Up in one of the caves. Perhaps you would like to retire?"

I rubbed my eyes again, feeling the grit of salt on my cheeks. Exhaustion already dragged at my body; the fuel of fury did not last long. I suddenly yearned for solitude. For years I had been among the untouchables, more often than not left on my own with my ill fortune. Now I was never alone.

My sleeping chamber was, it seemed, someone else's living quarters hastily surrendered for the use of the Dragoneye. I crossed the patchwork of rugs on the stone floor, barely registering the humble interior.

"Look at those hangings," Vida said brightly, following me across the dim cavern. The only light came from the sun streaming through the entrance, half of which was blocked by an ill-fitting wooden door. She reached out and touched a wall tapestry. "Aren't they lovely, my lady? I've never seen work like it."

Irritated, I eyed the depiction of a long necked crane snapping at an embroidered fish, the light catching the glow of gold threads. It was not the usual kind of woven hanging. Instead, delicately cutout shapes had been sewn to an undercloth, with fine embroidery worked over them.

"Beautiful," I said sourly.

I did not want to admire art. I wanted to break something or scream or hit someone. No, not just "someone": Kygo. I ground my hands together, trying to work the impulse out of my joints. Why did he say he trusted me when he obviously did not?

I spun on my heel and paced across the room again, finally taking in my surroundings. Apart from the rich wall hangings, the furnishings were basic: a low wooden stool, a woven chest for clothes, and two bedrolls—one prepared with blankets, the other tidily tucked away against the wall. A couple's chamber. The thought brought another spike of fury and sent me back across the room, my fists clenched.

"My lady, perhaps you should rest," Vida said. "You look very tired." She tested the bed's abundant wadding with her foot. "It's good and thick," she added encouragingly.

I took a steadying breath, the moment of calm bringing bone-aching fatigue in its wake. Perhaps I *should* lie down. The last time I'd had a chance to sleep properly had been in the forest. I remembered Kygo sitting beside me, his warm hand on my arm. It was where he had asked me to be *Naiso*. Where I had first touched the pearl. The sting of tears made me blink. Was I really no longer his *Naiso*? I turned quickly to hide my face and my feelings.

"All right, I'll try," I said, ungraciously. "You can go."

She bowed and headed toward the wooden door.

Wait," I said. "Will you do something for me?" She paused. "Will you find Ryko and make sure that he is all right? Do not tell him you ask at my bidding." My voice wavered. "I don't think you would be welcome if you did." I could not stop the sob that broke through me. "He will never forgive me now."

Vida hurried forward. "Forgive you for what, my lady?" More sobs tore at my chest in thick aching rasps. She took my arm, steering me down on to the bed, and knelt before me. "What happened?"

Through shuddering breaths I described the events of the morning. I tried to avoid telling her about the kiss, but the rest of the story made no sense until I had confessed that brief moment of desire. At the end of my stumbling recital, she sat back on her heels.

"Holy Shola," she said.

"And now he does not trust me." I pressed my hands against my eyes to stop another welling of tears.

"You don't mean Ryko, do you?" she asked.

I shook my head.

She made a soft sound of sympathy. "It always changes when you touch one another."

I lowered my hands. "What do you mean?"

"You two are no longer only Dragoneye and emperor, or even *Naiso* and emperor. You are also woman and man." Her smile was wry. "A powerful woman, and a powerful man. It is no wonder you do not trust one another."

"I trust him," I protested.

"Do you? Truly?"

I looked away from her searching gaze. The violence of his killing rage, the ambition in his eyes when he'd seen the black folio, his effect on my body—they all frightened me.

She let out a considering breath. "Watching my father plan and strategize for the resistance has taught me about trust." She leaned forward. "Personal trust is very different from political trust, my lady. The first thrives on faith. The second requires proof, whether it be upfront or covert." Awkwardly, she patted my hand. "His Majesty has always been a powerful man. Perhaps he has never had to distinguish between the two." She rose from the bed. "Take some rest, my lady."

"And you will see Ryko?"

"I will," she promised.

"Vida, thank you." I managed a watery smile. "You are very kind."

She cocked her head. "I am not that kind. You and the emperor must come to some kind of understanding. All of our lives depend upon it."

With a bow, she maneuvered the door closed behind her, the gaps in the wood letting in enough light to catch the gold and silver gleam of the fish in the wall hangings.

I stretched out on the bed. Vida's fine distinctions of trust were a jumble in my head; my mind was too tired to pick through them. The only certainty was that one kiss had snatched Kygo and me from the simpler world of friendship, and we could never go back. Or perhaps it was just I who could not go back. I turned my head, my eyes drawn by the gold of two jumping carp—the traditional symbol of love and harmony. Who was I to think of an emperor in terms of love? I had been a fool.

But as sleep clouded my thoughts, one last notion flickered across my mind in a leap of red and gold: the carp also symbolized perseverance.

"Lady Eona, it is time to wake."

I opened my eyes and blinked into the soft glow of shielded lamplight, the languor of deep sleep still weighting my body. The figure before me came into focus: Madina. She smiled, the lines around her eyes and mouth deepening in well-worn paths. Beyond her, the open doorway was dark.

"Good evening, my lady."

"Have I slept the whole day?"

I sat up, all my ease ripped away by the sharp-edged memory of Kygo's distrust. Every bitter word felt as if it had happened only a minute ago.

"It is just past dusk," Madina answered. "There is a point when an exhausted body must rest, and you had reached it. My husband did not want you to be woken, even now, but I told him it was time for food."

She held out a pottery bowl, a meaty steam fragrancing the air between us. My stomach rumbled loudly.

"It seems I was right," she said, her gentle humor easing my embarrassment.

She placed the bowl in my hands. The first salty sip seemed to reach into every corner of my parched body. I gulped down three large mouthfuls and felt the herbed heat purl through me.

"That's very good."

She acknowledged the compliment. "My restorative soup. My husband prescribed it for you." Her graceful wave urged me to lift the bowl again. "You must gather your strength."

I looked over the pottery rim. She had something to tell me; the burden of it was in her soft voice. "Is something wrong, Madina?" A knot tightened in my gut, around the warm food. "Is the emperor all right?"

She patted my hand. "The emperor is well enough, although he ignores my husband's entreaties to sleep." She smiled, but I could tell there was more. "Finish the soup, please."

I drained the bowl and handed it back, my eyes not leaving her face.

"What is wrong, Madina?"

She eyed me as if gauging my fortitude. "Two more of your party have been found," she finally said. "Dela and Solly. They were brought in while you were asleep."

"Are they alive?" I caught her arm. "Tell me. Is Dela alive?"

"It's all right, Eona." Dela's voice spun me around to face the doorway. "I am here."

She limped across the room, the lamplight showing dark

scrapes and cuts down one side of her face. I caught her outstretched hands, squeezing them too tight in place of the words that were locked in my chest.

"Eona, you are breaking my hands," she laughed. Her lips were blistered and flaking, her skin reddened from the sun.

"You've hurt your leg," I finally managed to say, easing my hold.

"I was pinned under a tree, but I'm all right."

"I'm so glad to see you. I had this awful feeling—"

It was her turn to grip tightly. "Eona, it is not all good news," she said, her smile gone. "Solly is dead. He drowned. Probably in the first rush of water."

Her words brought a sharp image of the deluge. I had seen Solly go under. I had seen the water swallow him whole. Did he die at that moment? I shivered, yet all I could find in my heart was a glancing regret. Was I now so used to death that I could not mourn a good man? Solly and I had fought together. I had relied upon his fierce courage and quiet efficiency, been warmed by his gruff kindness. He had been stoic and loyal and deserving of my grief. Yet I was dry. I had felt more sorrow for Lieutenant Haddo, our enemy.

"Does Ryko know?" I whispered, ashamed of my arid spirit. "Does Vida?" Both had fought alongside Solly far longer. Perhaps they would have tears enough for us all.

Dela nodded. "They are sitting the ghost watch together." She countered the flat note in her voice with a squeeze of my hand. She looked across at Madina. "Thank you for your help. Could you leave us, please?"

Dela waited until the woman had backed out of the chamber, then said, "The physician insisted you eat something before I saw you. He said it would buffer the shock to the spirit. Are you all right?"

I bit my lip. It seemed my spirit was in no need of a buffer. "They should have woken me when you arrived."

She shook her head. "No, they were right to let you sleep. There was nothing you could have done."

"I could have been there. I could have . . ." I faltered. There *was* nothing I could have done, and the powerlessness left a bitter taste in my mouth.

Dela stepped closer, gathering me against her body. I buried my face in the hard muscle of her chest. She wore a borrowed tunic and trousers, and had obviously bathed. Still, I caught a shadow scent of mud as she moved. Doubtless the flood was still ingrained in my skin, too. Perhaps its stink would never leave any of us now.

"May Solly's spirit walk in the garden of heaven," Dela whispered.

"And his honor live through his line," I finished. The traditional words did nothing to soothe me.

"There is more I must tell you," Dela said. "About what happened to me after the water hit us." She released me and limped to the door, peering outside for a moment before pulling it closed.

Finally, something broke through my numbness: a sharp foreboding. I sat on the bed as she dragged the low stool across the floor and sat opposite me.

"Hold out your arm," she ordered.

I obeyed. She pressed her large knuckles lightly against mine, then drew up her loose sleeve. The rope of black pearls rattled down her arm. Before I could even flinch, the coils had tightened around my wrist, hauled the red folio over our hands, and bound it to my forearm. I pulled my arm back.

"You know I don't want to carry it."

"They recognize you," she said, ignoring my protest. "Maybe you'll think I'm mad, but those pearls have a mind of their own. They pulled me out of the water." She shook her head. "I didn't imagine it. They saved me from drowning—although they couldn't do much about the tree that came down on top of me." She raised an elegant eyebrow. "But you're not surprised."

I touched the warm black coils around my arm. "I saw the pearls on the black folio save Dillon. I think both sets of pearls are made of *Gan Hua*, and are meant to keep the books safe, whatever happens to them."

"Ah, that would explain it. And whoever is attached to them is kept safe, too." Dela smiled. "Thank the gods." The smile faded. "Ryko told me that Dillon and the black folio are missing and the emperor has sent out every able-bodied man to search for them."

"His Majesty has decided that it is more important to find the black folio than to rescue Ido."

"Well, he is wrong." Dela leaned forward. "I was pinned under that tree for many, many hours. Every time I tried to free myself, I made things worse; nearly buried myself alive in mud."

She shuddered. "To keep my mind focused, I tried to decipher more of your ancestor's folio."

"You found something?"

Dela licked her cracked lips. "I think I have worked out two coded verses on the first page."

"What do they say? Show me." I yanked at the black pearls. The smooth rope released and pooled into my cupped hand, bringing the folio with it. I opened the red leather cover, flicking over the page with its elegant dragon, to the first page full of Woman Script.

"This one," Dela said, pointing to the faded characters. "If I am correct, it says:

> *"The She of the dragon will return and ascend*
> *When the cycle of twelve draws to an end. . . ."*

I lifted my head. "An end? Does that mean the dragons?"

"There's more." Dela's fingertip traced down the page.

> *"The She of the Dragoneye will restore and defend*
> *When the dark force is mastered with the* Hua *of All Men."*

I stared at the graceful calligraphy, trying to glean its meaning, although I did not know each character's sense. "Say the first verse again."

Dela repeated it.

"The 'She of the dragon' means the Mirror Dragon, since there is only one female dragon," I said slowly. "And she has now returned and ascended." I met Dela's eyes, unwilling to voice the meaning of the next line.

"Her return means the dragons' power is coming to an end," she supplied softly.

I shook my head, trying to deny the enormity of the portent. If the dragons came to an end, then so did my power—before I had even truly wielded it. There would be no glorious link with the red dragon. No rank. No worth. I would be just a girl again. I would be nothing. Useless.

"It can't be true," I whispered.

"The land is in upheaval," Dela pointed out, "and there are ten dragons without Dragoneyes."

"But that doesn't prove that their power is ending," I said sharply. "The Mirror Dragon returned before Ido killed the Dragoneyes."

"Then maybe the dragon power was coming to an end even before Ido murdered the Dragon Lords. And you cannot deny that the land is in peril."

I pressed my hands against my eyes and tried to follow the terrifying pathways of possibility, looking for a reason to deny the truth of Kinra's warning. But there was no getting past the first line: the Mirror Dragon had returned and ascended, and that meant the dragon power was ending.

"What is the second verse?" I demanded.

Again, Dela read it out.

"The 'She of the Dragoneye' has to be me," I said, my unease deepening. "It says I can restore and defend. Does that mean I can stop the dragons losing their power?"

How could I stop such a thing? The impossibility of the task was like a huge hand squeezing all the hope and courage from me.

"I pray that is what it means," Dela said. She touched a character on the parchment, its sharp angles in ugly contrast to the rest of the flowing calligraphy. "What is the dark force? *Gan Hua*?"

"It seems likely."

"Then what is the '*Hua* of All Men'?"

"I don't know," I said bleakly. "But it sounds final."

I closed the red folio, as if hiding the words would stop the crushing burden of their meaning. "I dread what you will find next, but we need to know more." I held out the journal. With a short nod, Dela took it back.

"At least we know that *Gan Hua* must be mastered." Dela stood up and limped toward the door. "Lord Ido is the only one who can teach you how to control your power. Can he teach you how to master *Gan Hua*, too?"

"Oh, yes," I said dryly. "Ido is a master of *Gan Hua*."

"Then we must rescue him."

"But His Majesty is fixed on finding the black folio."

Dela beckoned me to the door. "His Majesty cannot ignore the red folio, Eona. This is the voice of a Mirror Dragoneye. And she has given us due warning."

"Who is this Dragoneye ancestress?" demanded Kygo.

I had been expecting the question, but it still tightened my innards. The emperor paced across the strategy chamber and turned for my answer, his eyes ringed with blue fatigue. Although he had dismissed the section leaders from the cavern at my request, I did not take that as a sign of my return to favor. On the contrary. He had not allowed either Dela or me to rise from our knees, and there was a brittleness about him that I recognized: his body and mind had been pushed too far for too long. I glanced at Dela beside me. From the wary hunch of her shoulders, I could tell that she recognized it too; she would have felt the wrath of an overstrained master in her time. Still, I had no way of preparing her for what I was about to say—and hopefully she would have the sense to stay silent.

"She was the last Mirror Dragoneye before the Mirror Dragon fled," I said. "Her name was Charra."

Dela stiffened, her hand tightening on the red folio.

I held my breath, but she said nothing. No doubt she would vent her disapproval later, but even she would have to admit I could not tell him the truth. Kygo knew Kinra as a traitor. He would not accept any words that she had written, nor act upon them. And with such an ancestor he would trust me even less.

"Do we know why the dragon fled?"

"No, Your Majesty. Lady Dela has not yet found that information in the folio."

He closed his eyes and tilted his head back. "But now we

know what the return of the Mirror Dragon really means. My father wanted us to believe that you and the dragon are the symbols of hope and a blessing on my reign. But you are not." His eyes opened. The exhaustion in them sharpened into certainty. "You are the bringers of doom."

"That is not true," I gasped. "You cannot say that!"

"Ten Dragoneyes dead, my empire poised for a war, the land unprotected and ripping itself apart." His full mouth thinned into accusation. "And it all started when you brought back the Mirror Dragon."

I glared at him. "I did not bring her back. She just . . . appeared."

"But you were in the arena, where a girl should not have been. You gave her the chance to come back."

I dug my fingernails into my thighs, wanting to claw at his face and force him to say he was wrong. He had to be wrong. Otherwise, it meant I had somehow caused Ido's slaughter of the Dragoneyes—and Sethon's coup, and the war that was to come. He could not lay all of that on my shoulders.

"It is not all doom, Your Majesty," Dela said into the fraught silence. Her skin had paled under the sunburn, either from the pain of kneeling on her injured leg or the risk of speaking. She held up the folio, the black pearls wrapped tightly around it. "The second verse gives hope. Lady Eona can restore the dragons' power."

"Hope?" He gave a bitter laugh. "I do not find much hope in the words '*Hua* of All Men.'" He strode across the room again.

For all his exhaustion, he still moved with authority. "Go, Lady Dela."

She looked at me and hesitated—a dangerous show of loyalty.

"*Now!*" Kygo shouted.

With an agonized apology in her eyes, Dela struggled to her feet, bowed, then backed out of the chamber.

"Stand up, Eona," Kygo said.

I rose, my legs trembling with rage. He began to pace again, his quick steps taking him behind me, out of my sight line. Every other sense strained to keep hold of his position as he circled. "Why should I believe this portent, Eona?" He was at my left. "I cannot read ancient Woman Script. The Contraire could be lying for you."

"Lady Dela is loyal to you. As I am." I should have stopped, but my resentment surged into more words. "As I have always been."

He closed the distance between us until he was less than a hand-span in front of me. Too close. I did not raise my eyes, but I could smell the hot male tang of his anger—and I could sense something beyond words filling the space between us.

"Loyal? You are loyal only to your own goals," he said. "From the very beginning you manipulated everyone to get into the arena, and you have not stopped since."

I looked up at the unfair judgment. "Everything I have done has been in your service," I said hotly. "You are jumping at shadows that do not exist. You blame me because you are afraid of things you do not understand."

Blood rushed to his face. "You think me afraid?"

He might not want me as his *Naiso* any more, but he was still going to get the truth. "Yes," I hissed. "You are afraid because you are out of your depth."

He raised his fist. I tensed, waiting for the blow, but he turned away. Three strides and he was at the laden table. He grabbed its edge and flipped it over in a crack of wood and slither of parchment. "Do you know what all that is?" he demanded. "That is our numbers. We have one trained man to every twenty of my uncle's. One horse to ten. Most of our weapons are not swords, not even *Ji*, but farm tools!"

"Then maybe the bringer of doom is you." I saw the barb hit home. A small uneasiness pricked at my anger, but I ignored it. "Doesn't feel good, does it, Kygo? To be a bringer of doom."

He came toward me. "I am emperor," he yelled. "You are just a woman. And *you know nothing*."

"Yet you made me your *Naiso*," I shouted, his scorn pushing me into reckless challenge. "You said you wanted the truth? Well, here it is. You tell yourself stories about how I lie and self-serve, but everything I have done has been in your interest." I counted off on my fingers. "I told you the truth about my sex; I pulled you out of your killing rage; I woke you from the shadow world. I did *not* heal you and compromise your will. Yet you still distrust me." A roar of intuition burst through my fury. "Because you are afraid of me!"

The words felt like a leap into an abyss.

He stopped in front of me, his eyes alight with his own fury. We stared at one another, locked in a moment that held either a new beginning or an end.

"I am not afraid of you," he finally said. "I am afraid of what your power means." The tension dropped from his body, making him sway.

I nodded, suddenly exhausted myself. "I am, too. I know so little, and yet now I must save the dragons."

He touched the pearl at his throat. "Yes."

"It is too much." I flung my hand out, as if I could push it all away.

Kygo caught my wrist. "Yet it is your burden, as mine is the empire."

At his touch, all my anger shifted. I gasped as his hand tightened, the same shift searing the fatigue from his eyes. He pulled me closer.

"We do not have a choice, Eona," he said.

Were his words of our duty, or the energy that leaped between us? I turned my head, seeking refuge from the intensity in his eyes, but only found the sensuous curve of the Imperial Pearl and the shift of light across it. The memory of our lips and bodies touching shivered through me.

"I know." I lifted my other hand toward the glowing gem. Was it Kinra pulling me toward the pearl, or was it my own desire?

"Do you know what happens—what it does to me, when you touch it?" He was breathing through his mouth, hard and quick. "It is like a thousand lightning strikes through my body, all tipped with pleasure."

"I think the pearl is linked to the energy world," I whispered. And maybe to an ancient traitor, but my fear of Kinra's influence was lost in the drum of my blood.

He gave a low laugh. "You know it is linked to more than the energy world."

His wry tone pulled an answering laugh from me, but the entreaty behind his words sent a soft answering surge deep into the delta of my body.

He looked up at the cave roof, his teeth clenching for a moment. "If you touch the pearl, could it bring the ten dragons?"

"Perhaps," I said, but I could not pull my hand away. "I don't know."

I saw his battle against caution, duty against desire. It was my own battle. We stood leaning toward one another, my fingertips hovering above the pearl, our only connection his hand around my wrist. Yet I felt as if his whole body was holding mine.

His head strained back, the pulse in his throat pounding. "*Gods' venom!*" he swore, and pushed me away.

I staggered, still caught in the moment, my body reaching toward him.

"Eona, no!" He lowered his head, eyes fierce. "Do not step closer."

"You do not want to?" I demanded, the shameless words coming from somewhere ancient and thwarted.

"Of course I do," he ground out. "Are you blind?" He pressed the heel of his hand against his mouth and turned away. This time his laugh was harsh. "It would almost be worth it."

I balled my fists, trying to find some control of the turmoil that raged through my *Hua*.

Kygo strode to the upturned table, bent, and, with a deep sound of effort, picked it up and slammed it back onto its legs. For a moment, he stared at the split top, then drove his fist into its edge, pushing the whole table across the floor in a squeal of wood against stone. I winced. He cradled his hand, a trickle of blood between his knuckles.

"Always duty," I said, my voice caught between tears and resentment.

With his back to me, he leaned both hands on the tabletop, his head bowed. My eyes followed the broad line of his shoulders down to his slim hips.

"We may wish the portent and Sethon's greater resources away, but we cannot ignore them, *Naiso*," he said, his voice rough and deliberate.

Naiso. I closed my eyes. Before, the word had brought sweet unity. Now it was designed for distance.

"We'll head east again. It is our best fighting ground," he said. His bloodied hand circled his throat. "And we will get Ido, so you can master *Gan Hua*."

A mix of fear and relief pounded through me in time to my heartbeat. "And when I have mastered my power . . . ?" I wet my lips, not sure what I was offering, but offering nonetheless.

He looked around at me, half of his face in shadow. "Then everything changes."

I bowed my head. Of that I had no doubt.

CHAPTER TWELVE

THE CART HIT a deep rut in the road, jerking me against Vida's sturdy shoulder. I tightened my grip on the low railing at my back. It had taken us two hot, airless days to reach the city, and although the plan to retrieve Ido had been discussed over and over again, I felt a constant misgiving at its many risks. Not least was the city gate checkpoint ahead.

"You are so bony," Vida said, her usual forthright tone high and peevish.

We were both dressed in thin, ragged gowns, our hair unbound and matted, skin smeared with dirt. Beside me, Ryko looked up with a frown. He wore the deep blue headscarf of a Trang Dein man—the rebel islanders who had been ruthlessly subdued by the army a year ago—and his heavily muscled torso was bare except for a braided leather band that crossed his chest. He lowered his head over his bound hands. I had not liked that part of the plan; binding our best fighter was madness. Still, we were meant to be a delivery of flesh to the Pleasure Ward, and a Trang Dein man would not go quietly.

"You take too much room," I whined.

"Better than being a skinny slut," Vida shot back, for the benefit of the two soldiers approaching the cart.

I pressed myself into the front corner, my heart quickening at the purposeful stride of the men. Dela looked back at us from the driver's seat. Her hair hung in two greasy hanks from under a cap, and her face was rough with stubble. The cap's brim was pulled down low to hide the elegant arch of her eyebrows. To all appearances, she was a hired thug. Her eyes flickered over Ryko's slumped shoulders and raw wrists. He had insisted on having the rope tied so tight it cut into his skin; otherwise it would look suspicious, he'd said. Dela had offered to do it, but he had taken the rope to Yuso.

"Shut up," Dela snapped at us. "Or you'll feel my whip."

A heavy-set soldier raised his hand, and Dela brought the cart to a stop. Behind us, Yuso reined his horse to a standstill and dismounted, tying the animal to the end rail. He bowed to the soldiers. His role was the flesh trader, and I almost believed it myself. A thin beard transformed his seamed face, and the cold look he cast across us held all the concern of a man checking his livestock.

"Where are you heading?" the soldier asked. Narrow, crusted eyes took in Vida and me. His partner walked around the cart, bending to check beneath it.

"Pleasure Ward," Yuso said.

"You selling these two?"

Yuso nodded.

The soldier brushed a fly from his face. "Who they going to?"

"Mama Momo."

He grinned. "Maybe I'll come and visit you, hey, girl?" The soldier poked my bare arm.

I cringed, the hard rails of the cart digging into my back. His damp touch and foul breath brought back the night of the palace coup—Sethon's soldiers baying with bloodlust, only Ryko standing between me and their brutality.

The soldier gave a low hoot and glanced across at his scrawny comrade. "I reckon no one's had her."

"That's why she worth more than you can afford, friend," Yuso said, but I could see his jaw tighten. The second soldier laughed.

"I can wait till the price comes down," the crusty-eyed soldier said. He walked around the end of the cart, his attention turning to Ryko. "Big fellow. You selling him to Momo, too?"

Yuso followed him. They both stood surveying Ryko as if he were horseflesh. "Jumped his bond. The old lady is offering a good reward."

"Ah." The soldier glanced down at the islander's bound wrists, then leaned across and slammed the flat of his hand against Ryko's forehead, forcing his head up. "You're lucky *I* didn't find you, prickless dog."

Ryko's hands lifted, his lips drawn back from his teeth.

Before I could take a breath, Yuso had a knife at the islander's throat. "Put your hands down." Ryko lowered his fists. There was no pretense in the violence that raged in his eyes.

"Punchy," the soldier remarked.

Yuso grabbed the back of Ryko's neck and shoved his head back down. "Momo probably whores him out, too."

The soldier laughed uneasily. "I wouldn't put it past the old witch." He stepped back and glanced at his companion. "All clear?" The other man nodded and waved us forward.

Yuso resheathed the knife, then untied his horse and swung back into the saddle. He motioned lazily to Dela who, with a click of tongue and sharp prod of the switch, urged the cart horse into reluctant movement. It was a stubborn bay that Yuso had bought along with his own mount to replace two of the three horses we had lost on the flooded slope. Only Kygo's Ju-Long had survived the mud, the battle horse's big heart and stamina overcoming the shock of the water.

We bumped across the cobbles toward the huge tunneled gate. Two sweating guards flanked each side, watching our approach. By their smirks, they must have heard Yuso's conversation. At least their close scrutiny vindicated the hours that Yuso, Dela, and I had spent convincing Kygo that it was too dangerous for him to enter the city with us. Just the way he moved would have raised the guards' interest, let alone the imperial cast of his features. He had finally agreed to ride out with Caido and his resistance troop and wait with them in the nearby hills until their part of the plan came into play.

Until a few hours ago, those heated discussions alongside Yuso and Dela had been the closest I'd come to Kygo in three days. He had not sought any time alone with me since the impasse in the strategy chamber, although I had often looked up during the final tactical meetings in the resistance camp to find his gaze fixed upon my face. He always looked away, leaving me stranded in half-smiles and uncertainty—I had no map of this new territory between us. On the hard journey to the city, he had stayed among Caido and his men. It was only at our parting on a deserted dirt track at the outskirts of the city that he finally called me over, away from the others.

He took my hand, and I felt the tension in his body as he pressed a small metal weight into my palm. It was the thick gold ring studded with red jade. His blood amulet.

"I want you to take this for protection from harm." He closed my fingers around it. "My father had it made on my twelfth birthday," he said. "It was forged with my blood, and the blood of my first kill, in honor of Bross." He shifted his shoulders, as if feeling the touch of the man he had killed.

I opened my hand and looked down at the ring. Perhaps it was my fancy, but the gold did seem to have a pink hue. "Who was he?"

"A soldier who tried to assassinate Sethon. I executed him." The irony of it edged his voice. "Take the traitor's blood with you, Eona. And mine." His eyes clouded. "Today is the last day of Rightful Claim."

"Your uncle was never going to honor your claim. Never!" I said, as if my vehemence could shift the weight from his spirit.

He nodded. "Still, tomorrow I officially become a traitor. A rebel." His thumb brushed the back of my hand. "Be careful, Eona."

I watched him walk away, my hard grip on the ring pressing its edges into my flesh. The boundaries between us had shifted again, and I did not know where I stood. Only one landmark on our map felt fixed: the truth in our kiss.

Our cart rumbled into the cooler shade of the tunneled gate. One of the guards peered around the edge of the thick marble wall. "I'm saving up my pay, gorgeous," he called, hot faced and grinning.

My fingers found the ring through the cloth of my gown, hidden from view on a long leather thong around my neck. I sent a prayer to Bross: *Protect us, and protect Kygo, wherever he may be.*

Then I leaned my shoulder against the top rail of the cart and played the wide-eyed newcomer, gawking at the heavy carvings on the inner walls. Most of them were the usual huge guardian door gods and symbols of prosperity, but there were also worn inscriptions in other languages. I was sure I had seen one of the strange left-to-right-running scripts at Ari the Foreigner's coffee stall. As we broke out of the tunnel into the bright heat and the tumult of the old town, it occurred to me that the inscriptions had probably been left by ancient invaders. Perhaps we should etch our names into the stone, too—a foolhardy army of five trying to penetrate the Heavenly City.

I glanced at Ryko. He remained bent over his hands, but watched the passing stalls and shifting crowd from under his brow with an intensity that told me his blood was still high. After the quiet of the road, the calls of vendors, shrieks of children, and barking of dogs made me flinch. We were in the southwest Monkey Ward, the most squalid section of the city, and it was crawling with soldiers. I pulled back from the edge of the cart and drew my legs up under the curl of my arms, trying to make myself less visible. Vida dug her fingernails into her thighs, watching the bustle of the city from under the veil of her wild hair.

Along the narrow street, shredded red paper lamps from the New Year celebration still swung from crossbraces, and some shop-house doors displayed the long, red banners of New Year's couplets hung to attract wealth and good fortune. They should have come down days ago in respect for the old emperor's death. No doubt the merchants hoped the special wishes would help protect their businesses from Sethon's soldiers.

A roar of male laughter rose above the clamor of hawker calls and shrill bargaining. I did not move my head but found the source at the edge of my sight. A large group of off-duty soldiers sprawled across the wooden benches of an oyster stew stall, shouting down a comrade's joke. Although they took no notice of our slow progress, Ryko's hands flexed against his bonds.

For a few lengths, a sesame cake vendor walked alongside us, beating a wooden tablet hung from the basket pole across his shoulders. The nutty sweetness of his wares filled the air and I swallowed a sudden rush of saliva; for two days I had only eaten salty dried road rations. He glanced across at me and, seeing no chance of a sale, hurried past, adding his raucous voice to his drum.

Behind us, Yuso's horse sidled at the harsh sound, the captain holding the animal in check with firm knees and hands. I watched him manage the horse's fear, soothing it back into submission. After the last few days in Yuso's company, I had finally seen what prompted Ryko's loyalty and Kygo's respect. It was not only his command of tactical deception, although that had come to the fore as we planned this venture. It was also his concern for his men. On our last day at the resistance camp we had entombed Solly, and as we gathered for the death procession at dawn, Yuso had arrived carrying Tiron on his back. The injured guard was no lightweight, and both of his legs were splinted, but Yuso had borne him up to the hillside tomb to help send Solly to his ancestors. And that was not his only kindness. I saw him pass a small pouch to Tiron as we said our good-byes to the camp people. Later, when I asked him what he had given the young guard, he had eyed me in his usual dour manner and said, "If it is any of your business, my lady, I gave him the rest of my Sun Drug. Better that the boy not withdraw while his bones are mending. I can get more when we reach the city."

"Get your head down," he said now, through his teeth, as he eased the horse past me. Abashed, I obeyed. I had to remember my role.

He drew level with Dela. "Go over that bridge." he ordered, pointing to the wooden arch across a narrow canal, "and then right. Got it?"

Dela nodded and prodded the bay into a trot. As we thudded over the bridge, I caught a glimpse of opaque brown water and the sleek arrow of a water rat cutting through the sluggish current.

We turned into a wide road, each side a jumble of open-front taverns and sprawling eateries clustered around fire pits. Cooks bent over hissing pans, and the fatty smoke of roast pork flavored the air, briefly overriding the stench of sun-warmed urine and rotting cabbage. A few calls and jeers from early patrons followed us as we headed toward the tall red gates of the Blossom World.

I had never been in the Pleasure Ward, although I had heard many stories about it from the other boys when I was a Dragoneye candidate. Mainly it had been whispers about strange contraptions and impossible positions, but one boy's master had actually taken him inside the Blossom World. He had told us that every man who passed through the gates had to wear a mask and a disguise; it was the symbolic shedding of self, he'd said loftily, to become whoever you wanted to be, or to put down the burden of who you already were. For a night, farmers could be lords, and lords could be peasants. All men were equal, and no one was allowed to carry a weapon inside the gates. Except, he'd added with a knowing grin that made us lean closer, the infamous Sword Lilies, who practiced the art of pain.

"Greetings!" Yuso called to a gateman as we drew up to the ornate entrance. He dismounted and led the horse up to the neat annex that jutted from the towering wall.

The wooden gates—too high for a man or even a man on his friend's shoulders to look over—were heavily carved with stylized flowers: peony, apple blossom, lily, and orchid. I searched the sinuous tangle of stems and leaves for the lewd figures that were supposed to be hidden among them. All I could see was the faint outline of a smaller door set into the left panel.

The gateman ambled out of his gatehouse and surveyed us. "Expected, or touting?" he asked.

"Mama Momo," Yuso said. "Tell her Heron from Siroko Province is here."

It was the code name that Kygo had given us. Mama Momo, it seemed, was more than just Queen of the Blossom World. If the code name failed, we had Ryko as backup: he had admitted he'd known her long ago, in another lifetime. I knew he had once been a thief and hired muscle. Perhaps it had been for this woman who now held our way into the palace.

The gateman straightened. "Mama Momo?" He snapped his fingers, and a boy hurried out of the gatehouse, wiping crumbs from his mouth. "Run up to the big house, Tik, and tell Mama—who are you again?" Yuso repeated the code name. The boy nodded his understanding. "And wait for her instructions," the gateman called as Tik pushed open the smaller door in the gate and stepped through. It banged shut behind him.

The gateman smiled brown-stained reassurance. "He shouldn't be long."

He wasn't. Tik returned with a plump man whose winged black hat and soft body marked him as a scribe eunuch.

"I am Stoll, Mama Momo's secretary," he said, bowing to Yuso. His eyes passed over me and found Ryko. Thin plucked brows lifted with interest. "Please come this way."

He pointed to the far end of the high wall at a plain wooden gate—a delivery entrance. The beautiful front gates of the Blossom World did not open for a flesh trader and his wares.

The delivery gate was dragged open by two boys as we approached. Not eunuchs—at least not yet. Stoll waved us into an alley that ran alongside the far wall of the Pleasure Ward. Courtyard after courtyard backed onto the narrow roadway, the rear living areas of huge houses that must have faced onto the main thoroughfare of the Blossom World. Large quantities of washing hung from ropes strung between walls and trees, all of it sheets and drying cloths. As we passed each courtyard, women in loose gowns looked up from cooking on small braziers, throwing fortune sticks, mending gowns, and drying their wet hair in the noon sun. A few were even chasing the dragon, the smoke from the drug curling around their heads like the tail of one of the great beasts. I recognized the pungent smell from the teahouses around the market. The women's interest was fleeting, mainly centered upon Ryko; then they turned back to their own start-of-day concerns. The only fixed gaze came from a tiny girl crouched at the feet of a woman who strummed scales on a long lute. The plaintive rise and fall of the notes caught on a faint breeze that stirred the heavy air and brought the perfume of soap and the succulence of grilled fish. The little girl smiled and waved. I lifted my hand in response and watched her jump up in delight.

As we neared the summit of a small hill, the tiled roof and elegant shutters of a large house rose above its more squat neighbors. It was obviously our destination, for Stoll hurried ahead and turned to wave us into its courtyard. I wiped the sweat from my neck and touched the blood ring again—for luck, and for the hope that Kygo was safe.

Unlike the other courtyards, this one was not full of washing or the out-spillings of cramped living. Instead, it was cobbled and clean, with a stable at the left and a small walled garden to the right. A low platform ran along the length of the house, creating a deep step up to a wall of paneled screen doors. One was open, allowing a framed glimpse of the interior: traditional straw matting, low table, and the abrupt angles of a formal orchid arrangement.

A feminine figure moved into the frame and stood silhouetted for a moment, slender and erect, then stepped out on to the platform. She was older than her elegant bearing had led me to expect: perhaps around sixty, with deep lines that carved fierceness into a face that still had the graceful bones of beauty. She lifted the green silk hem of her gown and walked to the edge of the platform. Stoll hurried forward, but she stopped him with a raised hand.

"You are not the Master Heron I was expecting," she said as Yuso dismounted. Dela pulled our cart up beside him. The cart horse shook its head, the jangle of its harness loud in the sudden wary silence.

Yuso's eyes darted to the stable. I followed his gaze into the dim interior: two large Trang Dein men holding lethal double hooks waited inside the doorway. Across the yard, another two armed men watched from the shadows of an outhouse. So much for the policy of no weapons.

"Who are you?" Mama Momo demanded.

Yuso glanced back at us. "Ryko, what are you waiting for?" he said through his teeth.

Beside me, the islander straightened and cleared his throat. "Hello, Momota. It's been a long time."

"Ryko? Is that really you?" Her narrowed gaze dropped to his bound wrists, then back to Yuso. "Boys, we've got trouble," she said, and it was an order.

The Trang Dein men stepped out of the shadows, their sword hooks slicing through the air in soft whirring circles.

Yuso drew his knife. "Ryko, I thought you said she'd help you!"

I sucked in a breath. There was nothing in the cart to use as a weapon; my swords were with Kygo, along with the folio and compass. I scanned the courtyard. The nearest thing was a wooden shovel. Vida edged between me and the approaching men.

"Get ready to run," she whispered.

"Momo," Ryko said, "I swear on Layla's grave that we are from the true Master Heron. He needs your help."

"You are not being forced?"

"No!"

Momo held up both hands. "Wait," she ordered, halting her men. They lowered their weapons. She stared at Ryko. "If you just lied on Layla's name, I'll have them rip you apart. You know that."

Ryko nodded. "I know it."

"All right, then. Come in. Explain yourself." She pointed at Yuso. "And you, knife-boy, cut Ryko free."

Mama Momo sat back from passing around bowls of tea and studied us. She had also offered small crescent New Year cakes, but Yuso's warning glance had stopped me reaching for one, although my stomach squirmed with hunger. Distrust flowed both ways. I looked around the room. It was on the second story of the house but had no windows and, strangely, the walls were covered with straw matting. The ceiling was covered with matting, too.

"Soundproof," Momo said, following my upward gaze. "Completely." She smiled as she picked up a blue porcelain bowl and made a show of sipping the tea.

I took a hurried sip from my own bowl, remembering my fellow candidate's lurid stories. Across the low table, Yuso shifted his weight, a crimp of pain between his eyebrows; kneeling did not agree with a leg wound.

"So you claim to be friends of Master Heron," Momo said to him. "I know Ryko. But who are you?"

"I am Yuso, captain of His Majesty's imperial guard."

She shot a glance at Ryko, who nodded. She leaned forward. "And you say His Majesty is alive? Sethon proclaimed his death more than a week ago, and my normal channels have picked up only wind-whispers that he survived the coup."

"We got him out in time. He is alive and preparing to fight for his throne," Yuso said. "We left him this morning."

"Preparing?" She frowned. "Today is the last day of Rightful Claim. Does he not make his move?"

Yuso shook his head. "Not yet."

"I see." Her shrewd gaze rested upon me. "And who are you, to be so carefully watched over by your comrades?"

Yuso bowed toward me. "This is Lady Eona, Mirror Dragoneye."

"Lady Eona?" Momo sat back on her heels. "Ah, I see. Lord Eon." She bowed. "It is a good disguise, my lord."

"No," I said quickly. "I really am Lady Eona. The Mirror Dragon is female, as am I."

She pressed her hand to her mouth. "Truly?" Her fierce face folded into deep carved laughter lines. "How wonderful, a female Dragoneye. That would have put the wind up those Dragoneye Lords." She sobered. "Of course, they are all dead now, may they walk in the garden of heaven." She turned to Ryko. "You do realize how dangerous it is to bring Lady Eona into the city? I didn't raise a fool, did I?"

We all froze, staring at Ryko. He looked around the table, his glare finally resting on Momo. "Lady Eona is integral to our plan," he said flatly.

"Are you Ryko's mother?" Dela asked Momo, her own fierceness softening into a small, surprised smile.

Momo snorted. "Of course not. I took him in when he was eight." She glanced across at the islander. "Trouble from day one."

Ryko's glare intensified.

Ignoring him, Momo turned to Yuso. "What is this plan that is so important that you would risk a Dragoneye? Do you try to assassinate Sethon? You will die before you get near him."

"We have to get Lord Ido out of the palace," Yuso said.

She took a sip of tea, eyeing us. "That's almost as difficult. He is in the cells."

"You're sure he's still alive?" I asked urgently.

"He was this morning," Momo said. "The soldiers take my girls to look at him like some kind of freak show: the great Dragoneye Lord bowed and bloody. My girls have seen a lot in their lives, and even they are shocked by what Sethon has done. From all accounts, if you try to move him, you'll kill him."

"That is why I am here," I said. "I can heal him."

It was one of the biggest risks in our plan. I had to heal Ido fast enough for him to gather his strength and hold off the ten bereft dragons before they tore me apart with power. Again, I touched Kygo's ring: not only for luck, but for comfort, too.

"You can heal?" Momo shook her head in wonder.

"You say the soldiers take your girls to look at him," Dela said. "That could work to our advantage."

Momo tilted her head. "You're eastern," she said.

"I am Lady Dela. I was—"

"The Contraire?" Momo sat up straight.

Dela nodded, smoothing back her greasy hair with a self-conscious hand.

The old woman pressed her thin lips together. "We may have a problem. I have an eastern girl here, from the Haya Ro, and if she recognizes you . . ."

"She may," Dela said. "I am the only twin soul among the Highland Tribes, and well known."

Momo crooked a finger at Stoll. "Tell Hina she can take those two days off to see her son. As long as she goes now."

Stoll bowed and left to deliver the good news. As the sliding door closed behind him, I glimpsed one of the Trang Dein man on the landing, armed and alert.

"And who are you?" Momo asked Vida dryly. "The Sun Empress?"

Vida shook her head. "I am a resistance fighter," she said, undaunted by the old woman's sarcasm.

Dela circled her hands around her tea bowl. "Why would Sethon torture Ido?" she asked. "It doesn't make sense. He needs Ido."

"No doubt Sethon is trying to get information out of him," Yuso said.

Momo grunted. "I don't like Lord Ido. I never have. He is twenty-four now, but I've known him since he was sixteen, and right from the beginning he has had something within him that is"—she paused—"keyed differently. If Sethon wanted something out of him, he would have to push past what a normal man could endure."

I knew what Ido was trying to keep from Sethon: how to use the black folio to control a Dragoneye and his power. Or *her* power.

"You think Sethon has just gone too far with him?" Dela asked.

"I have seen Sethon's methods," Yuso said grimly. "They do not err on the side of restraint."

"It is even beyond that," Momo said. "We get imperial orders to send girls to the palace for our new esteemed emperor. Sometimes they don't come back." She glanced around the table, her eyes hard with anger. "Three bodies in the canal so far; one of them a girl from my house. He enjoys having power over life and death. I've tried to stop supplying, as have the other houses, but he just sends his men to get them."

We sat in silence.

"Why do you want Ido so badly?" Momo finally asked. "It's going to be a hellish job to get him out, and I can see you are here to ask for my help."

It seemed we had finally passed her scrutiny. Yuso looked across at me, questioning. I shrugged: *Why not?*

"Lady Eona needs training," he said. "Without Ido, she will not be able to control her power. And His Majesty needs her power to win his throne."

Momo leaned forward, pinning me with her bright gaze. "What makes you think Ido will do what you want? From gratitude?" Her thin body shook in a silent laugh. "Ido doesn't know what the word means. I should know."

"When Lady Eona heals someone, she can control their will," Ryko said. "She has healed Ido once already."

My skin heated at the edge in his voice. Momo heard it, too; her attention snapped to the islander.

She sat back and sucked on her teeth. "She's healed you, too, hasn't she, Ry?"

His nod was almost imperceptible, his eyes fixed on the table. For a moment, Momo's face softened.

"Well, then, Lady Eona." She turned to me, once again Queen of the Blossom World. "If you can control a will like Ryko's, you might be able to control Lord Ido. What is your plan, Yuso?"

"We cannot go in by force, so we must go in by deception. Lady Eona and Vida will masquerade as Blossom Women for one of these gatherings."

Momo stared at him. "That is a very dangerous proposition."

"Not so dangerous if they go in as high-ranked girls," Yuso said.

She crossed her arms and inspected me, then Vida. "Possible, with a bit of work," she conceded. "Although the refined arts of an Orchid or Peony are not often requested by soldiers. They do not want music or dance. They are more your Jasmine or

Cherry Blossom type of men." She drummed her fingers on the table. "We can work around it, though."

"We do not expect Lady Eona or Vida to actually have to perform," Yuso said quickly. "And Ryko, Lady Dela, and I will go in as their protectors, or something along those lines."

"Could you and Ryko be recognized, captain?" Momo asked.

"Not unless some of the imperial guard have survived and turned," he said.

Momo shook her head. "Executed. Every one of them."

Yuso and Ryko looked at one another—a moment of shared anger—then Yuso bowed his head. Ryko pressed his fist to his chest, his face tight.

After a moment's respectful silence, Momo said, "If you go in as my men, you will be stopped and held back outside the rooms, but at least you will be inside the palace walls. How quickly do you want to move?"

"As soon as we can," I said.

"There's an officer's party tonight. Is that soon enough?"

I took a deep breath and looked around at the others. I saw the same tension in them that shifted through me: we had all stepped up to the edge.

Yuso smiled, hard and grim. One by one, we all smiled back.

"I'll take that as a yes," Momo said dryly.

It was good to have hot fish and rice in my belly and to be clean again, even if the bath had been rushed and the scrubbing delivered by a maid with the touch of a net-hauler. I pulled the still-damp drying cloth higher up on my chest and shifted on the hard wooden stool as Mama Momo and Moon Orchid examined me.

The young Blossom Woman reached across and pushed my wet hair behind my ear, then pursed her lips thoughtfully. I tried not to stare, but it was hard to resist the draw of her face. Madina had spoken of the four seats of beauty, and Moon Orchid had them all, in abundance. Thick, soft hair dressed high to accentuate her broad forehead; wide eyes with a hint of clever mischief in them; lips that called for a fingertip to trace their shape; and a long, smooth throat, all in a harmony of spirit that brought a pang to the heart.

"I don't think she can be an Orchid," Momo said. "Her face and voice would pass, but she moves like a delivery boy." She glanced down at me. "No offense, my lady."

I hitched up the drying cloth again and shrugged. Compared to Moon Orchid's languorous grace, I did move like a boy.

Moon Orchid tilted her head. "It will have to be a Peony, and we will hope that she is not asked to play for them." She eyed me for a moment. "I don't suppose you have any skill with a lute?"

I shook my head.

Momo reached across and tilted my face, inspecting my jaw. "The Peony paint will also cover that bruise. We do not want the vultures to circle." She touched Moon Orchid's arm. "Will you begin? I'll see to Vida."

She crossed the room to where the resistance woman sat on her own stool. "You, my dear, will be a Safflower. But let me give you a few words of warning about . . ."

"I think Mama Momo is too harsh," Moon Orchid whispered, diverting my attention. "You could pass as an Orchid." She smiled and handed me a long strip of cloth. "Please pull your hair back, my lady, and we'll get started."

I wrapped the cloth around my head, tucking in the loose strands of hair.

"You should take off your pendant, too, or it may get paint on it."

I lifted the leather thong over my head, pulling Kygo's amulet from under the edge of the drying cloth. For a moment, Moon Orchid's eyes fixed on the swinging gold ring. Her long throat convulsed in a hard swallow.

"Kygo's—I mean, His Majesty's blood ring," she said. "Why do you have it? Is he all right?"

I pulled it back from her avid gaze. "He gave it to me," I said.

How did she know it was Kygo's ring? The obvious answer was like a slap across the face. We stared at each other, her beauty sending another pang through me, discordant and sour.

"Is he well?" she asked.

"He was this morning." I closed my fingers around the ring.

Moon Orchid turned and pressed a brush into the white face paint, her smooth brow creased. Even a frown did not detract from her beauty. She took a deeper breath, withdrew the brush, and wiped the excess on the side of the pot. When she turned back to me, her face was once again serene. She placed the brush alongside my nose and gently stroked the cool paint onto my skin.

"The ring is very important to him," she said. Her eyes flicked up from her task. "He must think highly of you."

No doubt she saw my cheeks redden.

"It is to protect us on the mission," I said.

"Yes, of course." She smiled and charged the brush again. A small silence settled as she painted the other side of my face and my forehead in broad strokes.

I wet my lips. "How long have you known him?"

She looked up from under her long lashes. "I have not seen him since Her Majesty, the Empress Cela, walked the golden path to her ancestors."

She had not answered my question, but something narrow-eyed within me was pleased that she had not seen him for a year.

Moon Orchid turned from the paint pot again. "He is a very handsome man." Another long stroke ended at my chin. "Although his heavenly rank creates tension for his earthly body."

I pulled back from the brush. Its white tip hung between us, pointed like her comment.

"How is that?" I finally asked, curiosity overwhelming my unease.

"To be so sacred that one cannot be touched. It builds both a hunger and a restraint." The soft brush followed the shape of my mouth. "A conflict that is mirrored in his spirit." She stopped painting, her face polite. "Or perhaps you disagree, my lady?"

For a searing moment, I felt Kygo's hand around my wrist again and saw the strong line of his jaw as his head strained back, fighting for control. I drew in a breath, meeting Moon Orchid's watchful gaze. "You know him well, then."

A small shrug, and the brush swirled through the paint again. "Well enough to know that he has given you more than just a god's protection with that ring."

I opened my hand and we both looked down at the thick band. I knew it meant more—it had been in the touch of his hand and the soft urgency of his voice—but I still wanted to know what she thought he had given me.

There was no need for me to ask: Moon Orchid was a practiced reader of desire. She put down the brush, her dark eyes suddenly much older than the smooth beauty of her face.

"He has given you his blood, and the moment when he crossed into manhood," she said, and pressed my fingers around the ring again. Her smile was as tight as my heart.

For a moment I felt victorious, as though I had won some silent battle between us. Then I looked down at her hand enclosing my own, and in my mind all I could see were those long, pale fingers moving slowly across Kygo's sacred skin.

I had not even stepped into the arena.

After what seemed an age, Mama Momo circled me again, Dela by her side.

"You have done a beautiful job, my dear," she said to Moon Orchid. "Do you not agree, Lady Dela?"

Dela smiled her agreement, although her face was troubled. She had joined us early in the preparations, like a moth drawn to the flame of femininity in the room. She had sat beside me as Moon Orchid finished painting my face, and I had watched her large-knuckled hands hover over the brushes and paint, her eyes judging the deft darkening of my lashes and reddening of my lips. I could almost feel the ache in her to shave off her stubble and paint back the contours of her true self.

"Are you all right?" I whispered, when Moon Orchid had stepped away for a moment.

Dela had put down the pot she was holding, her lip caught between her teeth. "Every day, Ryko sees me in this man's garb. It is difficult enough for me, let alone him."

I touched her arm. "It does not matter. He knows who you really are."

"Then why do I see him withdrawing from me?" she asked.

"I don't think it is you," I had said grimly. "I think it is me."

Across the room, Vida stared at her completed Safflower reflection in a large mirror that stood against the wall. She touched the glass, pulling back as her finger met the hard surface. I remembered my own shock at seeing the whole length of my body for the first time in the arena mirror; the sudden shift from living within flesh to viewing it, a collection of form and contour that was myself, but at the same time outside myself. Quickly, Vida averted her eyes from those in the precious glass; perhaps she did not want to see her spirit in its depths. She watched her reflected hand trace the curve of her waist. Her body was swathed in diaphanous blue cloth that in some places was only one layer thick, showing the sheen of oiled skin, and in others, three or four layers, hiding everything but shape. She frowned and stepped back, her cheeks flushed.

"It will be hard to fight in this," she said. "It is very tight. And I cannot hide a weapon."

"You would not get one past the guards anyway," Momo said. "Come, Lady Eona." She beckoned me over to the mirror. "See yourself transformed."

I gathered the skirt of my pink and green gown and walked over to the mirror, both eager and afraid to see my reflection.

A fine-boned woman watched me warily from the smooth glass, her large eyes made larger by the charcoal definition of lashes and brows. Her thick hair, braided into three crown coils and pinned with a beautiful fall of gold flowers, added height to her small frame. Her mouth was painted into a stylized flower bud that was oddly melancholy, its natural upward curve hidden in the white paint that softened a stubborn chin and created an elegant length of throat.

I blinked, bringing the separate parts of my face into a whole. The woman before me was pretty, but not beautiful like Moon Orchid. My eyes followed the downward sweep of white paint to the hollow of my throat. It had been left unpainted, a jewel of smooth, natural skin that hinted at what lay beneath the clinging sheath of pink and green silk and the tight binding of the embroidered sash.

"Although she is completely covered, the message is still very obvious," Dela said wryly.

"That is our art," Momo said.

I shook my head. "I cannot do this." I stepped away from the mirror. "I am not feminine enough. I will walk like a boy and give us away."

"Nonsense. You were skilled enough to fool everyone into believing you were a boy for years. I'm sure you can now manage a Peony." Momo led me back to the mirror and stood me in front of it again. "Look at yourself. You are a beautiful Peony, a highly skilled artist whose company is reserved for the rich and powerful. Every other man will be busy unwrapping you with his eyes. They will not see anything beyond that."

I pressed my lips together, tasting the waxy red ocher of the paint. I knew Momo was right: the soldiers would not see anything beyond the promise of my body. Not at first, anyway. Even Kygo's gaze had changed when I had finally told him I was a girl. He had been furious, of course, but as he recast me in the mold of woman, I had felt my body became a possibility to him, and my flesh the sum of what I was. At the time, it had shamed and infuriated me.

I stared into the mirror and a small smile shifted across the reddened flower-bud mouth. Part of me wished Kygo were here to see me in the gown and paint. Would he think me beautiful? I glanced across at Moon Orchid. Not if she was in the room. Still, he had made me his *Naiso*, and kissed me even when I had been stinking of horse and sweat, and covered in mud. I *was* more than just a body to him.

A small doubt slid through my thoughts like a honed dagger. It was possible that my body had never had anything to do with it. Perhaps he did not want Eona—just "the thousand lightning strikes tipped with pleasure." Was that why he had not sought my company on the ride to the city—since I dared not touch the pearl, I was of no use? I looked at Moon Orchid again. He could have any woman he wanted. Why would he choose me?

Perhaps he did not even see Eona when he looked at me. Perhaps all he could see was dragon power.

Mama Momo guided me away from the mirror. "If all goes smoothly, you won't be in the company of the officers for long, anyway," she said. "Tell me the plan again."

We had been through it twice already while I was being painted, but she was right to insist. "One of Sethon's half-brothers is hosting the party—High Lord Haio. He has requested only lower rank girls, so when he sees me among the others, he will complain."

Momo nodded. "He is tighter than a fish's bum and won't want to pay for a Peony he did not order."

"I then explain that there has been a mistake, and that Vida and I are a gift for the emperor from the Blossom Houses: a Peony for music and song, and a Safflower for the more base arts." I paused. "What if Haio decides he wants a Peony after all?" I did not have a clear idea of what would happen at such a party, but I knew it would not be safe for either of us.

"He will not want to interfere with his brother's pleasure—

with good reason. Haio will have a steward escort you to Sethon."

"Ryko, Yuso, and Dela will intercept us," I continued. "We'll get rid of the steward and make our way to Ido."

"Do not miss that opportunity." Momo gripped my arm to emphasize the warning.

"We know," Vida said.

"We get into Ido's cell. I heal him, then we make our way to the east wall of the palace, where the resistance will be waiting with horses and an escape route out of the city." I looked at the somber faces around me. "Let's hope the gods are with us."

"They should smile upon you just for the sheer audacity of it all," Momo said. She turned to Dela. "Are you sure you cannot do this without risking Lady Eona? I could have her meet you outside the palace."

"I have to be there to heal Ido and control him," I said, before Dela could answer. I was afraid of going into the palace, but I was just as frightened of losing my one chance of rescuing the only man who could train me in my dragon power.

Momo sighed, then beckoned to Moon Orchid. "Take Vida and Lady Dela to the top room, my dear. Yuso and Ryko are waiting." She smiled at me. "Lady Eona, will you stay a few moments longer?"

I crossed my arms. "What for?"

Did she think she could persuade me to stay out of the palace?

"I would speak to you about Ryko," she said in an undertone.

Dela turned back, ignoring Moon Orchid's gentle ushering toward the door. "Ryko? What about Ryko?"

Momo's eyebrows rose at her tone. "It is a matter between Lady Eona and myself."

Dela's chin lifted. "Ryko is my guard. I will stay, too."

"Your guard?" Momo echoed.

It was no longer strictly true, but both Dela and Ryko seemed to be clinging to the formal bond that had first brought them together. I caught the silent plea in Dela's eyes.

"Lady Dela will stay," I said. My support was not all for Dela's sake; I did not want to face Momo alone. Especially about Ryko.

Momo's lips thinned, but she nodded and waved Moon Orchid and Vida from the room.

"You are killing him," she said flatly when the door had slid shut behind them. "This possession of his will—it is withering his spirit."

I tightened my arms across my chest. "I did not ask for it."

"Yet you keep on doing it. I have spoken to him."

"Only twice," Dela said. "And Lady Eona has promised—"

"Three times," Momo said. "At least."

Dela focus snapped to me. "Three?"

"His Majesty made me. It was a test." I lowered my head. "I did not want to."

"Eona!"

I did not look up; the disillusion in her voice was clear enough. "You were not there," I said. "Do not judge me."

Momo clicked her tongue in irritation. "It does not matter

how many times. Ryko is a man who lives by his own code, and if he cannot have that, he would rather die. I should know. His damned code drove a wedge between us."

"How?" Dela asked.

"His mother, Layla, and I were friends. We worked in the same house. She wanted to get out and take Ryko back to the islands, and she was so close to repaying her bond. Then she was killed by a client, right in front of him."

Dela pressed her hand to her mouth. "Killed in front of him?"

Momo nodded. "He tried to stop it, but he was only eight. I took him in after that. Then when he was sixteen and I had my own house, he helped one of my girls break her bond. She manipulated him, but that's not the point." She waved away the girl's importance. "He just wanted to save her, like he couldn't save his mother." Momo turned to me. "For Ryko, your control is a bond that can never be repaid or escaped. You have his spirit in chains."

I glanced at Dela. "Maybe he should leave us."

Her jaw tightened. "You know he will not."

"It is only going to get worse," I whispered. "If our plan works and I heal Lord Ido, then Ryko will be caught up in my control of him."

Momo shook her head. "Does he know this?"

"Yes."

"Then it is his own choice. And that is the crux of the matter, isn't it," she said grimly. "If Ryko cannot make his own choices, by his sense of duty and honor, he would rather die."

"I am hoping that once I am trained by Lord Ido, I can end this bond," I said.

Momo grunted. "You are pinning a lot of hope on Lord Ido," she said. "I pray that you can control him, as you say. Let me show you something, as a warning."

She loosened her sash and pushed her robe off her right shoulder, exposing the bony flat of her back. A long ridged scar, old and deep, slashed the skin—the mark of a whip.

"That was Ido?" Dela whispered.

Momo nodded. "When he was seventeen. I turned my back on him," she said. "Never make that mistake, Lady Eona. He will strike as fast as a scorpion and with just as much venom."

"Why did he do it?" I asked.

"Because he could," Momo said. "It is his nature."

Yet she had not seen the remorse that shook Ido's body after I had healed him, nor witnessed the terrible pain he had suffered to hold back the ten dragons from tearing me apart. Surely it was possible his nature had changed. Why else would he put himself in such danger?

CHAPTER THIRTEEN

TWELVE GIRLS; AN auspicious number. As we gathered at the Gate of Good Service, I scanned the faces around me in the twilight. Some of the women were tense—no doubt the three bodies in the canal were playing on their minds—while others had the glazed eyes of dragon chasers, the drug loosening their minds as well as their bodies. Momo had told us to stay well away from those girls; they had no sense of their own safety or anyone else's, she'd said. The warmth of the day still held, and the smell of sweat was barely masked by the clash of perfumes on the bodies around me. We were corralled between the men who were our "protectors" and the soldiers who manned the gate. I shifted my sweaty grip on the neck of my lute and leaned over to Vida. She was standing, feet apart, arms crossed.

"You look like you are on guard duty," I whispered.

She unwound her arms and pressed her hands together. "What is the delay?"

A woman sidled up to us. "I didn't know there was going to be a Peony," she said loudly, directing the attention of all the other women to me. She was dressed in a gown similar to Vida's, although considerably more skin showed, and when she smiled, I saw her teeth had been dyed black, the custom marking her as a married woman from the far southeast coast. How had she got so far from her home and husband? "We'll have music," she added. "We can dance."

"What? Are you trying to be an Orchid?" another Safflower scoffed.

The two women began a soft exchange of insults, pulling the focus of the others away from me. I looked back at Yuso; the stern commander I knew was hidden beneath a ratty beard and worn clothes and a slouch. He yawned, affecting boredom, but his eyes met mine in swift reassurance. Dela stood beside him, absently scratching the stubble on her face. She hawked and spat.

I rocked forward on my toes and watched two of the gate soldiers search a dragon chaser. The girl giggled and draped herself against them until they finally pushed her face-first and limp against the raw boards of the new gate. Only twelve days ago, Ryko and I had followed a battering ram through that gate, fighting our way into the courtyard on the back of a horse. I shivered, remembering our beast trampling a soldier, the man's chest caving under its hooves. Was Ryko also remembering that same desperate night? His face held only impatience as he lounged beside a Trang Dein man, the two of them a wall of islander muscle.

"Little Sister Peony, please give me your lute." I jumped as a very young, pock-marked soldier held out his hand. The old-fashioned courtesy matched his shy smile. "I will be careful with it."

I passed him the instrument. He gently shook it and peered into the exquisitely carved sound holes, then handed it back.

"I am sorry, Little Sister, but I will have to search you." The pits on his face stood out white against the vivid scarlet of his blush. "Orders."

I bit the inside of my cheek as I felt his hesitant hands pat my chest and waist, then around my hips. Beside me, Vida was getting the same treatment from another guard, but with far less deference.

My young soldier ducked his head. "You can go in now."

I tried a Peony smile—slow and mysterious, as Moon Orchid had taught me—and saw him flush again.

Vida fell in beside me, and we walked through the gate into the courtyard that ran alongside the huge kitchens. I circled my hand around my wrist and felt the shape of Kygo's ring, hidden under the leather thong that was wrapped and tied into a thick bracelet. It had been Moon Orchid's idea, and the care she had taken to wind it around my moon wrist had felt like a silent blessing.

I glanced back; Ryko was walking through the gate. We had all made it into the palace. I sent a quick prayer to Tu-Xang, the oldest god of luck. He was known to protect fools and thieves.

Four men bustled up, barely acknowledging our ragged bows. Their black caps and the green feathers pinned to their robes marked them as stewards. Momo had been right: we had no guards once we were inside the walls, only eunuchs. On the terrible night of the coup, Ryko and I had seen many of the eunuch attendants hacked to death, but these four seemed officious and self-satisfied, as though such atrocities had never happened. It seemed the change of an emperor—even a brutal change—did not stop the bureaucracy of the palace.

"Follow me," one of them called. "Keep together."

A few women hooked arms, their soft whispers breaking into quick nervous laughter. I glanced at Vida and caught her hand, partly to keep our paces matched, but mainly for the comfort of another human touch. She squeezed my fingers. We rounded the kitchen buildings, the salty slick of fish stock on the warm night air, and passed the wall that enclosed the imperial guest apartments, the former home of Lord Eon. For more than a month I had lived as a Dragoneye Lord in the Peony Apartment, and here I was, back as a Peony Blossom. A mad desire to laugh bubbled through me.

We turned along the avenue that led past the lesser banquet hall. This part of the palace had not sustained much damage. There was more destruction, I knew, on the other side, around the central harem where Lord Ido had used his dragon power to blast through the sanctuary wall. Perhaps his torture was the gods' way of punishing him for his transgression against the Covenant of Service.

The eunuchs led us past the hall to the third guest apartment: the House of the Five Color Cloud. It was our destination, for we were ushered into the formal garden, and the lead eunuch dropped back to walk beside Yuso and Dela.

"You and your men cannot enter," the eunuch told them. "At any time. Do you understand?"

Yuso shrugged. "We understand." He opened his hand, showing a set of dice. "We are used to waiting."

As we approached the elegant door screen, the energy within the group of women shifted. Even the dragon chasers straightened, and I felt Vida tense through our linked hands. It was up to me now to get us past the next obstacle: Sethon's brother. Momo had been certain he would call for a steward. She knew him and this world, but what if he decided he did want a Peony, after all? A stark memory from the coup—a maidservant screaming, struggling under a soldier—shuddered through me. I tightened my grip on the lute. Ahead, the soft murmurs of the women ceased as the steward clapped to announce our arrival, the glow from a pair of brass lanterns casting his shadow long across the raked pebble path.

The black-toothed Safflower turned to face me. "You should be at the front," she said in the silence. "What are you doing back here?"

I stared at her surprise, unable to come up with a quick answer.

"Well, if you get your fat arse out of the way," Vida said tartly, "Fortune Peony will be able to take her proper place."

Black Teeth scowled at Vida, but she moved aside. "Fat arse?" she muttered as we passed. "Look who's talking."

Vida quelled her with a look. I forced a serene smile as the other women shifted for us, a few murmurs of discontent fading at Vida's silent belligerence. We took our places at the front of the straggling line and stepped onto the low wooden viewing platform. The screen door snapped open. A plump servant glanced at us, then bowed to the steward.

"They're late," he said. He jerked his head back to the sounds of male laughter inside. "They are already drunk as newts."

A whisper rustled through the women, the tension rising.

"Then let them in," the steward said.

With a parting sniff, the servant bowed and led us into an elegant foyer, our footsteps muffled by fine straw matting. I recognized the layout; it was the same as the Peony apartment, with a formal reception room at the front and private chambers at the rear. From the murmuring and sharp bursts of laughter, it was clear that the men waited in the reception room.

The servant clapped at the screen door and the sounds of conversation stopped. My mouth dried, parched of everything except fear. Beside me, Vida pressed her hands against her chest.

"Vida," I whispered. She looked at me, my own panic mirrored in her eyes.

"Enter," called a male voice.

The servant pulled back the screen, his portly body folded into a low bow.

My blood roared in my ears. Before me, men in the dark blue tunics of the cavalry lounged around a low table, its polished surface littered with long-necked decanters and platters of food. My eyes skipped across the faces, some assessing, some leering. And one, surprised—no doubt High Lord Haio. The smell of cooked meat and male sweat was overwhelming.

Forcing a smile, I bent into a walking bow and led the women into the room. I did not dare look up at the circle of men; they would see my fear as if it were a black mark upon my face. I kneeled, placed the lute before me, and sank into a kowtow, the other women following my lead. The straw matting stank of spilled rice wine and brought a rise of nausea into my throat. I clenched my jaw, fighting for poise. A Peony would not shift with nerves or spew vomit on the feet of her clients.

"Rise."

I sat back and met the frown of High Lord Haio. His features held the echo of his two older half-brothers'—the forehead was the same as the old emperor's, and the eyes were as cold as Sethon's, but set closer. Haio's mouth, however, was all his own: small and mean and currently pursed into petulance.

"Who are you?" he demanded.

For a moment my mind scrabbled—*What am I called, what am I called?* Then my memory found a foothold: Vida snapping at Black Teeth.

"I am Fortune Peony." Relief brought a real smile. I bowed again.

"Well, I didn't order a Peony," he said. "Is this some kind of ploy to create business?"

Momo was right, thank the gods. He *was* a tight arse. "There seems to be have been a misunderstanding, my lord."

I motioned to Vida, kneeling at my side. "My house sister and I are meant as a gift for your brother, His Royal Majesty, the emperor. A token of goodwill from the houses of the Blossom World."

Behind me, I felt unease ripple through the women. A soft vibration of dread.

Haio grunted. "A gift, you say?"

"Why didn't *we* think of such a gift?" a red-faced man said. He and his neighbor clinked their wine bowls together. "We could do with a bit of His Majesty's favor, general. We always get the dregs of gear and men."

Haio looked across at his officers. "You are right in that." He wiped his nose with a thick finger and studied me. "We could take this gift to my brother ourselves," he said slowly. "He doesn't need to know it came from the Blossom World."

I stiffened and heard Vida's sharp intake of air as the men around the table laughed.

I clasped my hands together. "My lord—"

Haio pointed at me. "And you can shut up about who sent you, or I'll find you and cut up that pretty face so you're no good anymore. Understand?"

I ducked my head.

"We could keep the Safflower," Red Face said, peering at Vida. "Just give His Majesty the Peony."

"Keep her?" Haio mused.

"My lord," I said, fighting to keep my voice calm, "my house sister is one of His Majesty's favorites. I would not want your lordship to unknowingly cross your revered brother. "

Haio rubbed at his jaw. "Favorite." He picked up a wine bowl and tossed back its contents. "There's enough flesh here for everyone." He scowled at the men in the circle. "No need to be greedy." He hauled himself onto his feet, swayed slightly, and pointed at Red Face and three other subordinates. "Let's give my brother a late New Year's gift." Haio beckoned to Vida and me. "Come on." He glared at the men still kneeling at the table, his finger swinging around in warning. "Don't you dogs start without us."

I glanced across at Vida. What could we do? Her shoulder lifted slightly. We could do nothing. Not yet. I bent into a low bow again, drew back, and picked up the lute. It would be good for one blow, at least—if I got the chance. It did not look likely; we would be surrounded by five experienced soldiers, not just one or two stewards. I blinked through a sudden blur of panic and forced myself to stand. First things first: get out of the apartment.

I walked around the kneeling women, Vida close behind me. For a moment, I met the wide eyes of Black Teeth. There was such fear in her face—fear for us.

Haio slammed back the screen door and lurched into the foyer. Two of the men fell in behind Vida, their looming presence pushing us both into a faster walk. I glanced back. They were not drunk—their focus was too sharp—and each had a dagger sheathed at his waist. I checked Red Face's waist. He had one, too. It must be part of their uniform. I took a steadying breath and followed Haio out of the front door, every sense primed to find Yuso and give him some sign of what had happened.

I did not have to search far; he was squatting at the end of the wooden platform, throwing dice into a ring made up of Ryko, the Trang Dein man, and two kitchen servants. As Haio called a lewd joke to Red Face, Yuso's head snapped up, hand suspended mid-throw. I saw his mouth tighten in comprehension, and felt a leap of gratitude for his quick intelligence. Barely missing a beat, he finished the throw and eased back, watching us with a grim smile. Beside him, Ryko glanced up, seemingly unconcerned, but both hands tightened on his thighs. Dela was nowhere to be seen.

I shifted the lute to face them and spread four fingers flat across the strings: *Armed.* Then I closed my hand into a fist around the wood: *Sethon.* Would Yuso or Ryko see it and understand? We were already past their position, and I did not dare look back. I did not even dare look back at Vida.

The night air seemed to have focused Haio. His stride lengthened as he led us back toward the lesser banquet hall, our way lit by white paper lanterns strung between the buildings. Soldiers stationed at doorways and corners saluted him as we passed, their presence stoking my dread. I risked a glance at Vida; her head was bowed meekly, but her eyes noted positions, possibilities.

There were none.

From our left, the silhouettes of two men emerged from between the halls, and for a moment my heart hammered with hope—Yuso and Ryko! But the bodies were wrong; lax and soft. Two eunuchs. They hunched into low bows.

"You," Haio called. "Is my brother still dining?"

"He is, your lordship," the senior man answered, bowing even lower.

We climbed the marble steps to the gilded double doors of the banquet hall. The soldier guards on either side saluted and opened them as we approached. I touched my face, feeling the soft, chalky powder over the white paint. High Lord Sethon had met Lord Eon only once, during the triumphal procession where my master had succumbed to poison. I had prostrated myself before the High Lord, begging for assistance. It had not been that long ago. Could he have marked my features enough to recognize me under this Peony mask? My arms and legs fired with the urge to run from such danger, but I forced back the instinct.

"High Lord Haio approaches," another eunuch called as we stepped over the raised threshold and entered the dining hall. The sweet, shivering notes of a flute suddenly stopped, leaving the murmur of male voices. Gradually, that ceased too as we walked into the presence of Emperor Sethon.

He was on a gilded dais at the far end of the chamber, his yellow robes thick with gold embroidery and gems that shimmered in the lamplight. Guests sat below him along two long tables that faced each other. A sharp prod from Red Face hurried me onto my knees, the lute voicing a soft twang as I placed it on the marble floor. I stole a quick glance at the men seated nearby—all senior military. We were in the middle of Sethon's central command. I pressed myself into a flat kowtow, the cold stone against my forehead echoing the freezing fear in my body.

Haio's footsteps clipped an uneven beat as he strode up to the imperial platform. Just behind me, Vida's breathing quickened. I closed my eyes and prayed to Bross. *Courage, give me courage.*

"Greetings, brother, you may rise." Sethon's voice was the same impassive monotone I remembered. "I thought you dined with your men this evening."

"I do, Your Majesty," Haio's voice had shifted from bluff bully to a younger brother's diffidence. "I have brought you a gift. A Peony and one of your favorite Safflowers."

My breath caught. Would Sethon deny having a favorite? He had never seen Vida before. It took all of my control to keep my head down.

"And what has occasioned such a gift?"

Thank the gods—he was more concerned with what lay behind Haio's generosity.

"Nothing, brother. Nothing." Haio cleared his throat. "It is just a gift. For the New Year."

"They have no bearing on your current dissatisfaction?"

His words sent a stir through the men at the tables.

"There is no dissatisfaction, brother," Haio said quickly.

Sethon's disbelief sat heavily in the silence.

"I am glad of it," he finally said. "Stewards, bring my gift to me."

A soft *shush* of slippers on the marble grew closer. A touch to my shoulder brought me back onto my heels. I looked up into the face of a very young eunuch. A long, half-healed gash across his cheekbone marred his smooth skin. He met my gaze and a moment of sympathy flickered across his careful composure. Behind us, an older eunuch helped Vida onto her feet. I picked up the lute and rose, myself. There was no way to stop the momentum that was driving us toward this deadly audience.

I kept my head lowered and followed the young eunuch to the dais. As we passed the tables, I saw the men shift for a better view. We were another part of the evening's entertainment.

The two eunuchs bowed to Sethon and left us at the edge of the platform. I sank to my knees, but still did not lift my head; every moment he did not see my face was a moment that still held hope. I could see the boots of a soldier standing guard behind the gilded chair, and the pearl-and-diamond-encrusted hem of Sethon's long tunic. I swallowed, fear crackling in my ears. Beside me, Vida's hands were clasped so tightly in her lap that the outline of knucklebones showed through the stretched skin.

"Come here, Peony," Sethon said.

My whole body became a heartbeat: all I could feel and hear was the vibrating drum of my fear.

"Now!"

I lurched up the two steps that took me before the false emperor, then sank to my knees again. The gold flowers on my hairpin chimed like a tiny toll as I bowed my head. My hand tightened around the neck of the lute. If only I had Kinra's swords instead. From under my brow I watched a flick of his hand bring four attendants to the table in front of him. They picked it up and carried it off the platform with smooth efficiency. He stretched back in his carved and gilded chair, the action showing the breadth of his warrior body, then pushed himself out of it and stood over me.

"Look up. I wish to see your face."

He was so close that I could see the delicate stitches of gold thread that held the gems to his tunic, and smell the herbs that had been used to sweeten the silk. There could be no more delay. Slowly I raised my head, my gaze fixed on the jade inlaid panel behind him. Even so, his features were framed in the corner of my sight: he was Kygo and the old emperor cast in a scarred, crueler mold.

"You may look at me," he said.

And so I met the eyes of the man who wanted to kill everyone I loved and enslave me. And in their flat stare was a frown of recognition that chilled me to my very core. He reached across and cupped my chin in his calloused hand.

"Have I seen you before?"

Did he remember Lord Eon kneeling before him in the same way, begging for his help? I blinked, praying he did not see the memory in my eyes.

I forced a measured tone. "I have not had that honor, Your Majesty."

He tilted his head, studying me, then pressed his thumb into my cheek and wiped away the white paint over my bruised jaw.

The hard pressure made me flinch. An avid expression crossed his face, like the half-seen flick of a serpent's tail in the grass.

"Someone has been here before me," he said. He turned to Haio. "Have you been tenderizing the meat for me, brother?"

"No," Haio said through the uneasy laughter of the seated men. He held up his hands. "She came straight from her house to you, brother. I would not dream . . ."

Sethon waved him into silence, then tapped my jaw. "Well now, damaged goods no longer have to be handled with care." He released me. "I thank you for your gift, High Lord Haio," he said formally.

Haio bowed. "It is my honor to have pleased Your Majesty."

Sethon beckoned to the two eunuchs who had brought us to the dais. "Take her and the other one to my apartments." Another flick of his hand brought forward one of the soldiers standing behind his chair. "Guard them," he ordered. Then he smiled down at me. "We will be alone soon, little bruised Peony."

His fingertip traced my jaw again and pressed into the heart of the bruise. I winced, but did not dare pull away. The thin smile broadened. "Tell me," he said to the two tables of men below him. "Who was it who said that a flower's true perfume can only be found when it is crushed?"

"The great poet Cho, Your Majesty," someone called, through more laughter.

"Yes," Sethon said, "and we must always follow the truth of our poets."

The two attendants stepped up to flank me. Only habit

bent me into a bow, and only the blind need to get as far from Sethon as possible brought me to my feet.

I backed away, sour bile burning the back of my throat.

"Stay, brother, and have a bowl of wine," Sethon said to Haio.

The two attendants and the guard ushered the two of us along the left wall; we no longer warranted a procession back between the tables. Vida's face was white and rigid, a mirror of my own horror. I touched her hand, but she did not rouse from her eerie, unblinking stare.

We could not afford to lose ourselves in fear. We had to rally—and quickly—or we would end up in Sethon's apartments, at his mercy. Ruthlessly, I caught a pinch of skin on her arm and twisted. Her eyes flickered and refocused. Thank the gods she was still with me. Alone, I could not fight off two eunuchs and a guard, but together we had a chance.

Many of the officers turned to watch us pass, their callous amusement sending another chill through me. A few faces, however, were grim, with lips pressed together in pity. Perhaps those were the men who had daughters and wives.

As we came out onto the front steps, I took Vida's hand in mine. Our guard marked it, but he did not stop my womanly reach for comfort. After all, we were just Blossom Women, and unarmed. He, on the other hand, had a knife and sword, and wore leather armor. Very slowly I curled my hand inside Vida's: the sign for *Attack*. She squeezed my fingers: *Ready*.

But where to make our bid? I dredged up my patchy mental

map of the palace. The most likely route to the royal apartments was the wide path alongside the harem wall. That meant there was only one place we would have a chance to escape: the small passage between the harem and the wall of the West Temple. I made the sign for *Wait* within Vida's damp grip and felt the quick press of acknowledgment.

The two eunuchs led the way, their soft-slippered pace quick and businesslike. My guess had been right; they were taking us in the direction of the harem wall. The young one with the cut face glanced back at us with a frown of unease. Could he sense our plans, or was he just troubled by his duty? I scanned the courtyard, noting the soldiers at the corners of each building. A flicker of movement jerked my attention to a large lion statue guarding a doorway. Did its shadow shift, or was it just my hopeful imagination? Our pace put it behind me before I could doublecheck.

We turned right onto the pathway, and I saw the destruction caused by Ido during the coup. Piles of bricks and debris marked the breach in the harem wall, and I counted at least four soldiers stationed around it. Were they close enough to hear a struggle in the passageway? It did not matter. We had to risk it.

Vida tapped my hand, then flicked her eyes back at our guard, claiming her target. I gave a slight shake of my head and shifted the lute against my chest; it was the only thing we had that approached a weapon. It made more sense for me to attack the armed man. Although her jaw jutted mulishly, she conceded with a soft exhale.

Ahead, the West Temple wall cornered and ran alongside the harem as I had remembered, creating the dark passageway. It curved into a shadowy bend that was perfect for an attack. My back prickled with the presence of the soldier behind me, and the weight of the next minute.

According to Xsu-Ree, surprise is far more important than outnumbering your enemy. Slowly, I tightened my grip around the neck of the lute as the path began to narrow and squeezed Vida's hand again: *Ready.*

As the two eunuchs rounded the bend, I grabbed the lute neck in both hands and swung the sound box at the soldier's head. It slammed into his jaw, the lacquered wood splintering in a sour chord. He staggered back against the temple wall. Vida punched the old eunuch to the cobbles, and grabbed the younger by his queue. He rammed an elbow into her stomach, the two of them hurtling toward me. I jumped out of the way as they slammed against the harem wall, grappling.

I spun to face the soldier. The force of the blow was already receding from his eyes. He drew his knife, blinking me back into focus. I tensed into readiness, all of my attention fixed on the blade.

"No knife!" the old eunuch on the ground gasped. "He'll have us killed if you cut them."

The soldier hesitated. It was all I needed; I drove the jagged end of the lute into the side of his neck, above the armor. The sharp wood pierced flesh and vein, the impact snapping its length in half. A spurt of blood arced into the air; he choked and slashed wildly at me as I jumped backward. His blade caught my forearm, my own momentum pulling it through my flesh in a wash of blood and searing pain. A thousand pinpoints of light exploded across my sight. My back hit the harem wall, its hard surface a mooring in the sudden gray, swirling haze.

A dark figure rose from the ground and came at me. The old eunuch? I swung a fist, but he was suddenly gone. Then came the thud of flesh hitting brick and a low, wet moan. I crouched against the wall, only registering dark shapes and the sounds of movement. My whole arm was a burning pulse of agony.

"Is she all right?" Vida's voice.

A shape loomed through my fog. Instinctively, I hit out at it again, my fingers grazing skin.

"It's all right, Eona."

A hand caught my wrist, and held me still. The gray haze ebbed into Dela's shadowy face. I gasped in relief.

"Let's have a look." Dela pulled my arm away from the brace of my body. We both looked down at the deep gash from elbow to wrist. It immediately welled with fresh blood. "I've seen worse," she said with a quick smile of reassurance, but there was worry in her eyes. "Are you sure you cannot use your healing power?"

"It would bring the ten dragons," I said. "Like in the fisher village." I took a deep, shaking breath. "When I heal Ido, the power should heal me, too."

At least that is what I hoped would happen.

Dela quickly ripped a strip of cloth from her tunic. A few

folds made it a field dressing. She pressed it to the wound, then deftly bound the rest of the cloth over it, the firm pressure sending a surge of pain up my arm. "Keep a tight grip on it," she said.

Nearby, Vida held the young eunuch at knifepoint against the temple wall. The slumped form of the soldier was at their feet. Dela edged back the way we had come and peered out, then did the same for the path ahead.

"No one coming," she whispered. She bent to check the guard.

"Dead?" I asked. But the overpowering stench of urine and bowels had already answered me.

"Yes." Dela rose and crossed to the other eunuch. "This one, too." She grabbed the dead attendant under the arms and dragged him farther back into the shadows, then rolled the body against the red brick wall. "We need to get out of here. This passage is too well used."

I tried to force my mind beyond the stinking presence of death and the pain humming through my head. We had to get to the Pavilion of Autumnal Justice; the cells were part of its compound. I closed my eyes and pictured the layout of the palace again. The fastest route was across the forecourt of the royal apartments, but it was also well lit and well guarded. My inner map showed another possibility. The servants' path ran the whole way around the palace wall—a hidden track for the low and menial to navigate without being seen. And it was never guarded.

"The servants' path will be safest," I said. "We can get to it up past the royal apartments. Or we could go around the front of the West Temple and beside the kitchens."

"Both have soldiers posted," Dela said.

"Apartments," the young eunuch whispered.

Vida jerked the knife closer to his throat. "Shut up."

Dela walked over to him. "Why do you say that?"

He lifted his chin. "Blossom Women are brought to the royal apartments all the time. They never go to the kitchens."

"Why do you offer this?"

"I am already dead," he said, eyeing the knife. "If you do not kill me, His Majesty will, and not as quickly." The round curves of his face sharpened. "If I must die, I will at least deny him two more victims of his sick pleasure."

"He is right," Dela said. "The royal apartments are closer, and we will have a better chance of deceiving the guards."

"Take me with you," the eunuch said quickly. "It will look more authentic."

Vida leaned in. "You will just call for help."

"No, no—please! Take me with you. I cannot stay here anymore."

Dela stared intently at him. "All right, we'll take you," she said, stopping Vida's protest with a raised hand. "But you have said it yourself—Sethon will kill you as surely as I take my next breath. We are your best chance of survival, so do as we say."

"And I will have this knife at your back the whole time," Vida added.

I remembered the sympathy in the young man's face as he led me toward his royal master, and felt a leap of grim intuition.

Sethon did not limit himself to Blossom Women. "You will not give us up," I said to the eunuch. "Will you."

He met the knowledge in my eyes. "No."

Vida snorted with disbelief. I levered myself upright and leaned against the wall. "Where are Ryko and Yuso?"

Dela looked up from removing the dead guard's helmet, her eyes bleak. "I saw two soldiers join their dice game." She bent to untie the man's leather vest armor. "If they can get rid of them, they know where to meet us."

The god of luck was playing his own games. Mustering my strength, I pushed myself off the wall. The world pitched and spun, then settled again into gray shadows. At least the haze had not returned. I cradled my arm against my ribcage, my fingers still clamped over the wet, pulsing wound.

With a soft grunt, Dela pulled the vest over the dead man's head. His body flopped back against the wall, a sickening reminder of Yuso pulling his sword from Lieutenant Haddo's chest. I shivered, but it was not all from horror. I felt hot and cold at the same time.

Dela slid the vest over her head and knotted the side ties. Although she hated dressing as a man, she made a convincing soldier. Her movements were always quicker and bolder in men's garb. All the womanly control and grace—gone.

She looked up at the walls on either side of us, topped with slanting tiles. "Too high to throw the bodies over," she said, tucking her greased hair under the helmet. "We'll have to leave them, but they'll be found soon." She picked up the sword. "Ready?"

I nodded and stepped beside Vida, the simple action bringing a wave of nausea. Although a deep breath steadied me, fresh blood oozed through the field bandage and my fingers. I shifted my good arm over the wound; the wide silk sleeve would hide most of the blood from view. Hopefully, I would not drip a trail behind us.

Vida held the knife poised behind the eunuch, the end of his sash wrapped around her other hand. She smiled reassuringly at me, then prodded him between his shoulder blades.

"Walk normally," she ordered.

I heard him whisper a prayer. Then he moved forward, leading us out of the shadowy protection of the passage.

We rounded the corner of the harem; before us rose the two enormous red and gold palaces that formed the royal apartments. Each was raised on a marble terrace with a staircase guarded by two gilded lions. Heavy brass braziers lined the steps, creating two majestic paths of light up to the identical porticos. Twelve red columns—topped by carved jade emblems—supported each gold tiled roof that curved up toward the heavens: a harmonious meeting of the earthly and celestial planes. And to enhance the good fortune of the Heavenly Son and his empress, a water garden stretched between the two residences, the pale moonlight picking out the arch of a formal bridge and the answering genuflection of twelve ghostly water trees.

Yet it was not this grandiose beauty that caught my breath. It was the soldiers posted every few lengths around the terrace walls.

"Holy Shola," I whispered. "So many."

The eunuch glanced back at me. "There are fewer alongside the empress's residence," he said softly.

It was logical; the residence was empty. Sethon had not summoned his old wife to sit by his side as empress. Still, even with fewer guards, the avenue between the residence and the West Temple would make an excellent trap if the eunuch planned to betray us, after all.

Vida's hand tightened around her knife; she must have come to the same conclusion. If it came to a fight, there would not be much I could do. Every step I took brought a fresh welling of blood through my fingers, and a chill had settled on my skin. Even worse, there was a lightness in my head that made the world pitch and sway.

We crossed the perimeter of the forecourt, the eunuch keeping us at the edge of the light thrown by the bronze braziers. The two soldiers at the corner of the empress's residence shifted to watch us walk by. I clamped my fingers more tightly around my arm, hoping they could not see the dark saturation of blood on my silk sleeve. A strange sound brought my head up. One of the soldiers was kissing the air, gesturing at his groin. His partner snorted, the noise attracting the attention of two sentries farther along the wall. The eunuch looked back at us, his eyes wide with terror.

"Turn around," Vida whispered urgently. He obeyed, but his body was stiff with fear.

From the corner of my eye, I saw Dela gesture obscenely at the gyrating kisser. "You wish," she called, her voice rough.

He gestured back, but subsided.

I lifted my chin, fighting to keep my breath even.

"Keep moving," Dela urged softly.

We turned into the wide lane that ran between the temple and the empress's residence. At the very end was the main palace wall, and beneath it, the dark track of the servants' path. So far away. We had to pass at least ten more sentries along the terrace wall. I fixed my eyes on the ground and concentrated on keeping up with the eunuch's brisk pace. A mesmerizing pattern of light and dark stones passed beneath my feet. I counted the sentries, trying to focus past the racing rhythm of my heart. Four . . . five . . . six. My whole being listened for a shout or the hiss of a drawn blade, but all I could hear was my hard breathing and the shrill, throbbing song of the frogs in the water garden.

The palace wall loomed ahead. We passed the last sentry and I saw his head turn to follow our progress. The urge to run the last few lengths surged through me. I grabbed Vida's arm, praying I would not stagger. We finally crunched onto the rough gravel of the servants' path—dark, narrow, and thank the gods, deserted.

Dela ushered us behind the thick hedge grown to hide the passage of the palace menials. Vida half carried me along the dim, pot-holed path until I stumbled and pitched forward, kicking up a spray of dirt and pebbles. Strong hands caught me under my arms and eased me onto the uneven ground.

"Put your head between your knees," Dela said, pressing my head down. She crouched in front of me and pulled my hand off my arm. The wet dressing stuck to my palm and yanked the cloth out of the wound, ripping a gasp from me.

"Sorry," Dela whispered. "Vida, I think she's still bleeding. Get something else to bind it."

I hung my head, breathing through the pain. The world was spinning around me again.

Vida took Dela's place in front of me. "Let me have a look."

The eunuch peered over her shoulder. She took my arm in a firm grasp and peeled back a larger section of the cloth with a low grunt of concern. "There's not enough light to see properly, but from the feel of this bandage, you've lost a lot of blood."

She unwound the sash from her waist and folded it into a pad, then pressed it over the wet dressing, using the ends to tie it in place.

"Hold it up against your chest," she said, lifting my arm across my body. The weak moonlight caught her frown. "Your skin is cold."

I caught her sleeve. "Don't let me pass out. If I pass out, I won't be able to heal Ido. Everything will be lost."

At Ido's name the eunuch stepped back. "Do you mean Lord Ido, the Dragoneye? The prisoner?" He retreated a few more steps, pebbles clinking loudly in the sudden tense silence. "I thought you were Blossom Women. Who are you?"

Dela stepped up to him, her hands held out as though she were calming a nervous horse.

"It's all right," she said, then punched him in the face, the snapping blow so fast and so heavy that he staggered backward, sat down on the pebbles, then toppled over.

I gaped at the still figure lying in front of me. Knocked on his arse like the eunuch clown in the fool's opera.

The ludicrous comparison rose through my shock in a quivering curl of laughter. I bit down on the building wave of whimsy—it was callous and wrong—but it broke out of me in uncontrollable giggles. I clamped my hand over my mouth. It had to stop. The poor eunuch had been punched senseless. We were in extreme danger. Which was suddenly hilarious. I rocked forward and shoved my bloodied knuckles into my mouth, trying to force back the spasms that caught my breath into snorting gasps.

Vida stared at me, a horrified smile pulling at her lips.

"Stop it," she hissed. The words hiccupped into a snuffling giggle. She pressed both hands against her mouth. "Stop it." But her shoulders shook, her eyes filling with tears. The sight pushed me further into gulping spasms.

Dela's hands caught my shoulders, holding me still.

"Eona, calm down. You've lost a lot of blood. You need to *calm down!*"

The low urgency in her voice broke through my hysteria. I sucked in a breath, fighting for control. The fluttering crest of a giggle ebbed away, leaving only the thudding pain in my arm.

Dela looked at Vida. "I don't know what *your* excuse is," she said acidly.

Vida wiped her eyes. "Sorry."

"Get up and help me roll him under the hedge."

"Is he all right?" I asked.

"He's still alive, if that's what you mean." Dela hooked her hands under my armpits and helped me to my feet. For a moment everything was still, then the hedge and the wall rushed past me in a spin of nausea. I swayed and fell back into the tight embrace of Dela's arms.

"Eona?" Her face blurred in and out of focus.

My heartbeat resonated in my ears, fast and labored. At the base of my skull, a sick ache drummed in the same ominous rhythm.

"Get me to Ido, quick," I said, the words like sludge in my mouth.

CHAPTER FOURTEEN

DELA HITCHED ME up higher on her back and edged into the shadowy portico of the Pavilion of Autumnal Justice. Under the tight hook of my good arm, I felt her chest still heaving from the effort of sprinting from the Pavilion of Five Ghosts. I blinked through my own weariness; I had to stay awake. Already I had half stepped into the shadow world twice; only Vida's vigilant pinches had pulled me back from crossing into oblivion.

Dela's quick breathing lengthened into a sigh. The portico was empty. Yuso and Ryko had not yet arrived. Had they been caught? Were they still alive? I pushed the grim rush of possibilities away. They must make it to the pavilion: without them, our soldier and Blossom Woman ruse would not succeed.

I licked my lips, trying to find some spittle in my mouth. The last time I'd felt such thirst had been at the salt farm. Dela pointed to a tall, heavily carved recess: its dark alcove held the promise of good concealment and a decent view of the courtyard and cells. With Vida leading, we crept to our new vantage point using the thick columns that fronted the portico as cover. Vida pressed herself into the corner of the deep niche, shifting position until she had a sightline of the cells.

"Let me down," I whispered against Dela's ear.

Her head turned, stubbled cheek brushing mine. "Are you sure?"

She had carried me all the way from the servants' path and the trembling in her shoulders and legs vibrated through me.

"I'll be all right." It was more of a hope than a certainty.

She relaxed her arms and let me drop to my feet. For a moment, all was steady—then the world lurched, and a gray haze billowed across my vision.

"She's going again," Vida hissed.

Her voice sounded far away. My legs folded.

Dela spun and caught me. "I've got you."

I nodded, although the pain in my arm lodged in my throat like a dry retch. How was I going to get past the cell guards if I could not even stand? Dela gently maneuvered me against the carved wooden wall of the pavilion. With the solid support behind me, I rode the wave of dizziness.

"Rest." Dela eased me down the wall until I sat on the stone floor. She crouched beside me. "You're so cold." Her arm circled my shoulders. The smell of leather and grease rose from the damp heat of her body.

And so the wait for Yuso and Ryko began. Although my body yearned for rest, I tensed at every night noise and flickering shadow. At some point, three lamp-eunuchs filed into the courtyard and lit the large pedestal lanterns set at intervals in a raked pebble border, the flare of each wick accompanied by a chime of thanks from a small prayer bell. Although they did not come near the portico, I still retreated farther into our hiding place, glad of its deep, shadowed embrace. From my position, I could see only one of the two guards posted outside the cell doorway; he wore a leather and iron vest and held a *Ji*, his dutiful scrutiny of the wide courtyard interrupted by yawns and a bottle shared with his partner. Both bored, then, and open to breaking the rules.

We waited, every passing minute adding another lead weight of fear.

"What if they don't make it?" Vida finally whispered beside us.

"They will." Dela was firm. "Ryko will move the heavens to get here."

A heavy silence settled over us. Vida shifted uncomfortably, her attention still on Dela. She gave a small nod—as if coming to a hard decision—then touched Dela's arm. "Ryko loves you," she whispered.

"What?" Dela's body tensed against mine.

"You love him," Vida said. "Don't waste time. Men die fast in war."

Her eyes flicked to me, their stark sorrow pinning me against the pavilion wall. I looked away from the grief I had caused.

"This is hardly the place," Dela said through her teeth. She turned back to scanning the courtyard, her disquiet like a thrum through her body.

We all turned at the soft scuff of boots on stone.

Vida half rose, knife in hand. Dela's arm tightened around my shoulder, ready to lift me, as two dark figures paused in the shadows cast by the columns. But there was no mistaking the broad shape of Ryko, or lean Yuso. Dela's hold relaxed as Vida beckoned the two men across the portico.

Darting from column to column, Ryko and Yuso made their way toward us. They wore uniforms; no doubt the two soldiers who had joined the dice game were either dead or trussed up somewhere. Hard on them, but a victory for us. We were now three soldiers and two Blossom Women eager to see the Dragoneye in the cells.

"Are you all right?" Ryko whispered to Dela.

I could feel the softening within her at the sound of his voice.

"Lady Eona is hurt," she reported. "Knife to the forearm. Lost a lot of blood."

The news sent Yuso squatting before me, his face intent. "Can you still go ahead?"

I nodded, but closed my eyes as the world swirled again. I felt Yuso's calloused hand brush my cheek, his thumb finding the race of my pulse. His touch felt so like Sethon's that I flinched.

He pulled back with a frown. "We won't wait for the shift change. We go in now."

"That will only give us a half bell before the new guards," Ryko whispered.

"It can't be helped. Lady Eona does not have the strength to wait." Yuso clasped my good arm and pulled me upright. "Ryko, carry her."

Hands helped me onto Ryko's broad back. I rested my chin against the solid beam of his shoulders, my useless arm dangling over his chest. The whole limb was numb now. A small blessing, except I could feel the numbness spreading through my body. Everything was distant; sounds muffled, objects blurred, even the heat of Ryko's body against mine barely penetrated the cold armor of my exhaustion.

It seemed to take forever to edge from column to column. The guards were sharing another illicit drink, and Ryko moved only when their attention was on the pass of the bottle. I counted my breaths between each wait, trying to turn my mind from the shivering weakness that kept loosening my grip around Ryko's neck. We finally edged around the corner of the pavilion, beyond the guards' sightline. Ryko scanned the training compound before us—the dark hall and the raked expanse of the training sands were deserted—then ran across to the narrow set of rear steps.

One by one the others ran from the shadowed portico and joined us. Ryko tightened his hold around my waist and turned his head, our noses almost touching.

"All right?" he whispered.

"All right," I lied.

He nodded, but he was not fooled.

Yuso signed us forward. We skirted the training sands and headed toward the long rear wall of the imperial guard barracks. Before the coup, Ryko and Yuso had been quartered there along with the other imperial guards, but now it housed over two hundred soldiers. Or even more, according to Mama Momo. The dark wall bordered the whole length of the training compound and reached beyond the Pavilion of Autumnal Justice. I had not realized how close the barracks were to the cells. Dangerously within yelling distance.

At the edge of the training compound, Yuso signed a halt.

"From here," he whispered.

Ryko eased me down onto my feet. I swayed and felt hands grab the silk at my back—Dela, an anchor in the swirling, pitching world.

"She can't walk by herself," Dela hissed over my shoulder.

"Between you two, then," Yuso ordered.

Dela circled her arm across my shoulders, Ryko around my waist. Between them I was held upright, my injured arm hidden from view.

Yuso draped his arm over Vida's shoulders, then glanced back at us. "Ready?"

And so we stepped through the elegant gateway that separated the training compound from the courtyard of justice: three drunken soldiers and their giggling companions looking for fresh entertainment.

The iron grips of Ryko and Dela kept me moving forward. I smiled up at their laughing banter, hoping the strain did not show on my face. We passed the Pavilion of Autumnal Justice, the pools of lamplight hollowing Dela's eyes and catching the gleam of sweat at Ryko's temples.

I chanced a look at the guards. Our stumbling, giggling progress across the courtyard had drawn them close together in front of the doorway. They watched our approach, all evidence of boredom and bottle gone.

Ryko nuzzled my hair. "Almost there," he breathed. "Almost there."

Beside the door, a bronze gong hung from a sturdy wooden frame, ready to alert the men in the barracks if we made one misstep. For a moment, I closed my eyes, overwhelmed by the hazards ahead. Even if we did get inside the cell to Ido and I managed to heal him, we also had to get past those two hundred men.

I opened my eyes as Yuso bowed to the guards. "Evening." He swayed on the return, his drunken grin perfectly judged. "The lovely Dara and Sela here"—he pointed a wavering finger at Vida, then spun around and jabbed it toward me—"would like to view the mighty Dragoneye." He squinted at the two men. "They've never seen one."

Yuso was a convincing liar.

The older sentry shook his head. "My apologies, honored Leopard. As you must know, it is not possible." He wore a Bear ranked badge, lower than Yuso's stolen seventh-rank uniform.

Yuso grinned. "Come on, I've heard otherwise," he said.

"Don't disappoint the girls. We promised them." He caught Vida by the waist and pulled her against him. She squealed and giggled. "Say please, Dara."

"Please," Vida said. "Let us go on. We could make it worth your while . . . afterward."

Bear looked across at his younger partner badged with a Snake, the lowest rank.

"We get off in a quarter bell, sir," Snake murmured. He eyed Vida and smiled.

"That one looks sick," Bear said, jerking his head at me. I felt Ryko's arm pull me closer.

Dela snorted. "Sela chases the dragon a bit hard, don't you, sweetheart?"

I smiled dreamily and lolled my head against Ryko's chest. With the courtyard pitching around me, it was not hard to emulate the boneless distraction of a dragon chaser.

Bear peered more closely at my face. "Is she a real Peony?" Suspicion colored his voice. "A real Peony costs a Tiger coin."

"Of course she's not," Dela said quickly. "We can't afford a real Peony."

"What is she doing in Peony makeup, then?" Bear shifted his *Ji* forward.

I felt Ryko's heart quicken through the padding of his vest. For all of our planning, we had not prepared a reason why a Peony would be with low-ranked soldiers.

With the dregs of my strength, I mustered a high-pitched giggle and raised my head. "It's an extra half-coin for the makeup. I do Orchids, too. That's a full coin, but it includes a dance." Clumsily I circled my hips, glad of Ryko's arm bracing me.

"A dance?" Young Snake said, his eyes lingering on my body.

I summoned another smile. "Not boring dances like the real Orchids. A *real* dance."

Bear cleared his throat, his eyes cutting to his subordinate. "We could never afford such attentions, even at that price." He scratched his chin. "Not on our very, very low pay." He made the statement a question.

Yuso smiled. "How much, then, to see the Dragoneye?"

"A sixth. Per person," Bear said promptly.

"Outrageous," Yuso countered. "A twelfth per person."

"Done." Bear licked his lips and exchanged a smug glance with Snake. "Keep it short, though. We're relieved at the full bell."

Yuso handed over the coins, the ringing clink of their fall like one of the small prayer chimes.

Bear opened the wooden door and peered into the dimly lit chamber. "Got five for you. They've paid."

He stepped back, ushering us in with a broad smile. "Enjoy."

Yuso entered first with Vida, her giggling thanks diverting the guards' attention. As Ryko and I followed them over the raised threshold, Dela quickly stepped behind us and threw her arms over our shoulders; the embrace of a drunken friend, and a shield for my bloodied arm.

We were inside. As the wooden door shut, the rush of relief made me stumble. Dela caught my upper arm and pulled me into the support of her body. I remembered to giggle, but a freeze of fear locked in my gut. Ido was so close . . . and I could barely stand on my own. Did I have enough strength to help him? To even help myself?

"A few rules." The harsh voice came from a squat, jowled man behind a desk in the corner of the small chamber. Every one of his features—lips, nose, even eyelids—was overly thick, as though swollen with water. "You can only look through the door bars. And only two at a time. Got it?"

With a grunt, he pushed himself out of his chair and reached for a lamp hanging from a hook in the wall behind him—one of two handsome bronze lanterns that cast good light over the desk's orderly collection of scrolls, pens, and a deeply grooved ink block. Nearby, a small ceramic stove held glowing coals, the bitterness of burned rice and over-brewed tea barely covering another smell that made my stomach turn—the sour stink of suffering.

He held the lamp close to his face, the yellowed light sculpting the jut of his nose and rubbery lips. "Through the door bars. Two at time. Got it?"

"Got it," Yuso said. "Are there any other interesting prisoners in there?"

"No, he's got the whole place to himself," the warden said. "Nothing too good for the Dragoneye Lord, eh?" He offered the lamp to Vida. "Hold this for me, my dear, while I let you in."

With a pretty smile, she took the lamp and followed him to the sturdy inner door. Yuso stepped out of their way as the warden unhooked a set of heavy keys from his belt and held them up to the light, their polished brass tops glinting in his thick fingers.

"This one will get you into the cell itself," he said. "Maybe if you play your cards right, you can have a closer look."

Behind him, a duller gleam of metal caught my eye: Yuso's blade sliding silently from its sheath.

"I'd like that," Vida said. A tilt of the captain's head edged her back a step.

The warden inserted the key into the lock. "Me, too." He gave a low laugh as the lock clicked and the door swung open. "You just give me a call and—"

With savage speed, Yuso clamped his arm around the man's chest and thrust the knife into the sacral point, low and hard. The warden arched back, the brutal flex of his throat stifling his cry. Yuso yanked out the bloodied blade, raised it again, and plunged it over the man's shoulder, hard into his chest. The only sounds were the soft thud of hilt hitting home and a tiny wet gasp. The man's weight sagged against Yuso.

I let out a long, ragged breath—I had not even realized I was holding it. Ryko had spun around to cover the entrance, knife ready. But the door did not open; neither guard had heard the muted sounds of death.

Yuso eased the warden's body to the ground and dragged it out of the inner doorway. He looked around at us, the violence still raging in his eyes.

"Get going," he ordered.

Vida ripped the ring of keys from the lock, then forged down the shallow set of steps, lamp held up to light the way. I started to follow, but my knees buckled, the fall stopped by Dela's quick reflexes.

"I've got you," she said. "Just lean on me."

Together, we lurched down the steps into a stone corridor. Ahead, Vida's lamp showed a narrow downward slope and low ceiling. The stench of human pain—sweat, vomit, blood—caught in my throat, some primal part of me fighting the descent toward it.

"Holy gods, that's foul," Ryko said behind us.

"Here! He's in here," Vida called from the far end of the corridor, the ring of keys jangling as she fitted one into a lock.

Dela hauled me past three empty cells, the dark maws of their open doorways waiting for new flesh. The stink seemed embedded in the stone around us, our movements stirring small currents of air like fetid breath. We reached Vida as she pushed Ido's cell door open and held up the lamp.

The light found him against the back wall: naked, starved body curled side-on against the stone, his forehead pressed into the cradle of his shackled hands. The slow rise and fall of his chest rasped with effort, but he did not stir. His head had been shorn, the two sleek Dragoneye queues reduced to matted spikes. The one eye visible to us was swollen, the strong shape of cheekbone and jaw below it lost in a dark mess of blood and bruising. His nose, too, had been broken, its thin patrician length smashed and swollen. But the worst injuries were on his body: someone had taken a cane to his back and legs and the soles of his feet, and they had not stopped at shredding skin and muscle. The exposed bone and sinew across his shoulders caught the light like slivers of pearl.

"How could he survive that?" Vida whispered.

An image of the Rat Dragon—pale and agonized—leaped into my mind. Was the beast keeping him alive?

Vida pressed her hand over her nose and led us into the cell. A slops bucket, from the smell of it, sat in the far corner. In sharp contrast, an elegant table—its legs carved into four dragons—stood against the left wall. It held a porcelain bowl, the delicate gold edge encrusted with dark ooze, and a jumble of sharp metal objects that my eyes skipped across but my body registered with a shiver. A bamboo cane—half of its length stained with blood—lay on the floor beside a water bucket.

Vida put the lamp down next to Ido as Dela lowered me into a crouch beside him. I had not noted it before, but his beard was gone. Its absence, together with the close crop of his hair, made his face seem strangely young. Vida drew in a shocked breath as the concentration of lamplight showed more injuries. Both shackled feet were broken—the delicate fan of bones smashed and protruding through the skin—and a large character had been carved on his chest: *Traitor.* I leaned against the wall beside him. How could I heal such terrible damage while I was so weak?

"He's going to need some clothes," Dela said tightly. "I'll get the warden's." She squeezed my shoulder. "Be quick. Even Ido doesn't deserve this."

Across the room, Ryko picked up the bowl and sniffed the

contents. He thrust it away with a grimace. "Black Dragon."

I looked up at him blankly. Vida crossed the room and sniffed the bowl, too, nodding her confirmation.

"It constricts blood," she said. "That must be why he hasn't bled to death."

"That's not the only thing it does." Ryko put the bowl down on the table. "I've seen it used to heighten pain and unleash demons in the mind." The islander had more reason than anyone to hate Ido—the Dragoneye had tortured him—but there was something akin to pity in his voice. "If they've been feeding this to him, he won't know what's real and what's not."

I looked at Lord Ido's ruined, sweat-filmed face. If he could not distinguish between reality and nightmare, he would not be able to hold back the ten bereft dragons.

"We've got to wake him," I said, panic rising into a surge of desperate energy. "I need him awake."

I reached across and touched his hand. Even more chilled and clammy than my own.

"Lord Ido?"

No response. I shook his cold arm.

Not even a flicker.

"Lord Ido," I shook him harder. "It's me, Eona."

Nothing. He was far beyond a simple touch and call. More drastic measures were needed—more brutality. The thought of adding to such pain made me nauseous. But if he and I were to be healed, he had to be woken. Pushing past my own pity, I dug my fingers into the ridged, weeping damage across his shoulder.

His whole body flinched under my grip, his hands convulsing against the shackles. I jerked back. Surely that would wake him. But his eyes remained closed, no twitch of animation upon his drawn face.

"He's not waking," I said.

"Try again." Vida crossed the room.

I dug my fingers in harder. "Lord Ido!"

This time the pain flung him back against the wall, the raw contact shuddering through him. Even that did not open his eyes.

"He's deep in the shadow world. Probably a blessing," Vida said. She held up the warden's ring of keys. "I'll undo the shackles. Maybe that will speak to his spirit."

She fitted a slim key into the wrist irons, the heavy cuffs separating with a hollow click. Ido's hands dropped, their raw, bloodied weight slapping against his thighs. The freedom did not stir him. Vida bent and unlocked the ankle irons. "I can't pull them free." Her voice was small. "I think they've broken his feet in them."

Ryko squatted beside me and set the water bucket on the stones between us. He grabbed a handful of ragged hair and pulled Ido's head up. His pity, it seemed, did not translate into gentleness. "Lord Dragoneye. *Wake up.*"

The harsh, slow breathing did not alter.

Ryko pushed Ido's head back against the wall, then stood and picked up the bucket. "You might want to move," he said to me.

The water hit Ido in the face with a drenching force that caught me in its cold backsplash. I gasped, wiping the wet sting out of my eyes. It had certainly roused me from my exhaustion. I blinked and focused on Ido. The dripping water tracked through the crusted filth and blood on his face, but he was still beyond us.

I turned away as Ryko swung the bucket again. The water slapped and streamed over the Dragoneye. We all leaned forward, watching for any flicker across the closed eyes, or change in the rasping rise and fall of his chest.

"He's too far gone," Ryko said.

"No!" Frantically I shook Ido again, the back of his head thudding against the wall. "Wake up!"

Vida pulled my hand away. "Eona, stop!"

"If he's not awake, I can't risk healing him," I said through my teeth. "The other dragons will come, and he won't be there to stop them."

Ryko stood. "He's not going to wake any time soon. We're going to have to carry him out."

"It'll kill him," Vida protested.

"Maybe, but we can't leave him here."

The sound of running footsteps turned us toward the doorway. Dela rounded the corner, clothes piled in her arms. "Yuso is keeping watch in the front room," she panted. "But he says hurry, we've only got a few minutes before the new guard shift."

"We can't get Ido awake," I said. "I can't heal him."

She dumped the clothes on the filthy stone floor. "Let me have a look."

Ryko made way as she leaned over and peeled back Ido's left eyelid. The pale amber iris was almost all black pupil. Then something moved across the dark dilation—a slide of silver.

Dela recoiled. "What was that?"

Hua.

I lunged forward, lifting his eyelid again. The silver was dull and its shift across his eye slower than I had ever seen before, but it was definitely his power. "He's not in the shadow world. He's in the energy world."

"Is that good?" Vida asked.

"It means he's probably with his dragon already." I released his eyelid and sat back, remembering the blue dragon reaching toward me. Was it possible that Ido had taken refuge *in* his spirit beast?

"Does that mean you can heal him?" Ryko demanded.

I looked down at my bound arm. A slow throb was building through the numbness, leaching energy with every pulsing ache. I was not sure I had enough strength to get into the energy world. And even if I did, the ten bereft dragons were so *fast.* By my reckoning, I had less than a minute to find Ido and heal him before they attacked.

"I have to try," I said. "Everyone stand back. You saw what happened last time."

All three edged away to the other side of the cell.

Help me, I prayed to any god who listened, and pressed my hand flat against Ido's wet chest, above the brutally carved character. His labored heartbeat thudded under my palm. A tight knot of terror clamped my breath. What if I could not do it? What if I killed us all?

I forced my way through the fear, each deep inhalation easing my chest open until I found a familiar, deepening rhythm: the pathway to the energy world. My exhaustion dragged at me, a treacherous riptide that I had to fight with every breath. Under my hand, Ido's heartbeat began to match mine, the ragged rise and fall of his chest blending into my own steady measure. The dim physical world around us twisted and bent into bright colors and streaming *Hua*.

Before me, the solid suffering of Ido's body shifted into patterns of energy. Pain slashed and spun through his meridians in sharp, jagged bursts of *Hua*. Each of his seven points of power circled slowly, the silver pathways hampered by a thick black ooze. I looked closer. The points, from red sacrum to purple crown, turned in the wrong direction. I had seen it before in Dillon.

Ido was using *Gan Hua*.

Ryko, Dela, and Vida braced themselves in the far corner, *Hua* pumping through their transparent bodies in dazzling streams of silver. They could not see the Mirror Dragon above them or sense her power, but to me her vibrant energy radiated like a small sun, searing away the shadows of the dank cell. She focused her otherworldly eyes upon me and I felt my *Hua* leap to meet her huge, shimmering presence. Her sinuous neck stretched toward me, the gold pearl under her chin alive with surging flames. Cinnamon flooded my mouth, her warm, joyous invitation bringing tears to my eyes.

But I could not accept it. Not yet.

I dragged my attention from her glowing beauty and focused on the Rat Dragon crouched in the north-northeast corner, his wedged head bowed and pale flanks heaving. The power from the beast was sour and dull, a muddy energy creating pockets of darkness within the streams of bright color that flowed from my dragon.

Lord Ido? I called silently. *Are you in there?*

The beast slowly lifted his head. The large eyes were not depthless, like the Mirror Dragon's. They were amber and clouded with pain.

Ido's eyes.

"By the gods, you *are* in your beast!" I said, shocked into speaking aloud. "How is that possible?"

Eona. Ido's hoarse mind-voice was full of disbelief. *What are you doing here?*

I pushed past my own astonishment and answered him mind to mind. *I'm here to heal you.*

Heal me?

Yes, but I need your help. The other dragons will come and I can't hold them back. I need you to block them like you did before. In the fisher village.

Ido's dragon eyes met mine, their sudden human shrewdness at odds with the ferocious blue-scaled head and fanged muzzle. *Why do you take this risk? What do you want?*

For all his torment, he had not lost any sharpness of mind.

I want you to train me.

Ahh. The big wedge head slowly cocked to one side. *And what do I get from this bargain?*

You get your life! What more do you want? Yet part of me admired his attempt to shift even this dire situation to his advantage.

The thin dragon tongue flicked. *I will have one other thing.*

You have no power to bargain, Lord Ido.

You have no power without me.

The blunt truth jerked my hand off his human chest. Across the cell, the dragon's head lowered, watching me. Ido knew he had hit home. I could call his bluff, but we were both running out of time.

What do you want? I asked.

The red folio.

Of course. Ido had always wanted the folio. He had stolen it twice already, but had never got past its black pearl guardians. Rapidly, I gauged the risk; the Woman Script and codes would keep any secrets I did not want to share. Even so, I knew Ido could use information like an assassin's knife. A compromise, then.

You cannot have the folio, but I will tell you what it holds.

Agreed. But I could feel his dissatisfaction.

Are you ready?

The huge opal talons spread, bracing for my power. *Be very fast, Eona. I am almost too long gone.*

For the first time, I heard a note of fear in his mind-voice. I pressed my hand against his cold, bloodied chest and gathered all of my own waning strength into the call to my dragon. Even as the first vowel of our shared name rang out in the cell, her power rushed through me, filling my seven points of power with raw golden energy that thrummed in a song of joyous union.

My vision split between heaven and earth, the cell heaving with bright *Hua* around the darkened shape of Ido. *Heal him*, I thought. *Heal him, before they come*. No time to slowly sing the body whole. No time to delicately knit flesh and bone. *Heal him, now!* Through dragon eyes, we saw the gossamer threads that stretched between the man and his beast, the earth world and energy. Too frail, too dark. In the distance, we heard the shriek of sorrow ten times over—the other dragons were on their way, keening the loss of their Dragoneyes. And under their shrill song came another sound: a bell, ringing over and over again.

The pulsing patterns of *Hua* that we knew as Ryko ran to the doorway. "The alarm! They must have discovered us. Eona, hurry!"

We felt our power coil, tight and strong, drawing energy from every point—the earth, the air, the waters, the heartbeats of a thousand living things—into one huge, pulsing, healing howl. We were *Hua*, and we slammed our raw song into Ido's earthly form.

He screamed as our power wrenched him back into his tortured body, then exploded through every inner pathway. *Hua* roared through him, a fireball that fused torn flesh together, welded bone, and purified his leaden life force back into bright silver streams.

Ido fell on to his hands and knees, gasping. He looked up at us, and for a moment the planes of his energy face shifted into solid flesh, his shoulders and back once more dense muscle and smooth skin. Then his features shivered and shaped back into the rush of healing *Hua*. The silver coursed through his seven points of power, the orbs once more spinning in the right direction. My eyes found the heart point I had healed before; although it was now flowing with strong *Hua*, it was once again smaller and duller than the others. Did he still have the compassion I had forced upon him? And there was another difference that drew my gaze up to his crown point, the seat of the spirit. Deep within its whirling purple sphere was a small gap, black and malignant. I had never seen such darkness before in a point of power.

Beyond him, the vibrant form of the Rat Dragon stretched into sinuous strength. The beast's sky blue body expanded and rippled, pulsing with the exchange of energy. He swung his head up, delicate nostrils flaring, and then we heard it, too: shrieking grief, its pressure building around us. Our heavy muscles bunched, ready for battle.

"*Get out!*" I yelled at Ryko.

The ten dragons burst into the cramped space, their brutal power gouging huge chunks of stone from the walls that spun and smashed across the floor. Through dragon eyes, we saw Ryko wrench Dela and Vida into the corridor as choking dust billowed through the cell. My earthly body doubled over, coughing, as the grieving beasts hurled themselves at us.

The Rat Dragon arrowed across the path of the western beasts, slashing with opal claws that drew gushes of bright *Hua* from the Dog and Pig Dragons. They pulled away, screaming. Our big red body rammed the green Tiger Dragon and our ruby claws raked across the rose pink hide of the Rabbit Dragon. We twisted, muscles straining to duck beyond the amethyst claws of the Ox, the wall behind the purple beast exploding into rubble. The blue dragon leaped in front of us, sweeping in a snarling circle, claws connecting, driving back the other ducking, diving, howling beasts.

Eona, like we did before. Ido's mind-voice was strong, the orange taste of his bright power laced with sweet vanilla. *Together!*

His earthly hand grabbed mine. His touch pulled me from my dragon-sight and I saw him on his knees, head thrown back, amber eyes alight with battle. Then I was back with the Mirror Dragon, our huge red body rolling under the crushing need of the circling beasts. This time there was no hesitation: we opened our pathways, feeling the rush of orange energy. It blazed through us, drawing our golden power into a huge wave of *Hua* bound with spinning stone and rock, barely held in check by Ido's iron control.

His hand tightened around mine. With a roar, he let our power loose, a booming explosion that ripped through the roof and outer walls of the cell and slammed the ten dragons backward. For a moment, the glut of power turned the celestial plane vibrant red—the beasts were fighting the force—then the shimmering circle of dragon bodies screamed as one and disappeared.

The energy world buckled and snapped away from my sight. I was back in my own body, the glorious power of my dragon like a distant hum in my head and a hollow absence in my spirit.

Ido yanked me down to the ground beside him, his arm across my body. An aftershock slammed across us, pressing me against the stone and punching through the walls of the other cells, bringing a hard stinging rain of dust and dirt.

Slowly, I lifted my head. Half of the outside wall was missing, showing scattered bodies among the rubble: soldiers, called by the alarm and caught in the blast. A few shadowy figures were gathering at a wary distance. More would come.

"Are you all right?" Ido croaked. "That was too close. Either the ten are stronger, or we are weaker."

I ducked out from under his hold, both my arms holding my weight. All my pain was gone. I tore away the field dressing—under the caked blood, the savage gash had knitted together as though it had never been.

Ido sat back, his full restoration also plain to see. He stared down at the smooth expanse of his chest and brushed his fingers across the uncarved skin, then twisted to see the condition of his back. I, too, could not help staring at his body and the marvel of my dragon's healing power. All the damage was gone, his powerful breadth of shoulder and long legs unmarred by brutality. His musculature, however, was stark on the strong bones. Dragon power could not heal days of near starvation. Ido saw my attention, but did not move to cover his nakedness. "What is our number?"

I looked away, fixing on the dark figures outside the cell. Already the few had become many. "We are six, counting you."

He rubbed his hand down his face. "Six? Is that all?"

"Eona?" It was Ryko's voice, rough and urgent.

"Here," I called, pushing myself up on to my feet. "We are unhurt."

I touched my arm again. Better than unhurt.

"You've healed yourself, too?" Ido's eyes ran along my body. "You are not crippled anymore."

"No," I said, flushing under his scrutiny.

"A useful power to have," he said.

More useful than he knew.

"Soldiers," Ryko said as he picked his way through the haze of dust and the tumble of stones that lay across the doorway. "We're surrounded."

Behind him, Vida, Dela, and Yuso struggled over the sliding, clinking rubble. I saw Vida pause at the sight of Ido's healed body.

"They must have found the two men we killed," Yuso said. He wiped at a wide, bloody gash above his eye, smearing blood across his forehead. "More are coming."

"It does not matter." Slowly, Ido pushed himself upright. He stared down at his feet and flexed his toes, then glanced across at me and gave one short nod—probably the closest he could come to gratitude. "Now that I'm whole, I'll clear the way."

"With your power? It is against the Covenant."

Even as I said it, I realized how foolish I sounded. Ido had killed all of the other Dragoneyes. He would not care about the sacred Covenant of the Dragoneye Council.

His teeth showed in a wolf's smile. "Don't lie to yourself, girl. You know the Covenant is dead."

"It is not." The denial was hollow even to my own ears.

From the debris, Dela hauled out the clothes she had dumped earlier and handed them to Ido, grit cascading from their folds. "Since Lord Ido has already broken the Covenant in the service of Sethon," she said, her voice hard, "the least he can do is break it again in our service."

Ido eyed her as he pulled on the dusty trousers and tied the drawstring around his waist. "You have become very pragmatic, Contraire." He pulled the loose shirt over his head.

"Necessity." She licked her lips. "Will your power get us out of the palace?"

He looked down at his wasted body. "I should have enough in me to get past these men."

"Do you have enough to kill Sethon?" she asked.

What was she thinking? We were here to free Ido to train me, not assassinate Sethon.

Ido shook his head. "I am not part of your resistance, Contraire."

"But he tortured you. Surely you want to kill him."

Ido's jaw shifted. "I will kill him in my own time. Not at the convenience of your cause."

Yuso stepped forward. "We all want Sethon dead, Lady Dela. But this is not the time. It is not our mission. We are here to get Lord Ido out."

"The captain is right," I urged.

"They are forming battle lines outside," Vida reported.

A clipped voice of command and the ominous thud of running feet spun us all around to face the gaping hole in the wall. Troops were gathering around the building.

"We have men and horses waiting for us beyond the imperial guards' gate," Yuso said. "You know the direction?"

Ido nodded. "Everyone stay close to me," he ordered. "If any of you stray beyond my protection, I will not stop."

We clustered behind him, Dela and Vida huddling at either side of me, Ryko and Yuso at the rear. Ido's breathing changed, the slight lift and fall of his shoulders sinking into the deep, slow measure that would ease him into the energy world.

This was the moment to test my link with him: I had to be sure I could control him.

Tentatively, I reached out with my *Hua*, seeking the pulse of his life force, ready to pull back at the first sign of connection. With Ryko, my link was fast and brutal, but Ido's energy was guarded, layered, mixed with the vanilla orange of his dragon. As his mind moved closer to the energy world, I felt a pathway open, the distant beat of his strong heart drawing toward my own rhythm. Quickly, I retreated before his pulse melded to mine.

He looked back at me, amber eyes threaded with silver. Had he had sensed my presence? But a shout from the courtyard refocused his attention. The troops were advancing. He stepped through the hole in the cell wall—the rest of us moving as one behind him—and with an upheld hand, he hardened the light breeze into a sudden wind that raised the dust into violent eddies. They swirled around our tight huddle but did not touch us, their howling force building with every step we took toward the troops.

Soldiers raised their *Ji* only to have them ripped from their hands and spear the men behind. We walked toward them as the power of the screaming wind snatched up the bodies of the dead and slammed them into the living, the horror breaking the line as much as the damage from the heavy human missiles. Those who remained staunch were hurled backward, the wind like a battering ram that pounded them into their comrades and the walls of the guards' quarters. Pebbles from the raked border lacerated their skin into bloodied shreds, their screams lost in the shrieking gale.

How could I control the will of a man with such immense power?

We passed the Pavilion of Autumnal Justice, Ido reaming the earth on either side of us with a flick of his hands. The ground heaved under the next wave of soldiers, the cobbles ripped out from under them as they ran toward us. The stones arced in the air, then rained down on their heads with sickening thuds. Vida grabbed my arm and turned her head away as one by one the large oil lamps burst across another rank of troops, setting them alight, the wind whipping the flames across the oil-splattered, screaming men.

As we headed toward the palace wall, I caught sight of soldiers rounding the far corner of the guards' quarters. Ido saw them, too. With a lift of his hand, he raised the sands from the training arena. I ducked, although I knew the pale cloud that arrowed over our heads would not touch us. It hit the men like a thousand tiny knives, shearing away skin and stifling screams with suffocating force. Behind me I heard Ryko's soft moan of horror.

Ahead, a section of the palace wall exploded outward in a crash and tumble of stone and dust. Ido's pace did not falter. We climbed through the hole after him and across the debris-strewn riding track, all of us fighting the urge to run from the screaming devastation in our wake.

Before us spread the formal pathways and cultivated groves of the Emerald Ring—the lavish gardens that separated the palace from its surrounding circle of twelve Dragon Halls. We had emerged near the Lucky Frog Pond, its famed frog-house pavilion rising from the gilded waters like a miniature temple. The burning palace cast a burnished glow upon its surface, and caught the wet jewel eyes of the frogs crouched within it. Beyond the pond, a round moon gate framed a raked pebble garden, the pale stones gleaming in the reddened light like a pathway of gold.

Ryko hooked his fingers into his mouth and gave a series of

shrill whistles that pierced even the cracking, shouting chaos behind us. The inky shapes of men and horses emerged from a stand of cypress trees to our right. I saw the pale, dappled hide of Ju-long and my heart leapt. Was Kygo among the men? Surely he would not risk it.

"The god of luck is with us," Vida whispered.

"He had nothing to do with it," Ido said, his voice rough with fatigue. "I saw their *Hua* through the eyes of my dragon."

He led us past the pond toward them, the silhouettes coalescing into the wiry figure of Caido and four of his men battling to control the string of horses. No Kygo: he had given Ju-Long over to our rescue. The beasts had caught the scent of fire and burnt flesh, and all six were balking at the attempts to move them forward.

"Walk them back until they settle," Caido ordered, the mountain lilt in his voice flattened by urgency.

The men pulled the horses around and led them farther into the gardens. Caido strode across to us. For a moment, he stood transfixed by Ido, confusion pressing him into a hesitant bow. He knew Ido was supposed to be our prisoner, yet there was no mistaking the silver power that still pulsed through the man's eyes, nor his natural command.

Yuso stepped forward. "Is His Majesty safe?" he demanded, breaking Caido's thrall.

"He is waiting with the rest of my men at the rendezvous," the resistance man said, but his attention had shifted to the ruins of the palace wall. He squinted into the billowing smoke, then pointed to the dark shapes of soldiers climbing cautiously over the shattered stonework. "More are coming. We must go!"

"They do not learn, do they," Ido said. He whirled around to face the palace, then pressed his hands outward. The gravel riding track buckled and exploded upward. I ducked as the earth split with a tearing roar along the palace wall, opening up underneath scrambling, shrieking soldiers and consuming them in a sudden collapse of dirt and stone. More and more earth fell away in a thundering rush as the huge crack spread beyond the palace boundaries, ripping the gardens in half until the two sides were separated by an impassable, gaping chasm.

The rumbling died away, leaving an eerie silence and a heavy cloud of dust. Then the screaming started; men shrieking in pain and terror.

Ido looked across at me, then started to walk away. The captain lunged for him, but Ido clenched his fist, and the ground heaved beneath the Shadow Man. Yuso staggered and landed on his back with a pained grunt.

"Lord Ido," I yelled. "We have a deal. You said you would train me."

Although his gaunt face was hollow with exhaustion, power still threaded across his amber eyes. "What did you expect, Eona? That I would trot behind you like your islander dog?" He gestured at Ryko who had started to close in on him, alongside Vida and Dela. Ido raised a warning hand, stopping their wary approach. "If you want to learn, Eona, you must come with me. On my terms." He smiled, and I felt as if the weight of his body was already on mine.

"You know I would never go with you. Never!"

"I know how much you want your power—it is like a hunger in you," he said. "And I know that without me, you will never have it. So make your choice. Learn how to raze palaces to the ground, or be a useless girl without the steel to follow the path of her power."

I stepped forward. He was right—I did want my power, so much that it was like a constant ache within my spirit—but he was so very wrong about me not having steel.

With savage anticipation, I rammed my *Hua* outward, seeking the silvery pathway into Ido's will. I felt my life force roll over another pulse, a familiar heartbeat sliding under mine in a rush of unstoppable energy. Ryko.

Beside me, the islander dropped to the ground, gasping. I faltered; I had not even thought of him.

Ido crouched, sensing the threat. I saw the burst of silver across his eyes as he gathered his power. No time for hesitation. I punched my *Hua* through his exhaustion, the taste of him flooding my mouth in a rich wave of pulsing orange power that drove him to his knees.

What are you doing? His fury was like the cut of acid.

I fought to draw his heartbeat to mine, his resistance like a roar through my blood. Slowly, like hauling on a heavy net, I pulled his life rhythm closer and closer to my own. He struggled, the pounding of his rage fighting the grip of my *Hua*. Slowly, he forced his way through my power and staggered to his feet. The battle cost him: his pulse slid under mine—one beat of unity—then broke free again.

Instinctively I sought more power. *Ryko.* He writhed on the ground nearby, his frantic energy waiting to be tapped. I grabbed at it, drawing up his bright *Hua*. Ryko screamed, a terrible rattling sound, but I could not stop. The sudden surge of energy within me leaped like a howling beast and hammered Ido back to his knees.

Sweat soaked the back of the Dragoneye's shirt as he tried to fend off the savage onslaught, every desperate block ripped apart by the teeth of my power. It was dark energy, raw and shrieking, and it wrenched his *Hua* into mine, pinning his pulsing rage under the thundering beat of my heart. With the brutal strength of victory, I slammed him onto his hands and knees.

"Your will is mine. Do you understand?"

He strained upward, his mouth drawn back into a snarl. Beside me, Ryko groaned, caught in the backlash.

"Lord Ido, do you understand?"

He raised his head—the effort rippled through my stranglehold. His eyes were dark gold with fury, all silver gone. I slammed him down again until his forehead was pressed into the grass and dirt.

"Do you understand?"

"Yes," he gasped. "Yes."

My body roared with exhilaration; I had control of Lord Ido—all of his power and all of his pride. Now *he* knew the agony of enslavement. I could make him do anything—

"Eona, stop it! Now!" A blurred face rose in front of me, all screaming mouth. "You are killing Ryko!"

My head snapped back, the sharp impact of a hand breaking my thrall. Dela's stern features burst into focus. I cupped my stinging cheek as the rush of power drained from my body. Yet the savage joy lingered like a soft hum in my blood. My grip on Ido's *Hua* was gone, but I knew the pathway to it had been blazed into him. And into me.

I stepped back, trembling.

Ido slowly lifted his head, testing his freedom. I knew that feeling: the relief of being in control again. With a deep breath, he pushed himself back on to his heels and spat, wiping his mouth free of dirt. The shaking curl of his fingers was the only sign of his fury.

"That is not dragon power," he rasped. "What is it?"

Warily, I watched him, ready to clamp down again. "If I heal someone, I can take their will," I said. "Whenever I want." But he was right; it was not dragon power. Whatever it was, it came through the connection that had been forged between us when I had healed him, just as it had been forged with Ryko at the fisher village. A thin gold thread of each man's *Hua* entwined with my own. Yet I did not truly know where the power came from.

Or maybe I just did not want to know.

He pressed the heel of his hand against his forehead. "It nearly split my skull open." He looked up at me. "You enjoyed it. I could feel your pleasure."

"No." I crossed my arms.

He smiled grimly. "Liar."

"My lady," Caido said, "please, we must go now!" The resistance man's thin face was sharp with anxiety and awe and, I realized, fear of me.

I nodded and turned back to Ido. "Get up."

Ido's mouth tightened at the order, but he hauled himself to his feet.

Dela and Vida squatted on either side of Ryko. With a gentle hand, Dela rolled the big man onto his side. Ryko groaned, his face gray. I had almost ripped too much *Hua* from him. It had won me control over Ido, but I had nearly killed my friend.

"Dela, is he all right?" I moved toward them. "He just got caught up in it. I didn't—"

"Just let him be!" Her fury was like a brick wall between us. She turned back to Ryko and helped him sit up.

"Maybe I was wrong about you," Ido said, watching the islander tense and double over, shivering with pain.

"What do you mean?"

Ido's face angled toward me. The play of light from the flames carved deep hollows under his cheekbones and emphasized the long, patrician nose. "Last time we met, you surrendered to spare your islander pain. You could not bear to see him hurt." His eyes narrowed in a malicious smile. "Now you rip his *Hua* from him to compel me. Maybe you have enough steel to follow the path of your power, after all."

CHAPTER FIFTEEN

THROUGHOUT THE NIGHT we crossed the city using a chain of safe houses, staying only a few minutes in some and over a half bell in others to avoid patrols, all of it a blur of dark rooms, shadowy faces, and urgent whispers. Caido and his lieutenant led us from house to house. The rest of his troop were riding across the city in the opposite direction, brave decoys for the inevitable search.

In one house, Vida and I changed into more modest gowns, and I washed the white paint from my face. In another—the stable of a walled family compound—we stayed long enough to eat soup, brought by the sympathizer's goggle-eyed wife. By that time, Ido and Ryko were in desperate need of food and rest. The compulsion I had forced upon both men had weakened them, and Caido's relentless pace was beginning to tell on all of us.

The woman left the iron soup pot on the floor and bowed

out of the stable, her eyes fixed on Ido. He was slumped against the far wall, as far from the bristling distrust of the others as possible. Instead of the warden's ill-fitting clothes, he now wore the dun trousers and tunic of a workman, but the trousers were too short, and Dela had ripped out the tunic sleeves to accommodate his shoulders. Perhaps the goggle-eyed wife was not just overwhelmed by his Dragoneye rank.

In the dim light from the courtyard lanterns, Vida stirred the soup, then ladled out two bowls and passed them to me.

"Don't let him eat too much." She measured a small amount between thumb and forefinger. "Otherwise he'll just be sick."

Ido, it seemed, had fallen into my care. Not through any desire of mine—more from the refusal of the others to interact with him. I did not blame them. Even starved and exhausted, Ido could strike with venom at any time. His insinuation that I had become ruthless, even to my friends, still pricked at me like a burr caught on my spirit.

I carried the bowls and squatted in front of the Dragoneye. His shorn head was tilted back against the rough wood wall, eyes closed against a shaft of moonlight that slanted across his face.

"Soup," I said.

He flinched. I had obviously pulled him from the cusp of sleep. The broad planes of his face sharpened into fierce hunger. "Food?"

I held up his portion. Eagerly, he cupped his long fingers around the bowl, but his hands shook so much that he couldn't raise it to his lips. He bent his head and sucked at the liquid.

"Vida says you should eat sparingly, or you'll bring it back up."

He grimaced over the rim. "Shouldn't be a problem. I can't even get a mouthful."

"Here, let me hold it." I reached for the bowl again.

"No." He clenched his teeth and slowly raised the soup, the liquid slopping onto his fingers. Finally, he took a mouthful and smiled. Genuine pleasure. It was the first time I had seen him without the arrogance that usually hardened his features, and it stripped years from his face. I had always thought of him as being much older than I, yet Momo had said he was only twenty-four, and if I had ever counted the dragon cycles, I would have known his true age. How did someone get so old in his spirit? The easy answers were brutality and ambition. But perhaps it was impossible to know the truth of another person's spirit.

I thought of the black gap I had seen in Ido's crown point of power. Surely such a breach in the seat of insight and enlightenment would affect his spirit in some essential way. And his heart point had shrunk again, too. Did that mean he no longer felt the sense of compassion I had forced upon him?

I took a sip of my own soup—the thin taste almost overpowered by the stink of the sleeping pigs penned nearby—and watched Ido eat with the intensity of a starving wolf.

"Do you still feel remorse for all you have done?" I asked. "I know you felt it in the palace alleyway, and compassion, too. But do you still feel it?"

It was probably a foolish question—he had no reason to admit he was once more without conscience, and every reason to assure me that he was a reformed man.

Slowly, he looked up from his food. "After one hour in Sethon's company, I stopped feeling anything except pain," he said flatly. "Do not ask me about remorse or compassion. They did not exist in that cell."

The memory of his brutalized body leaped into my mind. After what he'd suffered, no wonder his heart point had shrunk again. Perhaps Sethon's cruelty had created the black gap as well. I watched him again over the rim of my bowl. From the slight turn of his body, it was obvious he did not want to talk of his ordeal. For a moment, I was caught between my own compassion and a sense of macabre curiosity.

"When I healed you, I saw a black gap in your crown point," I finally said. "Do you know what it is?

"A black gap?" He touched the top of his head, his face suddenly strained. "It is most probably *payment exacted*." The wry edge in his voice was softened by resignation.

"Payment?"

"You should know by now that there is always some kind of payment for power." Tiredly, he rubbed his eyes. "I used a lot of power to survive Sethon."

"What will such a gap do to you?"

"That remains to be seen." He gave a harsh laugh. "Perhaps I will never achieve spiritual enlightenment."

"What did Sethon want from you?" I asked.

The sarcastic smile faded. For a moment he toyed with not answering—the reluctance plain in his face—then he said, "The black folio. And you."

I had thought as much. "Did you tell him anything?"

"I don't know." His eyes met mine and I drew back from the cold accusation within them. "When you called your dragon that first time, you not only ripped my heart point open—you blocked me from my power. I was at Sethon's mercy for three days." His voice was a hard monotone. "By the third day I didn't know what I was saying. Maybe I told him. I would have said anything to stop it."

I took refuge from his blame in a sip of my soup. I didn't know I had blocked him from his dragon. Fear feathered down my spine. I had left him powerless against Sethon. Just the memory of the man's cold touch made me feel sick—even with Ido's injuries still fresh in my mind, my imagination failed at what he must have endured at Sethon's hands. I steeled myself against the impulse to apologize. It had been Ido's own ruthless grab for my power that had blocked him from his dragon. And his own treacherous plans for the throne that had enraged Sethon.

"I think it is safe to assume that Sethon knows everything I know about you and the black folio," he added.

"You know where it is, then?'

"Dillon has it."

"He survived the flood?" The news brought a confusion of gladness and foreboding.

Ido smiled grimly. "The black folio looks after its own."

"But if Sethon knows where it is, he will just go and get it."

Ido shook his head. "Sethon knows where it *was*. Dillon is long gone." With a sigh, he put the bowl on the floor. "Your servant is right. I cannot eat any more."

"She's not my servant. Vida is a resistance fighter."

"And what about you, Eona?" he asked. "Do you fight for the Pearl Emperor?"

I paused, sensing a bite in the question that I could not see. "Yes."

"And will you fight with your power when I teach you how to control it?"

"No, I abide by the Covenant. As does Kygo."

"'Kygo,' is it?" He crossed his arms, the moonlight showing the stark curve of muscle. "You should watch yourself, girl. Just because you are a Dragoneye does not mean you can call an emperor by his first name. Not even a usurped emperor."

I lifted my chin. "I am his *Naiso*."

Ido's heavy brows met over the high bridge of his nose. I pressed my lips together, half of me enjoying his astonishment, the other half tensing for the inevitable jeer.

"You are his *Naiso*? His truth bringer?" His shoulders started to shake with silent laughter. "You do not have a truthful bone in your body."

"Kygo trusts me," I said, hoping my vehemence would persuade him. And me.

He lowered his voice. "Then tell me, have you told *Kygo* that royal blood and the black folio can bind a Dragoneye's will and power?"

I hesitated, not wanting to give him the satisfaction of the answer.

He smiled, his old arrogance lifting one corner of his mouth. "I didn't think so. You may be misguided, but you are not a fool."

"I haven't kept it from him," I said through my teeth, although I also spoke more softly. A habit: too many years lived with too many secrets. "I just haven't told him. He would not use it against me."

Ido gave a snort of derision. "He is royal and he wants the throne. Of course he will use it." He leaned forward. "Ask yourself why you haven't told him. It is because deep down you know he is a threat to us."

In my mind, I once again saw that moment of hard ambition on Kygo's face as he stared at the black folio on Dillon's wrist; the book held such tempting riches for us all—the secrets of *Gan Hua*, the String of Pearls, and even how to stop the ten grieving dragons—but the cost was so high. Insanity and, in the wrong hands, enslavement.

"Kygo is not the threat," I said. "The threat is Sethon."

Ido sat back, a small smile playing across his lips. "You lie even to yourself. Now *that* is the mark of a fool."

I stood up. "You do not know Kygo," I said. "And you do not know me."

I turned and walked the length of the stable, my unease driving me as far from the man as possible. I stopped at the edge of the doorway and gulped at the cleaner air, ignoring the curious glance from Dela, seated on a bale of hay nearby.

As my mind quieted, a sick realization crept through me. Ido was right; I was a fool.

He had just manipulated me into admitting that we were Dragoneye allies against the threat of royal blood.

It was a full bell after dawn before we neared the rendezvous in the hills outside the city. The hot weight of the monsoon was back in the air, its presence like a hand pressing on my chest. Or maybe the tightness across my heart was from the prospect of seeing Kygo again. I circled my fingers around the leather thong tied to my other wrist. The hard lump of the blood ring gave no reassurance. We had been physically apart little more than a day and a night, but I felt as though a chasm had opened up between us. As Xan, the poet of a thousand sighs, once wrote: *Too many doubts grow in the cracks of silence and separation.*

Caido's lieutenant was scouting ahead, his forest skills rendering him invisible and silent. In front of me, Ido walked between Yuso and Caido. Although the Dragoneye was stooped with fatigue, he was still a head taller than the two men guarding him, and the overhang of trees forced him to duck under branches.

We were winding our way through dense bushland, Yuso's eyes sweeping over the ever-changing shift of light and shadow in the tangled undergrowth. Behind me, Dela and Vida helped Ryko, the islander still weak from my use of his *Hua*. We had only shared one brief exchange of words during our flight from the city. I had tried to apologize—again—but Ryko had caught my arm and, in a hoarse whisper, said, "He was strong. You needed me to quell him. I'm glad you made him suffer." I nodded, relieved that my friend was talking to me again, but I knew I did not deserve such a generous reading of my actions.

Ahead, the Dragoneye suddenly stopped and stared up at the sky, squinting as if he could see something in the heavy cloud cover. He looked over his shoulder at me with a frown.

"Do you feel it?" he asked.

I glanced up through the branches at the dark, bilious sky. Was he testing me? I paused and considered. "I feel something. It's thick. More than just monsoon."

"Good," Ido said. "From what direction?"

Yuso stepped in closer, his hand on his sword. "Keep moving," he ordered the Dragoneye.

Ido looked sideways at him. "Keep moving, *my lord*," he corrected, his voice cold.

"Just keep moving," Yuso said. "Or you will feel the hilt of a sword, *my lord*."

"Wait, captain. Lord Ido has something I wish to hear." I turned back to the Dragoneye, ignoring Yuso's tight-lipped scowl at my defection. "How do I find out what direction it is from?"

"You already know," Ido said, but his attention was still on Yuso, a sly smile baiting the guard.

"No, I don't." Then I realized something *was* in my mind, colored red with anxiety. I focused on it, trying to catch its sense. Slowly it floated up from its deep mooring. "West. It's coming from the west."

"Yes. Well done." Ido finally pulled his gaze from Yuso and glanced up at the dark collection of clouds again. "West. The wrong direction for this time of year."

"Wrong direction? What does that mean?" Dela asked behind me.

"It means a cyclone." His frown deepened.

"Here?" Vida's horror mirrored my own. "When?"

"Lady Eona, you tell us," Ido said.

Another test. "How?"

"It is in the *Hua* of the earth. Sense it."

I had no idea what he meant. "With my power? But that will bring the dragons."

"No, just feel it. Like you do when you trace the pathways of your own *Hua*."

"Really?" I took a breath, still unsure. I knew the land had inner pathways like our meridians—they were the energy lines that crisscrossed the earth in bright bands. But how was I to sense them without shifting into the celestial plane? All I could feel was the heat on my skin, and the thud of my own heartbeat, and the draw of my breath into my chest, and the soft, soughing breeze across my skin, and the pulse of the insects in my ears and—

"Five days," I whispered.

Ido smiled. "Five days," he agreed.

I laughed. "How did I do that?"

He looked at me quizzically. "You are a Dragoneye. It is what we do."

I grinned, unable to contain my delight. I had listened to the land like a Dragoneye!

Then a sobering thought struck me. "But we can't stop it, can we?" That was the real work of a Dragoneye.

He looked up at the sky again. "No. You will need training for that. And we will need more power. But at least we can get out of its way."

Silenced by the news, we started pushing through the undergrowth again. For all the danger of an impending cyclone, I could not help marveling at my new ability to listen to the land. Ido was already unlocking so much in me. I looked at the man's broad back, trying to divine what was in his serpentine mind. He glanced back as if he had felt my thoughts, and for a heartbeat I was caught in the questioning amber of his eyes. Although there was no slide of silver through them, I still felt the draw of his power. I looked away. Yet from the corner of my sight I saw him smile, and my own lips rose into the ghost of an answer.

Less than a half bell later, Yuso tensed and raised his hand. We stopped, watching the undergrowth.

"Sir!" Caido's lieutenant edged through a patch of bushes to our right. I would not even have guessed he was there. "They are a hundred lengths or so northeast."

"Has everything gone according to plan?" Caido asked.

The man nodded. "His Majesty is waiting for us."

My skin prickled. Kygo was ahead. The news affected Ido, too. He drew back his shoulders as if preparing to face an overwhelming enemy. In a way, he was: Kygo would have little welcome for the man who had helped Sethon slay his family and seize his throne.

I wiped sweat from my hairline. As I drew my hand away, I caught a flash of bright white on my finger: Moon Orchid's paint. How much was still left on my face? I probably looked like a piebald horse.

"Dela," I whispered, glancing back at the Contraire. "Have I still got paint on my face?"

With a smile, she studied me, then delicately flicked her thumb under my eye and along the dip of my chin. "There, it's all gone."

We passed two sentries—Caido's men, almost invisible in the undergrowth until they rose and sketched quick bows—and then the bushes and trees opened out into a spread of grassland.

In its center, Kygo stood facing us, two men guarding him, with others spaced around the edge of the clearing. There were new faces among them; no doubt local resistance. Yuso led us forward, and with a lift to my heart, I saw Kygo's eyes seek me first—a fleeting connection of relief and gladness. Then his attention cut to Ido, his expression hardening. Even I felt chilled by the cold rancor in Kygo's face, although his stern beauty caught in my chest like a missed heartbeat.

The ground underfoot already held the warmth of the heavy air, the sweet acidic smell of crushed grass rising around us. Kygo had undone the high collar of his tunic, and the milky sheen of the Imperial Pearl was framed against the dark cloth like a royal banner.

A length from him, we stopped. Behind me, Dela and the others dropped to their knees. I lowered myself into my own obeisance, but, beside me, Ido did not move. I looked up, dread creeping across my shoulders. The Dragoneye stood in front of Kygo. The two men watched one another silently. They were almost matched in height, each locked in the other's stare.

"Bow," Kygo said.

Ido's eyes flicked from Kygo to the two guards behind him. "You do not want me to bow."

What was he doing?

Kygo frowned. "Bow, Lord Ido."

"No." I saw the subtle shift of Ido's feet as he pressed his weight into the ground. He was bracing.

Yuso's head rose from his kowtow. Ryko's, too.

"I said, *bow*!" In an instant, Kygo's cold control was obliterated by savage fury.

"I will not bow to you, boy."

I flinched even before I heard the dull crack of Kygo's fist slamming into Ido's face. Another blow, in the gut, hammered away Ido's breath and doubled him over. He fell to his knees beside me, gasping. A vicious kick caught him in the ribs and dropped him into a hunched kowtow. Kygo stood over him, fist still clenched, the intention to keep punishing the Dragoneye in every line of his body.

"Your Majesty," I half rose from my bow. "Lord Ido is here to train me."

For a terrible moment, I thought he would just keep kicking.

His eyes—dark with rage and grief—found mine. It was like the village inn again.

"Kygo, he is no use to us dead!"

The killing rage snapped out of his face, although the dark grief stayed within his eyes. With a nod, he stepped back, breathing hard.

Still hunched over, head bowed, Ido looked across at me. Why had he deliberately provoked Kygo? He lifted an eyebrow. But before I could react, he looked back down and spat blood on the ground.

"Lady Eona," Kygo said. He was forcing calm into his voice. "Rise."

I stood, reeling from the calculation in Ido's face.

Kygo took my hand and drew me a few steps away. His knuckles were sticky with blood. "Do you have the same link with him that you have with Ryko?"

We both glanced back at the bowed Dragoneye.

I nodded, unease hollowing my gut. "I think he is provoking you, Kygo."

"Why would he do that?" His voice still held the sharp edge of violence. "I could have killed him."

"I don't know."

Kygo shook his head. "He has nothing to gain by it. Stand beside me, *Naiso*." He turned. "Everyone get up. Get back. Lord Ido, stay on your knees."

The others scrambled to their feet as ordered, forming a ragged half-circle around the Dragoneye. Among all the hostile anticipation, only Dela's face was troubled.

"Look at me, Dragoneye," Kygo ordered.

Ido lifted his head. His top lip was split, bleeding into his mouth and down his chin.

"Where is the black folio? Does Sethon have it?"

Ido's eyes flicked to mine. *See*, his expression said, *this is all he wants.*

I chewed on the inside of my mouth. Of course Kygo wanted the folio—it was logical. We could not afford to have it fall into the hands of Sethon. Yet some deep part of me—the Dragoneye—did not want it in Kygo's hands, either. But maybe that was just Ido's mind games playing upon me. I could not think straight.

"The folio is safe from Sethon," Ido said. "My apprentice has it."

"Bring it to us."

Ido shook his head. "No. It is safe. That is enough."

"I do not ask, Dragoneye. I command."

"No."

Yuso stepped forward. "Your Majesty, let me explain obedience to *Lord Ido*."

"I understand your enthusiasm, captain," Kygo said. "But there is no need." He turned to me. "Force him, Lady Eona. Make him call the boy to us."

My gut froze. "Your Majesty," I whispered, turning my head away from the circle of avid faces. "Do not ask me to do that."

"Why not?"

"You are asking me to torture him."

He grabbed my arm and pulled me across the clearing. I stumbled after him, his iron grip wrenching me through the thick grass. He stopped and rounded on me. "What are you talking about, Eona? I am only asking what you have done before."

"I did it before because you threatened Ryko," I hissed. "I will stop Ido from using his power against us, but I will not use my power for coercion and torture." I pulled my arm out of his grip. "It should not even be an option. I thought you were better than that."

"That is a fine line you draw," he snapped. "Did Ido come willingly with you? Or did you coerce him?"

"I showed him I had the link."

"So when does it become coercion? When I ask you to do it?"

"Yes!"

"That doesn't make sense."

"I don't care. I just know that what you ask is wrong. You know it, too."

He sucked in a breath. "We need the black folio, Eona. Sethon must not get it."

I pressed my hands to either side of my head. "Kygo, if I force Ido to get the folio, do you think he will train me?" I lowered my voice. "If I am to fulfill the portent and save the dragons, I need Ido's knowledge." I touched his arm. "Trust me; we will get the black folio."

He looked across at the kneeling Dragoneye. Ido had raised his head and was watching us. "Every part of me wants to hurt him," Kygo said, his voice low.

"I know."

He closed his eyes and sighed. When he opened them again, the darkness had receded. He took my hand. "All right, we will do it your way, *Naiso*."

I returned the pressure of his fingers. "Thank you."

Kygo was an enlightened man, his father's son, yet as he led me back to the silent ring of men and women, Ido's taunt in the stable echoed in my mind: *Why haven't you told him?*

The Dragoneye watched us approach, his jaw set.

"Captain," Kygo said. Yuso stepped forward. "We stay here for the day and move out tonight. Bind Lord Ido and put a guard on him. Then report."

His order broke the tension around the ring of onlookers. Bowing, they backed away from the presence of their emperor, heading, no doubt, toward food and sleep. As Dela walked past me, she touched my arm lightly.

"Be careful," she whispered, and glanced back at the Dragoneye. "He does not have only dragon power."

"Get up," Yuso ordered Ido.

With slow insolence, Ido stood and looked at me as Yuso pulled his wrists together and bound them with rope. The steady hold of his eyes sent a wash of hot unease through me.

"I must hear the captain's report," Kygo said. He watched dispassionately as Ido was shoved into a stumbling walk between two guards. "But please join me afterward."

"Of course, Your Majesty." I bowed and backed away as Yuso approached.

I headed toward the clump of trees where food and water were laid out. Although I kept my eyes fixed on the mill of people ahead, I could feel Ido's gaze upon me like the press of a hand along the length of my spine. Dela was right. I had to be careful.

A quarter bell later, I stood in front of Ido. My excuse was a cup of water and a strip of dried beef for the prisoner. But really, I needed to know why he had provoked Kygo.

The morning sun had broken through the clouds and added a burning heat to the heavy air. Ido was on his knees under its full glare, forced into a punishment kneel that I knew was ironically called the Blessing: back rigid, bound hands held up at chin level. Sweat dripped from under his ragged hair and into his eyes. Although his face was impassive, the strain was evident in the trembling along his arms.

I held out the cup.

Awkwardly, he held up his bound hands and took the water. "This is becoming a habit," he said.

The guard leaning on a nearby tree trunk straightened. "My lady, Captain Yuso has ordered that Lord Ido does not get food or water until he says so."

"Apparently I'm learning about obedience," Ido said, his voice hoarse. "The captain is keen to know the whereabouts of the black folio."

I glanced at Yuso, still in close conference with Kygo across the clearing. Was this Yuso's own idea, or was he under orders? The thought was disquieting either way.

"What is your name?" I asked the guard. He was one of Caido's men; a skilled bowman, if I remembered rightly. He certainly had the shoulders and muscled forearms of an archer.

"Jun, my lady." He dipped into a bow.

"Jun, do not make the mistake of thinking your captain's orders outweigh mine. I wish to speak to Lord Ido about Dragoneye business." I waved the man away. "It is not for your ears."

With an anxious glance at Yuso, Jun bowed again and edged out of earshot. Ido drained the cup and wiped his mouth with his thumb, the action making him wince. His top lip was swollen and the tight rope had already chafed a raw ring around his wrists.

"Sit back," I said.

He sank on to his heels with a small sigh of relief. "I'm out of condition. My master used to make me hold a Staminata position for hours." He rolled his shoulders. "We will start your training there: I don't think you have done much Staminata work, and it is the cornerstone of energy manipulation."

I resisted the tantalizing call of his knowledge. "Why did you provoke Kygo?" I asked, keeping my voice low. "He could have killed you."

Ido squinted across at the emperor. "His mother and brother were murdered with my help. Of course he wants to kill me."

In the distance, Kygo raised his head as if he felt our attention, his sudden stillness a clear message.

Ido gave a low laugh. "He doesn't like you being here, either."

Nor did Yuso. The captain had also looked up, and I could feel the wave of fury from him.

"Why did you provoke Kygo?" I repeated.

Ido wiped the sweat out of his eyes with the back of one bound hand. "At some point, he was going to try to kill me. If it didn't happen now, it was going to happen later, with even more heat behind it. Better that I gave him a reason to unleash it as soon as he saw me." He touched his lip with a light finger. "Now it is done. He checked his rage. He has missed his kill moment."

I remembered the vicious brutality in Kygo's eyes at the village inn. I wasn't so sure the moment was lost. "It was a big gamble," I said.

"No. The dice were loaded in my favor."

"How?"

"You."

I frowned. "You knew I would stop the emperor?"

He tilted his head, watching me. "Yes."

Was I so transparent to him? The thought sent a small jab of fear through me.

"It is obvious that he wants you," Ido added. "He wants your power—and he wants your body."

My skin flushed under his blunt words. He made Kygo's desire sound like his own attempt on my body and power in the harem—brutal and self-centered. I remembered the suffocating weight of his body pinning me against the wall, and his hunger for the Mirror Dragon's power.

As if he could see my thoughts, he said softly, "You have good reason to kill me, too."

"I have many good reasons," I said crisply. "But I also have a good reason to keep you alive."

"I know. You want your world of power. That is why I knew you'd stop him."

I drew back, but he shook his head. "You don't need to pretend with me, Eona. If there is one thing I understand, it is the need for power."

"I do not *need* power," I said quickly.

He studied the rope around his wrists. "Need. Want. Desire." He shrugged. "You and I both know what it is like to have immense power. And we also know what it is like to be truly powerless." He lifted his hands. "Not this kind of feeble restraint. You know what I mean: true and utter powerlessness. Whether it be the kind we have inflicted upon each other, or the kind that Sethon"—his hands clenched involuntarily—"deals in so masterfully. I will do whatever I must to never feel that powerless again. And you are the same."

"We are *not* the same," I said vehemently. "And you are powerless now. I can compel you any time I want. Crush you, like that." I closed my fist.

He shook his head. "You've missed your kill moment, too, Eona."

I opened my mouth to deny it, but his knowing eyes silenced

me. He was right. I'd had two chances to avenge my master and the other Dragoneye lords—on the night of the coup, and last night. I had failed both times.

He gestured at the food in my hand. "Of course, you could very well kill me with frustration if you don't give me that dried meat."

With a reluctant smile, I handed over the strip of beef. He crammed it into his mouth. Out of the corner of my eye, I saw Yuso striding toward us, almost vibrating with rage.

Ido swallowed the mouthful, a quick sideways glance also taking in the captain's approach. "Tell me, Eona," he said, almost casually. "What is going to happen when you sleep? How will you compel me then?"

I met his keen scrutiny with my best bluffing face. "We are always linked. If you call your dragon, I will feel it." It was half true: we *were* linked by that single thread of his *Hua*, just as I was linked to Ryko. But I could not feel the connection all the time, and not while I was asleep.

"Always linked?" he echoed. "Perhaps you will feel my touch in your dreams."

"If I do, it will be a nightmare," I said sharply.

He laughed, amber eyes at their most wolfish. I turned to meet Yuso's bristling arrival by my side.

"Lady Eona!" The captain's voice was icily courteous. "I have given explicit orders regarding Lord Ido. Please do not interfere."

"Lord Ido is here to train me, captain," I said, just as icily.

"He is of no use to me if he is starving and exhausted. Do not deny him food and rest. Do you understand?"

Yuso glared at me.

"Do you understand, captain?" I snapped.

"As you wish, Lady Eona." He bent his neck in a stiff bow.

"Is that what obedience looks like, captain?" Ido asked blandly, but his eyes met mine in lightning amusement.

I quickly turned and walked away. It would do me no good if either man saw my smothered smile.

One of the new faces—a young man with the flatter features of the high plains people—bowed as Vida poured me a cup of water under the trees. I sipped the tepid liquid, then poured a little into my cupped palm and patted its wet relief onto the nape of my neck. I was glad to be out of the sun, and just as glad to be away from the keen mind of Ido: he played us all as if we were the Revered Strategy Game.

Nearby, Dela sat on the grass, the red folio open and her brow creased with concentration as she traced the ancient script with her fingertips. She did not even look up when Ryko brought her a cup of water. The big man placed it beside her, then sat a few lengths away, a silent sentinel guarding her back as she worked.

I found myself watching Ido again, as if he were a lodestone drawing my attention. Jun had finally escorted him to the shade of a tree a good distance from the rest of us. The Dragoneye sat hunched at its base, his bound hands held awkwardly before him. He looked in my direction; the angle of his dark head held a strange intimacy.

"My lady," the young plainsman at my side said. "His Majesty wishes to see you now."

With a start, I turned to face Kygo's level gaze, my skin prickling as if I had been caught doing something wrong. He was seated on a fallen log that had been rolled under the shade of a large tree and covered with a blanket: the throne of a usurped emperor. Even at rest, there was a coiled vigilance in the trained grace of his body.

He pulled the long braid of his imperial queue over his shoulder, and smoothed his hand along its length; something he did, I realized, when he was perturbed. I smiled, and was relieved to see the immediate answer in his face. After Ido's game-playing, the warmth in Kygo's smile was like a sweet balm. Holding back the absurd desire to run to him, I crossed the grass with as much stately poise as I could muster.

"Your Majesty," I said, and bowed.

"Lady Eona," he said, just as formally.

For a moment we both hesitated, still caught in the hours spent apart. Then he took my hands and pressed his lips against my fingers. In that quick, hard gesture I felt the distance between us close. And I felt something new: possession.

"I could not give you a proper welcome before," he said, glancing across at Ido. "I underestimated my dislike of the man."

"Did you order Yuso to punish him, Your Majesty?"

He blinked at the sudden question. I had not meant to ask so abruptly, but the needling disquiet had forced its way out.

"You mean the Blessing? No, I did not order it."

"Then Yuso is acting alone?"

"Yuso knows how important the black folio is to us. But perhaps I did not make it clear that Ido is to be left alone. For now, anyway." He lifted my hand. "Come, sit by me."

The honor of the invitation and the soft lilt in his voice overwhelmed my lingering unease. I rose from my knees. As I settled on to the log, the draw of his fingers guided me close to him, until our thighs almost touched. He rested our interlocked hands across the sliver of space between us. A bridge across our bodies.

Dela looked up from her study of the red folio with a frown. For a moment, I thought she disapproved of my position beside the emperor, but then I realized she was staring past us in thought. She must have found something. Hopefully, it was not another dark portent.

"I have had some good news," Kygo said. Excitement had stripped away the new, harder lines of command in his face. "Word from the Mountain Resistance. Our strategy of attacking soft targets is beginning to succeed."

It was the plan he had put in place during our last days in the crater. Using the wisdom of Xsu-Ree, he had ordered the resistance groups to attack weaker outposts and lure Sethon's forces to defend them. By the time the army reached the position with reinforcements, the resistance would have already moved on to attack the next target. According to Xsu-Ree, it would not only keep Sethon's forces shifting around, frustrating and exhausting them, it would also provide an insight into Sethon's own strategy.

"That is excellent news, Kygo." I tightened my hand around his fingers and smiled at the quick, ardent return. The Imperial Pearl at the base of his strong throat glowed in the periphery of my vision: a pale reminder of our kiss.

"For the moment it seems Sethon's arrogance does not see us as a coherent threat," he added. "That will change, but for the time being we will strike and harass his forces and attack the *Hua-do* of his men."

His words prompted an image of High Lord Haio and his table of red-faced, sweating officers. "I think Sethon is already losing the *Hua-do* of his men," I said. "What was the line in Xsu-Ree about the signs of an enemy's will?"

"'Men huddled in small groups, with voices low, give sign of disaffection and dying *Hua-do*,'" Kygo recited.

"Yes. When we were in the palace, High Lord Haio—" I stopped, realizing the man was another of Kygo's uncles.

He smiled grimly. "Go on."

"High Lord Haio and his officers seemed bitter. And when I was brought before Sethon, it was obvious even his top men were afraid of him."

"That was well observed." His thumb stroked my finger. "Yuso said you had come face to face with Sethon. Thank the gods he did not recognize you."

"He is a vile man," I said, shuddering. "I pity anyone in his power."

"I have some good news on that front, too," Kygo said. "A messenger from Master Tozay has caught up with us." He nodded toward a dusty young man talking to Ryko. "Tozay has found your mother. She is safe from Sethon."

"My mother?" My heart quickened so fast it brought a pain to my chest.

"Yes. Tozay is sailing to meet us farther along the coast with supplies. He is bringing your mother with him."

"I will see her?" I could not focus through the tumult raging in me. After so many years, would she recognize me? What if she did not like me? What if she had sold me because I was—

"In four days, if all goes to plan. We can sail out before the cyclone hits," Kygo said. He squeezed my hand again. "Are you all right?"

I cleared the ache in my throat. "Was there mention of my father and brother, too?"

Regret pulled at his mouth. "There was no word of them."

At least my mother was safe. I touched the word again, letting it settle into calmer meaning. *Mother.* All I could remember was a woman crouched beside me, the weight of her arm around my shoulders, and a smile that held the same curve as my own. "I have not seen her since I was about six."

"She will be very proud of you," Kygo said. "You have brought great honor to your family."

A cold shadow fell across my excitement. If Kygo knew the full history of my family, he would not be so gracious.

"There is no possible way she cannot be proud," he added, misreading my frown. "You are not only the Mirror Dragoneye—the first in over five hundred years—but also the imperial *Naiso*. You are the most powerful woman in the empire, Eona."

I looked across at Ido, his head cradled in his arms. I had not yet attained my true power. But I would soon.

Kygo followed my gaze. "He puts us all on edge. I hope he is worth the trouble you took to get him." He reached over and, with a gentle finger, lifted one of the coils of my bedraggled Peony hairstyle. The warm musk of his skin opened through me like a flower. "Yuso said you played your part brilliantly."

I flushed. "Being Lord Eon was much easier. At least it had fewer hairpins and a lot less paint."

He laughed. "But I like Lady Eona much more." His finger dropped from my hair and traced the sweep of my jaw. "Truly, you look very beautiful." The blatant appreciation in his eyes brought a flash of heat to my face.

I focused on our clasped hands. The leather thong still bound his ring against my wrist. Although something within me knew I should not say it, I could not stop the words. "I had a lot of help. From Moon Orchid."

His fingers around mine tensed. I glanced up, almost afraid to see what was in his face. The soft smile sent a shard of ice into my heart.

"Moon Orchid helped you? How is she?"

"She is well. Very beautiful," I said tightly.

He pulled his hand free and rubbed the back of his neck. "Good. That's good."

"She recognized your blood ring." I forced my finger through the knot tied by Moon Orchid. With a yank, I unwrapped the leather and pulled it free from my wrist. "Here. I brought it back."

We both stared at the ring swinging between us.

"Keep it," he said.

"Moon Orchid said it meant a lot to you."

"It does."

"Your 'step into manhood,' she called it," I said, with too much edge in my voice.

His fingers closed around the ring, stopping its arc. "Did you think I had lived as a monk, Eona?"

"Of course not," I said, but I did not look up from his fist. I was a fool. He was an emperor, required by the law of his land to marry royalty, keep a harem, and sire many, many sons.

"I have not seen her for a year," he added.

"It does not matter, does it?" I said, a terrible realization breaking over me. I let go of the leather, the two long strands falling over his hand. "I am not royal. And I will not be a concubine. There is no place for me."

"There is a place for you if I say so." He opened his fist. The ring had pressed a dark red indentation into his skin. "Your power changes everything. It has its own rules."

It always came back to my power. Ido was right.

"What if I said you could have either me or my power? Which one would you choose?"

"What kind of question is that?"

"Which would you choose?"

"It is not even a real choice, Eona. Your power is part of you."

I lifted my chin. "Which one, Kygo? Tell me!"

His mouth tightened. "I would choose your power." I pulled back, but he caught my shoulder. "I would choose your power because I choose for the empire. I can never just choose for myself. You said you understood."

"I understand perfectly." I knelt, dislodging his hand, and bowed my head. "May I withdraw, Your Majesty?"

"You are not just your power, I know that," he said. "Eona, why are you creating a problem where there is none?"

I kept my head bowed.

"You are being ridiculous." His voice snapped into exasperation.

"May I withdraw?"

He hissed out a breath. "All right, go."

I backed away out of the shelter of the tree into the sun, the burning heat on my nape the only warmth in the whole of my frozen body.

I did not want company. Nor did I want the hunk of bread that Dela held out. But she would not go away. She crouched in front of me, blocking the sightline of my target, a tree stump a few lengths away. I leaned around her and threw another rock, hitting the wood with a satisfying *clunk*.

My retreat was not the most comfortable or prettiest of

places—the small, raised outcrop of stones and dirt amid the lush grassland was like a scab on the earth, and it had no protection from the blazing sun—but it did have the advantage of being as far from Kygo as possible within the confines of our camp.

Dela dusted off a half-buried rock and placed the bread on it. "I hear that Master Tozay has found your mother," she said.

I grunted and threw a smaller pebble. It ricocheted off the stump. Ten points, if I was keeping score.

"Finding your mother; that's good, isn't it?" she ventured.

I grunted again. If I said something, she would think it was an invitation to stay and talk. I'd had enough talk. And enough thinking. And definitely enough feeling.

"You seem to have had another disagreement with His Majesty," she tried.

I chose the largest rock in reach and, with a hard flick of my wrist, spun it at the stump. It carved a chunk out of the wood, the sliver flying up in a high arc. That had to be at least twenty points.

"Was it about Lord Ido?" She edged over again, her brows drawn into a worried knit.

"No."

"What was it, then? You cannot just sit here in the sun, throwing rocks. The perimeter guards are getting edgy. And you are ruining your complexion."

I fingered the smooth stone in my hand. "What did you find in the folio?"

She looked down at the red journal, its pearls wrapped around her wrist. "How do you know I found something?"

I aimed again. The stone hit square and bounced into the bushes. If I were playing for coins—like I used to with the other Dragoneye candidates—I would be making a fortune.

"I found out who the other man was in the triangle with Kinra and Emperor Dao," she said softly, breaking the silence.

I flicked over a few rock possibilities and chose a nasty edged piece of flint.

"It was Lord Somo," Dela said.

"Never heard of him."

"He was the Rat Dragoneye."

I paused, my hand drawn back midthrow. "Kinra was in league with the *Rat Dragoneye?*" I looked across the clearing at Ido, the irony of it welling up into a harsh laugh.

"What do you think it means?" Dela asked.

"Nothing," I said flatly. "The book is a history, not a prophecy." I threw the flint. It completely missed the stump.

"But it does have the portent in it," she said. I shrugged, unwilling to concede the point. "It is just a coincidence, then?"

"Yes," I said firmly.

"I don't think so." Dela was just as firm. "Look at me, Eona."

I finally met the worry in her deep-set eyes. "All right, then. What do *you* think it means?"

"I don't know," she said. "But Lord Ido is here, and His Majesty is here. And you are between them. A Rat Dragoneye, an emperor, and a Mirror Dragoneye."

"I am not between them. Lord Ido is here to train me. And Kygo is here to use me," I said bitterly.

"Use you?"

I cursed my tongue and the tears that had come to my eyes. "It doesn't matter."

"What happened?"

"Nothing." I groped for a change of subject. "Have you spoken to Ryko yet? Now that you know he returns your regard."

She squinted at me, finally giving in to the clumsy deflection. "Yes, I spoke to him."

"And?"

"He said that he has nothing to offer me. No rank, no land. Not even his free will." She sighed.

I leaned forward. "But that doesn't matter, does it? You would take him with nothing, because you love him."

"Yes, of course."

I picked up another rock and lined up the stump. "Lucky Ryko," I said.

CHAPTER SIXTEEN

OUR GOAL WAS the coast. Master Tozay had nominated Sokayo, a small village with resistance sympathies and a good harbor for our rendezvous. It was at least three nights of hard traveling away, even without the added complication of Sethon's patrols sweeping the land.

Twice during the first night we crouched among the dense foliage, praying to the gods as troops passed by only a few lengths away. And on a dawn scouting mission, Yuso came face to face with a young foraging soldier. Yuso's description of the encounter was predictably terse; he held up a precious map of the area and two dead rabbits, adding that no one would find the man's body. The gods, it seemed, were not only hearing our prayers, they were answering them.

Between the tense hours of night travel and snatched hours of sleep during the day, Ido began to teach me the Staminata:

the slow-moving combination of meditation and movement that helped to counteract the energy drain of communing with a dragon. I'd had only one Staminata lesson before the coup, but even that had helped me understand the transfer of energy throughout my body. Ido said the training was as much for him as for me. If he was to have any chance of holding back the ten bereft beasts while I practiced the dragon arts, he needed to restore the balance of energy in his own body.

And it was becoming painfully apparent by our second session that balance was the essence of the Staminata.

"Make your moon palm flatter," Ido ordered, beside me.

We were more or less alone—if two silent, invisible sentries ten or so lengths away could be called alone—and the morning heat had not yet descended. Even so, as I drew back my left hand I felt a trickle of sweat slide down my neck. I'd been holding the starting position for more than a full bell—a deceptively easy stance of palms faced out, knees slightly bent, and bare feet pressed into the earth—and my arms and legs were shaking with the strain. Ido held the same position. From the corner of my eye, I could see that he was sweating just as much, his bare torso slick with effort, although I could discern no trembling in his arm muscles. Just two days of travel rations and patchy rest had remedied the gaunt exhaustion in his body.

"Keep your eyes ahead and breathe. Let your mind trace the inner pathways," Ido said. "And keep that palm flat."

I refocused on the wild jasmine bush a few lengths in front of us and tried to turn my mind inward. All I could think of was the heavy perfume of the jasmine in my throat. And the itchy track of sweat down my back. And the fire that crept up my calf muscles.

And the hard press of Kygo's lips against my hand.

I swayed, the sudden lurch of the world jolting me into an awkward half hop backward. Ido straightened, his break of the stance just as graceful as the hold.

"What happened?" he asked, running his hands through his sweat-soaked hair.

"I lost concentration."

"Obviously. I meant, what did your mind throw in your way?"

I pushed away the image of Kygo. "Sweat and aching muscles."

"At least your mind is concentrating on the moment." He picked up his tunic. I looked away as he wiped his chest. "We'll stop soon. We both need rest."

I let out a relieved breath. We had started training as soon as Yuso had called a halt. Everyone else was either asleep or taking a short turn on guard duty.

Ido dropped his tunic back to the ground. "Give me your hands." He held out his own, each wrist still ringed with the cut of rope.

Except for the two times I'd healed him, I had never touched Ido. He had, however, touched me. With force.

He saw my hesitation. "If I do something you don't like, you can always slam me into the ground again."

True. I wiped my hands down the bodice of my gown and held them out. He turned them over and very gently pressed each of his thumbs into the center of my palms.

"Do you feel that soft part in the dip, under the bone?"

I nodded.

"That is a gateway of energy." He looked down, past the calf-high gathered knot of my hem. "There is one in each foot, too, in the soft center below the ball. Four gateways where the body can draw in *Hua* from the earth and everything around it. The fifth is in the crown of the head."

"In the seat of the spirit?" I asked, watching him. "Where you have the dark gap."

"No, above it," he said shortly.

He released my moon hand and pressed his palm against the flat of his abdomen. Under his fingers, the vertical interlock of muscle on each side of the central meridian was carved in hard relief. "Behind the navel is where the five gateways are united. It is the center of balance and the focal point of *Hua*. It is called the Axis."

He was still holding my other hand.

"The Axis?"

"Where all balance begins: physical, mental, and spiritual."

He drew my hand down and pressed it against my own belly, over the Axis point. The thin cloth of the gown stuck to my damp skin.

"Behind there," he said. "That is the place where *Hua* must be drawn. Do you feel it?"

"Yes." But all I could feel was the warm weight of his hand covering mine.

"Breathe," he said. "Center your inner awareness on that point."

Looking over his shoulder, I focused on the jasmine bush, but my body felt like a single thundering pulse resonating through our hands. I drew in air and the scent of hours of exertion and control on his body, the earthy maleness mixing with the jasmine perfume. I looked up, my eyes flickering over the cut lip and flared nose. The pale gold of his eyes was almost engulfed by black pupil.

"Good," he said tightly. "As you exhale, hold the *Hua* in the Axis."

I breathed out, feeling our hands move together. He leaned closer, his head bent to mine.

"Are you sure you want to do that, Eona?"

"What?"

He licked his lips. "You are compelling me."

"No, I'm not," I said.

"Yes, you are."

He drew my hand against his chest. Through the curve of damp muscle, I could feel his heartbeat quickening under my palm. I swallowed, my mouth suddenly dry. His rhythm was in my own blood. I *was* compelling him, in a different way. A call, not a coercion.

"I'm sorry." I tried to pull my hand free, but he locked it against his chest.

"I'm not complaining."

I shook my head. It was wrong. A dark attraction. It felt even more wrong than hurting him. Yet it pushed me toward him, just as much as it pulled him to me. I snatched my hand away and stepped back, the subtle link breaking.

Ido released a long, ragged breath.

"That was some kind of *Gan Hua*, wasn't it?" I said.

He touched his chest. "It would seem so."

"I don't know how to control it." I grabbed his arm. "You have to teach me."

He looked down at my desperate hold. "Don't be afraid of your power, Eona. It is a gift."

"It doesn't feel like a gift. It feels out of control."

"Of course it is out of control," he said. "*Gan Hua* is chaos."

"But it is dangerous," I said. "In my candidate training—"

"That is nonsense fed to you by frightened men." He dismissed the training with a flick of his hand. "We can distill *Hua* into either *Gan* or *Lin*—chaos or order—and neither force is intrinsically dangerous, or good or bad. They just *are*. The Dragoneye Council was full of fools." He shook his head. "They never understood the extraordinary power that comes out of chaos. But you understand. You use *Gan Hua* in a way that I never thought possible. I only wish I had your ability."

"But you used *Gan Hua* to go into your dragon."

He rubbed his hand across his mouth. "A clumsy attempt compared to yours, and only as a last resort."

"But how did you do it? How did you control it?"

He hesitated. "Pain is energy. I transferred it to my dragon and used *Gan Hua* to hold myself in the beast, away from what was happening to my physical body."

For all the heat of the new day, a chill swept over my damp skin. "Is that why your dragon was in such agony?"

"I said it was a last resort." His voice hardened. "And, as you saw"—he touched his crown—"the damage was not only to the dragon. I stayed too long and drew on too much of my dragon's power without the requisite return."

"I would never inflict such pain on my dragon," I said.

"And yet you inflict pain on me and your friend Ryko," he said. "It is easy to say 'never,' Eona. But you have already stepped over a line, and you did not even see it in your rush to get what you wanted."

I glared at him. "You have no idea what I want."

"Tell me, then."

"I want to master *Gan Hua*. As quickly as possible."

"For all your fear, you still want more power?" He smiled. "You are a true queen."

"No, you don't understand," I said, twisting my hands together. "I need to master *Gan Hua* because the dragons are not immortal. At least, their power is not without end."

He stilled. "What makes you say that?"

"There is a portent in the red folio. It says that when the Mirror Dragon rises, it is a sign of the end of the dragons."

"What?" He grabbed my arm. "Show it to me. Now!"

"I know every word of it." I tapped my head; it was inscribed upon my mind in fire. Slowly, I recited it:

"The She of the dragon will return and ascend
When the cycle of twelve draws to an end.
The She of the Dragoneye will restore and defend
When the dark force is mastered with the Hua *of All Men."*

"Say that last line again," Ido demanded.

I repeated it.

"Lady Dela and I think 'the dark force' means *Gan Hua*," I added.

"Yes, that is what our ancestors called it." His eyes scanned the clear space around us, his whole body tense.

"But we don't know what 'the *Hua* of All Men' means."

"I know what it means," he said.

"What?"

He leaned closer until his lips were against my ear. "'The *Hua* of All Men' is the old name for the Imperial Pearl."

I swayed as his words wrenched everything into a terrifying pattern of inevitability: the pearl—the emperor's symbol of sovereignty—was the way to save the dragons.

I shook my head. "No. That cannot be."

Ido's grip tightened into support. "I have seen the phrase in ancient scrolls."

Was this why Kinra had tried to steal the pearl from

Emperor Dao—to save the dragons? It took another moment for the horror to build to its full meaning. If that was the reason for Kinra's so-called treachery—the reason she risked everything to attack a king—then that meant the pearl had to come out of the emperor's throat to save the dragons. It had to come out of Kygo's throat. And that would kill him.

I looked up at Ido. "You are lying!"

"It is the truth, Eona." His grim face was only a handspan from mine. "In the ancient records that have survived, one dragoneye could look after a province by himself. Now it takes all the dragoneyes to work the same level of energies. Dragon power *is* fading. And according to your portent, the Imperial Pearl is the way to save it."

No. It could not be true.

Yet I had felt Kinra's drive for the pearl. I had almost ripped it from Kygo's throat twice under her thrall. Five hundred years ago, my ancestor and Lord Somo had tried to steal the pearl from Emperor Dao. Was I somehow locked into the same journey with Ido and Kygo?

No coincidence, Dela had said.

I tore my arm out of Ido's grip. "I don't believe you," I whispered. "It is another of your sick games."

Ido gave a harsh laugh. "This is no game, Eona. I am not lying. That is what the pearl was called."

"Prove it."

"All of the proof is locked in my library. But I swear; I have read it in some of the oldest scrolls."

I pressed my hand over my mouth—there was a scream building within me that was five hundred years old. I had to find some way to prove Ido wrong.

He sucked in a sharp breath. "Does the emperor know about the portent?"

"Yes."

"Then, if you value your life, do not tell him about this," he whispered.

I turned away from the fear in his voice. There was too much truth in it. "You said there is proof in the ancient scrolls."

"Yes."

"Is it in the black folio?"

His silence gave me my answer.

I spun around. "Bring it to me."

"No." He stepped back. "Not yet. It is the only thing that guarantees my life. And Dillon is even more dangerous now. I will bring him and the folio to us when you have more control of your power. Then we can restrain him together."

"Bring it now!"

"No. It is too soon."

"*Bring it!*"

"No!" He braced; he knew what was coming.

The roaring fury of my *Hua* slammed through his pathways like a crashing wave, dragging his pounding heartbeat under mine. He staggered backward under its force then lowered his head, teeth clenched. I felt something gather within him: a sudden resistance that rose like a wall of rock. The collision of *Hua* against *Hua* dammed the rush of my power, jarring through me like a physical blow. I gasped as my grip loosened around his will.

"Eona, it is too soon to bring the folio. We are not strong enough," he panted. Blood trickled from his nose. He had stopped me, but it was costing him.

I rammed my *Hua* into the barricade of power again. The strike recoiled through both of us, pushing me back a step and knocking him on to his knees. Another buffeting blow forced a grunt from him, but I could not break through. Throwing all of my fear-fueled rage into the rush of power, I rammed him once more. The pressure doubled him over, but he caught his weight on his hands, the strain ridging the tendons in his arms. His block still stood strong. He looked up, the silver sliding across his eyes.

"See. Not so easy this time, is it?" he said. "I can already hold you back."

Ido had found a way to stop my compulsion. He was no longer starved, no longer taken unaware. I could not even reach for Ryko's *Hua* to boost my power; I could feel the islander, but he was too far away.

And last time I had nearly killed him.

I stared into Ido's face, his taunting smile bringing a barrage of memory. I had seen the same smile as he pressed the knife-edge of his Dragoneye compass deep into his own flesh. And after the King Monsoon, when he'd hit me. And, most sharply, I had seen it when he had driven his sword through Ryko's hand.

A dark intuition quickened within me: there was another route to his will. One that I had stumbled across only minutes ago. A call in the blood that had drawn Ido toward me. But it had also drawn me toward him. A dangerous and double-edged weapon, made of pleasure and pain. I did not entirely understand it, but somehow I knew it would defeat him. He would be at my mercy.

Did I really want to have that kind of power over Ido? Yet he was already pushing against my *Hua*, looking for a way to turn it against me.

I had no choice. With a sob, I released my fury through the pathways of desire so newly blazed. Ido gasped as my power rolled over his defenses, burning away the silver in his eyes. The shock rocked his body forward. He collapsed flat on to the ground, his silent scream ripping through my *Hua* in a backlash of pained pleasure.

Ido's will was mine for the taking, and I took it, fusing his hammering heartbeat to mine.

"Eona!" His voice cracked; part plea, part warning.

I forced his head up, the amber eyes wide and dark.

"Call Dillon," I said.

His command to the Rat Dragon shifted through me like a hand sliding across my skin. The power reached, searched, found its goal. I felt Dillon's hate respond, its sharp barbs clawing into Ido like a soldier's grappling hook, anchoring the boy to his master and pulling him inexorably toward us. Dillon and the black folio were on their way.

Then the power curled back upon me, its razor edge sending a shiver of pleasure through my body.

Abruptly, I released my hold on Ido's will. He slumped, the rasp of his breath loud in the sudden, eerie quiet. All the birds and clicking insects around us were silent as if they marked some irrevocable event.

Ido slowly raised his head, but I turned on my heel, unable to look him in the eye. I got as far as the jasmine bush, its white blooms hanging heavily in the hot air. The cloying perfume caught in my throat. I could still feel his presence in my *Hua*.

"Addictive, isn't it, Eona?"

I knew I should ignore his soft voice. Just keep walking. Yet I stopped and looked over my shoulder. He was on his knees, the back of his hand stemming the flow of blood from his nose.

"What's addictive?" I asked.

His smile was a caress. "Getting what you want."

As I pushed my way through the bushes toward camp, my mind was caught in a loop of horror: the pearl, Kygo, Kinra, Ido, me, all of it circling around and around the red folio's portent. I slapped past branches, feeling the sting as they lashed back against my skin. Was Ido telling the truth? A bird flew up from the bushes at my feet, screaming an alarm. No! I had to believe he was lying. The alternative was too terrible. I ground my teeth. His presence still hummed in my blood.

"Eona, are you all right?"

Kygo stopped in front of me, sword drawn; a tall blur through my tears. I reared back and lost my balance. He caught my arm with his free hand and held me upright, the strain digging his fingers into my flesh. Behind him, Caido and Vida crashed through the scrub, swords at the ready.

"What's wrong?" Kygo said. "Did Ido do something? Ryko felt you compel him."

My eyes locked on the pearl. *The* Hua *of All Men.*

"It was nothing." I pulled my arm free. "Just training."

Kygo lowered his sword and turned to Vida and Caido, sunlight sliding across the pearl in a shimmer of colors. "False alarm," he said.

Caido scanned the bushes around us. "We shall escort you and Lady Eona back, Your Majesty."

"No." Kygo waved them away. "It is only a few lengths."

They bowed and retreated through the bushes, leaving the smell of churned earth and the green snap of broken twigs.

Kygo resheathed his sword. "Are you sure you are all right?"

I stared down at my dirt-smeared feet, away from the lustrous power at his throat. Did Kinra try to steal the pearl in order to save the dragons? It would mean that the energy beasts had been losing their strength even in her time. I was so new to the Mirror Dragon I did not even know if she was diminished. The thought that she could be fading sent a piercing pain through my spirit.

I pressed my hand against my forehead. "I'm sorry to have disturbed you, Your Majesty."

The pearl was too close to me. He was too close. What if Ido was right?

"I wanted to speak to you anyway," he said. "Alone."

I lifted my head and forced my eyes past the pale glow to the sensuous curve of his mouth. The memory of his lips against mine reverberated through me. I stepped back. "Your Majesty, I beg pardon, but I am very tired."

"It will not take long." He cleared his throat, the hard swallow forcing my gaze back to the jewel at its base. "I have come to understand that I have offended you with my honesty about your power," he said. "I am not accustomed—" He paused and rubbed his chin. "I mean, apart from my father, there has been no one whose opinion I was required to consider. And I've never had to"—his finger traced the edge of the pearl—"pursue a woman."

Was the emperor apologizing to me?

He took a deep breath. "I cannot take back those words—we both know they were the truth—but I regret that they caused you hurt." He reached across and took my hand. "And they did not take into account the importance I place upon your role as *Naiso*. Eona, you are the moon balance to my sun."

For a moment, I could not speak. His balance? My heart ached with the trust in his words. I wanted to be his balance, but I was more likely to be his death.

"I am honored, Your Majesty," I stammered.

"Kygo," he corrected softly. "I am sorry I hurt you, Eona."

His sincerity sliced through me like a knife. I tightened my hold on his hand and felt hard metal pressing into my skin; the blood ring was back on his finger. Good. He needed the protection. "You know I would never hurt you, Kygo."

"I know." His head tilted; a smile quickly suppressed. "Of course, you have already punched me in the throat and tried to stab me with a sword, but I know you would never hurt me."

I closed my eyes, but it did not stop the tears. He did not know how much truth was in his jest: at the inn, I had barely held back Kinra's murderous desire for the pearl. And that was even before I had been touched by the madness of the black folio.

"Eona, I'm only teasing," he said. The soft touch of his fingers stopped the track of my tears.

I pressed my wet cheek into his hand, unwilling to open my eyes and see the pearl. Unwilling to see the truth. But I knew Ido was right. The pearl was the way to save the dragons. To save our power. Even as he had said it—even as I had denied it—I had known it to be true. Like a part of a wooden puzzle locking into place, creating a picture of pain.

I took a shaking breath. Kinra had not been a power-hungry traitor, after all; she had been trying to save the dragons. There was no taint of treachery in my blood. Yet that did not change the fact that she was still trying to take the pearl through me—her Dragoneye descendant—and it was endangering Kygo's life. I was not going to be a puppet of my ancestor or the gods or whoever held the rods of this shadow play. Not without a fight. There had to be another way to save the dragons. Another way of mastering *Gan Hua*. And I could think of only one place it might be: the black folio.

I opened my eyes. "I know," I said, but my gaze had already locked onto the pearl.

Always the pull of its power nestled in the back of my mind. Now I knew why. Kinra. I had to protect Kygo and the pearl until Dillon brought the black folio. Until I found a way to save the dragons without the *Hua* of All Men.

I had to protect Kygo from Kinra. And I had to protect him from me.

I pressed my lips against his palm, into the soft gateway of energy, imprinting his touch and smell upon my spirit. Then, forcing a smile, I stepped back. Away from the sun that balanced my moon.

Ryko was the first person I saw as I followed Kygo back into the circle of our camp. Apart from the sentries stationed around the edge, the islander was the only one on his feet. Everyone else was preparing for sleep or hunched over food and eating with tired intensity. In contrast, Ryko was shifting from foot to foot, all of his attention focused on Ido at the other side of the scrubby clearing. The Dragoneye had been escorted back from our training session, and one of the guards—Jun the archer—was tying his wrists again. Ido looked across at me as a rustle of soft greetings announced our arrival, but I turned away from his scrutiny. I did not want to see what was in his face.

With a quick bow to Kygo, I headed toward Lady Dela. She was leaning against a supply pack slowly eating a dried plum, her fatigue like a heavy cloak across her shoulders. "I have a favor to ask," I said.

She wiped her mouth delicately with two fingers. "Anything, as long as I don't have to get up."

I leaned closer, lowering my voice to a mere breath. "I need you to find out if the folio has the reason why Kinra was executed."

Dela frowned. "We know why," she whispered, touching the book bound to her wrist. "For treason."

I had not told Dela that I believed Kinra had attempted to steal the Imperial Pearl. If it was in the red folio, then she would find it. And if it was not, then she did not have to know. Not yet, anyway. For a moment, I felt an overwhelming urge to tell her the meaning of the *Hua* of All Men. To share the horror. But she would tell Kygo—that was a certainty—and he would have to protect the pearl.

Unbidden, a terrible thought shivered through me: Emperor Dao had executed Kinra to protect the pearl. Love against power, and power had won.

I needed more time to master *Gan Hua*. More time to find another way to save the dragons. Then I would tell Kygo everything.

"Yes, we know it was treason," I said softly. "But I need to know exactly what she did, and why."

Especially *why*. I needed proof.

Dela nodded. "I'll look. There were no specifics in the note at the back, but it might be within the coded sections." She started to unwind the pearls, then paused. "I did glean another piece of information. At the very beginning of our bargain with the dragons, there were always *two* ascendant dragons each year, not just one—the male dragon who was in his Ascendant year of the cycle *and* the Mirror Dragon. She was always ascendant—whether with a male dragon or on her own in the Mirror Dragon year—until she went missing after Kinra's death."

Another piece of the puzzle, but where did it fit?

"If she was always ascendant, does it mean that dragon power has been halved since she left?" I mused. "Is that part of the reason why the dragons need to be saved?"

Dela shook her head. "I don't know," she said tiredly. "I just decode it."

"And I appreciate all your hard work." I clasped her arm in thanks.

As I withdrew, she caught my hand. "You're upset, and so is Ryko. Has something happened?"

I squeezed her fingers. "Everything is fine."

I turned to leave, but was stopped by Ryko. "Lady Eona, can I speak to you?"

I was fairly sure it was nothing I wanted to hear, but I allowed him to steer me away from Dela. He led me to the edge of the camp at a careful distance between two perimeter guards.

"What was that?" he demanded. All of his usual stolid composure was gone.

"What?"

He leaned down. "Don't treat me like an idiot. I know what it feels like to be compelled by you. You have done it to me enough times. And I know you compelled Ido just now, in such a way that"—he pressed his two fists together—"Eona, what have you *done?*"

Heat rushed to my face. "I did what I had to do," I said, lowering my voice. "Lord Ido found a way to block my compulsion. I found another way to his will. It is no different."

"No different?" His long islander eyes held mine. "Do you really believe that? You must know you are playing with fire. You heard what Momo said."

"Would you prefer that I not have any power over him?"

His chin jutted mulishly. "I would prefer him dead."

I glared at him.

He conceded with a reluctant tilt of his head. "Just be careful. Dela is worried sick about you."

"She is worried sick about you, too." His hard stare warned me away, but right then I had no patience for unnecessary suffering. "You are a fool if you think she cares about rank and fortune."

"I know she does not."

"Is it because she is physically a man?"

He gave a sharp laugh. "I grew up around stranger couplings. That is not the reason."

I crossed my arms. "What is, then?"

He rocked on his feet and, for a moment, I thought he was going to walk away.

"I am not meant to be alive," he finally said. "Shola allowed you to pull me back from my death. Do you think it was out of pity?"

I swallowed, remembering the fisher village. He had truly been walking the pathway to his ancestors.

"I am here for a reason," he said with determination. "I do not know what it is, but I doubt it is to find my own happiness. I am marked by Shola, and she will reclaim me when my part is played in this gods' game. I do not have the right to pull Dela close or make plans. It would not be honorable."

"You are here because I healed you, Ryko. My power brought you back from death. If anyone has a say in your life, it is me." I jabbed my finger into my chest. "And I say take happiness while you can."

At least one of us could have it.

"Are you so powerful now that you count yourself with gods?" he demanded.

"No! You know I did not mean that."

"You may have control of my will, Lady Eona, but you do not have control of my honor. It is all that I have left. It is all that I can give Dela." He gave a stiff bow. "With your permission." Without waiting, he turned and walked away.

I watched Dela's pale face turn to follow him as he strode across the camp. So much unhappiness in the name of duty and honor.

The village of Sokayo had a bathhouse.

It was a small, foolish thing to be excited about, but the report from Caido—recently returned from scouting the village—still lifted my spirits. We were less than a full bell's walk away, and had taken temporary refuge in a ravine with a small stream at its base. Although it was midmorning, Kygo had decided we could cautiously cross the final distance. Opposite me in the circle of intent listeners, Vida was grinning too, although I doubted it was from the thought of a hot bath; she would soon be reunited with her father.

And with Master Tozay would come my mother.

As Caido continued his report, I rubbed at the dust and sweat ingrained on the skin of my arms, flicking off tiny rolls of dirt. The shallow stream had provided a welcome drink and a quick cooling splash, but only a long, hot soak was going to budge the result of three days of hard training and traveling. Hopefully the bath house would have some kind of soap or washing sand. I did not want to look like a slattern.

"I can see why Master Tozay elected to use the harbor. It is sheltered and deep," Caido said. "But the village has strategic problems; it is in a cove between cliffs, with limited routes in and out."

Beside me, Kygo brushed away a spiral of persistent flies. "How much risk?" he asked Yuso.

The captain shook his head. "I would say low. The villagers support the resistance, do they not?" Caido nodded. "Then it will be manageable."

"My father has charted all of the coastline. He knows the harbors as well as he knows his own children," Vida added. "This will be the best one for him to use with the tides."

Kygo turned to me. "And the cyclone?"

I glanced up at the strange sky. The dark clouds were high but held the oppressive weight of a low storm, with the occasional flash of dry lightning. A hot inland wind had brought the swarms of tiny flies that surrounded us.

"Still two days away," I said.

Outside the circle, I saw Ido nod his agreement. We had not spoken since I had compelled him to call Dillon. Dela told me that his gaze followed me everywhere, but so far I had managed to avoid meeting his eyes. The intimacy of that new compulsion was still in my blood. No doubt it lingered within him, too.

"Cannot Lord Ido stop the development of this cyclone?" Kygo asked me. He refused to give Ido the favor of direct communication.

Ido leaned forward. "No, Lord Ido cannot stop it by himself," he said, with an edge in his voice.

Kygo angled his face away from the Dragoneye and waited for me to answer.

"No," I said brusquely.

It felt stupid repeating what everyone else had already heard. I grabbed on to the minor irritation—anything to stop the ache I felt whenever I looked at Kygo. Distracted by the hardship of traveling fast and covertly, he had not yet noticed the careful space I was keeping between us.

"My father will be able to outrun it, if all goes to plan and we board at dusk," Vida said.

"Then let's go in," Kygo said. "We don't want to miss our boat."

We were met outside the village by a keen-eyed lookout. With an apologetic bow, he explained that his orders were to lead us along the cliff path to the house of Elder Rito. As we followed the young man in single file along a track suited more to goats than men, the cove below came into view between the coarse bushes—a white sand crescent dotted with a few beached boats and drying nets. I stopped, overtaken by the image of another white beach and a woman holding out her hand. My mother. I almost had a clear picture of her face. But it was gone in an instant, only an echo of emotion left behind—and even that was blurred. Batting away a sticky fly, I hurried along the path to close the gap behind Dela, still caught in the soft-edged pull of my memory.

Elder Rito's cottage was set on a slope overlooking the cove. The small wooden dwelling was so faded by wind, rain, and salt that its silvered silhouette looked as if it was made of the gray sea below it. Inside, the furnishings in the single room were as worn as the exterior, but there was a scent of spicy fish stew that brought saliva to my mouth, and a pleasing order to the sparse belongings. As we gathered in the cramped space, three old men bent into kowtows on the worn straw matting: the elders of Sokayo.

"You may rise," Kygo said.

All three sat back stiffly on their heels. Each had the dark, weathered skin of the coastal dweller and gnarled hands from years of hauling nets. The man kneeling in the center—Rito, their spokesman—also had the distinction of a hideous scar that ran straight across his cheeks and nose. "An encounter with a sea ray," our young guide had thoughtfully informed us before we entered the house. Even warned, it was hard not to stare at the puckered ruin of his face.

"You are Elder Rito?" Kygo asked. The old man nodded. "We are grateful for your village's hospitality."

"It is our honor, Your Majesty," Rito said. His eyes flicked to the Imperial Pearl. "Our loyalty is to you and the memory of your revered father, who walks among the golden gods. We know you are the true heir to his enlightened throne." Rito bowed, then turned to me. "We are honored to welcome you, too, Lady Dragoneye."

"You know who I am?" I asked.

"Your true identity is widespread now, my lady. Tacked to trees and whispered in taverns. As is the tragic news of the slaying of your ten Dragoneye brothers."

His eyes went to Ido's bound hands, then traveled up to the Dragoneye's face. For such an old man, the threat within that slow gaze was palpable. Perhaps it was the scar across his face that intensified the menace; only a fierce and strong-willed man could have survived that injury. Ido's fingers curled into fists.

"For the time being, Lord Ido is under our protection, Elder Rito," Kygo said.

"Of course, Your Majesty," Rito said, bowing again.

"Have there been more troops in the area than usual?" Yuso asked.

"Activity has been increasing everywhere," Rito said. "We have had our share of scrutiny, but nothing that differs from other villages in the area. Probably less, since we are farther from the main thoroughfare and do not have grain or livestock for the taking."

"You have extra sentries posted?"

"Of course, but you are welcome to review them if you wish."

Yuso nodded. "Thank you. I will."

Rito turned his attention back to me. "You have seen the flies, my lady?" I nodded. "The dogs are also crying at night. And the children have seen ants climbing trees with their eggs on their backs—signs that a cyclone is coming from an unseemly direction."

"Yes," I said. "From the west. It will arrive here in two days."

He leaned forward, his face sharpening. "Can you stop it, my lady?" His eyes went to Ido, then back to me.

I licked my lips, mouth suddenly dry. "I'm sorry, Elder Rito. Lord Ido and I cannot stop it."

"Ahh." The slow exhale was full of crushed hope. Rito glanced to the elder at his right and jerked his head toward the doorway.

The other man nodded, then bowed to Kygo. "May I withdraw, Your Majesty?" His voice cracked with urgency. "We need to bring our cyclone preparations forward."

"Of course."

As the elder rose and retreated from the room, it felt as though all eyes were upon me. *Still useless*, they seemed to say.

"Your Majesty, we have hot food ready and have prepared places for sleep," Rito finally said. "If there is anything else you or Lady Eona require, please let me know."

There *was* something else I required: solitude. Just for a short time, I needed to be away from the silent judgment of the world, from the watchful eyes of Ido, and from the endless questions and fears that seethed through my mind.

"I believe you have a bathhouse," I said.

The old woman bowed, the arc of her mottled hand urging Vida and me through the blue door flags at the entrance of the communal bathhouse.

"I will wait out here and make sure you are not disturbed, my lady," she said with a shy smile. "And inside, you will find all that you requested."

"Thank you." I returned the smile and pushed through the flags.

Vida followed a step behind. After a hurried bowl of fish stew, I had spent almost a quarter bell courteously resisting the elders' pressure to be bathed by the senior village women. I could not, however, refuse Kygo's insistence that Vida escort me into the bathhouse. Her company was the closest I was going to get to time alone.

We both stopped inside the compact foyer. The attendant's small platform, edged by a thick carved railing, was set between two wooden doors that led into the bathing areas: faded blue for men on the right, red for women on the left. A set of shoe shelves stood on either side of the small area. I slipped my sandals off and pushed them onto the rough shelf next to me. Vida followed suit, placing hers next to mine.

"I do not have any training as a body servant, my lady," she said. "I will need instruction."

I shook my head. "I'll look after myself, Vida. You may bathe, too. I'm sure you'd like to honor your father's arrival."

"Truly?" She looked down at her feet. Tide marks of dirt showed the outline of her sandal straps. My feet were just as filthy. "That would be wonderful."

"Come, let's go in."

I crossed the rough straw matting and slid open the red door. The small dressing room was furnished with a wooden bench and more shelving. Steam from the baths had seeped into the room through a connecting door at the far end, giving the air a damp, velvety warmth. As I had requested, a stack of washing and drying cloths had been laid out on the bench, together with a ceramic pot of rough milled soap, combs, and, most importantly, fresh clothing. I picked up the neatly folded top layer of the first pile: a long woman's tunic, the brown weave close and soft. Below were the accompanying ankle-length trousers and a stack of underthings. A similar pile sat beside it.

"Clean clothes for both of us." I grinned at Vida as she closed the red door behind us. "Tunic and trousers. Finally!"

Vida eyed the second pile. "A set for me, too? Really?"

I nodded, gratified by her wide smile of pleasure. She did not smile very often around me.

It did not take us long to shed the now dirt-encrusted clothes we had been given in the city. I averted my eyes from the curves of Vida's naked form. It had been a long time since I had bathed in a communal bath. For nearly five years my maimed body had made me untouchable, forcing me to bathe alone. I looked down at my now-straight leg and smoothed my palm across the strong lock of bone and muscle and unscarred skin that formed my hip. It still filled me with wonder.

I picked up one of the washing cloths from the pile and held it modestly across my groin, then collected the pot of soap. "Vida, you bring the rest of the cloths."

Eagerly, I slid open the door to the baths, the heavier heat settling against my skin. Although it was humid outside, I still longed for the cleanliness that came only from hot water. A long wooden partition down the middle of the room separated the men and women's bathing areas, but it did not reach the roof, and steam had collected near the high ceiling in a soft haze. At the far end was the women's bath, a large sunken pool with pale drifts rising into the still, thick air.

But first, the washing station. I crossed to the narrow trough that stood along the wall with a series of low stools and small buckets in front of it. A terra-cotta pipe trickled continuously into its catch, the sound like a tiny waterfall.

I chose a middle stool, placed the pot of soap beside it on the wooden floor, then picked up a bucket. One deep scoop the length of the trough filled it with water on the satisfying side of hot.

Vida closed the dressing room door. "Shall I wait until you are finished, my lady?"

I lowered the bucket to the floor. "No, join me."

Vida smiled and bowed.

With full buckets and plenty of soap, we got to work. Vida picked the remaining pins from my heavy, oiled hair, the remnants of Moon Orchid's careful styling finally gone. Then I returned the service, freeing Vida's hair from the intricate Safflower braids into a frizz of kinks.

"That feels good," Vida said, digging her fingers into her scalp. She giggled as she felt the volume of hair around her head. "I must look like a wild woman."

I crossed my eyes and held out the thick tangle of my own hair. "Or a madwoman." Vida's giggle broke into a snort.

We dumped buckets of water over each other, the streaming heat slowly softening the days of collected grime. I worked up a lather from the rough, grainy soap that smelled of sweet grass, and massaged it from my toes to my crown, scrubbing with a cloth and sluicing with water until the suds that ran off my body was no longer gray. Beside me, Vida did the same, softly humming an old folk song that I vaguely remembered from the salt farm. We hummed the chorus together, breaking into laughter as our different versions ended in a clash of notes.

"Shall I wash your back, my lady?" Vida asked.

"Yes, please." I shifted around on my stool, then felt the wet, sodden warmth of a cloth against my back, and the gentle pressure as Vida worked it along my shoulders and spine. I sighed as tensions melted under her firm scrubbing. It had been so long since I'd had the pleasure of "skinship": that sweet, gentle bond of physical freedom and camaraderie that came with bathing among other girls and women. I had not realized how much I had missed it.

Eventually, we were both clean enough to enter the bath. I led the way down the three steps, the water rising from ankle to knee and then hip in delicious stings of heat. I sank down and found the stone sitting-step along the edge. Vida waded in and, with a sigh, sat opposite me.

"Thank you for this, my lady," she said.

"You must be excited to see your father again."

She nodded, lowering her strong shoulders farther into the water. "And you must be excited to be reunited with your mother."

I shrugged. "I have not seen her since I was six. I will be a stranger to her, as she is to me." I paused, then finally gave voice to my thoughts. "Perhaps there will be no feeling between us."

Or perhaps she'd not had enough feeling to keep me, so long ago.

Vida shook her head. "She is your family. There is always a bond."

"Maybe," I said. "I cannot remember what it is like to have a family."

Vida tilted her head. "But you have had people who have cared for you? Who care for you now, like Lady Dela and Ryko."

"I'm not sure Ryko would still want to be in that count," I said dryly.

But Dela definitely cared. When I was small, there had been Dolana, at the salt farm, before she was taken by the coughing sickness. And later, of course, Rilla and Chart. Even my master, in his own cold way. In all truth, I wished it were Rilla and Chart who had been found by Tozay's men, and not the stranger who was on her way. I missed Rilla's common sense and sharp-tongued affection and Chart's lewd humor. I sent a swift prayer to the gods to keep them safe. And to bring them to me.

Vida raised her leg in the water, contemplating the pale row of toes as they emerged above the surface. "It is obvious His Majesty cares for you, too."

I pretended to peer into the water to avoid her amused glance.

"And Lord Ido," she added.

That brought my head up. "He does not care about me."

"He watches you all the time," she said. "He is a handsome man, don't you think?"

"Not as handsome as His Majesty," I said firmly, but I smiled, too. I did not want to curb Vida's sudden friendliness. This was the skinship I remembered: women's talk, and laughter, and the gentle teasing about life and love.

"Perhaps. They are handsome in different ways. His Majesty is . . ." She paused, obviously searching for the right word, then gave a small shrug. "Beautiful, in that way that touches the spirit."

"And Lord Ido?" I prompted.

"Lord Ido is *very* male," she said with slow emphasis.

I nodded, meeting her grin. It was a good description.

She shot me a sharp look. "Are you attracted to him?"

"Of course not." I shook my head, but I felt my face flush.

"I can see why you would be. You have a lot in common."

"No, we don't!" I said quickly. "He is a traitor and a murderer."

Her gaze dropped from mine. Although I sat in a hot bath, I felt a chill: in Vida's eyes, I was also a killer.

All our ease gone; what a fool I was.

She cupped her hands and splashed water over her face, breaking the silence.

"You are the last two Dragoneyes," she said, smoothing back her wet hair. "It must be a strong bond. And he has more than just his dragon power."

I frowned: her phrasing seemed familiar. An echo of another voice within the words. I half rose from the water, driven by a terrible intuition. "Did His Majesty tell you to talk about Lord Ido?"

She shook her head. Too fast. "No, my lady."

I stood up. "He did. I can see it in your face."

"No, my lady."

"You are spying for him!" I raised my hand, wanting to slap away her betrayal.

She shrank back against the wall. "No, my lady. It was not His Majesty! It was Lady Dela. I'm sorry. I didn't want to do it. I told her I was no good at this kind of thing."

"Dela?" Shock stilled my hand. She was my friend. "Why would she do that?"

"She says you are shutting her out, my lady."

I waded to the steps and stumbled up them, catching my shin on a stone edge. Sharp pain spiked through me, opening my fury into full flame.

Vida stood up in the water. "Lady Dela is worried about you," she called after me. "You have to spend a lot of time with Lord Ido, and she knows what he is like. She was at court with him for years."

I turned around. "I'm doing it all for His Majesty," I yelled. "No other reason. Tell her *that*!"

I grabbed a drying cloth and ran, dripping, to the dressing room, snapping the door shut behind me. The cooler air in the connecting space shivered across my body. I jammed my hand against my mouth, trying to press back the sob in my throat. Even Dela did not trust me.

I had never felt so alone.

With frantic speed, I pulled on the fresh clothes, tying the tunic as I ran through the foyer, my wet hair unbound and hanging like a loose woman's. I grabbed my sandals from the shelf and pushed my way through the door flags. The old attendant was still waiting outside the entrance, with a man. I recognized the stringy frame: Caido. What was he doing here? They both turned at my abrupt appearance.

The old woman gasped. "My lady, do you need assistance? Did I forget combs?"

"No." I dropped my sandals and forced my feet into them, then gathered my hair back into my fist.

Caido turned his face away from my immodesty. "My lady," he said. "I am here to deliver a message from Lord Ido. He asks that you join him on the beach for training."

"That is the last thing I want to do." I pushed past him and the attendant and quickened my walk into a half-jog, although there was no place to go.

Caido's longer legs caught me up in a few strides. "Please, my lady. Lord Ido said to tell you that you are both strong enough to start working with your dragon now."

I stopped, all my pain and anger gone, obliterated by one thought: my dragon. Her glory was always with me. I was not alone. I was never alone.

"Take me to Ido," I said.

CHAPTER SEVENTEEN

LORD IDO WAS crouched a length beyond the tide line, sifting sand through his fingers under the gaze of his two guards. As I approached, he released the handful in a glistening slip and stood to watch my awkward progress across the soft beach. Each step squeaked and, along with the persistent flies and my sore spirit, I was finding it difficult to maintain any dignity.

I stopped in front of him. "Lord Ido."

"Lady Eona," he answered, bowing.

Gathering knots of villagers watched us from beyond the seawall. Most of the able-bodied men were out on the fishing boats, but it was wise to never underestimate the power of a mob, even if it was made of the elderly, women, and children. "Is it a good idea to be so conspicuous, Lord Ido? There is a great deal of ill feeling toward you in this village."

He shrugged. "His Majesty has agreed to us working on the beach."

I glanced at the two men behind him. Their startled eyes were fixed on my unbound hair.

"Wait over there," I said, waving them to the end of the seawall where Caido still stood. "And keep watch on the villagers. Do not let them approach."

They bowed and left, their retreat marked by the strange squeaking.

"I like your hair like that," Ido said.

I opened my fist and smoothed out the leather string that the old attendant had beseechingly pressed into my hand, for my modesty. With deliberate show, I gathered my hair at the back and tied the thong around it.

He smiled. "I like it like that, too."

Crossing my arms, I said, "You told Caido I was strong enough to work with my dragon now."

"No. I said *we* were strong enough to work with your dragon." He took a few steps toward the seawall. "Come. I'll show you how to catch lightning."

Catch lightning? Intrigued, I followed. He stopped midway between wall and water and sat on the sand near a small overturned boat, a tilt of his head inviting me to join him. Driven by a sense of unease, I scanned the beach and cliffs around us. Along the seawall, a lumpy expanse of draped fishing net had flipped back at one end, exposing the unmistakable outline of *tuaga*: long, sharpened bamboo stakes bound crosswise to form portable defense walls. It was the first sign of any fortification I had seen. What else did the villagers have hidden? I lifted my shoulders, trying to throw off my misgivings. They were resistance, and obedient to Kygo. Yet I could not forget the Elder's hostility toward Ido. The Dragoneye was hated here; he was a collaborator and had orchestrated the slaying of their Dragoneye protectors. I hoped Kygo's command was strong enough to hold back a mob's desire for revenge.

I settled opposite Ido, feeling the sand's heat seep through my tunic and trousers. The Dragoneye picked up another silky handful and watched it trickle through his fingers, the curve of his eyelashes dark against the pale strain under his eyes. The symmetry of his face was not gut-wrenchingly harmonious like Kygo's, but every line was strong and bold and brutally confident. Very male. Vida's description was perfect.

"You have surprised me, Eona," he said softly. "I was not expecting such"—he looked up at me with a wry smile—"*inventiveness* in your power manipulation. Or such strength."

I shifted uncomfortably. "You forced me to go that way."

"I forced you to find more strength. You chose that particular way yourself."

I did not look away from his challenge. "Yes."

His smile broadened. "Good. Don't ever be ashamed of the course your power takes."

"You say that, even after I used those pathways?"

"You did what you had to do, Eona. Just as I did," he said. "This time, however, I lost, and now Dillon and the black folio are coming. Although we are not ready for them."

I refused the bait. "Is he near?"

"No. It will take him a while to reach us."

"How will he follow us over water?"

Ido shrugged. "The black folio will find a way. If there is no boat, the boy will track us along the coast." He squinted up at the thick, dark clouds. "Our power is diminishing, I am sure of it. " My shift of alarm brought his eyes back to me. "Do not panic—it is diminishing slowly, not draining away," he added. "Still, we need to find a way to contain the ten dragons so you can use all the power that you have before Dillon arrives. Then we can both hold him off and get the black folio. It is ironic that once we have the book, you will have no problem with the other dragons—the black folio seems to repel them."

"Very ironic," I said dryly. "You really think Dillon will be that strong?"

Ido nodded. "By the time we meet him again, he will be completely taken over by the black folio. I can already feel its presence through the Rat Dragon."

I shivered, remembering the acid reach of its words. "What is it? What makes it so powerful?"

"Someone wove pure *Gan Hua* into its pages to protect the secret of the String of Pearls and the way to take all of the dragon power," he said. "Only a very strong Dragoneye can read the folio without their mind being burned into madness." He looked at me from under hooded lids. "And only two *ascendant* Dragoneyes could ever have the combined strength to take all of the dragon power and wield it."

I leaned forward. "You've read the whole folio."

He bent to meet me. "Then I must be mad or very strong."

"Most would say you are mad."

"What do you say, Eona?"

"I think you are very strong, Ido."

His eyes flickered. "Since when am I just 'Ido,' Eona? Since you showed me your true strength? Or since you called my body to yours?"

Abruptly, I pulled back. "How is the String of Pearls made, *Lord* Ido?"

He followed my retreat until his lips were a breath away from mine. "Nothing is free, *Lady* Eona," he said softly. "Especially not that kind of information."

I licked my lips, my heart quickening.

He laughed and leaned back. "I was thinking more along the lines of an information trade."

"What kind of information?" I snapped.

"Our bargain was that I would train you, and you would tell me what was in the red folio."

"I told you about the portent. There is not much else to know."

"Surely you know who wrote the folio?"

I was loath to tell him, but I needed to know more about the String of Pearls. "It is the journal of my ancestress, Kinra."

He seemed genuinely taken aback. "The Blossom Woman?"

"No," I said, shaking my head slowly. "The Ascendant Mirror Dragoneye."

"Ah." He smoothed back his ragged hair, eyes fixed on the

sand in thought. "Now I understand. As Rat Dragoneye, I hold Lord Somo's records—or what is left of them—and she is mentioned in them. Often." He turned his attention back to me with a sly smile. "They were lovers."

"Ancient history." I shrugged, hoping he could not see the flush of heat that prickled across my skin. "So, how is the String of Pearls made?"

With his forefinger, he drew in the sand between us: twelve small circles, one slightly larger than the others, connected to create one big circle. "Look familiar?" he asked.

"That's on the front of the black folio. The symbol for the String of Pearls."

"It is more than a symbol. It is a representation of the weapon. The dragons form a circle and release the pearls from beneath their chins, so each pearl touches the next. Once they have done so, the combined power is collected into all twelve pearls. As soon as *that* occurs, the power must be contained or it will destroy everything." He looked up. "The old scrolls sometimes call it the Necklace of the Gods. More poetic, I think, than the String of Pearls."

"What happens to the dragons?"

"Once the beasts are separated from their pearls, they cannot reclaim them," he explained. "It is Dragoneye lore that spirit beasts are immortal. But now your portent makes me think that the String of Pearls could destroy them."

"Then why would they ever give up their pearls?"

"I don't know." With one wipe, he obliterated the sand

circle. "Perhaps we will find out when Dillon arrives with the black folio."

Even if I believed what Ido said, he was probably not telling the whole truth. I had no doubt he wanted the power from the String of Pearls: he had already killed the other Dragoneyes in his quest for it. During the palace coup he had told me he was going to unite dragon power with the dragon throne, and I was the key to his ascension. He had wanted to rule both earth *and* the heavens. Did he still hold such grandiose plans? Perhaps his capture by Sethon had tempered his ambition. Or maybe the fires of suffering had branded it deeper into his heart. Whatever the case, I had the feeling that he, too, did not understand all the pieces of the puzzle.

The black folio held the secret of a weapon that took all the dragons' power, and the red held a portent that foretold the way to save that power. There was obviously some deeper connection between them, but I could not see it. I dug my fingers into the sand and raked my frustration through the grainy warmth. If felt as if every new bit of information curled back upon itself, seeming to get closer to the truth but in fact adding another veil of obscurity. Why was our Dragoneye power diminishing? And how could the *Hua* of All Men save the dragons? Did it have something to do with the String of Pearls? But if what Ido said was true, the String of Pearls was an agent of destruction—not an avenue of rescue.

One thing I knew with certainty: I could never tear the Imperial Pearl from Kygo's throat.

A sudden tension in Ido's body brought me back to myself. I followed his gaze to the seawall; the number of villagers behind it had doubled. Caido and his men had each taken a position on top of the stacked stones. Three men against fifty villagers, at least. And from the looks of it, not all of the men had gone out with the fishing boats.

Ido frowned. "Do they think I am defenseless?"

"We should go," I said, rising.

"No." Ido grabbed my arm, pulling me back down to the sand. "We are Dragoneyes. We do not get run off by peasants. Don't worry. What I am about to show you will keep them in check."

He pressed his palms—the gateways of energy—onto the sand and took a deep breath, tilting his head back. Almost immediately I saw the silver power slide through his eyes. Another breath swelled his broad chest. He released it and repeated the cycle in a smooth, regular rhythm. Then I saw the glory of communion strip the strain from his face. The joyous energy within him pulsed, its pleasure reaching me like a distant drum deep inside my body.

His silvered eyes locked on mine. "You are feeling this too, aren't you?" he said.

I did not want to give him the satisfaction of an answer.

Then his attention was elsewhere, beyond the physical world. Around us the air sang, building into a shriek that pushed the villagers back from the seawall in a wave of fear. Energy cracked and shivered across the sky. A long, pale jag of lightning split the dark clouds with a boom and flashed toward the sea. Then, as if a huge hand had grasped it, the bolt stopped. Slowly it turned, point aimed straight at the village, its power held suspended above us. I heard screams, but I was transfixed by the frozen flame of energy hanging in the air.

"Shall I teach these villagers some respect?" Ido said. "There are more of them across the hill."

"No!"

He gave a soft laugh. With it, the lightning was released. I flinched as it ripped through the air and slammed deep into the sand a few lengths from us with a heavy thud. The impact rippled under the surface like the track of a creature slithering below.

"Holy Shola." I scrabbled away from the shifting ground. A harsh smell burned the back of my nose and throat. Then all was quiet.

With a dismissive glance at the villagers cowering behind the seawall, Ido stood and dusted the sand off his trousers. "Come." He waved me over to the fused indentation in the sand where the lightning had struck. "This is the best part."

He crouched and carefully dug, clearing the sand away in two piles behind him. Cautiously, I crossed the short space and peered into the hole he had made.

"There," he said. Something white poked up from the sand. "Help me get it out."

"What is it?" I dropped to my knees and dug on the other side of the protrusion.

"Careful. It's brittle."

We dug down, clearing the cooler sand away. Finally, he gently withdrew a jagged white rod, as long as the stretch of my arms and encrusted with sand. It was no wider than my wrist, and hollow, like a length of bamboo.

"Listen." He gently flicked his fingernail against the top, causing a sharp, ringing *chink*.

"That sounds like glass."

"It is." He held it out to me. "Glass lightning." His head bent in a small bow. "A gift, Lady Dragoneye."

He placed it in my outstretched hands. It was very light and delicate, the rough, sandy surface edged with long ridges. I turned it on end; inside, it was a lustrous milky color, with tiny bubbles caught in pools of translucent glass. I smiled at its beauty. And its promise of power.

"Can I make one of these, too?"

"Of course," Ido said. "This is how I was taught to separate energy. Lightning is concentrated and has a definite form as it comes to earth, so it is easier to recognize and catch."

"How do you do it?"

"It is always about balance. Lightning is hot energy, so you catch it with cold." He flicked the captured lightning again, making the glass ring. "You will see when we are in the energy world. I'll block the ten dragons while you practice."

I flexed my hands. The desire to commune with my dragon and finally use my true power was overwhelming, but so was my mistrust of Ido. What if he did not hold back the other dragons?

"You don't trust me," he said. "It is written plain on your face."

"Why should I?"

"True," he said. "Never rely on trust. Rely on the fact that neither of us wants to lose our power. And we cannot save it without each other."

"Mutual survival," I whispered. It was my original pledge to Kygo. The echo brought an ache to my throat.

Ido's keen eyes watched me. "Exactly."

I placed the glass lightning on the sand between us. "Show me how to make one of these."

"Take your sandals off and press your feet into the earth's energy, as well as your hands," Ido ordered. "Use the gateways."

I settled opposite him and dug my soles and palms past the warmth of the top sand to the cooler depths.

Ido gave a nod of approval and did the same. "Wait until I have united with my dragon, then follow." He gave a knowing half-smile. "I believe you can now feel that moment within me."

I stared down at the sand, bristling at his snort of amusement.

His breathing smoothed into the rhythm of mind-sight as silver flooded his eyes again. Then, deep within my body, I felt his joy as he called the Rat Dragon.

My turn.

Trying to ignore the sensual link to him, I focused on my own pathways of *Hua*. The air I drew in was warm and salty, the acrid remnants from the lightning strike lingering at its edges.

I held each breath in my Axis as Ido had taught me, the swell of energy slowly easing the tension in my body and opening the way into the celestial plane. Around me the beach shivered and folded into the streaming colors of the energy world: the surging silver of the water, the rainbow swirls of the earth and air, and the tiny specks of bright *Hua* that were the brief burn of circling flies.

"Good," Ido said.

I watched the flow of *Hua* through the long meridians of his transparent body, spinning the seven points of power into dense vitality. Yet the dark gap still cut into the purple glow of his crown. Beyond him the villagers watched, their energy bodies bright against the dull backdrop of their cottages.

Above, the Rat Dragon circled the glory of my Mirror Dragon. The blue brilliance of his scales was like flowing water around the fiery crimson of her sinuous body. I could not tell if their power was diminished in any way—they were both magnificent. As if suddenly aware of my attention, the Rat Dragon turned, his white beard half covering the iridescent blue pearl tucked beneath his chin.

But I was already lost in the depthless spirit eyes of my dragon. She lowered the immense wedge of her head to me, and I saw the golden glow of the pearl at her throat. I called our shared name, my joy leaping to meet the rush of her answer. Golden power, warmed with deep, woody notes of cinnamon, filled my senses.

My mind-sight split between earth and heaven. Ido's *Hua*

body sat before my own on the warm sand of the beach. At the same time, I was high above the cove and village, watching the swirl of energy colors and ancient pulsing ley lines through my dragon's eyes. Together, she and I looked inland, noting the *Hua* of many bodies moving toward the endless flux of the silvered sea. Around us the blue one circled, weaving power that blocked the relentless need of the other ten.

"The bereft dragons. They can't feel us!" I said.

"We are shielding your presence from them," Ido said. "We can't hold it for long. Show your dragon what you want in your mind, then use your dragon sight to find the lightning."

With a thrill of excitement, I pictured Ido's frozen flame of energy, then opened myself to the dizzying shift into full dragon sight, my earthly body dropping away from my senses.

Below us, the world separated into walking, crawling, flying, surging *Hua*. We felt the ebb and flow of energy through us and gloried in the delicate balance. We turned our ancient eyes to the dark clouds, tasting the molten energy that snapped across the cooler heights of the above-world. We watched the tiny rips in the cold *Hua*, each one birthing a streak of forked heat.

Find it. The voice was barely a whisper, deep within me. *Find it. Below.*

The soft insistence broke through my concentration, pulling me back into my body.

"Did you say something?" Yet it did not feel like Ido's mind-voice. Nor did it have the strength and pull of Kinra's need.

"No." Ido said. His silvery *Hua* leaped into a quicker flow through his meridians. "Is it the ten? Are they coming?"

"No!" I did not want to lose this chance to use my power. "It's not them. It's nothing."

I clenched my teeth and pictured the lightning again, straining to hold the image as I called the Mirror Dragon. She was there, waiting, the embrace of her power once again raising me above my earthbound body and narrow senses. We spiraled into the bright energy world. Power flowed in and out of us, the exchange strong and smooth, beating a rhythm of balance and harmony. Our ancient eyes searched the sky, waiting for the—

Find it, the voice whispered. *Below. Find it.*

Below? Our attention switched to the ground. Hundreds of points of *Hua* had gathered in a neat fan on the hill above the village. Ranks of them. Slowly moving down toward the sea. Toward us.

Ranks?

"Ido, those are soldiers!" The sudden understanding wrenched me out of the energy world. I squinted in the harsh sunlight and pitched forward, reeling from the abrupt loss of my dragon connection. "Soldiers, not villagers!"

Ido's hands caught me. "I know. I should have realized sooner." His eyes were clear amber: no silver threaded through them.

"We have to warn the others," I said. "I have to find Kygo." I hauled myself upright, lurching to one side on the soft sand. My senses were still half caught in the energy world.

Ido stood, blocking my way. "It's too late, Eona. There is no way they'll hold back that many soldiers. You and I will have to stop them."

His words pulled me up. "With our power? Like you did at the palace?" I shook my head, as much to stop the sickening memory of burning, screaming soldiers as to refuse. "I can't do that."

"You saw what's coming over the hill. We are totally outnumbered."

He was right. I looked up at the quiet village, spread around the crescent cove. In a few minutes it would be a battleground.

"I can't kill people with my power." I could barely carry the weight of the thirty-six who had already died at my hands.

"Not even to save your friends? Your beloved emperor?" He cocked his head. "Not even to save yourself, Eona?"

I looked back up at the village, my heart pounding. The dragons were for harmony, for life. Not killing. Not war.

"We can do it together," Ido said. "I'll hold off the ten dragons and you can use the lightn—"

I saw him register the same soft *zing* in the air as I did, a moment before the dull, wet thump of impact. He spun to the left and staggered a step, then crashed to his knees, eyes wide. An arrowhead protruded through his chest, blood seeping bright red into the dun cloth of his tunic. With an agonized gasp, he collapsed.

Yells erupted from behind the seawall as the villagers scattered. I dropped to the sand, instinct overriding shock. The arrow had come from high in the west cliffs. The closest cover was the upturned boat. I scrabbled to Ido on my hands and knees. He was on his side, hands pressed around the arrow shaft, panting. All color had drained from his face, and a soft sucking sound came from around the long metal arrowhead as blood welled between his fingers. The arrow had punctured his air. I had seen such wounds before: always fatal. I had to heal him. Fast.

"Ido, look at me." His eyes were muddy, the skin around his lips already tinged with blue. "We've got to get behind the boat."

Protest tightened his pale face, but I grabbed him under his left arm and pulled. The slight movement forced a groan out of him, and barely shifted his body. He was so heavy.

"Try," I urged. "Try."

He gulped for air and pushed his heels into the sand as I pulled on his arm again, but it did not help.

"Can't," he whispered. The effort to speak brought blood bubbling to the corner of his mouth.

"Eona!"

The frantic call jerked my head up. Two men were running across the sand toward us, swords drawn: Kygo, powering across the soft, sliding surface, and Caido, struggling to keep up with his emperor's speed. Beyond the seawall, the other two guards were marshaling the villagers.

"We are surrounded!" Kygo yelled.

"Get down!" I screamed, torn between relief and fear. I pointed behind them. "Arrows."

Immediately, both men ducked and zigzagged, but kept running. Kygo arrived first, showering Ido and me with sand, Caido close behind.

"Holy mother of Shola," Kygo swore, taking in Ido's injury. He grasped my arm. "Are you all right?"

I nodded. "I have to heal him. We don't have much time."

"You take one arm, I'll take the other," Kygo ordered Caido. "Get behind the boat, Eona." He pushed me toward it.

I heard Ido's wet moan as they hauled him to his feet and dragged him across the sand after me. I scrambled behind the boat and pressed myself against its solid shield. Kygo and Caido rounded the prow at a lopsided run, Ido slumped between them. Caido dropped his sword and braced Ido against his chest. With a small grunt of effort, he eased the Dragoneye down next to me. Kygo crouched at the end of the boat and cautiously peered around the edge.

"I'd say at least two companies, coming in from high ground," he said. "And so far, only one arrow." He looked back at Ido. "Straight for the main threat."

"We've been betrayed," Caido said.

"But is it one of the villagers?" Kygo returned to his tense watch. "Or one of our own?"

I pressed my hands to Ido's ashen face. Icy skin, but damp with sweat. He was close to the shadow world.

"Ido, stay awake. I need you to block the ten dragons when I heal you."

He widened his eyes, trying to focus on me through his

shallow, labored breaths. "Again?" His smile was no more than a twitch of blue lips.

"Will your healing power destroy the arrow?" Caido asked.

I shook my head. "I don't think so."

"Then we'll have to get it out." He touched the sleek feathered end protruding from Ido's back. "That fletching has to come off before I can pull the shaft through his body," he said. "Your Majesty, I'll hold him still, if you cut."

Kygo nodded and shifted into position, sword raised. "That fletching is imperial," he said.

Caido nodded. "Short bolt for a mechanical bow." He pulled Ido's limp body against his chest, holding him in an iron grip. "Go," he said.

One downward slice of Kygo's blade and the fletching dropped to the sand. It was a clean, fast cut, but it still pushed the remaining shaft farther into Ido's body, ripping a muffled scream from him. I grabbed his clawed hands.

The distant, unmistakable clash of metal against metal sent Kygo crawling back to the end of the boat. "The villagers have put up *tuaga*, but it's not going to hold that many men back for long." He looked around at us. "They are going to drive everyone onto the beach. No way back and no way forward. A death ground." He picked up his sword. "Caido, guard Lady Eona."

"Kygo, what are you doing?"

"They've broken through!" He launched himself into a low zigzagging run across the sand.

I rose on my knees, enough to see over the boat. With sword

raised, Kygo was heading for three soldiers advancing across the beach. Along the seawall, villagers were using hooks and poles to defend their barricade against a vicious attack from ten or so pikemen. Ryko and Dela had marshaled a group of men to hold back more troops who were slowly forcing their way through the maze of *tuaga* spread across the main road. A line of longbow archers, some of them women, stood on the seawall, firing into the ranks caught in the bottleneck created by the bamboo spikes.

I swallowed my fear and turned back to the task. "Caido, get that arrow out of Lord Ido."

With a nod, Caido dug his knees farther into the sand, bracing himself. "My lady, at the moment it is plugging the puncture. When I pull it out you're not going to have much time."

"Do it."

Caido's thin face tensed. He reached around and hammered his palm against the stub of shaft in Ido's back, pushing it through his body. Ido gasped and arched against the agony. With brutal speed, Caido grabbed the barbed shaft from the front and wrenched it out of Ido's chest in a wet sucking release.

I dug my own feet into the sand, pressing the gateways into the earth's energy. "Quick, lie him down."

The Dragoneye grunted as his back hit the sand. I pressed my hands against the wound, blocking the escape of air, as Caido scooped up his sword and crawled to the edge of the boat.

The resistance man tensed, rising into a crouch. "My lady," he said urgently. "His Majesty is in trouble."

"Go," I said. "Go."

He pushed himself up as the sound of sword meeting sword clanged with quickening intensity. Caido roared a battle cry and ran to his emperor's aid. I snatched a glance over the boat again. Kygo was fighting three men, the desperate struggle sending up showers of sand. For a moment I was frozen, caught between Kygo and Ido, both fighting for their lives.

Under my hands, Ido's chest jerked in shallow pants, his blood warm and sticky on my skin. Right now, he was in more peril. I forced myself to take a shaking breath. I could do this; I had done it before. Another breath, this time steadier. Finally, on the third, I saw Ido's solid body shift into energy, his seven points of power dull and getting darker with each labored beat of his heart. There was no silvery flow through the meridians along the right side of his body. On the next breath I called the Mirror Dragon, opening myself to her power with the urgent command: *Heal.*

Hua tore through me in joyous union, filling my body with the ecstasy of golden song and the majesty of dragon-sight. Below us, the battle on the seafront was a swarm of bright dots coming together and breaking apart in a desperate dance. We saw the blue one—his thin tether to the earthly body fading—trying to circle us, trying to protect, but the other ten had already felt our presence.

Heal! We gathered power from the endless ebb and flow of the sea, from the wild energy of the approaching cyclone, from the crisscross of lines that pulsed deep in the earth. We were

Hua and our golden howl roared through the pathways of Ido's body, knitting flesh and sinew, fusing dark pathways back into the smooth silvery flow of life. As one, his seven points of power burst back into spinning bright vitality, the black gap in his crown still present, still resisting my influence. Ido gasped—a long, raw breath that leaped through his *Hua*. The Rat Dragon shrieked, power pulsing across his blue scales, opal claws spreading. His energized body coiled into readiness, his huge head swinging left to right, scanning the below-world. The ten dragons were coming—and their need was greater than ever before.

"Eona!" Ido pulled me down on top of him. The sudden contact wrenched me back into my earthly body. His eyes, so close to mine, were all silver. "We can use the ten to stop the soldiers."

Then I was back with the Mirror Dragon, the lift of her power pulling me into her sinuous strength. We rolled through the heavy clouds, our ruby claws slashing at the pressure that closed in on all sides. Beside us, the blue one shrieked again, twisting to meet the energy that circled in a high-pitched keen of ten sorrowing songs.

Their savage arrival slammed power across our body, knocking us backward through the air. We twisted, muscles straining to stop the impetus. A huge green body rammed us, emerald claws ripping through red scales. We screamed and ducked, our tail battering the bright green flank. The clash of *Hua* boomed across the sky. The Rabbit Dragon pounced, but the blue beast rammed him, and the huge pink body tumbled past.

Go lower. Ido's mind-voice cut through the fury of dragon battle. *To the soldiers.*

We found the ranks of bright *Hua* streaming down the hill and dived toward them. The ten followed behind us in a shrieking, ragged circle. The Rat Dragon twisted through the air, claws and teeth driving the Ox and Tiger out of formation, flattening the circle of dragons into a lopsided crescent.

Now!

We opened our pathways, the familiar orange taste of his power roaring through us, drawing up our energy. But this time we were not left behind. This time we were riding the roiling wave of *Hua* with Ido and the blue beast. Around us, the dragons were trying to re-form their circle. We had to stop them.

Bind the lightning, Ido ordered.

We felt the blue beast harvesting the tiny cold sparks of energy within the clouds, drawing them into the burning rush of our united power. We clawed at a bright flicker, pulling it into the rolling force. Deep within us we heard a howling song of destruction, a churning mix of gold and silver power spiked with the flashing fire of lightning.

Eona, aim it at the soldiers.

How?

Channel, like you do when you heal.

We felt our combined power gather into a crest, hanging for a moment as if offering the chance to step back. And then it broke, crashing into a rush of devastation.

With all our strength we tried to channel it downward, but

most of it flooded through our unpracticed grasp and slammed into the ten beasts around us. Their circle broke across the celestial plane. Shrieking, they vanished, leaving the bitter taste of despair.

Ido and the Rat Dragon were not so clumsy. With iron control, they sent destruction into the earth below. The fireball of lightning and power ripped through the bright points of *Hua* marching toward the village, obliterating the ranks of soldiers in its roaring path. Flames washed across the hill, the savage energy glowing through the celestial plane like a false dawn. Dirt and rock and ash spun upward into high arcs, then fell across the village and beach in a dark driving rain. The battle lines broke as screaming people ran for cover from the pelting debris.

I gasped, dragged back into my earthly body by the sudden sharp impact of a rock that sent hot pain through my shoulder. I blinked through a blur of tears, the heat and shape beneath me coalescing into Ido's body, the tight wrap of his arms holding me against his chest.

"It's not finished yet," he said.

He rolled over until I was under him, the full length of his body shielding me, his weight braced on his elbows. The aftershock boomed across the beach, the sand shifting under us, a fine layer of ash sweeping across our skin in a hot wind. Ido winced as stones thudded against his back and clumps of earth exploded around us in plumes of dust.

"It will stop in a moment," he said, glancing up at the leaden sky.

The wild savagery of the dragon battle and the exhilaration of power slipped away from me. I was hollow, a shell made of distant screaming, falling ash, and the dank stench of incinerated land and people.

"What did we do?" I whispered, horror locking me under him.

"We stopped Sethon from killing everybody and taking us." He touched my wet cheek with a bloodstained finger. The coppery tang echoed the drifting smell of death in the air. "You should be celebrating."

Celebrate? When all I could see was the image of all those soldiers on the hillside extinguished in just one fiery moment. "We killed them all. So fast."

He watched me, his brows drawn into a small frown. "It was us or them, Eona. Your power just saved all your friends."

Although it was true, I shook my head, unable to find words for the desolation that pierced my spirit.

"You are too tender." Hesitantly, he cupped my cheek in his hand. "You will be undone if you think of them as men. They are your enemy."

"Is that what you do?"

"No, I do this." He lowered his mouth to mine. I closed my eyes, part of me knowing I should push him away—the other part longing for a moment that held life, not death.

I felt Ido's body tense and opened my eyes. The tip of a sword slid along his jaw, forcing his head back. Kygo stood over us. Under the streaks of ash and sweat, his face was white with fury. "Get off her."

The shock in Ido's eyes hardened into rage. Slowly, he pushed himself away from my body, the sword guiding him back on to his knees.

"Are you all right?" Kygo asked me. His voice snapped like a whip.

I nodded. Somewhere in the village, a child wailed, the heartrending sound rising above the other calls and shouts; closer, the sporadic sounds of steel meeting steel echoed through the blanketing quiet of the drifting dust.

Kygo shifted the sword against Ido's throat. "Did you make that fireball?"

Ido's lips were drawn back into a snarl. "You should thank us," he said. "Lady Eona and I saved your precious resistance."

Kygo's eyes fixed on me. "You did that, Eona?"

I curled my body against the boat, away from the awe in his voice. "You were outnumbered. I didn't want you to get hurt."

Kygo stepped back from Ido and lowered the sword. The Dragoneye rubbed the thin line of blood that the blade had pressed from his skin.

"Now you have your army of two, Your Majesty," he said acidly. "Tried and tested."

I stared at the Dragoneye. "What do you mean?"

"Don't be naïve, Eona." Ido shot a malicious glance at Kygo. "Do you think he got me out of the palace to nurture crops and redirect rain? I am here as a weapon, and you are here to blunt or sharpen my blade at his command."

I looked at Kygo. "That's not true, is it?"

Kygo straightened. "You said it yourself, Eona—we are outnumbered. We will always be outnumbered. I swear I never wanted you to break the Covenant. I just wanted you to control *him.*" He nodded at Ido. "*He* has no problem killing people."

Ido laughed, a sharp bitter sound. "You are not so different from your uncle."

Kygo's hand tightened around the hilt of his sword.

"When were you going to tell me about this, Kygo?" My voice sounded distant, as if I stood lengths away from myself.

"When we got to the eastern rendezvous. Before the final strike."

I stood up. "Well, now I know." Beyond the boat, the bodies of three soldiers lay on the sand. Caido looked up from salvaging their fallen weapons as I rounded the prow.

"Eona," Kygo called behind me. "I was going to *ask* you."

I looked over my shoulder. "Thank you for that consideration, Your Majesty."

Wrapping my arms around my body, I walked steadily toward the battle-torn village, the huge blackened gouge in the hill above it like a long, deep scar.

CHAPTER EIGHTEEN

CAIDO STEPPED BETWEEN the two bodies sprawled across the narrow ridge above the beach. One man had no obvious marks on him, but his neck was bent at an ominous angle. The other had been stabbed in the heart, flies circling the knife embedded in his chest. A quiver of arrows was strapped across the man's back. Although I stood a few lengths away and the low light of dusk was approaching, I could see that their fletching was the same as on the arrow that had hit Ido.

"Yes, this is Jun, Your Majesty," Caido said, staring at the knifed man. He shook his head. "I can't believe it. He has been with the resistance from the start."

It was the young archer who had often guarded Ido. He had seemed loyal, but I had only spoken to him once or twice. Who knew what went on in the hearts of men? I certainly did not.

"Who is the other man?" Kygo asked.

"One of the village lookouts," Yuso said. "All the other village sentries are dead, shot with the same arrows as those in the quiver. An efficient job." He glanced at Caido questioningly.

Caido wiped his mouth. "Jun was our best bowman." He looked across the beach to the boat where we had sheltered. "Good enough to make that shot with ease." He sighed, the whole of his thin body lifting and falling with disillusion. "This is going to kill his father."

Ryko stood from his crouched survey of the area. "It looks as if the sentry surprised Jun." He pointed to a scuffed area behind two boulders. "The man got his knife home before Jun broke his neck."

"What say you, *Naiso*?" Kygo asked. His eyes did not quite meet mine.

The emperor had ordered his *Naiso* to accompany him, and his *Naiso* had obeyed. But if Kygo had hoped Eona was also at his side, he was wrong. She was buried somewhere deep within me, numb and silent.

"Was he ever in the army, Caido?" I asked.

The resistance man nodded. "It is where he learned his bow skills. He had some funny stories to tell around the fire." He cleared his throat. "I am sorry, Your Majesty, it is hard to reconcile the man and the deed."

Kygo grunted. "I fear there is not much room for doubt. Still, question the prisoners for confirmation, Yuso. Maybe they saw him in their camp. "

Yuso bowed, wincing slightly with pain. "Yes, Your Majesty."

Kygo glanced around the ridge again. "Leave his body for the scavengers and bring the villager back for burial." He gestured to me. "Come, *Naiso*."

I followed him down the narrow track. One of the soldiers on the beach had sliced into the long muscle of his thigh. Vida had efficiently stitched it, along with Yuso's nasty shoulder gash and Dela's slashed face, but she had no herbs that dulled pain. Kygo did not show it in face or manner, but the cant of his shoulders told me the injury stabbed with every step. Or perhaps it was the burden of Jun's betrayal and the deaths of the fourteen villagers who had perished defending their young emperor.

The black ash on the track muffled our footsteps. All the foliage on the bushes and trees around us was dusted with it, too, and the once-white beach below us was now gray. The tide was coming in with the setting sun, the water washing clean curves of white sand as it surged and ebbed. Master Tozay's boat was due into harbor soon. The village fishing fleet had already returned, drawn back early by the sight of the fireball. The hollow-eyed shock of the men as they had landed on the beach and seen the damage to the higher sections of the village had briefly pierced even my numb armor.

"For such a young man, this Jun had extraordinary spying skills," Kygo said. "He must have woven a dense web of lies."

"In my experience, young men lie with great skill and ease," I said dully.

Kygo stopped and faced me. "It was not a lie, Eona."

I felt my gaze pulled to the pale shine of the pearl, half covered by his tunic collar. "What was it, then?"

"It was me leading my army in the best way I know how." He pressed his fingers along his eye sockets, rubbing away the strain. "Yes, I want you to control Ido's power. But I swear it was never in my plan to ask you to break the Covenant and use the Mirror Dragon to kill. You and your dragon are our symbols of healing and renewal." He crossed his arms. "And hope."

"I did it to save you." If I said it enough times, maybe it would make me feel better.

"I know. When I found out we were surrounded, my first thought was getting to you." He reached out toward me but stopped, his hand dropping to his side. "You didn't push Ido away."

The abrupt accusation broke through my protective shell. "What?"

His jaw tightened. "He was on top of you, and you didn't push him away."

I flushed. "I had just killed hundreds of men with power that comes from my *Hua*. You cannot understand what that feels like—or what it takes from me."

"But he can." Kygo looked out across the water. "You and he are bound by power. Are you bound to him by anything else?" His voice was without inflection, as though the answer did not matter.

"What do you mean?" For a dizzying moment I thought he knew about the *Hua* of All Men. About the black folio.

He turned his head, his face a polite mask. "Do you desire Lord Ido?"

Relief—and uncertainty—made me hesitate a beat too long. "No!"

His look of disbelief was like a punch to my chest.

I stepped closer. "Kygo, you know Ido manipulates whenever he can. It is second nature to him. Please, do not let him come between us." The pearl glowed within the edge of my vision.

"Every time you are alone with him, it feels like you are moving further from me," Kygo whispered.

I shook my head in mute denial. He touched my face, the curve of his hand drawing me toward him. I closed my eyes and felt the soft press of his lips against mine. His hand shifted to the nape of my neck, guiding me closer against his mouth. I knew I should pull away—protect him—but I had to prove my certainty. To him. To me. We found the taste of each other at the same time; the sweet kiss forcing a soft sound of pleasure from him that shivered through my whole being. I laid my hands against his chest and felt the quick rhythm of his heart through the tunic.

He pulled me against his body, his hand at the small of my back, holding me against his hips. I shifted, trying to meld even closer to his warmth, his taste, his smell. His breath caught as I jarred his thigh wound. I started to move away, apologize, but he followed and captured my mouth again, his hand sliding around my waist and pulling me back into his embrace. A beat thundered through me, a pulsing, driving rhythm that was in my body—and, I realized, in the base of my skull. The pearl. I gave a shake of my head, trying to stop the pressure. The draw was not strong; I could contain it.

Kygo broke our kiss, the concern in his eyes holding back the desire. He'd misread the shake of my head. I brought my mouth to his again and felt him smile against my lips. The gentle press of his tongue parted my answering smile. His hand shifted from my nape to trace the curve of my throat and collarbone with exquisite slowness, his gentle touch leaving a path of pleasure across my skin.

He rested his forehead against my own, the rasp of his breaths echoing mine. His face was so close it was a blur, but I could still see the glow of the pearl between us. I slid my hand into the loosened cross-tie of his tunic, my fingers trailing across the flat muscle of his chest, toward the glowing prize. Toward the *Hua* of All Men. As my fingertips brushed the edge of the scar of stitches, he tilted his head back, eyes closed, the strong curve of his throat exposed. I could rip the pearl out now—

The pearl! A cold wash of understanding broke through the thrumming in my head. I snatched my hand back. With all my strength, I pushed Kygo away.

He staggered back. "What are you doing?"

I groped for a way to stop the confusion in his eyes. A reason that was not the pearl. "It's the dragons."

His confusion snapped into something more savage. "Is it? Or is it Ido?"

A sound from farther up the track wrenched us both around:

Yuso and Ryko, their guilty withdrawal making it obvious they had witnessed more than the last few moments. I turned and ran down the track toward the village, the muffled thud of my footsteps sending wisps of ash into the heavy air.

In the last of the daylight, Vida and I sat silently on the seawall and watched the arrival of Master Tozay's boat. It was an ocean junk with three lugsails, the horizontal bamboo battens across the sailcloth like the ribs of a folding fan. The white painted eyes on its prow—eerily lit by the lanterns on deck—stared at me with flat accusation. Silhouettes on board darted to and fro with the business of anchoring. I kept my gaze fixed on the three small figures at the front. Was one of them my mother, straining to see if I waited on the beach?

"Are you ready, my lady?" Vida asked, pushing herself off the low stone wall. "My father will want to turn on the high tide. The more distance we can put between us and the cyclone, the better."

Was I ready? We had at least four days ahead on the boat as we rounded the Dragon's Belly—the large mass of land in the southeast—to reach the rendezvous in the east. Four days with a mother I had not seen for ten years, two powerful men who hated each other, and friends who did not trust me. I turned to watch the trail of lanterns heading up the east cliffs: the villagers were shifting their lives into the nearby caves. Weathering a deadly cyclone and a vengeful army in a network of dark, dank caverns seemed far less daunting than the boat journey ahead.

A splash brought my attention back to the junk. A small tender had been lowered over the side. Four figures climbed down a rope ladder into the vessel and pushed off, an oarsman pulling strongly toward shore. None of the silhouettes looked like a woman.

Kygo and Elder Rito stepped down on to the beach, the rest of our troop gathering behind them. Beyond them, two men shoved Lord Ido onto his knees in the sand. Kygo called Dela to him and gave her low-voiced instructions that sent her heading toward us. She trod heavily across the sand, part of the right side of her face bandaged; a sword had sliced her cheek open and taken off half her ear.

She bowed. "His Majesty commands the presence of his *Naiso*."

As she raised her head, I saw the mute apology in her eyes. For a moment I could not understand her guilt, then I remembered the small bathhouse betrayal orchestrated between her and Vida. It seemed distant and pale in comparison to what had happened on the beach.

I stood and gently squeezed her shoulder, feeling the tension in her body ease a notch. "How are you, Dela? Vida tells me it is a nasty wound."

She touched the tight bandage. "It is not going to help my good looks." Although trying for lightness, her tone rang hollow. With a quick glance behind us, she pushed something into my hand: the small leather pouch that held my ancestors' death plaques. "You should take these for now." A shake of her head curbed my protest. "They are the only things your mother gave you. You should be carrying them when you meet. Show her you never forgot." She leaned closer, her voice lowering. "Maybe she will know more about your ancestress."

Reluctantly, I took the pouch and slid it into my tunic pocket. Wrapped in leather and hidden away, Kinra's plaque posed no real threat. Still, it made me uneasy to carry it.

Dela patted my hand. "Come. His Majesty is waiting and he is not happy."

"I can imagine," I muttered, and led the way back across the sand.

As we approached, Kygo's eyes stayed steadfastly on the approaching boat. Ido, however, kept his gaze on me. He had been bound again, this time with his hands behind his back and, judging by the awkward shifts of his shoulders, as painfully as possible—a deliberate show that Lord Ido and his power were still under the control of the Emperor. And perhaps Kygo was not above some private malice, too.

Forcing myself to ignore Ido, I bowed to Kygo, but he gave no flicker of acknowledgment. I took my position at his left shoulder. The tender bumped into the rise of the shore, and all four occupants vaulted out, grabbing the edges and pulling it on to the beach. The solid, stocky shape of Master Tozay strode across the sand, flanked by two other seamen. The fourth man stayed beside the beached boat.

Tozay's pace increased, pulling him away from his men.

Anxiously, he scanned the people behind us. I saw the moment he found Vida: his stern features softened, and his head bowed in relief, or maybe in a prayer of thanks. With a small nod to her, he continued toward us, his men at his side again. They dropped to their knees in the sand and bowed.

"Rise, Master Tozay," Kygo said. "You are indeed welcome."

Tozay sat back on his heels. "We were not sure what to expect, Your Majesty. We saw the fireball."

"An opportunistic betrayal that Lady Eona and Lord Ido quashed," Kygo said. "Together." Beyond its surface meaning, the single word clearly had some other importance between the two men.

Tozay took in the Dragoneye's kneeling, bound constraint. "I see," he said dryly. "And will Lord Ido require separate, lockable quarters, Your Majesty?"

"Yes," Kygo said shortly.

I cleared my throat, the sound turning Kygo's face toward me, eyes narrowed. Did he think I was going to intercede on Ido's behalf?

"Is my mother on board, Master Tozay?" I asked quickly. "Is she all right?"

Tozay bobbed his head. "Your mother is well, Lady Eona. She awaits your arrival eagerly." He glanced back at his ship. "If you please, Your Majesty, we must make a move if we are to sail on this high tide."

The man waiting with the tender bowed as Kygo, Tozay, and I approached. Kygo stepped into the small boat first, taking the stern seat. Tozay took my hand and helped me on board, the pressure of his hold directing me to the prow seat. He sprang in nimbly between us and took the oars as his men pushed us out into the water. With his strong strokes we were soon midway between shore and ship, a cooler sea breeze diluting the smell of burnt death that drifted from the land. "What news?" Kygo said.

Tozay glanced back at me.

"You can speak freely," Kygo said. "Lady Eona is now aware of the major part she will be playing in the events to come." We stared at each other: it was no small thing for him to trust me with whatever Tozay had to report. "Lady Eona is now my *Naiso*," Kygo added. His words felt like an apology and an absolution, all in one.

I caught the quick lift of Tozay's eyebrows as he turned back to his rowing. "We've had more reports of land disasters—floods, earthshakes, mudslides—particularly in the south and west regions."

I looked up at the darkening sky, the wheel and dip of a few white gulls bright against the heavy clouds. It made grim sense; all of the dragons connected to the pure south and west compass points were in exile, whereas the easterly and northern compass points still had the presence of the Mirror Dragon and the Rat Dragon to create some balance in the earth energy. Not a lot of balance, though, and not for long if Ido's judgment about the decline of our power was correct. Surely he would have known that killing the other Dragoneyes would create this turmoil.

"The tavern whispers are getting louder in their call for the

Right of Ill Fortune," Tozay added. "We are getting some good recruits."

I straightened on the hard bench. The Right of Ill Fortune proclaimed that an emperor whose reign was besieged by too many earth/water disasters could be denounced by the people and replaced with a ruler who was favored by the gods. A way to end Sethon's reign without war.

"The whispers are not loud enough, nor quick enough," Kygo said, squashing my hope. "If my uncle would not honor Rightful Claim, he would certainly quell any attempt at Ill Fortune. Still, such unease will work for us. The people are beginning to realize that he does not have the good will of either the gods or the last two Dragoneyes." His eyes flicked to me then back to Tozay. "What news of my uncle's progress?"

"The lure is working, Your Majesty. Sethon is personally marching his men to the east at a punishing pace for the final strike. The numbers, however, will be bigger than we anticipated."

"How much bigger?"

For a few moments there was just the rhythmic splash of oars and the slap of waves against the prow. "My spies estimate at least fifteen thousand," Tozay said.

I pressed my hand over my mouth. Fifteen thousand soldiers? Were Ido and I expected to kill so many? The cold sensation of killing four hundred a few hours ago slid down my spine.

Kygo's silence was eloquent. "Has he drawn from his other battalions?" he finally asked.

Tozay shook his head. "No. Mercenaries."

Kygo blew out a long breath. "It is not as good as him weakening his other forces, but it is better than an alliance. And bringing in paid foreigners will not endear him to the people, either."

Tozay snorted. "Sethon has never sought the *Hua-do* in any way."

Kygo tilted his head in agreement. "Is the east preparing? Stripping the land?"

"There is not much to strip after five hundred years without a dragon's blessing. But all is being done as you ordered," Tozay said. "There will be no food for his men. The tribes are preparing maps and scouting enclosed ground."

"Enclosed ground?" I asked.

"Areas that are reached through narrow gorges and paths," Kygo said. "It is where a small number can attack a large."

I leaned forward. "How small is our number, exactly?"

Kygo shot a glance at Tozay.

"We are four and half thousand," the master fisherman said. "And two Dragoneyes."

I licked my lips. "I don't know if even Ido will kill fifteen thousand men," I said.

Tozay stopped rowing, and looked over his shoulder at me. "He will if you compel him."

I swallowed the dryness in my throat. "What if I don't?"

Tozay's face hardened. "Lady Eona, when you stepped into my boat with the palace in flames behind us, you told me you wanted to join the resistance. What did you think you would be doing?" He glanced at the burned hillside. "Quickening crops?"

"Enough, Tozay." Kygo's voice snapped with command. "The Covenant of Service was put in place for a reason. It is better if Lady Eona finds it hard to break than if she does not. We don't want another power-hungry Dragoneye like Lord Ido, do we?"

I stiffened at the edge in his voice. Perhaps I was not completely absolved.

The master fisherman turned and began rowing again. The hull of the junk loomed ahead of us, one round painted eye watching our approach like a startled horse. I pressed my hands together, the grim war-mongering temporarily pushed back by the impending reunion with my mother.

"What is she like, Master Tozay?" I asked, breaking the heavy silence. "My mother, I mean. Has she said anything about me?"

"Lillia does not talk much," Tozay said gruffly. "But you are the image of her in face and body." He heaved once more on the oars, the impetus taking us to the side of the junk and the rope ladder. "You will see for yourself in a moment or two."

I craned back my head to look at the people watching over the raised side of the deck. The ship lanterns behind them cast their figures into silhouette and hid the details of face and form from me. There was, however, one small, slender shape mirroring my intense search.

A sailor quickly descended the ladder and landed lightly in the boat, his deferential bow rocking us to and fro. He took charge of the oars as Kygo mounted the ladder, all the people disappearing from the side as the emperor stepped on board. I followed, with Tozay close behind. The swinging, jolting journey up the wood rungs was, I'm sure, only a few moments, but it felt like a full bell.

Strong hands pulled me up onto the solid deck. I caught a quick image of rough faces and weathered skin before everyone lowered into bows before the Lady Dragoneye. Three rows of men—and one female figure—on their knees, heads bent, waiting for me to release them.

"Rise," I said, my voice cracking.

As Lillia sat back, our eyes met. I saw fear and hope and a strained smile that held ten years of loss. Tozay was right: we were the image of each other.

Lillia pressed herself against the bulkhead as the deck-boy set a tray down on the fixed table in Master Tozay's command cabin. The master fisherman had ushered Lillia and me to its spacious privacy once everyone else was on board, calling for tea as he led us down to the mid-deck. We had passed the locked compartment where Lord Ido was already incarcerated, the guard dipping into a duty bow and flattening himself back against the door as we made our way along the narrow passage. Tozay had glanced back at me, watching my reaction. Perhaps he thought I would wrench the door open and release the Dragoneye.

"Sir." The deck-boy's agonized whisper was loud in the thick silence that had descended across the command cabin. "I have forgotten the hot water."

Master Tozay jerked his head toward the hatchway. "Be quick."

I picked up one of the nautical instruments from the lipped shelf behind me. It was a brass compass of some sort, its dial gleaming in the extravagant glow of the three large wall lanterns lighting the cabin. I turned it over and over in my hands, glad to have somewhere to focus. Even through my unease, it was occurring to me that Master Tozay was not quite the simple fisherman turned resistance fighter that he professed to be. He cleared away the star charts spread across the table, his pace quickening as neither Lillia nor I made any move to speak. The boy returned, hurriedly mixed tea and retrieved water together, and with a bow backed out of the cabin.

"I will leave you two alone, my lady, to get acquainted," Master Tozay said, slipping the last scroll into one of the neat slots built into the bulkhead. He glanced across at Lillia's downturned face and clasped hands. A quick bow, and the door closed behind him.

Above us came the calls and creaks of the junk getting under way. I returned the instrument to the shelf.

"May I pour you some tea?" I asked.

She finally looked up. Although the weight of time had softened the taut lines of her face, it was more or less the same oval as my own. Perhaps her chin was less stubbornly set and her nose longer, but her mouth had my upward tilt and her eyes the same wide cast. I knew the expression on her face, too. I had worn it many times myself—an overly courteous mask designed to avoid irritating a master or mistress.

"No, please, allow me, my lady," she said and crossed to the table. She picked up the brewing dish, deftly pouring a measure into the first bowl.

I chewed my lip. She could not seem to scale the mountain of my rank. "Thank you," I said—then took a breath and climbed my own mountain. "Mother."

Her hand shook, spilling some of the tea onto the table. Slowly she placed the brewing dish down, carefully cupped the first bowl, and carried it to me. With a bow, she held it out. As I reached, we both paused, staring down at the meeting of our hands. Both were long-fingered, with a thumb almost at right angles.

"We have the same hands," I said, wincing at my too-bright tone as I took the bowl.

"They were my mother's hands, too," she said softly. She chanced a fleeting look up at me. "Charra. Your grandmother."

"Charra? I have her death plaque."

"You still have it?"

I silently thanked Dela. "Yes, and the *other one*, too."

My mother caught the emphasis and looked away. She knew something about Kinra.

I placed the bowl on the table and retrieved my leather pouch, upending it. The two plaques slipped out onto my palm. With a shaking forefinger, Lillia touched Charra's memorial, then pulled out a worn cloth bag that hung on a string around her neck. She opened it and withdrew another death plaque, a replica of Charra's.

"I had two made when my dear mother died—may she walk in the garden of the gods," she said. "I knew *he* wanted to get rid of you as soon as she died. I had to give you a link to your family. To me." She stroked the plaque again. "He was afraid of Charra."

A sour lump formed in my throat. "Do you mean my father?"

Lillia gave a strained laugh. "No, not your dear father. Charra loved him as if he was her own. No, he died—drowned in the terrible Pig Year storms. Do you not remember?"

I shook my head, and pain crossed her face.

"I'm sorry," I said. "I do not remember much at all."

"I suppose it is to be expected. You were only four when he joined the glory of his ancestors. I married another man, a year after." She studied me. "You do not remember your stepfather, either? Or what happened?"

"No."

"Probably a good thing," she said grimly. "He said he'd provide for all of us—you, me, your brother, even Charra—but when things got hard, he said he would not keep another man's useless daughter. It was enough, he said, to raise another man's son. He sold you to a bondsman."

"Why did you let him?" The question came out too harshly.

"'Let him'?" She frowned, puzzled. "He was my husband. How could I gainsay him?"

"Did you even try?"

I would have fought for my daughter. I would have fought as hard as possible.

She turned her head away from the veiled accusation. "I begged the bondsman to sell you into house service." Her voice dropped into a whisper. "Did he?"

"Yes." It was partly true—I did start off in the salt farmer's house as one of the kitchen drudges—but what would be the use of telling her the whole story? The farmer's wife who eventually sent us all to the salt when her husband noticed us, and the choking misery of the long days, and the nights spent with breaths held, listening for the tread of the whipmaster.

"What happened to my brother?" I asked.

In an instant, her face aged, the sweet tilt of her mouth lost in bitterness. "He took up soldiering a year ago and died in the Trang Dein raids."

I felt a cold, unexpected plunge of loss, although in truth this woman and her son were strangers to me. Yet there it was—an ache for the lost chance of a family. Or maybe it was the stark sorrow on my mother's face.

She looked up and forced a smile, touching my arm hesitantly. "I thought I had no one left. Until Master Tozay's men came."

"You know why you are here, don't you?"

She shook her head. "Master Tozay said that I could be used against you—although I do not see how. I am nothing."

"You are the Mirror Dragoneye's mother," I said, watching

her closely. "And you may be awed by the rank, but you are not shocked by a female Dragoneye like everyone else, are you?" I smiled, trying to take the edge out of my words. "Can you see the dragons too, Mother?"

Her eyes were steady on mine. "Daughter, until a few weeks ago, women who claimed to see dragons found themselves either chained to other madwomen or dead."

I clasped her shoulder. "Did you know I could see them?"

"All the women in our family can see them. It is our secret."

"What can you tell me about Kinra?" She stepped back, breaking my hold, but I followed her retreat. "Please, tell me what you know. It is more important than you think."

She licked her lips. "I gave you the plaque. I taught you the rhyme."

"What rhyme?"

She leaned closer. "The rhyme that is passed from mother to daughter.

"Rat turns, Dragon learns, Empire burns.
Rat takes, Dragon breaks, Empire wakes."

I froze. I did know it, or at least the first part of it: I remembered sitting opposite my master in his study, before the approach ceremony, and hearing its simple rhythm in my head. I had thought it was something I'd read in one of his history scrolls.

"We used to say the rhyme together—when we walked

along the beach where no one could hear," my mother added.

Kinra had tried two ways to send her message across time: a rhyme passed through generations, and a portent written in code in a Dragoneye's journal. I wished that she had not hidden her meaning so well, but I knew why; to protect the Mirror Dragoneye bloodline, exiled by her attempt on the Imperial Pearl.

"What does the rhyme mean?" I asked.

She shook her head. "I was told by Charra that it came from the same Kinra whose plaque had to be handed down from mother to daughter. It was our duty to pass along three things." She counted them off on her fingers. "The plaque, the rhyme, and the riddle—which, frankly, is not a true riddle, and does not bring any honor to her name."

I stared at her; I had no recollection of a riddle. Was this the missing piece of the puzzle?

I caught her arm. "What riddle?"

Startled, she looked down at my tight hold. "Her daughter had two fathers, but only one bloodline. Two into one is doubled."

"Two into one is doubled?" I echoed.

The words rang no sudden chime of understanding through me. The puzzle did not click into place. But I could at least guess the two fathers: Emperor Dao and Lord Somo. Only one bloodline. Two lovers, but only one was the father. My breath caught as an intuition gathered force, a roaring build of hope and possibility.

Kinra's line could have royal blood. Dao's blood.

I could have royal blood.

Kygo—we could be together. Truly together. My blood would be both royal and Dragoneye. And that would stop any other royal blood from binding me with the black folio. I would be invulnerable. I would have everything.

"Which one was the father?" I tightened my grip on Lillia's arm. "Which one? Do you know?"

She pulled away from me and stepped back against the bulkhead, eyes wide. I knew I was frightening her, but she had to answer me.

"Tell me!"

"'The one she loved.' That is the answer to the riddle. That is all I know!"

But I knew more than she did.

"No!" I clasped my hands on either side of my head, trying to stop the truth from forcing its way through my hope. "No!" But I knew Kinra had loved Lord Somo. Not Emperor Dao. Dela had told me that Somo was the nameless man in the journal, and Ido had read it in his records. Kinra had loved the Dragoneye, not the emperor. I did not have royal blood. I had double Dragoneye blood. It had probably given me my strong dragon sight, but it did not give me what I truly needed—a way to save both Kygo and the dragons.

I bent over, sobbing for breath under the crushing return of desperation. For just one glorious moment, I had seen a way out.

My mother edged closer, her hand hesitantly touching my

shoulder. "Why are you crying, daughter? What does the riddle mean?"

"She loved Somo." I took a shaking breath. "She loved the wrong man."

Her hand patted my back. "She will not have been the first," my mother said. "And she will not be the last." She peered into my face. "You are very pale. Come, sit down. When did you last eat? Or sleep?"

I let her usher me to a chair and press the cooled tea bowl into my hands.

"Tell me what all this means," she said.

In the clear golden liquid, I watched my reflection summon a mask of courtesy.

I smiled up into the face that was so very like my own. There was no denying that we were mother and daughter—but for the moment, we were also strangers. "You are right, I need to sleep. Perhaps we can talk about it later."

CHAPTER NINETEEN

I HAD NOT lied to my mother—I did need to sleep. Master Tozay assigned me the chief mate's quarters farther along the mid-deck. It was a cramped cabin, but one of the few private spaces on the ship. The narrow bunk was set into a nook created by two tall cupboards at head and foot, and a low bank of storage lockers above. I stretched out on the bed and tried to ignore the boxed-in sensation and the dank smell. If I'd not had the oil lamp burning, it would have felt like a tomb.

Under my fatigue and discomfort, another kind of restlessness scratched at my spirit and kept me awake. At first, I thought it was the enigma of my mother's rhyme. What would the Rat take—the pearl, or something else? And what would the dragon break to wake the empire? The Covenant, the pearl, my word . . . my heart? There was no doubt that it meant Ido and me, but was it a prophecy or a warning?

Even after I had exhausted the rhyme's grim possibilities, the scratchy unease kept my eyes wide open and my body shifting against the hemp mattress. The pitch of the junk had deepened, the plunge and sway not quite rhythmic enough to lull me to sleep. Finally, I gave in to the need to move and the hankering for fresh air.

I lurched along the creaking passageway, my approach watched by Ido's guard. The Dragoneye's jail—a hastily cleared storage compartment—was near the steps that led to both the upper deck and down below, where the crew lived and, for now, our troop was quartered. Under the junk's rolling progress, I heard the murmur of their voices and saw the dim glow of lamplight rising up the steps. The guard ducked his head in a duty bow as I passed and climbed into the night.

The slap of fresh air made me gasp. Those sailors on duty and watch marked my arrival in the swinging light of the lanterns, but turned back to their windblown tasks. I made my way across the deck to the thick railing, the dipping roll of the junk every now and again sending me into an inelegant lurch. I found the rail and pressed the lower half of my body against the security of its solid wall.

Spray from the cut of our passage dusted my face with water and the taste of salt. Above, the dark sky bore down upon us, the banks of cloud like a huge bulwark between heaven and earth. As I watched a fork of lightning flash deep within them, I realized the source of my driving need for space and air; the approaching cyclone was affecting my *Hua.* Was this something that always happened to a Dragoneye? If I was this unsettled, Ido must be crawling up the walls of his narrow prison.

A stocky figure strode along the deck toward me with practiced balance: Master Tozay. I lifted my hand in greeting.

He stopped beside me. "Good evening, Lady Eona."

"Not really, is it?" I said, tilting my head back at the sky.

"No." He followed my gaze. "We will outrun most of it, but I think the edge will catch us. These weather patterns are the most bizarre I have ever seen."

"Where is His Majesty?" I asked.

"Sleeping." Tozay turned toward me, his thickset body blocking the wind that snatched at our words. With a gesture to his ears, he ushered me to the three-sided shelter created by the high horseshoe-shaped stern deck.

We stepped into the windbreak, the sudden release from the spray and rushing air making me cough. A single lantern, fixed beside a hatch that led below, cast our shadows along the deck. Tozay signaled to a man coiling ropes nearby to move away.

"I have a question for you, Lady Eona," Tozay said, as the man obediently headed farther along the deck. "Why are you fighting for His Majesty?"

His tone was a return to our discussion in the boat. I settled my body more firmly into the rise and fall of the junk. "He is the true heir. He is—"

"No." Tozay lifted his hand, stopping me. "I am not looking for an avowal of loyalty or defense of his claim, Lady Eona. I am asking you why you think he is a better choice than Sethon. Why you have joined this fight."

The question held an intensity that demanded an answer in kind. I paused, and gave it thought.

"He is his father's son, but he is his own man, too," I said slowly. "He understands tradition, but he can step beyond it with the energy of renewal. He knows the strategies of war and power, but unlike Sethon, they are not his first love. His love is the land and the people, and he places his duty above all." I smiled wryly. "He once told me that an emperor should have one truth tattooed upon his body: *No nation has ever benefited from a protracted war.*"

"From the wisdom of Xsu-Ree," Tozay said. "Chapter Two."

"That is strange," I said sharply. "His Majesty also told me that only kings and generals were permitted to read Xsu-Ree's treatise."

I caught the flash of Tozay's rare smile. "That is my understanding, too." He leaned on the side partition that supported the small deck above us and looked out across the sea, his profile once more stern. "His Majesty will not ask you to break the Covenant again."

"Why do you say that?"

Tozay grunted. "I could give you his complicated explanation about you being a symbol of hope, and the need for something that is not tainted by the corruption of power, and the *Hua-do* of the people." He turned to face me. "But, in the end, it is because he loves you. He does not want you to suffer."

Although his statement of Kygo's love leaped through my blood, I shook my head. "His Majesty will not put his personal feelings above his land and his people. He has told me so."

"That is what I always thought, but that has changed. For you." Tozay's eyes met mine, their expression unreadable. "Xsu-Ree also says that one of the five essentials of victory is a competent general unhampered by his sovereign. As Kygo's general, my directive is to defeat Sethon. I am asking you for the power to help me do that."

I gripped a carved scroll on the side partition, steadying myself. "His general? I thought you were a simple fisherman, Master Tozay."

He gave a gruff laugh. "And I thought you were a lame boy with no chance of becoming a Dragoneye. We are all more—and less—than what we seem, Lady Eona."

I stared into the water swelling and surging around the junk as we cut through its night-dark depths. A pressure was building within me, a need to release the burden of all the secrets and lies. I could tell Tozay everything. I could tell him that the dragon power was ending and that the only way to save it seemed to be the Imperial Pearl. I could tell him that the black folio was on its way to us, and that maybe—hopefully—there was another way within it to save the dragon power that would not lead to Kygo's death. I could even tell him that the folio could bind Dragoneye power to the will of a king.

"Has His Majesty told you about the portent?" I asked, feeling my way. The slap of the water against the hull was like the beat of a drum.

Tozay nodded. "Do you think your portent is bound in any way to this war?"

"I don't know."

He lifted a dismissive shoulder. "Like Xsu-Ree, I do not put much stock in omens or portents. They create confusion and fear where there should be will and control. The ways of gods are for priests to unravel. I believe in strategy and the means to effect that strategy."

"And I am a means to your strategy," I said flatly.

He inclined his head. "As I am. As Lord Ido is, as we all are. History does not care about the suffering of the individual. Only the outcome of their struggles."

"And you will use all the means you have to defeat Sethon?"

Tozay's gaze did not waver. "To their utmost limits. And, if needs be, beyond."

I felt a chill at the innocuous word. *Beyond.* Who decided when *beyond* stopped? Part of me longed to tell Tozay everything—let him take on the burden of this knowledge and sort through its terrible intricacies and consequences. But another part drew back. Tozay would use everything he had to win, and the black folio had something within its pages that could force me into a *beyond* that I did not want to imagine.

"What is your answer, Lady Eona? Will you place all your power under his command—under *my* command?"

I felt the taste of ash rise into my mouth. Yet Kygo and the hope he brought were worth the fight. And maybe even the cost.

"I will, General Tozay," I said.

He bowed.

May the gods forgive me, I added silently. *May they forgive me for agreeing to break the Covenant again, and for not trusting even Tozay with the secret of the black folio.*

After my encounter with Tozay, I knew sleep was even more of a vain hope, but I stepped over the lip of the hatch onto the steep stairs that led to my cabin. Below me, in the gloom, a man sat hunched on the bottom step, bald head in hands. Ido's guard watched him, arms crossed. I trod heavily as I descended, the slap of my sandals twisting the seated man around. He looked up. Not bald—bandaged—and not a man. It was Dela. She stood as I reached the deck, her smile strained.

"I've been waiting for you."

I glanced at the guard's renewed interest and drew Dela back toward the steps that led down to the crew's quarters. In the soft light of the stair lamp, I saw the reddened edges of her eyes. "Is something wrong? Have you found something bad in the folio?"

"No." She licked her lips. "I have a favor to ask."

At the corner of my sight, I saw a shift of shadow on the steps below.

"Of course. What is it?"

"I want you to heal me." She touched the bandage along her cheek.

"Is it getting worse? Is your jaw locking?"

"No. I am all right."

"Why do you want me to heal you, then?" I pulled back.

"You know if I do, I'll have your will. Vida says your injury will right itself."

"I know." Her voice cracked. "But I still want you to do it."

"Not if I don't have to, Dela."

"Can't you just do it because I ask? Please."

"Are you afraid of being disfigured?"

"No, it is not that. " She angled her face away from me. "Can't you see? If you heal me, we will be the same. Ryko and I will be the same."

The flicker of shadow surged into a big body launching itself up the steps at us. The light caught the work of his muscles across his chest and the liquid dread in his eyes.

"No!" Ryko boomed, hauling himself onto the deck. "You will not do that."

Dela spun around. "Why not?"

The islander grabbed her shoulder. "Do you think I want that for you?" For a moment, his eyes caught mine, the fear in them snapping to fury. "Do you think I want you to be caught in her ghost world, too?"

Words rose to defend myself, but I quelled them and stepped back. This was their matter, and it was best they be alone.

"At least I would be with you!" Dela seized the edge of my tunic, stopping my retreat. "Do not leave, Eona. I want you to heal me."

"No!" Ryko said. "Please, Dela, don't do it. Not for me. I could not bear it."

She reached for his hand, but he snatched it away as if he

had touched royalty, and stepped back into a bow. "Forgive me."

"I cannot bear *this*, Ryko." Dela gestured at the careful space he had created. "This standing apart, to save later hurt. It doesn't work. I hurt now!"

"It is better this way." The torment on his face gave lie to his words.

"You know it is not." She closed the distance between them and laid her hand on his chest, her body swaying toward him. "I would be dead now if that sword had struck my head at a deeper angle. Do you think you would have saved yourself any hurt, Ryko?"

His eyes were fixed on her hand. Slowly he shook his head.

"Then stop being such a noble idiot," she whispered.

"I just want to keep you from any hurt."

"You can't."

She touched the pain on his face. Gently, he drew her against his chest, her head fitting neatly under his chin. She leaned into him, her slim body engulfed by the wrap of his arms. He kissed her bandaged forehead, the tenderness bringing an ache to my throat.

I quickly turned and saw Ido's guard peering around the rise of the steps.

"Return to your post," I ordered, blocking his view with my body.

With a bow, he backed away. I followed him, resisting the urge to glance over my shoulder. The guard took his position again in front of Ido's jail. Although I intended to walk straight past, I found myself stopping outside the wooden door. The back of my neck crawled with the energy of the approaching cyclone.

"Has Lord Ido said anything?" I asked the guard.

The man shook his head. "I've not heard a sound, my lady."

With a nod, I made my way down the passageway to the loneliness of my own narrow cell.

I woke with a jolt, my face only a fingertip away from the bunk wall. The cabin lamp was still alight, its yellow glow steadfastly fixed despite the steep rise and fall of the ship. The slap and boom of waves against the hull resonated through the wood, and I could hear the wind screaming, the eerie sound like a dragon in pain. I rolled onto my back, struggling to kick off the blanket, and saw a figure crouch down beside the bunk. With the energy of terror, I gathered my legs under me and levered myself to the top of the bed, every sense coming together to recognize Ido.

"*What are you doing?*" I gasped.

He held his finger to his lips. "Quietly, Eona. If I'm found here, Kygo will rip my heart out."

I lowered my voice. "How did you get out?"

"Your constant link to me seems to have broken," he said with a tense smile.

His other hand gripped the edge of the bed as the junk plunged and rose sharply, the wood groaning around us. Beneath all of Ido's smooth control, there was an uncharacteristic urgency that alarmed me almost as much as finding him crouched in my cabin.

"What do you want?"

"Right now, I want to survive the next few bells. Have you felt the cyclone?"

Involuntarily, I rubbed the back of my neck. The crawling sensation had hardened into pain.

He nodded. "It has doubled its pace and shifted. The edge will hit us in a bell or so. We are not going to outrun it."

My unease burst into cold fear. Nearly everyone I loved was on this ship. "We should tell Master Tozay."

Ido looked up as another grinding moan resonated through the wood. "It is already too late."

"Can we do something to stop it?"

"It is why I am here."

"I thought we weren't strong enough to do anything."

"We're not if I have to fend off ten dragons as well as work the elements."

"But you don't." A deep plunge rocked us. I grabbed the edge of the storage unit above. "The dragons only come for me. You could go in alone."

Ido rose and sat on the end of the bunk. "Eona, I am not strong enough to control the cyclone by myself. It usually takes all the beasts and Dragoneyes to redirect such force."

"So can we or can't we do something?"

"I have had an idea." He rubbed his mouth. "It is one that has unknown risks for both of us."

"What is it?"

"Bypass the ten dragons by compelling me." His eyes held mine. "But let me take that power and use it to get us out of the cyclone."

"You mean the compulsion I used when I made you call Dillon?" I flushed, remembering the way his pleasure had curled back upon me.

"That holds the most power between us."

Although I still wore my tunic and trousers, I pulled up the blanket. It would be a big risk; every time I used those pathways was a chance for Ido to find a way to block them.

"Will that work?" I asked.

"Possibly." He watched me. "But are you willing to do it without Kygo's knowledge?"

"Why should we keep it from him?"

"Did you tell him about your new way of controlling me?"

I looked away from his keen scrutiny. "No."

"Well, someone has. Perhaps your islander guard? He certainly felt the difference when you first used it."

I shifted uneasily. "What makes you think Ryko told him?"

Ido lifted his hands to his tunic collar, and in one smooth movement pulled the garment over his head.

"What are you doing?" I demanded, pressing myself back against the bunk head.

He threw the tunic onto the bed. The yellow lamplight highlighted the dark purple bruising across his ribs. "I would say Kygo is aware of your new way of controlling me." His voice was dry. "He will forbid you from doing this, and place his faith in

Tozay. Will you obey him like a good little girl? Or will you be the Ascendant Dragoneye and take control of your own power?"

I stared at the damage on Ido's body. "He did that?"

"Yuso, on his Majesty's behalf."

I shook my head. "No, that was Yuso, on his own behalf. Kygo would have done it himself." I ignored the Dragoneye's snort of disbelief. "If we do this, Ido, we do it with Kygo's knowledge. Tozay has asked me to place all of my power at Kygo's command—beyond the Covenant—and I have said yes."

"You've done what?" Ido stared at me, aghast. "You haven't told him about the black folio, have you?"

I lifted my chin. "Not yet."

He leaned across and gripped my forearm. "Not *ever*, girl."

I tried to wrench away, but he did not let go.

"Do I have to paint you a picture?" he said. "If Kygo gets the black folio, he will bind me first—that is without question—but it won't stop there. You are the Mirror Dragoneye. Your power will always be greater than anything he takes from me, and that will make you a threat. Perhaps not at first, but something will sour between you—maybe you'll not agree about a war, maybe he'll start seeing enemies where there used to be allies, or maybe he will just tire of you as a woman. But he will bind you, too." Ido released me. "In the end, power is always used to gain more power. That is the nature of the beast."

"You can't know that."

"I understand men, and I understand power, Eona." The ship pitched sharply. I grabbed the edge of the bed as he steadied himself with a hand against the wall. "He has already seen his opportunity and asked you to break the Covenant again. Even after he swore on the beach it was not his plan."

"Tozay asked me. Not Kygo."

"They are the same, Eona. Can't you see they are manipulating you?" He reached up and cupped my chin. "Poor Eona. His Majesty will press for more and more—through Tozay, or whoever else he uses—until he realizes he has created something that threatens his own power. We all know how that ends."

"That will not happen." My protest sounded too small against the howling storm outside. "He loves me."

"He has asked you to go against your spirit. Is that the act of a lover?"

I pulled away from his hold. "What do you know about love?"

His eyes flickered. "I know that love is about power, too. Who gives, who takes. Who is willing to risk showing their true self."

The intensity of his expression sent heat crashing through my body.

He bent his head, running his thumb across the rope-cut around his wrist. "You have forced your way into my *Hua*, Eona. Changed me. First, by your power—then, just by who you are." He raised his head and there was no guard upon his expression. The raw need caught my breath. "You have seen me at my worst and at my weakest. Let me show you my best. Help me save this boat and everyone on board like a true Dragoneye."

I gaped at him, unable to force my mind past the avowal of love. For that was what it was, wasn't it? Yet Lord Ido did not love anything except power.

"What are you saying?" I finally managed.

The intensity gave way to a smile that held his wry humor. "I was wondering if you would help me save our lives. The rest relies upon us surviving."

Had he really changed? And what did he mean by *the rest*?

"Eona?"

His urgent voice brought me back to the priority in front of us: survival. "All right."

Ido pushed himself back against the other end of the bunk, into the corner made by the three-sided enclosure, and braced himself. "I'll go into the energy world. As soon as I am with my dragon, compel me."

He was wasting no time. Each breath he took was smoother, deeper, until I felt the thrill of his communion with the Rat Dragon and saw the burst of silver across his eyes. The joy on his face sharpened my ever-present yearning for my own dragon. On a breath, I pushed past that deep ache and concentrated on the rhythm of my heart, reaching out with my *Hua* for the pulse of Ido's life-force. There was a moment of resistance and then his heartbeat slid under mine, the fusion so fast it made me gasp. This was the level of my control that he had already conquered; I could feel the history of it within his *Hua*, like a soft whispered defiance.

"We are ready," he said.

I found the desire within myself—too easily—and sought the route that would take me into the heart of his hungering. We both cried out as my compulsion locked in and roared across his energy, subjugating its fire with my own.

But how could I pass him the power? Instinct told me that the only way was physical touch. I hesitated, knowing the man's strength, then crawled across the bunk. His hands were flat against the wooden walls, his head craned back into the corner as he resisted the impulse to fight my control. I edged alongside him and reached to press my hands against his chest, but the boat plunged, jolting me backward. My reflexes caught the edge of the bunk wall in a wild grip, stopping my fall.

"Eona!" he rasped. "Hurry."

I had to anchor myself long enough to pass the power. The straining muscles across his bare chest and shoulders held both menace and a sensuality that pulled me closer. I straddled his legs, knowing his body was under my control, but also knowing that at any moment it could change. With a deep breath, I pressed my palms against his chest, the contact forcing a low grunt from him. But there was no shift of energy.

"Take it," I said.

"Can't." He forced his head down, the silver in his eyes threading thin enough for the amber to show through. "You have to give it."

"How?"

The answer thundered in my blood and the race of his heart under my hands.

The power was built on sensual desire. I had to give him my desire.

The peril of it was like another pulse pounding in my body. My desire for Ido was not the same as my desire for Kygo. With Ido, it felt dangerous and double-edged; one side honed by hate, the other a jagged edge of need, not love.

But we had to save the boat.

With a prayer to Kinra, I released my dark attraction to the man. It leapt through me, pushing me against him. I dug my fingers into his hair and wrenched his head back, slamming it against the wall. For a moment the silver of his eyes snapped into amber again, the pain flaring into pleasure, then his eyes silvered back into the energy world.

His response burst through me like a rush of victory. I bent and covered his mouth with mine, finding the taste of him—orange and vanilla, like his dragon—the sweetness doubled by his communion with the beast. He rocked forward and drew his legs up behind me. I met the rough demand of his tongue and teeth with my own. Power jumped through us like an arc of lightning, and I felt the heat of his low laugh against my lips. His body arched toward me, his hands gripping the curve of my hips and pulling me closer.

Our hearts pounded together, power rising through the melded beat and the ragged rhythm of our breathing. It was locked between us, a spiral of energy that was like molten metal pouring through my pathways into his *Hua*. I felt him gather its force, his sweet union with the Rat Dragon seeping into our shared power. I could feel the blue beast's presence, its own massive power boosted by the energy.

In a dizzying wrench, the cabin was gone. I was high above the boat, anchored in orange-vanilla power, the pleasure in my earthly body a distant thunder. Through ancient dragon eyes, I saw the raging silver water and violent swirling yellow of the cyclone winds roaring below me, bearing down on our tiny vessel. Driving rain slashed the building seas and claws of light stuttered across the dark sky, their flashes penetrating the celestial plane. Nearby, the Mirror Dragon shrieked, all her crimson beauty before me—so close, but unreachable.

Eona? Ido's mind-voice, shocked by my presence. As shocked as I was.

I am with you.

I felt the power between us surge into the blue dragon, his muscular body rippling with energy. Ido's joy flooded me as he and the beast amassed all our strength into one purpose—an arrow for the eye of the massive storm. With sinuous control, they harvested high ice, freezing winds, and sparks of new lightning, weaving them into a massive bolt of cold energy. I felt the huge effort of man and dragon as they drove it into the warm center of the circling winds, piercing the delicate balance of the cyclone's *Hua*.

For a terrifying moment, nothing happened, and then one side of the yellow maelstrom collapsed, pulling its deadly force away from our boat. Huge dragon muscles coiled and sprang, blocking the wild under-surge of winds. The cyclone swirled toward the land, its ragged edges curling around a smaller center. I felt every delicate shift of power between man and beast as they wrestled the remnants of its collapsed fury into a driving wind that pushed our tiny vessel across the silvered waves toward its far-off goal.

I reveled in Ido's command of his dragon and the majesty of their union. The Mirror Dragon and I could be like that—we could rule the elements, rule the *Hua* of the world.

For a heartbeat, I was back in the cabin—Ido's mouth on mine, the shift of his heavy muscles under my hands, and the rush of power mixed with the building heat of pleasure.

Then we were above the boat again, spinning into exhilaration, the tiny points of *Hua* on deck, crawling across its surface, safe, all safe. Out of the ravening fury of the circling winds and sweeping rains. So much power pulsing through us.

A painful grip on my shoulders yanked me back into my body, into the cabin. I was being dragged off the bunk. I hit out, my desperate punch catching my assailant in the chest.

"Stupid girl!"

Ryko's voice. I twisted around in his brutal grip and saw his snarl of disgust. He shoved me against the far wall, then turned back to the Dragoneye. Dela stood in the doorway, her face white.

Ido lunged at the islander. "What are you doing? What—"

His protest was stopped by Ryko's fist. Ido fell against the back of the bunk, hands to his face. The islander leaned in and grabbed him by the hair, hauling him out and slamming him against the wall in one savage move.

"Get your—"

"Shut up!" Ryko thrust his face up to the Dragoneye's, daring him to move or speak.

"Lord Ido! You must go back now," Dela said. "They will realize it is dragon power. If His Majesty finds you in here, you'll die!" She grabbed his arm, her courtier's eyes raking over the room. "Is that his tunic?"

I snatched up the garment and held it out. She snagged it from my hand, her mouth tightening. "I hope you know what you are doing."

"We were saving the boat!" I said.

The islander spun around to face me. "I know—I felt it!" He stabbed his finger at my dishevelment. "You'd better make up some story. Something that doesn't involve the two of you together."

Dela pulled Ido into the passage, Ryko casting one last scathing look at me before following them. I took a step toward the door, then stopped. What could I tell Kygo? Power still thrummed through my body, Ido's touch hot on my skin. I looked around the cabin. The mattress was askew. With shaking hands I pushed it back into place and straightened my tunic, trying to find composure—and a convincing lie. I wiped my mouth, feeling my torn lip. I pressed my finger against the damage, the tiny pain an echo of the sharp shame building within me.

I had paced the length of the cabin five times before the sounds of footsteps turned me back to the door. Kygo filled its narrow frame, Tozay behind him. Both men were soaked. Kygo had been up on the main deck, too—always rushing into the fray. An errant thought sent useless dread through my body—if he had stayed below, in Master Tozay's cabin, he would have heard us. I dropped into a low bow, glad to hide my face for a moment.

"Lady Eona, was that you? Did you calm the waters? Tozay says only dragon power could do that to the storm." I felt his hand touch my shoulder, drawing me out of the bow. I stood and forced myself to meet his elation. Surely he could read the truth in my eyes?

"Yes."

Kygo took my hand, his skin cold against my heat. "How did you do it? I thought you could not work your power without Ido's protection from the other dragons?"

I steeled myself; this lie was going to be difficult. "I can, for a short time, Your Majesty. Although I could only push us a little way from the storm." I looked past Kygo to Tozay. "I hope it is enough, Master Tozay. I cannot do any more."

"It is, Lady Eona," Tozay said. "You have saved us all. Thank you." He bowed.

"But how?" Kygo would not be deflected.

"I have learned a great deal from Lord Ido, Your Majesty." Four years of lying to survive kept my gaze steady and my voice calm. "It is why we rescued him from Sethon."

Kygo's gaze was just as steady. "It is good to know he is worth all the trouble." He smiled. "Your power is, indeed, becoming formidable."

"It is in your service, Your Majesty," I said.

I caught his glance back toward Tozay. "So I have heard."

Was Ido right? Was Kygo manipulating me?

"You have hurt your lip." He touched the fullness of his own mouth.

"I must have bitten myself," I said, glad he could not also see the race of my heart or the sharp rending of my spirit.

CHAPTER TWENTY

WITH THE FORCE of our illicit power, Ido and I had pushed the junk a day ahead of schedule and out of the range of the diminished cyclone. For the remainder of the journey, most of my time was spent in intense sessions of campaign planning with Kygo and Tozay. When I was not in the command cabin looking at maps or discussing strategy, either I sat with my mother—our conversation safely centered upon small talk and the father and brother I had never known—or I lay on my bunk in a dark cycle of shame and confusion that inevitably ended with me reliving Ido's mastery of the cyclone. And the rushing rise of our power, together.

The planning sessions at least brought me close to Kygo, although the fast approaching strike against Sethon and my role as weapon and trigger were building a constant dread within me. I was seeing Kygo the emperor, all of his energies centered on the war ahead. Only once, on the morning after the cyclone, did I have a few precious moments with Kygo the man. Tozay had withdrawn from the command cabin to attend to a course correction, and Kygo and I were left alone, on opposite sides of the fixed table, a map of the land between us.

"I did not tell him to ask you," he said abruptly.

I looked up from the map.

"To break the Covenant again. Tozay took that on himself. He brought it to me as a deal already struck."

I straightened, as if some of the weight in me had been lifted. "Tozay said that you would not ask me."

He nodded. "I know you do not wish to kill." He gestured at the map. "Yet you can see that we cannot do without you." His smile held no humor. "I find myself in one of the quandaries my father warned me about—principle versus pragmatism."

"I have said yes, Kygo. This time pragmatism wins."

"Pragmatism is like water against the rock of principle," Kygo said softly, quoting the great poet Cho. "If not channeled, it will eventually wear its own path through the spirit."

He walked around the table and drew me to him, his hand reaching up to stroke my face. Our kiss was slow, seeking, a gentle press of mute atonement on both sides. Yet in the midst of the tender union, the memory of Ido's savagery cut through my mind. The sudden intrusion brought a wash of shame, and I pulled away. Kygo let me—both of us, it seemed, caught in our own separate guilt.

I did not see much of Dela and Ryko during the rest of the

voyage. The islander, I think, was avoiding me, but then the two of them were avoiding everyone, using the short time on board to create their own brief haven. Dela sought me out once, as I took air on the main deck, to tell me that they had silenced Ido's guard with the knowledge that he'd left his post to watch their rendezvous, allowing Ido to escape.

"This alliance you have with Lord Ido frightens me," she said. "Do not forget what he has done."

"I haven't." The brisk sea wind caught my hair, whipping it across my face.

"He gave me a message for you." She tightened her lips as if the words soured her mouth.

"What is it?"

"That you are in his blood."

I looked down at the deck to hide the answering surge within my own blood.

"Those are the words of a lover, Eona."

"Lord Ido only loves power. I know that," I said, but she did not look convinced.

With a bow she turned toward the hatch.

"Dela." She looked back. "Does Ryko hate me?"

Her face softened. "Ryko doesn't hate you. He wants to save you, Eona. Like he wants to save everyone."

As I watched her walk away, my throat tensed with an ache of sadness. Ryko wanted to save everyone—except himself.

When we finally anchored in the deep cove harbor of our eastern rendezvous, a sense of relief quickened everyone's movements. I think we all wanted to get off the boat and face more than just the dark shadows in our own minds.

It is not often that the real world conjures worse than what we can imagine.

I stood against the railing and studied the vista before us, a mix of barren sand dunes, ocher rocks, and patches of low green growth bright in the late sun. This was the east—my dragon's stronghold of power—abandoned for five hundred years, cast into a hot wasteland of desert that only the border tribes inhabited. Now the Mirror Dragon had returned and, with her, the green blessing of renewal. And maybe, if we had the good will of the gods, victory.

"Lady Eona."

Ryko's voice pulled me out of my reverie. He held out a back sheath, the moonstone and jade hilts of Kinra's swords protruding from the two scabbards strapped into the leather brace.

"His Majesty has ordered that everyone be armed, at all times," he said. "I've greased the throats."

I hesitated, then took the sheath. I had not touched Kinra's swords since the village inn. It seemed so long ago. Ryko crossed his arms, waiting for me to test the oiled draw. Clenching my teeth, I grabbed one leather-bound grip and felt Kinra's rage roil through my blood. Still there, still strong.

"It's good," I managed, plunging the sword home again. The kiss of hilt against metal mouth released me from the fury.

"The other?"

"I trust you," I said.

"Test it, my lady."

I gripped and pulled, the smooth slide whispering death in its hissing release. I rammed the blade back, snatching my hand away. "Lovely. Thank you."

He bowed.

"Ryko."

He looked up, eyes wary.

"Thank you for looking after my swords." It was not what I wanted to say, but the real words were caught in the strain between us.

"It is my duty," he said. "I will always do my duty." He backed away.

Eventually, a loud "Hoy!" went up from the high mast lookout—the signal from the shore had been spotted, although I could see no people on the beach or in the dunes.

I took my place in the first tender, along with Kygo, Tozay, and two of Caido's bowmen. Another, larger boat followed, with Dela, Ryko, and more armed men, two of whom guarded Ido. We rowed the distance between junk and land in silence, the air eerily still and hot after the quick sea winds, and no sign of our allies on the broad expanse of sand.

"Where are they?" I whispered.

"Wait," Tozay said.

Both tenders beached at the same time, the bowmen covering us as we climbed out and splashed to shore through the warm water. Squinting in the glare, I scanned the undulating horizon of sand, my skin crawling with the certainty we were being watched. Tozay walked up beyond the tide line and stood with his hands on his hips, eyes fixed on the bank of dunes that curved and peaked before us. At the edge of my sight, something moved in the far dune. I swung around, reaching back for Kinra's swords, the bowmen catching my alarm and swinging with me. The sand convulsed and lifted, falling away to reveal human figures.

"Hold your fire," Tozay barked.

I lowered my hands. Twenty or so men dressed in bleached garments the same color as the dunes rose to their feet and watched us, their weapons drawn. One of them raised a fist, then smoothed it across the air in an arc.

Tozay returned the signal. "It is clear," he said to Kygo.

We had made contact with the Eastern Resistance army.

The soft-spoken leader pulled up his horse and turned in his saddle, waiting for Kygo to walk our sturdy dune beast up beside him. I was riding behind the emperor once again, but this time his hand covered mine as I held his waist, the press of our bodies moving together in mesmerizing harmony. We had been traveling through the night—the dune men and our troop—steadily heading to higher, more strategic ground. The moon-silvered sands had gradually given way to featureless plains and strange dark outcroppings of rock. Now the gray predawn light was giving definition back to the scrubby landscape, and to the faces around me.

Kygo reined in beside the dune leader. Tozay pulled his horse in behind us.

"As you requested, Your Majesty," the leader said with a bow. "We are now about a quarter bell from our camp." His words seemed to conjure the flavor of smoke on the cool dawn air, and I could see a faint glow that hinted at cooking fires.

Kygo nodded. "Which of your men has the most docile horse?"

The leader flicked his hand at a rider in the group of mounted men behind us. I turned to look back, smiling at Dela on a gray near the front, my mother clinging nervously to her waist. But my real attention was on Ido, in the periphery of my vision. He was astride one of the larger horses and, although his wrists were tied to the pommel, he still sat the animal with easy grace. He watched me from under half-closed lids, his smile as intimate as if his hands were around my hips instead of bound to a saddle. The memory of his hold swept heat across my skin. I quickly turned back to face the front.

The summoned rider dismounted and bowed to Kygo, his face still streaked with sand dust from the camouflage.

"Your mount will take a novice?" Kygo asked.

"Yes, Your Majesty. She is steady as a rock. Even my three-year-old rides her without saddle."

Kygo twisted to look at me. "Do you think you can manage her, Lady Eona? I wish you to ride into camp beside me."

Although it was a serious command, and there was obviously more to it than just protocol, I narrowed my eyes at the hint of humor that lifted the corners of his mouth.

"Of course," I said, although in truth I was not sure if I could stay on one of the beasts by myself. Still, I would try. At least I knew how to dismount. I swung my leg and slid off our horse, landing with reasonable grace on the loose gravel.

The dune man smiled encouragingly, inviting me to pat his mare. "Her name is Ren," he said. "It means 'forbearance' in my tribe's language."

I slid my hand along the silky nap of her neck. Forbearance: the poor creature would need a lot of it once I was on her back.

As we rode on, Ren was as good as the dune man had claimed—steady and eternally forgiving of my heavy hands and lack of skill. Kygo kept close beside me, our horses' shoulders almost touching. Ren, may the gods bless her sweet nature, seemed oblivious to Kygo's horse and its occasional nibble at her bridle.

"You are doing well," Kygo said.

"She is making me look good." I shot him a sharp look. "But then, that is what she is supposed to do, isn't she? What are you worried about?"

"Always so quick, *Naiso*." He shifted in his saddle, lowering his voice. "As commander of the army, Sethon has ruthlessly quelled the Eastern Tribes for years, so there is no love lost there. But they are not totally convinced of me, either. After all, my father allowed Sethon's eastern campaigns." He drew his hand down the length of his queue. "Nor do they have the same reverence for Dragoneyes as the rest of the land, since they have been without the blessing of one for five hundred years."

Ever since the Mirror Dragoneye was executed and the Mirror Dragon fled. Would the easterners have any legends about Kinra? Or had she been wiped from their stories, too?

"And now the Mirror Dragon is back, and the Mirror Dragoneye is about to arrive," I finished for him. "What do you think will happen?"

His eyes cut back to Tozay, riding a length or so behind us. "Tozay says the easterners respect only strength. So, we show strength." He turned back to me, his face somber. "Are you ready for that . . . my love?"

The soft, hesitant endearment blazed through me. Kygo had called me his love. I knew he was warning me about the easterners, but all I could focus on was that one sweet phrase. I could not stop the smile that sang from my spirit.

"Yes," I said. "Yes, I am ready."

I wanted to return the endearment, but I did not know what to say: I had never called anyone a heart-name. Yet it seemed my smile was enough, because he leaned across and took my hand, his own smile holding me in its embrace.

For one joyous moment I forgot I had lied to him about Ido and the cyclone. Then the Dragoneye was there again, in my mind: the memory of his hands touching me and his mouth on mine, and the glory of his power. If Kygo knew about that, he would not be calling me his love.

The dune leader reined his horse. "We are here," he announced, drawing Kygo's attention from me. A small mercy; I could no longer meet his eyes.

The man motioned ahead. "Your army awaits, Your Majesty." He bowed over his saddle, waiting for us to pass and lead the troops into the resistance camp.

I had never seen so many people gathered in one place—not even in the ceremony arena or the crater camp. Involuntarily my hands tightened around Ren's reins, yanking on her bit, as we made our way between two plains of bowed bodies that stretched for hundreds of lengths on either side into the pale shadows of morning. Behind them, low military tents and the taller, round tribal tents were built up row upon row like city streets, the outer ranks so far away they were just white dots in the glow of cooking fires.

All of this at Kygo's command. And under the protection of my power.

I glanced at Kygo. He did not look left or right, and his bearing had straightened from the relaxed meld of horse and man into regal authority. All of his attention was focused on the group of six men bowing to us outside a huge round tent, its position and size distinguishing it as a meetinghouse.

I had a moment of absurd pleasure as I reined Ren neatly in beside Kygo's horse. I had not fallen off, and I had managed to stop. Following Kygo's lead, I swung my leg over Ren's back and found the ground, the twist on the stirrup allowing me a quick view of Ido, still mounted behind us. One of the dune men was cutting him free from the saddle.

"Rise," Kygo ordered.

The six men climbed to their feet. I glanced over my shoulder, past the grips of Kinra's swords, and saw the royal command shift back like a wave through the sea of people behind us.

"This is Lady Eona, Mirror Dragoneye and my Imperial *Naiso*," Kygo said.

The men's eyes flicked over me. Although not one of their expressions changed, I could feel their disappointment as if it had been shouted in my face: *A girl*.

"You know General Tozay," Kygo continued. He turned his head, finding Ido. "And that is Lord Ido, Rat Dragoneye."

The introduction sent sharp glances among the six men. A ripple of whispers rose from the people around us. One of the six—a man of about thirty with a permanent sun squint and a meaty strength about him—stepped forward, his bright red coat adorned with an embroidered eagle on each sleeve. All of the six men wore intense colors—emerald green, sky blue, red, purple, orange—their clothes overbright among the bleached colors of the rest of the camp.

"Welcome Your Majesty and Lady Eona." He angled his face away from Ido. "I am Rulan, leader of the Haya Ro. Be welcomed on behalf of all the tribes."

"Rulan," Kygo said. "Lord Ido is the Rat Dragoneye. Acknowledge him."

The big man shifted. "He is a traitor."

"Acknowledge him!"

Rulan's mouth tightened. "And we acknowledge Lord Ido," he said through his teeth. Kygo had won the first round. Rulan gestured to the man in emerald green. "Here is Soran, leader of the Kotowi and tribe brother to the Haya Ro." He proceeded to name the remaining four men behind him and their affiliations, but the elaborate introductions blurred into a string of unfamiliar words. I had seen the ill feeling toward Ido at Sokayo village, but this held an even sharper edge of malevolence.

As Rulan finished with a bow, Soran, the first man introduced, stepped forward. "Your Majesty, may I have leave to greet my daughter-son, Dela?" he asked. "She has been away from us for six years."

This was Dela's father? On closer inspection, there was a resemblance—the proud nose and deep-set eyes, and the humor in his angular face.

Kygo smiled and nodded. "Of course, Soran. I know Dela came to my father's court as a ransom, but he was fond of her, and she was a valued courtier."

Soran bowed and backed away. I saw the wonderful moment on Dela's face when her father stepped into view—such love. And so much warmth between them as Soran folded Dela against his chest. My mother watched with a sad smile. Was she comparing our reunion with the joy of this one? She was a good woman and deserved more than the polite detachment I had shown on the boat. After all, we were blood.

I turned back to find Rulan ushering us toward the wooden door of the round tent. The structure was covered in pale cloth, and through a few gaps, I could make out the thick edges of a darker layer beneath. A woolen blanket perhaps, or felt. Both layers were bound onto the circular structure with neatly separated rounds of rope. I had heard that these buildings could be dismantled and moved within a full bell, yet were sturdy enough to withstand sandstorms.

As I followed Kygo into the tent, the sudden color and opulence made me pause. The walls were covered in bright cloth printed in red, white, and green diamonds, and the entire floor was made of layered woven rugs in a clash of reds and greens and yellows. Two long, elaborately carved poles in the center held up the crown of the tent, and between them stood an open-topped brazier, a high mound of glowing coals sending out heat and soft light. Long benches with padded seats made of printed and colored cloth were set up in ranks that curved with the walls and left a large round space in the center. One bench was raised higher than the rest and had no other seats set behind it: the position of power. Rulan led us toward it. The Emperor and his *Naiso* Dragoneye were to sit together.

It did not take long for the round room to fill with people. As there was only one door, I did not miss the entry of my mother, and behind her, Dela and Soran, their reunion evident in reddened eyes and Soran's protective clasp of Dela's shoulder. Nor did I miss the entry of Ido and the subtle shifting away from him as Yuso and Ryko led him through the benches. His hands were no longer bound with rope. They were shackled in heavy irons.

Noticing the fix of my gaze, Kygo leaned close to my ear, his breath warm. "The solid permanence of iron holds more effect for these people than just rope. They will kill him in a second if they think he is not under control."

Ido's chin was lifted, the amber eyes hardened into dark gold. Even when they fell upon me, their expression did not change. He was pushed onto the front bench at my right. I forced my attention away from him and scanned the meetinghouse. Rulan and his five cohorts were seated to our right. Apart from our people, the rest of the forty or so gathered seemed to be men—and a few women—who held some kind of rank. All of them were wearing the bright colors and intricate embroidery of celebration dress. And all of them were watching Kygo and me, the thick padded walls muffling the rise of their whispers.

From his lower seat, Rulan bowed to Kygo then clapped his hands, glaring around the tent for attention. "Our emperor is here and we have much to discuss," he said to the quieting room. "First we must honor Lady Eona, and the Mirror Dragon. Many generations have passed without a dragon in the east, and perhaps Lady Eona will not understand our ways. We have survived, and our independence may seem to offer insult. Yet we are not without respect, lady." He gestured to the two men at the door to open it again, then turned back to me. "Normally we would not allow such weakness to taint us with its ill-fortune, but we understand these people are important to you." He held up his hand to stop the rise of muttering. "A gesture of good will, if you like."

Bewildered, I watched the doorway.

For an instant, I did not recognize the woman's face. Then the rush of all that was Rilla flooded through me: safety and warmth and a smile that always held the truth. Behind her was Lon, the big body servant, and in his arms was the dear, twisted form of Chart. I launched myself forward as Rilla pushed her way past the benches, her hands reaching for me. As mine reached for her.

"You are safe!" My words were a half-sob as her tight embrace squeezed my voice away. Her cheek was soft against mine and I drew in her familiar smell—a mix of sweet soap and hard work.

"My lord"—she gave a breathy laugh—"I mean, my lady. We have heard so many different stories." She pulled back to look at me. Her joy did not stop a quick inspection. "You are tired, I think." I could see the shrewd observation in her face. She already knew it was more than fatigue. "And you are no longer limping."

"I will tell you all later," I said.

Lon stopped beside us, struggling to hold Chart as he thrashed his limbs in excitement. Although Chart's muscles had crabbed and curled him almost double, he still had a fifteen-year-old's body, and it could do some damage. A few of those sitting nearby leaned away from him, their fingers curled into ward-evil signs.

"Lady . . . Eon . . . a!" Chart slurred, holding out his hands.

I caught his bone-thin fingers. His liberation disc—the token of release from bond service that I had given him—swung on its leather thong around his neck. A symbol of his rank as freeman. It obviously meant nothing to these easterners, who saw only his twisted body.

An idea was forming. Could I heal Chart with my power? Make his body straight again?

His mouth stretched into his slow smile. "You . . . not . . . bad-looking . . . as a . . . girl."

I grinned and leaned closer. "Think of all those missed opportunities for a grope," I whispered.

Chart's mouth opened wide into his raucous laugh, his body straining upward in Lon's arms. I smiled at the big man. "Hello, Lon, how are you?" I lowered my voice. "Have you been treated well?"

"Yes, my lady," he said, ducking his head. "We are all well. And glad you are safe."

"Lady Eona." Kygo's call was crisp but he was smiling. "I understand your joy in the return of your friends and rejoice with you, but we must proceed."

Although his voice seemed easy, I heard the tension within it. Guiltily, I looked back at my mother; she would have seen my joy, too. Yet she smiled at me, the gentle understanding on her face bringing an answering smile to my own.

"Of course, Your Majesty, we must proceed," I said loudly, and turned to Rulan. "My thanks to you and your people for finding my friends." With a touch to Rilla's shoulder, I drew all three toward the raised bench. "Come, sit by me." My firm order stopped the approach of the door guards, obviously intent on removing Chart from the meetinghouse. They looked to Rulan, who waved them back. Ignoring the subtle shifting of dismay around the tent, I returned to my position beside Kygo, while Rilla and Lon seated themselves and Chart on the rugs near my feet.

"You have indeed survived well without the blessing of a dragon," Kygo said to the gathering. "And your courage and skill in battle are legendary." He touched the Imperial Pearl at his throat, its pale luminescence drawing everyone's eyes. "As you can see, I am the rightful heir to the throne. The pearl is within me, is a part of me. And with the might of the Mirror Dragon and the Rat Dragon behind us, we will be victorious in the struggle ahead."

Rulan cut through the rise of voices with a flat hand. "We acknowledge your right, Your Majesty," he said. "But with all due respect, you have brought us a girl barely beyond childhood, and a traitor who killed his Dragoneye brothers and sided with our enemy. We do not see how his power can be brought to our venture. Or how a little girl can be trusted to fight and not run from the battle."

On the bench to our left, I saw Tozay stiffen.

"Lady Eona does not run from a battle," Kygo said coldly. "She has as much courage as any man in this room. And she can compel Lord Ido's power. He will do as she commands. And she will do as I command."

The change of atmosphere in the tent sent danger prickling across my scalp. I straightened, not even daring to swallow, in case it was seen as weakness.

"Then show us this staunch chain of command, Your Majesty," Rulan demanded. "Prove that all of this power is under your control, and we will follow you to victory—or death—with joy in our hearts."

His words were greeted with yips of enthusiasm from around the room.

"Silence," Kygo commanded.

The noise stopped, its shrillness shifting into a sudden press of expectancy.

"You have something in mind, Rulan," Kygo said flatly. "What is it?"

Rulan looked around the tent with a smile, the delay in his answer sharpening his people's excitement. "Have Lady Eona compel Lord Ido." His eyes fixed on the Dragoneye, then found me. "Make him hold his arm in the brazier coals for a count of ten. One count each for the Dragoneye Lords he betrayed."

Beside me, Rilla gasped. I sucked in a hard breath, forcing myself to meet the challenge in Rulan's face. The demand was too brutal. I would not do it. Yet I had placed my power under Kygo's command, and I could not renege on that promise. Perhaps Kygo would refuse. If he loved me as much as Tozay had said—as much as his sweet endearment and caresses seemed to say—then surely he would not ask me to do this.

I turned from Rulan, praying that Kygo would see my reluctance. But he was staring at Ido, his jaw tensed into a brutal line. He needed the Eastern Tribes. He could not refuse, and he could not show weakness. And as his *Naiso* and Dragoneye, neither could I.

Ido's hard gaze moved to me. He was not a man to plead, but I saw something flick across his face. What he saw in mine made him close his eyes.

"For a count of ten," Kygo agreed.

Ido's hands clenched in the irons.

"Ryko," Kygo said. The islander looked up. "Take Lillia outside."

Ryko bowed, crossed the floor, and led my mother from the tent. A tiny spark of warmth penetrated my dread. Kygo had just protected Ryko from the full brunt of my compulsion, and Lillia from the truth. I turned to Rilla—she and Chart should go outside, too—but her face was already set into the stubborn lines I knew so well. She would not leave.

"Yuso," Kygo ordered, motioning to the brazier.

Yuso grasped Ido's arm, preparing to pull him upright, but the Dragoneye wrenched himself out of the captain's grip and stood under his own volition. He looked around the room, slowly and deliberately—and in that moment I understood the strength of Ido's will, for there was not one friendly face in that crowd. Not one place to find solace. Then he walked to the brazier.

Yuso followed.

"Lady Eona," Kygo said. He looked at me, and I finally saw what was in his heart: fury at Rulan for forcing his hand, and regret for me. "Show Rulan your power."

I stood as Yuso undid Ido's shackles, then pulled them off his wrists and stepped back. The tent was so quiet I could hear Ido's quickening breaths. Or perhaps they were just mine. I crossed the distance between us and stood opposite him. He had to have one pair of eyes that offered compassion, even if they belonged to his torturer.

"Again," I said, hoping he would understand.

The tilt of his head was almost imperceptible, his face paling with anticipation.

I reached with my *Hua* and found his heartbeat, folding his pulse into mine. Then I sought the deeper level; the pathways that flared so dark between us, the pathways that had fused pleasure and pain. This time there was resistance. Ruthlessly, I pushed through it, the compulsion rolling over him, his eyes widening with the energy that leaped through us.

"Lord Ido, put your arm into the brazier," I ordered, fighting back the rise of bile into my mouth.

I felt Ido's instinct rage against the command, the sinews ridging in his arm as he braced against my will. But he could not withstand the force behind it. He turned, and with head thrown back, plunged his arm into the glowing coals. His choked scream shuddered through me, his agony resonating through my *Hua*.

"One," Kygo said. "Two."

I heard the gasps from around the tent, but I was fixed on Ido, concentrating fiercely on the meld of pathways between us. I had a plan.

"Three," Kygo said above the growing calls of excitement. "Four."

Pain was just another kind of energy; Ido had said that. And energy could be directed, stopped, absorbed. I caught the torment that surged along the three meridian lines of his arm. Clenching my teeth against the backlash of boiling, blistering pain, I rammed my *Hua* against their convergence in his shoulder, blocking the flow. Blocking sensation.

Ido dropped to one knee. Around us, the calls had thickened into baying.

"Silence," Tozay roared. The mob subsided into whispers. I could smell the same stench that had been in the ash wind on the beach: pain and burning and fear.

"Five." Kygo's voice was flat, emotionless. "Six."

Damming the raw pain was like holding back a battering ram with my bare hands. But I felt Ido's breaths lengthen, the straining shock of his body ease a level.

"Seven . . . eight."

Pain seeped through my hold, long splinters of molten fire searing through our *Hua*.

"Nine," Kygo said. *"Ten!"*

I grabbed the back of Ido's tunic and pulled him free of the brazier. And my protection. He collapsed onto the rugs, gasping for breath. My gorge rose at the stink of burnt flesh and the terrible damage to his arm. But there was no time for horror. I gathered the rage that was building in me.

"This is not the purpose of dragon power!" I screamed at Rulan. *"I will show you the Mirror Dragon's true power!"*

I splayed my hands on Ido's chest and, with one breath, entered the energy world in a twisting buckle of color.

The tent was a seething mass of *Hua*. Silver savagery leaped through the transparent bodies of the mob around us, the swirl of violent energy streaming around the tent and between the two coiled dragons above. The blue beast shrieked as I felt Ido's union with his power burst through my core, the damage to his arm a small dark death in his energy body. I called the majesty of the Mirror Dragon, my fury meeting the cinnamon torrent of her golden glory in a slam of healing force. Our *Hua* closed over Ido's arm, restoring skin and flesh and charred bone with new authority. We heard the long drawn breath of agony finally released. Ido reached up and grabbed my earthly arm as the blue dragon uncoiled.

But we were not finished. These ignorant, savage people would see the true magnificence of the Mirror Dragon and her Dragoneye.

"Hold the ten beasts back," I said. "As long as possible."

Ido nodded as the blue beast launched himself into a sweeping circle around the pulsing crimson of my dragon.

I stood up and walked to Rilla and Chart. Silvered awe and fear pumped through their bodies as I kneeled beside them.

"Eona! What are you doing?" Rilla's voice leapt with her *Hua*.

Chart's body cringed from me as I placed my energy hands on the thin cage of his chest, the power centers along his spine spinning with vitality. Gold power flowed, searching, finding old damage—birth damage buried in the memory of his growth—knitted into the structures of muscle and bone and sinew, and even deeper in the tight twists of energy that flowed from mind to body. Our power dug and unraveled, rebuilt and connected. Our golden union thundered through us. We were *Hua* and we were the force of creation.

They are coming, Ido's mind-voice warned.

We felt them; the pressure of their keening approach was building in our energy.

I wrenched my hands off Chart's chest, and the swirl of the celestial plane collapsed into the fixed heat and stink and stunned hush of the tent. The abrupt separation from the glory of my dragon was like a freezing hand of loss around my heart. I looked down at Chart's face. His straining fight for control of muscle and sinew was gone, the planes and angles of his features settling into a familiar heart-stopping shape.

My breath caught. He was the image of my old master, the man who had found me in the salt farm and set me on this path of power. Chart lifted his hand and stared at the open splay of his fingers, the dazed incomprehension in his eyes dousing the last of my righteous fury.

Rilla's sob brought my head up. She touched Chart's cheek, her body shaking with shock.

"Lady Eona." I turned at Kygo's voice. He held out his hand, an anchor in the pounding wash of loss and fading power, and pulled me to my feet. Beyond us, Ido pushed himself up from the ground. The energy between us had left a small smile on his face.

Kygo's eyes swept around the tent. "You have seen Lady Eona's power and resolve," he said harshly. "Be thankful that you have also witnessed her compassion and restraint."

CHAPTER TWENTY-ONE

RULAN HELD BACK a branch for me as I followed Kygo past the scrubby stand of trees to the lookout that had the best view of Sethon's camp. The tribal leader and his people had certainly become more respectful since my display of power. I wiped the slip of sweat gathered at the base of my throat and blew a cooling breath upward. The day's heat was building to its peak, and Kygo's pace was relentless. He was set on gaining a rapid overview of the resistance resources and what we faced on the plain below.

I had not even had a chance to see Rilla and Chart and celebrate the wonder of my dragon's healing power. Or tell Chart about the effect of that power on his will. I rolled my shoulders, trying to shake off the dread of that moment; surely his joy would override any distress. And he knew me well enough to know that I had healed him out of love, even if it had looked as if it was done in anger. There had been no time to explain afterward; Kygo had wanted me by his side in the formal negotiations, and Chart had been too shocked to take much in. But I had at least promised him I would visit as soon as I could.

"What do you expect with these shackles?" Ido's low voice, behind me, was full of contempt. "If you want me to move faster, take them off."

I looked over my shoulder. Yuso was taunting him again, like a mongoose baiting a snake.

After the brutal events of the morning, I had not expected Ido's inclusion in the observation party. Yet, on reflection, it made sense. Both he and I needed to know the terrain of the battlefield and the scope of Sethon's preparation. And Kygo was no doubt reminding Rulan and the other tribal leaders that Ido was not only a murderous traitor—he was also a Dragoneye, and a key player in the battle to come.

Yuso prodded Ido in the back. "I doubt you will ever get out of shackles, *my lord*." He leaned closer, but I caught his soft words. "And you are the girl's bitch, forever."

Anger flared in Ido's face. He did not normally rise to Yuso's harassment. Uneasily, I realized my own anger had risen too. I shook it off; Ido did not need me to defend him.

"Lady Eona." I turned at Kygo's call. "Come look."

I forged through the thinning copse of trees. Kygo stood with Tozay under a shaded overhang of branches, a scout crouched at their feet. All three men observed the sweep of land below the precipice on which we stood. As I stepped up beside Kygo, the scout ducked his head into a quick bow.

The back of my neck prickled with the sight before me. Sethon's army was camped halfway along the massive plain. The stretch of tents and war machinery and horses and men was so great that, although I squinted, I could not see where the camp ended, its far reaches lost in distance. I had thought I was prepared for the battle ahead, but the plunging freeze in my gut told me otherwise. I'd had no true idea of what we were about to face.

Tozay gestured across the flat expanse of land that stretched between the precipice and the front line of the army camp. "Sethon has staked a battleground. But he will not attack us while we hold the high advantage."

"What will he do?" I asked.

Kygo rubbed his chin. "He will try to lure us to him so we surrender our high ground."

"Lure us? With what?"

Kygo nodded. "That is a good question, *Naiso*."

"So this is what fifteen thousand men look like," I said, my voice a little too hearty.

"No, my lady," the scout said. "This is eight thousand men. See those pockets of dust?" He pointed to tiny puffs on the horizon. "That is more men coming into camp."

Dry fear caked my throat. May the gods keep us: this was only half of them. "You have keen eyes," I said.

"Our best eyes," Rulan said, walking up beside me. He pointed to a large red pavilion tent set close to the front. "That is Sethon's tent. Arrogant prick."

A soft clink of metal announced Ido's arrival. He scanned the low plain, his heavy brows angled into a frown. With a shake of his head, he stepped back.

"You have something to say, Lord Ido?" Kygo said sharply.

The Dragoneye looked up as though roused from a daze. "No. Nothing."

He lifted his shackled hands and dug his fingers into his forehead. Almost all color had drained from his face, and his skin was sheened with sweat. Yet it did not look like fear or heat.

"When was Lord Ido last given water?" Kygo demanded.

Yuso stepped forward. "Before we got to camp, Your Majesty."

"Get him water." Kygo turned back to watch the plain.

Yuso bowed and headed to the young porter carrying the water skins. Ido grabbed my sleeve and edged me back a step, and another, until we had a slice of open ground between us and the men concentrating on the enemy below.

"Dillon is a day from us." His voice was barely a breath. "He is like a nail in my head." He pressed his fingers into his temple. My gaze fixed on his arm—the arm I had burned and healed.

He brushed his fingers against mine. "Never apologize for your power," he murmured.

I pulled away as Yuso approached with the water skin. He thrust it at Ido's hands.

"Is this one of your petty ideas, Yuso?" I said, trying to cover the rise of heat in my face. "Denying water?"

The Captain crossed his arms. "You are always very concerned for Lord Ido's welfare, my lady."

I had no answer to his sly insolence. Lifting my chin, I walked back to Kygo, the fear of Dillon's approach and the touch of Ido's fingers twining together into a hammering beat through my body.

It was late afternoon before I was able to make my way to the round tent assigned to Rilla, Lon, and Chart. Surrounded by a three-man escort, I walked through the rows of bleached-cloth-and-rope-bound dwellings. Curious onlookers gathered to watch the Dragoneye walk by, their hopeful murmurs following me like a long, whispered prayer. News of Chart's restoration had traveled fast in the camp, and a small crowd was outside his tent to catch sight of the evidence of my mighty power.

A few hours ago, the boy had been an untouchable demon of ill fortune. Now he was a symbol of power and hope. It was an effect of the healing that I had not considered.

I saw Rilla through a gap in the crowd, crouched next to a cooking fire. She was shaking a pan over the heat—goat meat, by the dank gaminess of the smoke—and staunchly ignoring the press of murmuring curiosity that followed her every move. Lon leaned against the sturdy frame of their tent next to the faded red door, his size and watchful demeanor sending a clear message.

"My lady, please wait," Caido said beside me.

He signaled to the other two men in my escort to clear a path through the onlookers. There was no need. A small girl jabbing a twig into the dirt caught sight of me, her yelp of excitement swinging all attention upon us and parting the throng into two ragged, bowing borders.

Rilla hastily placed the pan onto the ground and rose from her crouch, anxiously tucking a strand of graying hair into her coiled braid. She and Lon bowed.

"Lady Eona." Her face was a tense mixture of smile and tears.

"I am sorry I could not come before." I took her hands in mine. "How is Chart?"

"He is—" She looked around at the avid faces and turned away. "They will not leave," she whispered, drawing me closer to the tent. "My lady, Chart is . . . overwhelmed. As I am." She squeezed my fingers. "I think it will take us all more than just a day to feel the truth of your wonderful gift." She glanced at the red door. "He is"—her hand undulated through the air—"up and down, my lady. He has had fifteen years as he was, and in just a moment you have made him something different."

"But he is healed. He is whole again. Like me."

"Yes, his body is healed," she said slowly.

"Well, I will see him," I said, perplexed by her hesitancy.

"Of course, my lady." She cleared her throat. "Lady Dela and Ryko sit with him now."

"Ryko?" The islander had never met Chart. Why was he here? I could think of only one reason: to inform the boy about the compulsion. Did he truly think I would keep it from Chart?

"Ryko says he has also been healed by you." Rilla's voice was flat. I recognized the neutral tone: she had always used it when my master had done something questionable. Ryko must have told her, too. Resentment straightened my back. Her son was healed; surely that outweighed any cost.

Rilla ushered me forward as Lon swung the door open. Behind us, people craned to look inside the tent. I stepped over the high threshold, the door closing swiftly behind me. For a moment, the abrupt shift from harsh sunlight to dim interior reduced everything to featureless gray shapes. I paused, waiting as color and details sharpened into focus.

"Lady Eona."

Dela rose from a stool and bowed. She had exchanged her man's clothing for a long orange tunic cut in the full-skirted style of the eastern tribeswomen. Behind her, Chart was propped against a mound of cushions on a bed seat, one of three that were set around the edge of the small tent. Ryko stood next to him. The islander bowed stiffly to me and stepped back as I crossed the floor rugs. The stove set between the two central poles was unlit, but the tent was still stuffy, the day's heat trapped by the tightly closed door.

"Lady Eona, I hoped you would come," Chart said. Without the strain in his throat, his voice held the deeper timbre of manhood. He rocked forward on the bed, attempting to hoist himself to his feet, but his thin arms buckled. "Ryko, will you help me?"

The islander took Chart's arm and pulled him upright. I stared at the boy's sudden height; he was at least a head taller than me.

Braced by Ryko, Chart bowed. "See, my lady, I can stand." He grinned, the echo of my old master in his narrow features. "My muscles are too weak for much yet." He paused and took a wheezing breath. "But Lon says with practice I'll get stronger. He's already made me this." He held out a ball made of roughly bound leather strips. "To help my hands."

I smiled. "You're so tall!"

"I know, I know," Chart crowed. He coughed and swallowed hard. "Not used to having so many words at once," he rasped.

"Help him sit down again, Ryko," Dela said, reaching for the boy. "He looks pale."

"No!" The excitement in Chart's voice sharpened. "Do not talk over me as if I were still on the floor!"

Dela drew back.

"You have been through a lot, boy, but keep a civil tongue," Ryko warned.

Chart pulled his arm out of the islander's tight hold, swaying as he turned to face me. "Ryko says that you can control my will now. Is that true?"

I met his fierce gaze. "I was going to tell you myself." I glared at Ryko. "Did you think I would not tell him?"

"I no longer know what you will do," Ryko said. "Your ideas of right and wrong have changed since you have become so close to Lord Ido."

"Ryko!" Dela said. "This is not the way to do it. Not in front of the boy."

The islander and I turned away from the Contraire.

"What are you saying, Ryko?" I demanded.

His chin jutted forward. "I see the same love of power in you that I see in him. You did not heal Chart for his own sake. You healed him as a show of your might, with no thought to his wants or needs."

I bit down on my anger and glanced across at the boy. "You are happy to be healed, aren't you?"

Chart groped for the liberation disc around his neck. "Am I still a free man? I don't understand what this compulsion means."

"Of course you are free," I said.

Ryko snorted. "As free as a man whose will can be controlled at any time."

"I will not apologize for using my power," I snapped. My glance took in Chart and Dela, too. "You saw what happened in that meeting tent. I did what was best for the emperor."

"You always have a good reason ready," Ryko said. "You could have stopped once you'd healed Lord Ido. It was enough. But you did not."

I crossed my arms. "You were not even in the tent."

"No. But I felt you glorying in your power. You wanted to show your strength and fury and you used Chart to do it. Not so long ago, you would never have done that."

"Even if that were true, it doesn't matter." I swept my hand through his accusation. "Everything has changed. I have to do things now that I never thought I would."

"It matters to me," Chart said.

I swung around to face him. "What?"

The boy flinched but his gaze was steady. "This gift is truly a blessing from the gods, Lady Eona, and I thank you." He swallowed hard and held up the disc. "But you also gave me my liberation: the right to decide and choose for myself. In the meeting tent, you took that away." He coughed and lifted his chin, stretching his throat muscles for more words. "When you were just Eon, you were my friend. I was always a real person to you. Never a demon freak without voice or mind. But in that tent, you made me the freak." He drew himself up to his full height, the effort making his thin body shake. "You did not even look at my face until it was all over. I was just the thing you were using your power upon."

"No, it was not like that," I said, denying the sting of truth in his words. "You would have chosen to be healed, wouldn't you?"

"That is exactly the point," Ryko said acidly. "You did not give him the choice."

"I do not need you to speak on my behalf," Chart snapped at the islander. He turned back to me. "Have you already forgotten what it was like to be the cripple? To be allowed no feelings, no humanity? My friend Eon would not have forgotten."

"I have not forgotten," I said, trying to push down my own anger. "But I am not Eon anymore. Everything has changed. I am Lady Eona. I am the Mirror Dragoneye. I am the emperor's *Naiso*."

"Does that mean you no longer have to think of other people?" Ryko demanded. "Do you have your own rules now?"

I rounded on him. "That is unfair." My resentment gathered Dela and Chart into its bitterness. "I am always thinking of other people. None of you understand what it is like."

"You still should have asked me," Chart said stubbornly. "Eon would have asked me."

Dela touched my arm. "I know you are not easy with what happened in the meeting tent," she said. "You have gone against your own sense of right and wrong. Deep down you know it. Do not let all this power cloud your spirit, Eona."

I pulled my arm away. "Who are you to tell me about my power or my spirit? I am the Mirror Dragoneye and I will do as I see fit."

Ryko stared at me. "Listen to yourself. That is something Ido would say. He has got inside your mind as well as your body."

"Ryko!" Dela gasped.

"*That is not true!*" The heat of my fury reached toward him, seeking his *Hua*, seeking to force his words back down his throat. I felt my heartbeat engulf his life-force, doubling him over and dragging another faster, frightened rhythm with it. Chart. The boy clutched at the air, his knees buckling. Dela lunged for him and caught his frail weight against her body before he hit the floor.

What was I doing? Abruptly I broke the connection.

Ryko raised his head, panting. "Is this your answer to everything now?"

I turned on my heel and pushed all my anguish against the wooden door, feeling Lon shift aside. The sight of the watching crowd tipped my wretchedness back into fury.

"Go back to your tents," I yelled.

They gaped at me.

"Now!" I screamed. "Get out of here!"

Ducking into low bows, the mass of people backed away and broke into small groups, scurrying through the pathways between the tents.

Rilla stood up. "What has happened?"

"I am the Mirror Dragoneye," I said bitterly. "That is what has happened."

I looked back at the door. Lon had closed it again. "Tell Chart I am sorry."

"For what? Healing him?" Rilla said.

"No. Tell him I am sorry for not being Eon."

I walked away from her bewilderment, my escort hurrying into position around me. The Mirror Dragoneye did not apologize for her power.

The evening meal was a drawn-out affair, with the tribal leaders eager to show the emperor their local delicacies and entertainments. There seemed to be a lot of goat, and a sour rice wine called the Demon Killer, and dancing to drums, all bound together with an extravagant bravado that drove the laughter into hard shrieks, and the drinking into fierce competition. I sat at Kygo's left on the raised dais set up under the crescent moon and cloudless night sky, the dining circle surrounded by torches dug into the earth. There was little chance for private conversation, only a few snatched words in between the constant claims of the tribal leaders for our attention, and the loud relentless entertainments. In one moment of rare calm, Kygo leaned across to me, his hand finding mine under the low table. The gentle pressure of his fingers eased my wretchedness.

"You are pale." His breath was spiced with wine. "Is something wrong?"

I swallowed, trying to force down the oily nausea that I knew heralded the black folio. Unbidden, my gaze found Lord Ido, seated under guard across the circle. Kygo had insisted that he attend the dinner, but the Dragoneye had refused all food and drink. He sat very still as if any movement would break him apart, and his skin had a gray cast that added years to his face. My sickness came from just the approach of the folio, but Ido had a direct connection to it via the Rat Dragon and Dillon. I could not even imagine what he was suffering.

Kygo followed my gaze. "He looks unwell."

At some point very soon, I would have to tell him that I had forced Ido to call Dillon to us, but it was not a conversation to be tucked in between one goat dish and another.

At Kygo's throat, the Imperial Pearl caught the flickers of orange and red torchlight as though it held its own fire. What would happen if I told him the whole truth? That I had kept Dillon's arrival from him because the black folio held a way to bind my will and power. That I knew the *Hua* of All Men was the pearl stitched into his skin and his blood, and I had not told him because I hoped to find a way to save the dragons that did not make me a threat to his life. Any king in his right mind would kill me on the spot.

I shrugged. "Nothing is wrong with me," I said. "Except too much goat."

He smiled, squeezing my hand. "It is not my favorite meat, either, but it is certainly abundant." He lowered his voice. "The things we do in the name of duty."

His attention was claimed by Soran with yet another drunken story of battle prowess. I watched him graciously accept a piece of roasted goat from a fresh platter, his eyes meeting mine in a quick slide of amusement. The intimacy of the glance sent a wash of warmth through me that distilled into a single sharp ache of desire.

Where did my duty lie: with this powerful, beautiful man who held my hand and named me moon to his sun; or with the dragons, the source of my own magnificent power? Somehow I had to find a way to serve the interests of both. Yet what if it came to a choice between them? I shifted uneasily on the cushions: Ido was also bound up within that terrible question. As if he had heard my thoughts, the Dragoneye raised his head. There was fear in his eyes, and it chilled me with foreboding. Ido was as much in the balance as Kygo and the spirit beasts. He was tied just as tightly as I was to the dragons and their destiny. And that destiny was walking toward us with a black folio strapped to its arm and madness darkening its mind.

CHAPTER TWENTY-TWO

I WOKE THE NEXT morning to the sound of a shouting voice. Blearily, I focused on the tent roof above me, the open smoke circle at its peak pinked with dawn light. Pain drummed through my head, each spike sending a wave of nausea into my body. I struggled up on to my elbows and winced as loud barking erupted, the camp dogs roused into their own sharp rhythms of alarm.

Vida rose from her bed on the rugs, both daggers drawn, and crossed to the tent door. "Get up, my lady," she whispered. "Something is happening."

I swung my legs over the edge of the bed seat. "Is the battle starting?" The possibility closed a vise of fear around my gut.

"No, it's not the battle alarm." Vida pushed the door open a crack, her eye pressed against the slice of light, head cocked for listening. "It is one of the scouts. He is shouting something about a demon ripping through Sethon's camp."

It was no demon: the pain in my head told me it was Dillon. He had arrived, and with him had come hope—and dread. Snatching my trousers from the wooden press, I pulled them on, half hopping across the rugs to the airing rack. I scooped up my tunic and slid my arms into its wide sleeves.

"Vida, help me put on my swords." I knotted the inner laces of the tunic and wrapped the sash around my waist.

She held up the sheath. I plunged my arms through the brace and shrugged its weight into place on my back. Without the protection of a breast band, the straps dug into my chest, the sharp physical pressure a strange kind of anchor in the turmoil of my fear. Vida bent to secure the waist strap, clicking her tongue at the stiffness of the ties.

The door shuddered under a hard barrage of knocking. "Lady Eona, the emperor commands your presence. Now!" It was Yuso's voice.

"Done," Vida said, stepping back from me.

"My ancestors' plaques," I said. "Where are they? I must have them." Kinra had helped me hold off Dillon once before. Perhaps she would do it again.

Vida lunged across to a small basket on the ground and dug through it. "Here." She held out the leather pouch. "May your ancestors protect you, my lady."

"And yours, too, Vida."

As I took the pouch, her hand closed around mine. A brief press of hope and fellowship.

I tucked the pouch into my sash and pushed open the door. A blaze of pain rocked me on my feet. Captain Yuso bowed, his shrewd eyes noting my recoil. Beyond him, men ducked around shifting horses, tightening straps, and checking tack. I saw Ryko issuing orders, and Kygo in close conference with Tozay. The air still held the freshness of dawn, but an edge of heat was already in the bright sunlight.

And something else—a faint dankness that made me shudder.

"We ride to the lookout, my lady," Yuso said. "A scout has reported something in Sethon's camp." He watched me closely. "He says it is a demon."

Although I tried to hold firm, my eyes slid from his scrutiny. "A demon?"

The truth was finally bearing down with all the force of a mountain avalanche. I looked past Yuso at a figure crouched into a tense ball a few lengths away; a man with his arms wrapped over his head, his back heaving with each rasping breath. There was no mistaking that powerful line of shoulder or dark, ragged hair.

Ido.

I pushed past Yuso and sprinted toward the Dragoneye as one of his guards dragged at his arm.

"Leave him!" I shouted. The guard straightened.

"Ido?" I dropped to my knees beside him. "Ido, look at me." He did not raise his head. "Give him some air," I ordered, waving back the two guards.

Tentatively, I touched the dark hair. It was wet with sweat. He finally lifted his head.

"Eona." His shackled hands clasped mine, his skin hot and damp with fever. "He has arrived. Do you feel him?"

"Yes. Why is it so bad?"

"He is far stronger than I thought he'd be," he whispered. "He is using the death chant from the folio. I can feel death all around him."

"Can Sethon stop him and take the folio?"

"I don't think anyone can stop him. Not even us."

"We have to," I said. "He wants to kill you."

Ido's grasp tightened around my fingers. "He wants to kill both of us."

His face changed, a warning etched over the lines of pain. At the edge of my vision, I saw the two guards drop into kowtows. I whirled on my knees to face the emperor.

"What is wrong with him?" Kygo said, jerking his chin at Ido. "He looks worse."

I bowed, but before I could answer, Ido struggled to his feet. All of his grace was gone, stripped away by pain and the awkwardness of his shackled hands.

"There is nothing wrong with me," he said.

He bent his neck—almost a bow—and walked toward the horses. It must have cost him greatly to move as if his body was not wracked with agony. I dug my fingers into my forehead, pressing back my own pain.

"Come, *Naiso*." Kygo offered his hand and pulled me to my feet. "You will ride behind me."

Very soon, he would know that the demon was Dillon. Was

this the time to tell him everything? Truly be his *Naiso*? If I did, the love in his eyes would be gone forever, replaced by fury and betrayal. Yet it had to be done. I knew it had to be done.

"It will be all right," he said, drawing my hand to his lips.

His soft kiss on my palm broke my tenuous resolve. It was not going to be all right, but I could not bear to tell him. Not yet.

We rode at a flat gallop, the bone-grinding discomfort barely registering. Every part of me was fixed on the sensation of Kygo's body against mine: the work of his muscles beneath my hands, the braided rope of his queue pressed under my cheek, the smell of last night's smoke still in his hair. The ordeal of Dillon and the folio hung over me like a stone weight, but for that short ride, I held on to Kygo and lived within his breath and heartbeat, and the foolish wish that we could stay like this forever.

At the lookout, Ryko caught me as I slipped down from the horse, and held me steady as my trembling leg muscles recovered. My head was full of thick pain.

"Thank you," I managed.

He gave a quick nod. "My lady"—he pressed his lips together—"Dela says I went too far."

Before I could respond, Kygo swung neatly out of the saddle and took my hand. Ryko bowed and backed away, the moment gone.

Behind us, Ido dismounted, but his legs buckled beneath him. He rolled away from the horse's startled stamp, the reflex seeming to take the last of his energy.

"Get him up," Tozay ordered the guards.

The two men hauled the limp Dragoneye to his feet again, bracing him by his elbows.

No one spoke as we wove our way through the trees, led by the scout who had raised the alarm. I think we could all feel the presence of something dark ahead—a distant disturbance that shivered across the air and lodged in the teeth like a blade drawn across stone.

Another scout turned from his surveillance as we approached the edge of the precipice. It was the same keen-eyed man who had been on duty yesterday. He bobbed his head into a bow as we clustered around him. Everyone except Ido. I looked back at the Dragoneye. He had fallen to his knees, bent double, every breath holding a wheeze of pain.

"It started just before dawn," the scout said, pointing to a dark cloud of dust on the horizon.

Something was moving through Sethon's camp toward us, slicing through the soldiers as they tried to stop its progress. Every few moments a surge of men rushed at it, herded forward by a column of cavalry. And each time, the front line of foot soldiers broke against the force of the single moving figure and disappeared into dark dust like black foam on the crest of a wave. An ominous pink mist hung above it all, sweeping rain across the men that churned the mud beneath them red. Their distance from us stole any sound, but the morning breeze brought a stink of fear and offal and the dank metallic edge of blood.

Sethon wanted the black folio so much he had created a

death ground for his own men. My stomach lurched. I turned my face away, fighting back an acid rise of vomit.

"In Bross's name, what is that moving through them?" Kygo said, pressing his hand over his nose.

"It is a boy." The scout squared his shoulders. "I swear that is what I see, Your Majesty. Yet the soldiers that approach him shrivel into dust and a rain of blood." He shivered. "It must be a demon."

"Whatever it is, it's doing a good job of culling Sethon's men," Tozay said.

Kygo looked at Ido, hunched and panting, and then back down at the tiny figure carving its way through the army below. His quick mind was forging the link. He would soon arrive at the answer, and I would be left behind, forever caught in my silence. Forever caught in betrayal.

I had to offer this truth, before it was too late to offer him anything. The huge risk clawed at my breath. But it was now or never.

"It is Dillon and the black folio," I said. The momentum of truth quickened my words. "I compelled Lord Ido to call him to us. Before Sokayo."

Kygo's head snapped up. "Before Sokayo?" he echoed. The suspicion in his face was like a hand around my throat. I heard Ryko hiss.

"A long time for a *Naiso* to stay silent," Tozay said caustically.

Ido straightened on his knees, his face gray. "Eona, do not say any more."

I shook my head. "Dillon is here, Ido. It must all come out now."

Kygo turned on me. "Are you in league with him?"

"No!"

"Of course we are in league." Ido swayed with the effort of speaking through his pain. "We are the last two Dragoneyes. Our destinies are locked together, just like our power." His eyes flicked across to me. "And our desire."

I froze. What was he doing?

Kygo lunged and grabbed the Dragoneye by his hair, wrenching his head back. "*What do you mean by that?*"

Ido looked up into Kygo's face and bared his teeth in a smile. "Ask her what happens when she compels me."

"Your Majesty, please, we must focus on this boy and the folio," Tozay said. "He is killing everything in his path and heading straight for us!"

"Lady Eona has some questions to answer," Kygo snarled. He drew his short blade and laid it across Ido's straining throat. "Leave us." Kygo's hard glance swept the order around the circle of men. "Now!"

"Your Majesty," Tozay said sharply. "This is not the time—"

"Leave us!"

Tozay glanced around the circle and jerked his head back toward the copse of trees. With deep bows, they all backed away. My eyes skipped over Ryko's devastation, only to be caught by Tozay's savage mix of accusation and demand. This was my fault, and it was up to me to stop it.

I gritted my teeth; it was only the start of the truth. There was a lot more to come.

Kygo pulled Ido's head back harder, forcing a grunt from the Dragoneye. "I should have killed you the moment I saw you."

"We have been here before," Ido said, eyeing him steadily. "You will not kill me while you can use my power."

I flung my hand out at the plain below. "Kygo, Dillon is coming to destroy us. I cannot stop him by myself."

He glared across at me. "Why didn't you tell me the boy was on his way? Why are you keeping secrets with this whoreson?" He jerked the Dragoneye's head back even more. "Tell me everything, or I will cut his throat and be done with it."

"I *am* telling you everything," I snapped, my fear blazing into anger. "I made him call Dillon because I wanted to protect you!"

"From what?"

"From me, Kygo. I know what 'the *Hua* of All Men' means. It is the Imperial Pearl. I was hoping the black folio would have another way to save the dragons."

Kygo's jaw clenched, but it was not in shock.

Ido's labored breathing broke into a harsh laugh. "He already knew it was the pearl, Eona. You can see it in his face."

Ido was right: Kygo knew. I felt the last few weeks shift under me.

"Why didn't you tell me?" I gasped.

Kygo narrowed his eyes. "Why do I need to be protected from you, Eona? Are you about to rip the *Hua* of All Men from my throat?"

"He does not trust you," Ido said. "That is why he did not tell you."

"Hold your tongue, or I will cut it out!" Kygo pressed the sword harder against Ido's skin. The Dragoneye froze under the blade.

"It is not me who wants the pearl, Kygo. It is my ancestor." I dug my knuckles into the pain that clamped my skull, desperately searching for the right words to make him understand. "The red folio was written by Kinra. She was the last Mirror Dragoneye. The one who tried to steal the pearl from Emperor Dao."

"You lied even about that? Kinra was a traitor!"

"No, she wasn't, I am sure of it. She was just trying to save the dragons." I took a deep breath. "She is in my mind, Kygo. In my blood. Whispering, driving me to take the pearl and save the dragons. She's even in my swords. Remember at the village inn? She tried to take the pearl then. But I have always stopped her, always held her off. I have *always* kept you safe!"

"She is in the swords? In your mind?"

"Not all the time. Just when I am too close to the pearl."

"She is there when we kiss?" His hand went to his throat. "When you touch it?"

"Yes."

His voice hardened. "Is everything between us just this Kinra driving you toward the pearl?"

"No!" I stepped forward. "It is me. With you. I swear it."

"And what about me, Eona?" Ido said. "Was it an ancestor or you wrapping your legs around me in the cabin?"

Kygo stared down at him. "What?"

"She never told you about my visit to her cabin on the boat, did she?" Ido said.

"Kygo, that is not what—"

Ido raised his voice over mine. "We used the compulsion power to save the boat from the cyclone." His smile was a taunt. "You know the power I am talking about, Your Majesty."

"Is that true, Eona?" Kygo's voice was ragged.

"We saved the boat."

"Did you take pleasure from him?"

I could not help the rush of hot truth to my face. "It is in the power, Kygo. I know Ryko told you about it. We saved the boat; that is what matters."

"What if she did take pleasure?" Ido said. "She is an Ascendant Dragoneye, not one of your concubines. She takes whatever she wants. It is her due."

"It was not like that!" I clenched my fists. "It was the power that created it. I did not seek it."

"Do not hide behind your power," Kygo said. "You are using it for your own ambitions. Your own pleasure."

"I am not. I have always placed my power in your service. You know that's the truth."

His jaw set in disbelief.

There was one way I could show him I was loyal.

I jabbed my finger at the bloody slaughter in the distance. "That black folio can control my power."

"Eona, what are you doing?" Ido half rose on his knees, stopped by the blade. "You will destroy us."

I ignored his plea. "Anyone with royal blood can use it to bind a Dragoneye's will."

Kygo's blade dropped from Ido's throat. "What?"

"Your blood and the folio can compel our power." My voice cracked.

Kygo released his hold on Ido. The Dragoneye slumped, sucking in air. I could not meet the bleakness in Kygo's face.

"How long have you known that?" he asked.

"I told her when Sethon took the palace," Ido said savagely. "So much for your truth bringer. Your *Naiso*."

"Why didn't you tell me, Eona?" Kygo said.

I finally looked up at him. "Why didn't *you* tell *me* about the *Hua* of All Men?"

Within the lock of our eyes, the same reason stretched between us like a wasteland; neither he nor I trusted enough to place our power in the other's hands.

Kygo turned his face away. "And you have put all that power in reach of Sethon, in the middle of his army."

His words hollowed me into a cold husk. All he wanted was the folio and its power. I took a rough breath, fighting tears. Ido lifted his head, vindication in his haggard face. He had been right. Power always wanted more power. It was the nature of the beast.

"Sethon will not be able to stop Dillon," the Dragoneye said tightly. "The boy is using the *Righi*."

Kygo straightened his shoulders. "What is the *Righi*?"

"It is the folio's death chant. It rips every bit of moisture from a man's body and reduces him to dust."

"Is that what is happening to those men down there?" Kygo touched the blood ring on his finger. "May Bross protect us."

"Even Bross would find it difficult to stop him," Ido said.

I looked down at the red churn of Dillon's death march. He was coming for us. We had to face him or he would kill everything in his path—including the entire resistance army. His power drove a spike into my mind, over and over again, in time to my heartbeat. How could we possibly defeat a madness driven by hate and fed by the immeasurable power of the black folio? Even if we did, and wrenched the book from Dillon's mind and body, what would happen then?

I looked across at Kygo. He was watching me, and in his eyes I saw the same dark question.

Beside me, Yuso unshackled Ido, the irons clinking as he pulled them away from the Dragoneye's wrists. Ido slowly flexed his hands and rolled his shoulders, ignoring the captain's belligerent refusal to step back.

"Your Majesty!" The scout rose from his crouch and pointed across the plain. "Sethon's men have turned on each other!"

I hung back as Kygo crossed to the precipice edge. I did not know where to stand anymore. At his side? I doubted it.

"Lady Eona. Lord Ido. See this," he ordered brusquely.

I followed Ido across the small clearing. We both peered over the edge. Below us, the ragged waves of foot soldiers around Dillon had changed direction and were pushing back against the horsemen driving them to their death. I squinted, trying to gain more detail in the haze of red mist and flying mud. They were not only pushing; they were hacking at each other and trying to flee.

"The boy has forced his way through an entire army," Kygo said into the sickened silence.

"I would say Sethon has lost near to a thousand men," Tozay said. "And the *Hua-do* of those left. He will have a task ahead to regroup."

Kygo looked at Ido. "Are you sure you have to get near Dillon to defeat the folio?"

Ido nodded. "Dillon is draining the Rat Dragon's power. My power." Pain roughened his voice. "I will strike from that angle and block him from the beast in the celestial plane, but Lady Eona will have to strike the black folio. And that means contact with it."

I flinched, remembering the burn of its words in my mind.

"We will need to use every source of power we have," Ido added. "Including her compulsion over me."

Even now, he baited Kygo. The two men stared at one another in fierce silence.

"You are ignoring another source of power," Kygo finally said. "My blood and the black folio together can compel dragon power. If Lady Eona can get me close enough, I can stop Dillon."

"No!" Tozay and I said together.

"Your Majesty, you must not risk yourself," Tozay insisted.

"You want me to sit by while Lady—" He bit off what he

was about to say. "I cannot sit by while others face such horror."

A tiny glimmer of warmth broke across my desolation.

"That is what a king does," Tozay said flatly. "Your Majesty, if you attempt to go down there, I will stop you by force. Even if it means my execution."

Kygo glared at him. "I am not my father, Tozay. I do not blindly hand over my trust and my military because I cannot face the realities of war. I am not afraid of fighting."

I gasped. He would anger the gods with such disrespect.

Tozay drew himself up. "Your revered father was never afraid," he said. "He was devoted to this land and he did not want to see it plunged into eternal warmongering. I thought his son was the same."

"I am," Kygo ground out. "To a certain point."

"We are not at that point yet, Your Majesty. Believe me."

Kygo turned and walked a few paces across the clearing as if working the frustration from his body. "Then at least take some of my blood."

His blood.

I stared at his clenched hand, the glint of gold flaring into an idea. "Your ring," I said, the hope pushing me toward him. "Does it really hold your blood?"

He swung around, the possibility aflame in his face. "Yes." His voice lowered. "I told you the truth about *that*."

I bit my lip.

"There is not much in it." He measured a sliver between thumb and forefinger. "Will that be enough?"

I looked back at Ido. "Is it?"

"No one has ever seen the folio's blood power work. I do not know," Ido said.

Kygo twisted the ring from his finger. "Take it."

For a moment, I thought he was just going to drop it into my hand, but then he pressed it against my palm, the metal holding his body heat. With an ache in my throat, I remembered the last time he had pushed the ring into my hand. It had been his way of protecting me. Now it was his way of taking more power.

Yuso volunteered to take me on his horse to the plain below—no one dared suggest I ride behind Ido—and the three of us spent the short journey down the escarpment in grim silence. What was there to say? Either Ido and I stopped Dillon or everyone died.

After helping me dismount, Yuso hoisted himself back into the saddle, his attention on Ido. The Dragoneye had walked out a few lengths across the grassland to watch the distant dust cloud. Sethon's soldiers—both infantry and cavalry—had finally fallen back, leaving Dillon to his single-minded march toward us. Ido could now barely stand upright. No doubt Yuso was asking himself the same question that was on my mind: would the Dragoneye collapse before Dillon even arrived?

I passed Yuso the lead rope of Ido's horse, the animal tossing its head against the sudden pull on its bridle.

"Is it true what you said about your ancestor's swords?" Yuso said. "They have power, too?"

I stared up at him. What did that have to do with the ordeal ahead? Then I flushed—no doubt all the men had heard the painful revelations between myself, Kygo, and Ido. "Yes," I said tightly. "What of it?"

"It is a wondrous thing." He bowed and turned the horses. The bland response from the man was as strange as his question.

I turned from watching Yuso's retreat back up the escarpment and, with a deep breath, walked across the grass to join Ido. He was transfixed by the lone figure on the horizon and did not mark my arrival. Suddenly, he doubled over, hands on thighs, as a bout of shivering racked his body. I closed my eyes against a surge of pain in my head; as it subsided, I squinted Dillon back into view.

The boy seemed a lot closer than before. Far too close for the brief time that had elapsed. I craned my head forward, trying to make sense of it, and fear crawled across my scalp. Dillon was moving at a speed that was not quite human.

"Ido, look how fast he's moving," I said.

"I know." He straightened and sucked in a pained breath. "I think there is very little Dillon left now. He is all *Gan Hua*."

I touched the blood ring on my thumb. "There are too many maybes in this plan," I said. "Maybe the black folio will hold off the ten dragons. Maybe Dillon will have to get close to use the *Righi*. Maybe this ring will work."

Ido turned his head, the long angle of his profile and his steady eyes reminding me of a watchful wolf. "Eona, it is time that you faced the truth. If we can defeat Dillon and get the black folio, we must not give it to Kygo. We must keep it ourselves."

"What?"

"The black folio is our only chance to take the dragon power."

"What do you mean, 'take it'?"

"With the String of Pearls," Ido said. "We can have our power a hundredfold. Just think of what we could do."

I stepped back. "That's insane. It's a weapon."

"No, listen to me." He shot another glance at Dillon, gauging his approach. "We are the last two Ascendant Dragoneyes. If anyone can contain all the dragon power instead of releasing it as a weapon, it is us."

"Contain it? How?"

"In our bodies, together, like we do when you compel me." He licked his cracked lips. "Do you remember what I told you after the King Monsoon? What I read in the black folio? The String of Pearls requires the joining of sun and moon."

Sun and moon: it was Kygo's endearment. The resonance caught in my chest like a hand gripping my heart. "I remember you coercing me," I said, pushing my desolation into anger. "I remember you taking my will."

"I think you've had your revenge," Ido said dryly.

It was true; I had done the same to him, over and over again.

"We are a pair, Eona," he said. "I know you are as drawn to me as I am to you." The intensity of his eyes held me. "We are the sun and moon: the male Rat Dragoneye and the female Mirror Dragoneye. Together we can have all of the dragon power."

"To do what, Ido—rule the land? Is that your plan?"

"I told you before, chaos brings opportunity."

"So you brought chaos upon us to create your opportunity?"

"And yours," he said.

I shook my head at his arrogance. "Even if we get the folio, two Dragoneyes cannot control everything."

"If we take all the dragon power, we'll be far beyond Dragoneyes. We will be gods; it is the real promise of the black folio." Dillon was closing the distance rapidly: less than five hundred lengths. Ido's voice quickened. "You felt the hunger for more power when we moved the cyclone. Do not deny it."

I had felt it, and I knew he could see it on my face. "That does not mean I want *all* the power."

He gave a pained laugh. "Eona, wake up! The choice is either no power or all the power. There is no middle ground. Kygo will not give up the pearl, and that means our power will soon be gone with the beasts."

"But we would destroy the dragons."

He gripped my shoulder as if I was a young child having to hear a hard lesson. "You know by now that there is always a price."

"But we can't do that," I said. "They are part of the land."

"I do not wish to lose my power, Eona. Do you?" He doubled over again, struggling to keep his head up. "We must keep the folio." Urgency and pain stripped his voice into breath. "Are you ready?"

Dillon was less than fifty lengths away.

For a moment, fear sucked all sense from my mind. All I could see was a demon running toward me.

There was no flesh left on his bones. His face had been reduced to yellowed skin stretched across the sharp shape of his skull, his pumping arms and hands all swollen joints and knuckles. His eyes were dark holes of black power—ghost eyes—sunken into their sockets. Every step he took sprayed blood and matter, both feet worn to pulp from days and days of relentless running. Everything had been carved away by the driving force of the folio.

Ido grabbed my hand, bringing me back to myself. His hard grip dug the edge of the blood ring into my flesh. "Together," he said.

He took a breath, seeking a path to the celestial plane, his usual smooth rhythm broken by the ragged draw of pain. I held my own breath as he fought to shift into the energy world. Finally, his eyes silvered into union with the Rat Dragon. The moment echoed deep in my core, bringing an ominous wave of nausea.

Ido's hand convulsed around mine. "Holy gods!"

Black power surged across the silver in his eyes, like oil across water. I jerked back in reflex, but Ido's iron grip held me at the length of our outstretched arms. The black folio was inside his dragon power. I could feel the sour slide of its words, the whispering call of it through our linked hands.

I pushed through the seep of dark energy and found Ido's heartbeat. His pounding pulse folded into mine, our melded

Hua roaring through the deep pathways made of our desire, as dark and dangerous as the folio. I could taste acid as the folio's power surged from Dillon into Rat Dragon and Dragoneye, tainting the sweet vanilla orange of the union.

"The *Righi*," Ido panted. "He is chanting the *Righi* again."

Twisting around, I fixed on Dillon. He was only twenty lengths away, the black folio bound to his left arm, the white pearls shifting and heaving.

"My lord!" Dillon called, his voice like the hollow scrape of dried bamboo upon itself. "I am coming to you, my lord. I will watch your blood and dust scatter into the wind."

I felt him drop back into the deep chant of *Gan Hua*, the bitter song ripped from the earth and the air around us.

I took a shuddering breath, and another, focusing on the pulse of Ido's energy to guide me to the celestial plane. A third breath and the world shifted and buckled into violent, writhing color. Dillon's energy body swarmed with black, bloated power, every point spinning the wrong way, every pathway thick with darkness.

Ido's energy body was a battleground: pounding silver energy forced its way through the thick black veins of power that twisted and coiled around his pathways, anchoring themselves into his life-force. Screaming, he dropped to his knees as Dillon wove the blistering wind-song of the *Righi* across the water and blood of his body. I could feel it in my own pathways, whispering searing words of death.

"Eona!" Ido's body twisted in agony, his hand tightening around mine. "*Now!*"

Above us, the Rat Dragon thrashed in the sky against the hold of the black folio, his power streaming into Dillon. Beyond the shrieking blue beast, the Mirror Dragon was a swirl of crimson, her massive body contorted, ruby claws and slashing teeth aimed at the dark energy that pulled at her golden power. I screamed our shared name through the hissing words of the chant. Her huge spirit eyes locked on to mine as our union exploded through me in a pounding rush of strength. My earthly body rocked back against Ido's straining grip as golden union and sensual link fused into a torrent of power.

Dillon stood before me. "Too late, Eona," he said, his shriveled lips drawing back into a death's-head smile.

"No!" I lunged for him—trying to touch his dried flesh with the ring—but he was just out of reach. "No!"

His death song seared my body. Deadly heat boiled through me, slamming pressure into my head that drove spikes into my heart with every labored beat. I could taste blood in my mouth, my nose, feel it bubbling in my chest and pounding behind my eyes as if they would burst from my head. Everything blurred into a red haze. Above me, the Mirror Dragon roared as her golden power pushed against the blazing song, trying to dam its destruction. Screams—I could hear screams from Ido at my feet, and deep within my own blistering chest.

"Dillon, stop!"

"You want my power! Just like my lord."

Gathering my failing strength, I launched myself at him again, half blinded by the pulsing red heat in my head. Our bodies collided, my clawed hands raking wildly for connection.

I felt the hard leather of the folio, and then my fingers closed around papery skin and bone. The circle of gold around my thumb found his wizened flesh. *Please*, I prayed, *let it work.*

I tasted metal and the bitterness of the folio, melded into new power. Blood power. The ring was working.

"Stop chanting!" I screamed.

The whispering ceased. Immediately, the consuming heat dropped into dull warmth. My vision cleared. Dillon's face was inches from mine, his hot breath like the stink of rancid meat. I could feel his mind squirming against the force of the ring, his madness like a savage animal caught in a trap, snapping and clawing against it. So strong. So vicious.

My hold slipped—on his will and his arm.

The ring was not enough.

With a roar, he wrenched himself free and staggered back, the white pearls tightening around the folio in a pale stranglehold.

Searing heat exploded through me again. Ido screamed. Above, the Mirror Dragon bellowed, her golden power meeting the conflagration, holding back its deadly force.

A cold, clear thought pierced the scorching pain in my head. *Do not fight it. Take it.* As I had on the mountainside. The folio had wanted me, not Dillon. Its madness had reached for my mind, whispering promises of perfect power.

Madness. It would bring madness.

But it was better than this burning death.

"Come," I screamed and held out my arm. "Come to me."

"No!" Dillon shrieked. "The power is mine!"

I saw the dark energy gather in him like a snake coiling to strike. The white pearls unraveled from his arm in a spinning snap and leaped at me. They writhed through the air, dragging the folio behind them, then wrapped around my wrist in a slam of weight, binding the book against my skin. Power pulsed up my arm like acid through my veins. Dillon ran for me, his bone fingers ripping and dragging at the folio's defection. His chanting broke into a howl as its ancient power drained from him into me.

I gasped as the killing heat disappeared. Below me, Ido groaned, his body slumping with relief. "You have it. Kill him."

I tried to focus past the words that ate into my mind—dark secrets that scored my spirit with old power. The song of the *Righi* settled on my tongue, hissing into soft sibilance. Its power was a bitter vinegar, drying my mouth, sucking away softness and hope. The chant was in my head, spilling from my mouth, lifting power from the *Hua* around me—from the earth, the air, the dragons—building into a fire of destruction that bowed to my bidding. I heard the distant screaming protest of the crimson beast, but her power was mine. All power was mine.

Dillon pulled at the folio, yammering with rage. My chant quickened, weaving the power into more and more heat, every whispered word stoking the scorching energy into his destruction. He arched back, screaming, but I kept singing the song of his death.

Clapping his hands to his head, he fell to his knees. Blood

streamed from his nose, his ears, from the black pits of his eyes. The words fell from me into him, building and building into a furnace of annihilation. I was killing him, and I could not stop.

Help me, I prayed. *Help me, Kinra.* But it was too late.

Dillon's scream cut off, his body disintegrating into a sudden searing wind of dark ash and red mist that pelted my face with wet, gritty death.

I screamed, horror beating against my mind like leathery wings, but the acid words kept coming. Ido rolled away from me, crawling across the ground, coughing with pain.

Another song rose through me, pulling at my mind, bright and cool, a counterpoint to the words of the folio. I knew that song. I had sung its healing with the Mirror Dragon. I felt its golden harmony break through the bitter hiss of *Gan Hua*, easing the dark hold of its power. My breath broke into a sob as the terrible chanting faded from my throat, my mind. I dug my fingers under the pearls, my nails gouging the flesh of my arm. With the last of my strength I wrenched the folio free and flung it to the ground. It landed in the dirt, the pearls thrashing like a cut snake.

I fell to my knees and vomited over and over again, heaving my anguish into the earth. I had killed Dillon. The atrocity was still wet on my face and hands, the bitter taste of death still in my mouth. Maybe it would never leave me.

Nearby, Ido sat back on his heels, scanning the ground around us. "Where is the folio?" he rasped. "Do you have it?"

I managed a nod. It was beside me, the pearls coiled across the cover.

The sound of hooves resonated through the earth, galloping at speed. I raised my head to see Kygo, flanked by Ryko and Yuso, their horses lathered with effort.

"Eona!" Kygo wrenched the horse to a stop and dismounted into a flat run. His eyes were on me, not the folio. Behind him, Ryko and Yuso swung themselves from their saddles and followed their emperor.

"Eona!" Ido dived across the red-spattered grass. "Give the folio to me. Quick!"

"No!" I knocked it out of his reach with my forearm. The pearls heaved it across the dirt.

Ido scrabbled toward it again. "Eona, what are you doing?"

"Lord Ido, stop!" Kygo shouted.

Ryko grabbed Ido's tunic and hauled him backward. The Dragoneye twisted around, punching the islander. "Eona, it is the only way," he yelled. "Get the folio!"

I reached for the book, my hand hovering over the black leather binding and shifting pearls. Above me, Yuso drew his sword. The hissing release of the blade was loud in the sudden silence.

"Yuso, stand down!" Kygo roared.

The captain hesitated, then stepped back and lowered his sword.

I looked up at Kygo. "I promised you I would deliver the folio. It is yours."

"What!" Ido lunged forward on his knees, but Ryko jerked him back. "Don't be stupid, Eona! You are giving him our power."

Gritting my teeth, I picked up the folio; I could feel the golden song of my dragon and the force of the blood ring like a shield within my *Hua*. Slowly, I worked the ring off my thumb and placed it on top of the squirming wrap of pearls.

"Be still," I ordered. The rope quieted. Ryko sucked in a startled breath.

"Eona, please, no!" Ido struggled in the islander's grip. "He will compel us. We will lose everything."

Bowing on one knee, I held out the book and the ring in the cradle of my outstretched hands.

"Do not touch it, Your Majesty," Yuso said.

Kygo dismissed the man's counsel with a raised hand, but his eyes did not leave mine. "You are giving me your power? How do you know Lord Ido is not right?"

"You have always had my power, Kygo," I said. "Now I am giving you my trust."

He took the book and ring from my hands. "I know what this has cost you, Eona."

I looked down at the spread of dark ash that marked the place where I had killed Dillon. The place where I had felt the true power of the black folio.

He could not possibly know the cost.

The girl placed the steaming washbowl on the table set against the tent wall and backed away, her eyes never lifting from the lush overlap of rugs. I wondered what she had been told about me. That I was dangerous? A demon killer? I leaned over the bowl and breathed in the damp heat, the outline of my mouth and eyes reflected against the dark blue fish painted into the porcelain. I scooped my hands in the hot water. Curls of pale red unraveled across the surface as heavier black specks spun and surged around my fingers. The twisting patterns of blood and ash transfixed me.

"Eona!" Dela crossed the soft rugs, a drying cloth in her hand. "Wash it off. Now! You will feel better." She had already helped me out of my bloodied clothes and cleared them away as I dressed in a clean tunic and trousers. But I could still smell death.

I closed my eyes and splashed my face. The heat against my eyelids, my nose, my mouth was too much like the *Righi*. I straightened, the clamp of panic shortening my breath.

"Get me some cold water! Now!"

Dela motioned to the girl, who ran forward and picked up the bowl, carefully stepping with it to the tent doorway.

"Here." Dela held out the cloth to me. I wiped my eyes and mouth. The rough beige cotton came away stained with pink.

"Nothing will ever make me feel better about Dillon," I said.

"Ryko told me what he saw." Dela's face tightened with distaste. "That *thing* was not Dillon. Not anymore."

"It was once Dillon."

She clasped my arm. "He was probably in agony. You said yourself it was like hot acid in your head."

"Dela, I took the folio's power," I whispered. "I used it to kill him. What have I become?"

She pulled me against her chest. I pressed my forehead into

her muscular shoulder. "You are not Dillon," she said briskly, rubbing my back. "Do not even think it. You did what you had to do. And you got His Majesty the folio." She held me away from her for a moment, her dark eyes solemn. "You have restored Ryko's faith, too."

She folded me back against her shoulder.

"The folio is just death and destruction," I said.

"Well, Yuso has it under guard now," Dela said. "His Majesty and the leaders are discussing what to do with it."

I pulled away. "Now? Without me? But I am *Naiso*. I should be there."

Dela caught my arm. "Ryko told me what the folio can do, Eona. The leaders are discussing the potential of Lord Ido's power. His Majesty does not want you to be there."

The Dragoneye had been right; their first thought was to enslave him with the folio's blood power.

"No!" I jerked myself free and started toward the door. "I can compel Ido. They do not need to use the black folio on him."

Dela intercepted me, thrusting her body in front of the closed door. "Eona. I am not here only as your friend. I cannot let you go to that meeting."

"You are here to guard me?"

She placed her hand on my back, her man's strength steering me to the bed-seat opposite the door. "Just sit down. Sleep."

I pushed her hand away. "Sleep? For all I know, they could be deciding to compel my power, too!"

"You do not believe that, Eona. You are exhausted. Try to

rest." She picked up the red folio from a nearby table on which Vida had laid out my few other belongings: the pouch containing the Dragoneye compass, and my ancestor's plaques set around a small prayer candle. "Or if you cannot sleep, we could work on Kinra's folio together. I have found another name within it: Pia." The black pearls wrapped around Dela's hand in a rattle of recognition.

"It is probably another riddle," I snapped. "Just let me be." I turned from her, although I knew it was childish.

In all truth, I *was* exhausted, in both body and mind. Yet the terrible turmoil of my thoughts—about Ido and the folio and Dillon's death—kept me pacing the tent for a full bell while Dela sat by the door and kept her head bent over the red folio. At some point, the girl brought back a bowl of clean water, but her wide-eyed fear just made me angrier, and Dela dismissed her quickly. Rage and guilt, however, could not hold off my exhaustion forever. I finally lay down on the bed-seat, curling into my fatigue.

I woke with a sour mouth and a crick in my neck. The smoke circle in the roof of the tent held the dark mauve of dusk. I sat up, digging my thumbs into the cramped muscles at the base of my skull. I had slept the entire day.

"My lady, can I call for anything?" Vida asked from her cross-legged position on the floor. One jailer replaced with another.

"Some tea," I said ungraciously. "And some light."

Vida rose and opened the door, leaning out to murmur instructions to someone outside. She pulled back with a lamp in her hand, its glow brightening the wall coverings from shadowed pink to bright red. Dela had left the folio on the table. She was returning, then; a chance for me to apologize for my surliness.

I stood, smoothing down the ruck of my tunic. "Do the leaders still meet with His Majesty?"

Vida placed the lamp on the table. "They are finished."

"And?"

"I'm sorry, my lady, I do not know." From her tone, she knew the question had been about Ido's fate. "But the word in the camp is that we'll be fighting within the next few days," she offered.

"Is that really a rumor, or does it come from your father?" I asked.

"Let's just say that when I asked to be assigned to a platoon, I was told that I would be staying in camp to help with the injured, and I was to be ready for action soon."

We were both silent; no doubt there would be plenty of injured to be helped.

"Will you do something for me, Vida?" I asked.

"If I can, my lady."

"When the fighting starts, will you make sure Lillia is safe? And Rilla and Chart?"

She nodded. "I'll try."

A hard knock on the door sent her back across the carpets. I swished my hands through the water in the washbowl, the cool contact making me shiver. I had brought my mother and friends into such danger.

"My lady."

I turned at Yuso's clipped voice, my hands dripping.

The captain stood in the doorway, his lean body in shadow. "His Majesty wishes to see you."

I nodded. No doubt to tell me what had been decided. Vida grabbed a cloth and passed it to me. I dried my hands as Vida picked up my back sheath.

"No, my lady," Yuso said. "His Majesty wishes me to carry your swords."

Vida's eyes met mine. None of us went unarmed in the camp.

"Give Captain Yuso my swords, Vida," I said, overriding the mute objection in her face.

I recalled Yuso asking about their power. Did Kygo think they were a threat? Did he think *I* was a threat?

Yuso slung the back sheath over his shoulder. "My lady, you are expected now."

"She has just risen," Vida said quickly. She kneeled beside me, twitching the hem of my tunic into place. "She needs a few moments to prepare herself."

Yuso's gaze swept over the room, stopping on the table with my belongings. Perhaps Kygo thought everything I owned was a threat.

Yuso's eyes shifted back to me. "Lady Eona is expected *now*," he repeated.

"It's all right, Vida." I patted her hands, which were busy repleating my waist sash. Reluctantly, she pulled away.

I walked across to Yuso. He wore his usual dour expression, but there was energy coiled tight in him, distilled into the continual rub of his forefinger against his thumb. He knew something was about to happen.

"I will wait here, my lady," Vida said.

I looked back and smiled as reassuringly as I could, then stepped over the threshold. Yuso shut the door and silently led me across the large space outside the meeting tent. We passed small groups of people talking and laughing around fires, their warm camaraderie grating against my disquiet. I caught the slink of a shadow dog between two tents, only the white tip of its tail giving it substance in the gloom. A child howled in the distance, or maybe it was the keen of a night animal. It was soon obvious that we were headed beyond the heavily settled areas of the camp, toward a round tent set well apart from its neighbors, a guard stationed at its door.

"Is that where you are keeping the black folio?"

"Yes," Yuso said.

I stopped. "Why does His Majesty want to see me in there?"

"That is for him to tell you."

The guard saluted as we approached. Yuso opened the door, the wash of yellow lamplight casting his thin, lined face into seamed relief. He bowed and shifted aside for me to enter, hanging back a moment to give a murmured order to the sentry. With a crawl of unease across my shoulders, I stepped into the tent. Uncovered walls, no carpets. Just one man—another guard—standing beside a table that held a black lacquered box. No Kygo. The guard ducked his head in a duty bow.

Yuso ushered me farther inside.

"Sirk, your watch is over," Yuso said, dismissing the man,

who bowed again and backed out of the tent, closing the door behind him.

I walked over to the black box, its polish catching the lamplight in a slide of bright reflection. Why did Kygo want all the guards gone? Was he going to compel my power?

I turned to face Yuso. "What does His Maj—"

My head snapped back, the blow as solid as the man behind it. I staggered, my hands pressed into the pulsing agony across my cheekbone. The second blow into my stomach was so heavy it lifted me off my feet and punched away my air. I doubled over, gulping silently for breath, my vision blurred by shock and pain. He hooked his shin behind my knees. My legs buckled and I dropped on my back. The tent around me hazed into streaming lines of gray. Something slammed into my chest like a stone weight, pinning me to the ground; Yuso's knee. He bent over, his mouth set with the business at hand.

"Open up," he said.

He clamped my nostrils together. I gasped for air and saw the white porcelain of a herbalist's bottle in his hand. He forced it into my mouth, the cold ceramic edge clipping my teeth. Foul, briny liquid ran down the back of my throat. I wrenched away, coughing and gagging against the bitter draught, trying to spit it up. Trying to yell. He dug his fingers into either side of my jaw and forced my head back. I punched at him, connecting once onto a hard edge of bone, but the tent was already fading into soft blackness, the drug dragging me down into the thick silence of the shadow world.

CHAPTER TWENTY-THREE

A STINGING SLAP across my face hammered me back into myself. Another slap forced my eyes open. I gasped, a blurred face filling my vision. Bitter pain pounded in my head like a nail being driven into the base of my skull. Acid and metal in my mouth. I knew that taste. Panic burst through me into raw agony. It was the folio. And it was blood power.

"No!" I tried to raise my hands, but something gripped the need and held me still.

The blur in front of me sharpened into Yuso. I looked down; my wrists were bound with the white pearls, the black folio pressed between my palms. Blood smeared the gleaming rope. I tried to lift my hands again, but a clamp of compulsion locked them down. I could feel it around my mind, caging my arms and legs. I sucked in a long breath, groping wildly for the energy world, but a burning wall of acid blocked every pathway I tried.

"Yuso!" It came out as a croak, my mouth so parched I could barely dredge up sound. My hazed senses caught a backdrop of red and the smell of incense and roasted meat.

Yuso's eyes shifted from mine. "She is awake, Your Majesty," he said, straightening.

"Good."

The cold voice snaked into my mind, bowing my spine back against the wooden chair.

Sethon.

He was across the tent, back to me, the play of lamplight on his gilt armor emphasizing the breadth of his warrior body. Blood roared in my ears as understanding crushed me into a heartbeat and ragged breath. Sethon. Yuso had given me to Sethon. He had brought our enemy all of my power.

I was in a field tent, but the lush furnishings were suited to a palace chamber. The light from large gold lamps shone across carpets, elegant chairs, a lounging couch, and a large darkwood table with my swords on it. Four aides stood at attention, one against each wall, their curious eyes on me. At the base of the tent, I could see a sliver of darkness. It was still night. How long had I been senseless?

The High Lord turned, face impassive. His kinship to Kygo was carved into the clean modeling of his features, yet there was no warmth in his eyes nor mercy in the full lips. Everything was tight and twisted, like the scar that cut across his nose and cheek.

"Do you know where you are, girl?"

I nodded. At least I could move my head. I strained against the invisible hold of the black folio. Could I call its power as I had with Dillon? I focused on the energy pinning me down. *Come*, I called silently. *Come to me*. My desperation vibrated through the compulsion, but the folio did not answer. I was not strong enough to break the grip of Sethon's blood.

He crossed the short distance between us, every heavy step echoing in my chest. I flinched as he leaned down and threaded his thick forefinger under the bloodied pearls.

"And you can feel my hold on your will? My control of your body?"

"Yes," I whispered.

He tilted his head. "Let's test that, shall we? Let's see if this blood power truly works."

He pressed his calloused thumb along my little finger and bent it slowly back. The pain built, and built again. I gasped, the need to rip my hand from his grasp slamming into the wall of compulsion.

"I *will* break it," he said.

"No, please. I can't move!"

"Are you sure?" He smiled into my panting fear and pushed harder.

"I can't! I can't!"

He wrenched back. The bone snapped. Agony shot through the marrow of my arm. I screamed, my body jerking, mind raging with the need to snatch my hand against the safety of my chest.

He inhaled deeply, as if breathing in my pain. "Exhilarating," he said. "I can see why you enjoyed compelling Ido." He dropped my hands and the folio back into my lap, the raw impact making the world spin for a long, gray moment. "It is going to be most interesting to explore your capabilities, Lady Eona." He took my jaw in his thumb and forefinger and forced my head back.

"Your Majesty." Yuso stood to one side, hands clenched. "I have delivered Lady Eona and the folio. I have done as you wished."

Sethon waved him away. "Later, Yuso."

How had I not seen Yuso's treachery? My mind raced over the last few weeks, looking for missed signs.

"You raised the alarm at the palace, didn't you?" I said. "And the army at Sokaya. Did you shoot Ido, and kill Jun, too?"

Yuso angled his face away from me.

"Bastard!" I pushed all of my rage into the word.

"Your Majesty," he said through his teeth. "Please. You promised me my son as soon as I brought the girl and the book to you."

Sethon leaned closer to me, as if sharing a confidence. The smell of him—acrid and metallic—caught in my throat, an echo of the folio. "Unlike you, Lady Eona, Yuso's son does not have much fortitude," he said. "When I broke his fingers, he passed out. I'm sure a flogging brought on by his father's insolence would kill him."

A vein pulsed in Yuso's forehead.

Sethon nodded toward the wall of the tent. "Wait over there, captain. I still have work for you."

He watched as Yuso forced his fury into a bow and retreated.

"Love is such an exploitable weakness." Sethon turned his cold scrutiny back to me. "Yuso tells me that both my nephew and Lord Ido will come running to your aid." He dragged his thumb across my lips. "What do you have that brings two powerful men running to their annihilation? Is it just the dragon, or something else?"

"They will not come," I croaked.

He tapped my cheek lightly. "We both know they will come before the day is out. You are the perfect lure."

I clenched my teeth; he was right.

He leaned over to a small table set beside the chair. Around me, there was no lush carpet, just dirt floor. He picked up a long, thin knife. The shapes of blades, hooks, and a mallet flared at the corner of my eye. I had seen such implements before: in Ido's cell. The memory fired through my body, urging me to run. To fight. But I could not move.

"My nephew will come for you," Sethon said, "and in doing so, he will deliver the Imperial Pearl to me, safe under that strong, young pulse in his throat." He lifted the blade and examined the honed edge. "I would have preferred for Yuso to kill him and bring me the pearl, but all the lore says it must be transferred from one living host to the next in the space of twelve breaths." He shrugged. "One never knows if these stories are true or not."

He yanked at the edges of my tunic, exposing the skin above my breasts. In my mind, I punched and kicked, but my body stayed motionless under his hands.

"Ido truly believes you are the key to the String of Pearls," Sethon said. "He took a lot of damage before he gave up his secrets, but in the end, he was . . . very forthcoming about you and the black folio." He paused, his forefinger tracing my collarbone. "A leash made of your own dragons' *Hua*. The last thing he gave up before I lost him in the shadow world."

"What?"

Sethon eyed me. "Ido didn't tell you?" His body rocked with a silent laugh. "Still playing his games." He patted my cheek. "The black folio is made from the essence of all twelve dragons. Created by the first Dragoneyes. You are caught by your own kind."

"No!"

Yet the truth of his words crashed through me. From the first time I had touched the black folio, I'd felt its power reach for both of us—the Mirror Dragon and me. But why would the first Dragoneyes make such a thing?

I wondered what else Ido had not told me.

Then Sethon pressed the knife lightly into the base of my throat, and my whole world became that thin length of blade and the hand that held it.

"I understand from Yuso that you can heal yourself, Lady Eona. Over and over again." The hand arched and leaned into the blade, the edge just sinking into my skin. Blood rose around it, the pain leaping through my nerves a moment later. "Let us explore the extent of this leash."

I had been cut before—felt the quick shock of the battle

slash—but this was another kind of hurt. Slow and deliberate, a careful carving of flesh that dragged me behind its trail of blood into a crescendo of agony. I screamed, my head straining back, my body locked under the hand and knife, unable to run or fight or even press myself away from the malice slicing into my chest.

With a smile, Sethon lifted the blade and ground his other hand across the raw edges of the jagged, open wound. A different kind of agony. "Heal yourself with your dragon." He stroked my cheek again, his finger wet, the tang of metal on his skin this time the smell of my own blood.

All of my fury and pain and terror converged into one thought: *Kill him*.

I drew a deep breath and lunged for the energy world. The room twisted into streaming colors, the energy body of Sethon before me rushing with dark-edged excitement.

The red dragon writhed above me, her golden power locked into the crimson pulse of her huge body. Nearby, the blue beast roared its fury. Could Ido feel what was happening?

"Holy gods," Sethon whispered. "They are beautiful."

He could see them through the folio's power.

Sethon's energy body leaned down, the heat of his breath against my ear. The words he whispered were bitter and strong—an ancient command that closed around my *Hua* like a strangling hand. I clawed at it, my desperation useless against the implacable strength.

"Heal your wounds," Sethon ordered.

It was as if the hand opened for one precious moment, allowing a breath of the red dragon's golden power and a rush of healing ease. I opened my mouth to call her—*Turn the healing on him, take his will, kill him!*—but the hand clamped tight again, stifling my voice, blocking me from her glorious power. The energy planes of Sethon's face solidified into flesh and bone again, the streaming colors around me buckling back into the stillness of the tent.

I gasped, drawing in the sudden absence of pain. The carved mess of my chest was smooth again under the clotting blood, and the swollen ruin of my finger had knitted straight.

Sethon's head was thrown back as if at the end of an ecstasy. "So that is the energy world," he whispered. "Such power. No wonder Ido wanted it all." He broke into a rough laugh. "And when he comes for you, I will have his dragon, too. An army with two Dragoneyes. I will be unconquerable."

"*No!*"

He wiped his hand across my chest, smearing the blood. "You have no choice, Lady Eona. Your will is mine." He raised the knife again. "And, before long, your spirit will be, too."

Again, he lifted my chin, the shape of him blurred by blood and tears. He was never going to stop. Cutting me over and over again.

Hours must have passed—I could see the brightening of daylight at the base of the tent wall.

At the corner of my eye, I saw him pick up the mallet. He wanted my spirit, and he would have it soon; I could feel the loosening of hope, the ebb of strength and resolve.

I had to find a way beyond his reach. Before it was too late.

Ido had taken refuge in his dragon. But how? *With pain*, he'd said. Slowly, I found the memory in my clouded mind—we were training, the smell of jasmine, his thumbs pressed into the soft centers of my palms. Our first touch. He had told me that pain was an energy. I could use it to find the dragon. Not a true union. A last resort—and dangerous to the dragon and the Dragoneye.

But Ido had not been held by the bonds of royal blood and the black folio.

Sethon bent down, wrenched off my sandal, and pressed my foot onto the dirt; a solid backing for his mallet. Under my bare sole, I felt rough earth, the wetness of my blood. And something else: a tiny shiver through my foot's gateway of energy.

I stilled, focusing past the roar of pain in my body. It was earth energy; the oldest power. And my blood—my ancestors' blood—dripping from me into the dirt of the east, my dragon's heartland. Her center of power. I drew in a shaking breath to hide my desperate hope, waiting. And dreading.

The smashing blow exploded through me, every part of me gathered in its agony. Screaming, I opened myself to the earth's energy and the primal power of my blood—an ancient call to an ancient dragon.

Spinning. Weightless. Pain gone. All sensation gone. Only darkness—in my eyes, my nose, my mouth. A cocoon of blessed relief.

Was I dead?

Eona.

A voice. Familiar.

Eona. Come. I have been waiting for so long. We have all been waiting for so long.

Waiting? Who has been waiting?

Come.

The voice drew me out of darkness into the swirling reds and greens and blues of the celestial plane. Below me, my body sagged in the chair, silvery *Hua* still pumping through it, the pathways threaded with the black of the folio. Not dead, then.

Sethon's dark energy body bent over my limp form and hauled my head up by my hair. "She's in the shadow world." He slammed the mallet down onto the table.

I was in my dragon. Safe from him. The triumph gathered into cold intent: this was a chance to kill him. Rip his army apart.

Eona. The voice pulled me back from my hate.

You must make it right.

The voice was in me, beside me, above me. I knew its tone, its rage.

Kinra.

In the Mirror dragon, too. Had she been here since the dragon fled?

. . . waiting for so long. I am nearly gone, Eona. You are the last of my line. You must make it right. See my memories. See the truth.

The energy world suddenly fell away, plunging me into an assault of light and heat, a memory of flesh and bone and skin.

I am standing in hot sunlight in a courtyard, a tart citrus smell rising from the border of kumquat trees around the marble square. It is the courtyard of the Rat Dragon Hall and I am holding a man's hand. He stands before me, thin body tense. For a moment, I do not know his face, and then his sharp features shift into the face of—

—my beloved Somo.

"Are you sure, Kinra?" he demands. He looks over his shoulder, but we are alone.

I hold up the scroll. "I have found the proof. There is no bargain between us and the dragons. There never was any bargain. The first Dragoneyes stole their egg of renewal—the Imperial Pearl—and we still hold them here with it. A ransom for their power sewn into the throat of our emperors."

"No!" He shakes his head in disbelief. "If that is so, then why do I feel my dragon's joy when we unite?"

I touch his cheek. "Somo, I don't think that joy is for us." Hot tears sting my eyes. "I think it is because every union holds the hope that one of us will finally understand what we have done to them and make it right."

The energy world burst back into swirling brightness below me. Although my physical body was slumped in the chair, I felt as though my spirit was rigid with shock. The dragons were enslaved. There was no bargain between man and beast. We had stolen their egg, and Kinra had tried to return it. And like Somo, I had misread my dragon's joy, blinded by so much power at my command. Now I understood: the ten bereft dragons were not crying for their dead Dragoneyes. They were crying for their lost hope.

Sethon's energy body squatted down before my inert form, the dark flow of his *Hua* raging through his pathways. "She is crying," he said. "That is not possible in the shadow world." He grabbed my chin, lifting it. "So, where are you, Lady Eona?" For a moment, he watched me, then he closed his hand around the pearl rope binding my wrists. "Return to your body!"

His command opened a crack of searing pain in my safe cocoon.

No! You must see. You must know the truth.

Kinra's voice snatched me away from the agony, plunging me once more into another place, another time. A large bedchamber, shutters closed, bronze lamps burning oil scented with roses. A small girl kneeling on the floor, playing with a wooden horse—

—my sweet, beautiful Pia. Somo at the door, ordering my maid away. I place the black folio on the table and stifle a shiver. It has taken me so long and all of my resolve to read its dangerous words.

"This book and the Imperial Pearl are the ways we keep the dragons bound to us," I say as Somo crosses the room to me.

"I can feel the Gan Hua *in it." He rubs the base of his skull. "It makes me feel ill." He reaches for the folio, and snatches his hand back as the white pearls stir. "You say it has been woven with*

the Hua *of all of the dragons? Like a rope around their spirits?"*

"Yes. And if the dragons are to renew, their old Hua *must join with the Imperial Pearl, the new* Hua*. According to the scroll I found, they must be reborn every five hundred years or their power starts to weaken, and with it the balance they bring to the earth. Not so many cycles ago, one dragoneye could take care of his own province, by himself. You know that is not the case anymore. Now every wind and water disaster needs the power of at least two dragoneyes to quell it. Sometimes even three."*

"We only use three in the worst situations," he protests.

"See, you are downplaying it, too. Just like the rest of the Council."

For a moment he stares at me. Then, reluctantly, he nods. "How would this renewal be achieved?"

I lower my voice. "Somo, I think the dragons are reborn through the String of Pearls."

He steps back. "The weapon?" He gives an uneasy laugh. "Do you intend to kill us all to release all the dragon power?"

"No, it is not meant to be a weapon. It is supposed to be the way for the dragons to renew." I point to the symbol tooled into the book's black leather cover. "See, there are twelve interlocking circles. They symbolize the pearl that each dragon carries under its chin. They are not just pearls of wisdom, Somo. They are each dragon's new self, waiting to be born." I run my finger around the large circle created by the smaller interlocking circles. "And this, the thirteenth pearl. The Imperial Pearl—the catalyst—that brings their renewal. What we stole from them."

Somo stares at me. "If they are reborn, what will happen to our union with them?"

I straighten, knowing the pain I am about to cause, because I feel its deep ache myself. "It will go with the old beasts."

"Go? You mean for good?"

"Yes. We will lose our dragons forever."

"Kinra, we will lose our power!"

"It is a power built on the enslavement of the dragons, Somo! We are creating a massive imbalance in the land's Hua *by not allowing them to renew." I point to our daughter, click-clacking her horse across the parquetry. So innocent. "Do you want her children's children to bear the bad luck that our greed will bring upon them? They will curse our names as the land dies around them! And we will have no rest in the garden of the gods if we do not right this terrible wrong."*

The dim, rose-scented room snapped back into the bright ebb and flow of the celestial plane. Kinra's memory seared through me. I would lose my dragon. Ido had been right; there was no middle ground. It was all the power or nothing.

Far below me, the energy in the tent broke and swirled as someone burst through the doorway and knelt, every pathway in the newcomer's body rushing with frantic *Hua*.

Sethon turned. "What is it?"

"The resistance is massing at the top of the ridge, Your Majesty."

Sethon's dark energy surged. "Excellent. Prepare for engagement."

He circled the chair, pacing, then picked up a knife and sliced into the palm of his hand. *Hua* gathered at the pulsing leak. He closed his fist around the pearls. "Return to your body, *now*."

The blood command reached toward me, calling me back to my flesh.

Not yet!

Kinra's voice was desperate, dissolving the streaming colors around me into—

—the same bedchamber. Alone. Six months of preparations nearly complete.

Tonight, Emperor Dao will call for my body, and I will steal the pearl. He thinks he has finally seduced the Dragoneye Queen, the only woman in his empire who can reject him with impunity. He thinks he has won me away from Somo. I slot the calligraphy brush into its porcelain rest and press the back of my hand to my wet eyes, stemming the useless tears. Whether I succeed or not, tonight everything changes.

At least Pia is safe—hidden far away with a good family. Leaning down, I blow on the wet ink of the last entry in the red journal. Woman script and code; it should be safe. The journal is my letter to Pia, the only way she will ever know why she lost her mother and father and her Dragoneye heritage. And if we fail, it will show her the way to make it right.

I close the journal and watch the black pearls settle around the smooth red leather; an idea I have borrowed from the first Dragoneyes. They knew how to guard their secrets.

If all goes according to plan, I will take the pearl from Dao on the hour of the Ox and meet Somo outside the palace, where he will be waiting with the black folio. By the time I get to my beloved, the twelve breaths of the Imperial Pearl will be well past and the dragons will be forming the String of Pearls. It will be too late for anyone to stop their release.

The black folio is open on the table, ready for the final task. I touch the hilts of the jade and moonstone swords, feeling my rage woven into their steel. I have not told Somo this part of the plan, and the small deception settles in my heart like stone. But he would not have let me put my spirit at such risk. I pick up one of the swords and draw the tip of the blade across my palm in a hot sting of pain. Bright red wells in its wake. With a deep breath, I press my hand against the open pages and gather my Hua *through the flow of my blood. The black folio grabs at me, weaving my energy into the heat of the dark force that already holds the dragons. Bound together now. If I succeed, my* Hua *will be released with the dragons. If I fail, I will be locked alongside the dragons waiting for another chance. Waiting for Pia or another of my bloodline to make it right—*

"Return!"

Sethon's voice ripped me from my dragon and slammed me back into my brutalized body. I screamed, every part of me alight with pain. His hand snaked around my throat, fingertips digging into the round of my windpipe.

"If you try that again, I will not be so generous with the healing power," he said, choking off my sound.

My pulse pounded in my ears, its frantic rhythm holding Kinra's words.

Make it right.

CHAPTER TWENTY-FOUR

I SQUINTED ACROSS the battlefield, trying to recognize Kygo and Ido among the tiny figures that stood along the edge of the escarpment. Could they see me on this command tower, kneeling at Sethon's feet? They could hardly miss me: we were in the center of the assembled army, raised twelve tiered steps above it on a wooden platform. To add to that, we sat upon a small throne dais marked out by a tall canopy. The bait in plain sight.

Sethon reached down and stroked my hair, his touch making my skin crawl.

Perhaps Ido was not standing on the ridge at all. He no longer had the threat of my compulsion hanging over him, so why would he stay?

I glanced up at the purple silk canopy that billowed over us, its long fringe of red blessing banners snapping like whips.

There was some strange quality in the hot gusts that swept the flat grassland, and in the bank of silver clouds closing in around us. I wet my cracked lips, tasting the air: it held the harsh edge of dry lightning, the same acrid energy I had smelled and tasted on the beach with Ido. Every Dragoneye sense within me said he was making this searing wind. He had stayed, and he was going to fight alongside Kygo. The certainty straightened my spine.

"You have something else to say?" Sethon asked High Lord Tuy, who was bent on one knee before him at the base of the small dais. He was another of Sethon's half-brothers, closer in age, with wary, narrow eyes and deep lines cut from nose to mouth; a permanent sneer etched into his face.

"I have a concern, Your Majesty," he said. "This plan to take the ridge. All conventional wisdom says that attacking uphill is a fool's strategy."

Sethon's hand traced the moonstone and jade circles on the hilt of one of Kinra's swords, slung in the back sheath over the arm of his chair. "A fool's strategy?" he echoed softly.

"Xsu-Ree cautions against it specifically, brother," Tuy said, his fist clenching with the effort to moderate his tone. "Why go against his wisdom? It has always stood us in good stead."

My knees ached from kneeling on the hard wood, but I did not dare shift in case the movement brought Sethon's focus back to me. Except for my hands—still bound by the pearls, and useless—he had released my body from his physical control. I could not bear to lose that freedom again. As it was, I still felt his choking grip on my power like a tight rope around a dog's neck. Hot shame swept over me; this was what I had done to Ido, and what we were doing to the dragons.

"We should march around the escarpment," Tuy added. "Attack on equal ground with all our force. It will only take a week or so, and we will slaughter them with minimal loss."

Sethon's fingers curled into my hair and yanked my head back. I fixed my eyes on the canopy, trying not to show the pain that clawed across my scalp. "Look at what I have, brother," he said, shaking my head. "Dragon power. I don't need to attack on equal ground."

Tuy's eyes flitted across my face. "Everyone sees what you have, Your Majesty," he said tightly. "The Mirror Dragoneye is indeed a prize. But her presence is making the men uneasy. They fear you will bring bad luck upon the campaign by flouting the Covenant."

Sethon released my hair and gestured to the huge battalions below us, each division in its own painted armor—red, green, purple, yellow, blue—immense ranks of color that seemed to stretch forever toward the escarpment.

"The men will be glad enough of her dragon power when Lord Ido attacks," he said. "You will take the ridge while I take care of Ido and his dragon. Even if we lose five men to their one, we will soon overrun them." He crooked his finger at Yuso. "Remind my brother how many men we face."

Yuso stepped forward. "No more than four and half thousand, High Lord Tuy."

I bit down on my rage. Couldn't Yuso see that Sethon would never release his son? He had betrayed us for nothing, and now the resistance faced dragon power. My power.

"I am aware of the numbers, Your Majesty," Tuy said. "But—"

"No. I want this finished," Sethon said. "I waited long enough for the throne, and I have waited long enough for the pearl." He indicated a man kneeling at the far edge of the platform; a physician, by the maroon cap he wore and the red lacquered box beside him. "I want Kygo and Ido contained and captured, and I want the pearl sewn into my throat. *Today*. Do you understand?"

It was Kygo's death warrant. As soon as the pearl left his throat, he had only twelve breaths left to live. Less than a minute.

Tuy bowed. "Yes, Your Majesty."

"Give the signal to Tiger Division to move into position, and return to your battalion."

With his jaw set, Tuy bowed again and backed away. Sethon watched him issue the order to the twelve flagmen clad in leather armor who stood along the top terrace step of the platform. Immediately, two men at the far end of the line raised their large square pennants—one yellow and one white, on sturdy poles—and snapped them across the gusty air at right angles to their bodies. Below, the yellow division broke away from the main formations.

Sethon gave a grunt of satisfaction. "Now it is up to us, Lady Eona, to draw Lord Ido's focus." He stroked my hair again.

I pulled my head away. "You have had one day of dragon power," I said. "He has had twelve years. You will not defeat him."

I knew he would punish my defiance, but it was worth it. Strength came with bold words. I tensed, waiting for his blow. Instead, he laughed.

"When I had Lord Ido in that cell, I learned three important truths about him," Sethon said. "Firstly, he must be in possession of his full faculties to use his power. Secondly, he can only direct his power to one task at a time." Sethon leaned down until his face was close to mine. "The final truth is more about the man than the Dragoneye. After three days of my attentions, there was a moment in that cell when he regained both his faculties and his power. He could have razed the building to the ground. Instead, he directed his power elsewhere—to help you, I believe—and so he lost his chance to escape."

Understanding prickled across my back. Ido had used his power to save me from the bereft dragons at the fisher village, instead of escaping.

"Lord Ido will protect you at all cost," Sethon said. "It is why I know he is up on that ridge waiting to attack. Why I know this platform is safe. And why I know we will defeat him."

With bullish purpose, Sethon rose from the chair and hauled me to my feet. My legs were locked into stiff crooks, and only his hard grip kept me upright as I stumbled to the edge of the platform. The flagmen who lined the step below us dropped into bows as Sethon pointed to the ground. "Do you see that squad of men down there?"

I stood swaying on the edge. Below us, about fifty soldiers stood in formation, their leather armor dull gray, as if they had emerged from the shadows.

"I call them my hunters. Every one of them knows what Lord Ido looks like. And every one of them knows how to disrupt a man's *Hua* and render him senseless. They are here to capture Lord Ido and deliver him to me, safely contained by the shadow world. And you and I will keep Ido's power focused on other matters while they do it."

The strategy was simple and clever. Sethon did not need twelve years of dragon training; just fifty hunters who knew how to fight their way through a melee, and a distraction that would pull Lord Ido's attention away from his earthly body. It was well worthy of Xsu-Ree.

"Begin the attack," Sethon said to the flagmen.

Red, green, and yellow flags arced in a graceful sequence. A roar rose from the thousands of men below as the yellow division marched toward the ridge. I prayed to the gods that Kygo and Ido were ready.

Deep within my core I felt the rush of Ido's union with the blue dragon. The sensation was muted by the black folio, but it still held the dark, crisp flavor of the man and his spirit beast. The taste of hope.

Around us, the air suddenly compressed. The clouds above the battlefield contracted as if they were a huge flexing muscle. Three jagged spears of lightning ripped the sky, their crackling power slamming into the yellow battalion. Gouged earth sprayed upward, the pale flash of bodies visible in the dark churn. The impact surged across the battlefield, reaching us in a wave of sound that held the force of a punch. Sethon and I both staggered back a step, the flagmen below us crouching for cover. I turned to hide my exultation.

"Continue the advance," Sethon ordered.

The flags sent the order across the battlefield.

A thick rain of arrows flew from a line of archers across the ridge. The dark slivers momentarily filled the silver sky then were lost against the dull background of the ridge as they fell to earth. Only the sudden dips and gaps in the rush of men below showed their final destinations.

A low rumbling vibrated through my feet. To the left of the escarpment, a crack opened in the earth. On either side, the grassland collapsed inward, the chasm deepening and lengthening along the battlefield. It headed straight for us, as if two huge hands tore the earth apart. Screaming men fell into the heaving channel; half of the blue battalion was lost under convulsing earth and huge plumes of dust. I ducked as dirt and gravel pelted down in a stinging shower. Sethon was wrong: Ido was going to destroy the platform. Three of the flagmen dropped their pennants and scrambled down the steps.

"Hold your positions," Sethon yelled.

They froze as the roaring progress of the chasm shook the structure. A wave of heat swept over us. I gagged, dirt and fear caught in my throat.

It stopped. There was only the patter of falling dirt, and

Sethon's harsh breathing, then screaming, from below.

I blinked away the grit and tears. The chasm had sliced past the platform and run the length of the plain, splitting a third of Sethon's forces from the rest of the army.

"My nephew knows his Xsu-Ree," Sethon snarled. He closed his hand around the pearls binding my wrists. "Show me the dragons!" he said, his face so close I could smell the metallic power of the folio on his breath.

The blood compulsion propelled me into the energy world, the transparent shape of Sethon's features streaming with thick black *Hua*, the pathways along my arms riddled with dark veins. Sethon gasped at the sudden shift.

Below us, the battlefield whirled in violent iridescent reds and oranges—thousands and thousands of soldiers reduced to pulsing points of *Hua*, caught in the shock of the double attack from earth and air. The resonance of the lightning strikes lit the mangled earth in a fading white afterglow, and the dark scar of the chasm held the *Hua* of dying men flickering like the tiny glow of fireflies.

Above, the blue dragon circled the plain, his huge body doggedly resisting the folio. Another gossamer thread linked the beast to the ridge: Ido, working his power. The red dragon thrashed against the thicker stream of energy being pulled from her body, the dark return of *Hua* from the folio dulling her crimson scales. My eyes locked on the golden pearl under her chin. Her renewal.

Make it right. Kinra's plea pounded through my blood.

The Rat Dragon dived, his power tearing another gaping chasm on the right side of the battlefield, straight through the red and green battalions. Hundreds and hundreds of bright points of *Hua* flickered and disappeared, caught and consumed in the splitting earth. Ido was carving out two unbreachable chasms that divided Sethon's army into three. At the top of the ridge, bright lines of *Hua*—the resistance—surged down the steep slope to meet the remnants of the red and green battalions corralled between the deep trenches. I knew Kygo was among them, no doubt at the front, and I sent a desperate prayer to Bross to protect him. Ido's position was easy to see; his thin thread of power rose from the center of the advance straight to the dragon, the beast above him still ripping the earth at his command.

"Stop him!" Sethon yelled.

The compulsion surged through me and reached toward the red dragon. Bitter black energy hooked her power, forcing us into union. There was no glorious warmth or cinnamon joy; just rage and fear in both of us. I fought it, trying to wrench myself free from the union—to save her from Sethon's control—but the blood power burned its way through like acid eating another pathway to our bond.

"Stop Ido's dragon," Sethon ordered. "Attack it."

"No!" I gasped, feeling the howling denial echoed through my bond, but the Mirror Dragon and I were already coiling our strength toward the blue beast.

We spread our talons into weapons, our massive muscles

bunching into deadly intent. We launched ourselves at the Rat Dragon. He swung around and met our attack, shrieking, his power dragged away from the second chasm. It was not finished—a bridge of land still connected the two battalions. Our claws caught on blue scales, slicing open one flank into a gash of bright energy. He roared, his huge tail slamming into our chest and knocking us backward. The energy world spun past us in a blur of color as we strained to break free of the hold on us, but the tether was too tight. Circling upward, we swung around to face the blue beast again. He retreated through the air, but we followed, slashing at his deep chest.

Ido! I tried to force my mind-voice through the barrier of the folio, but it was like trying to call to him through a thick stone wall.

We charged, the blue dragon ducking under our impetus, one of his curled horns scraping along our belly. We twisted through the air.

Below us, the resistance streamed down the slope between the trenches Ido had carved into the earth. The soldiers caught in the corridor of land rushed to meet them. The two forces clashed, the tiny points of *Hua* smashing together into a morass of heaving energy. The gossamer thread between blue beast and Ido shone like an arrow pointing to his position.

"Send the hunters," I heard Sethon order the flagmen. "Ido is straight ahead."

The swish of the flags sent his command below. At the foot of the platform, the tight formation of the hunters broke apart, their bright points swallowed into the huge pulsing energy knot of the battle.

The blue dragon roared, turning with sinuous speed toward the unfinished chasm. We swept around, massive head down as we rammed him, the impact shuddering through the red dragon into my human body. Our huge jaws closed on his neck. Sethon laughed beside me as the blue dragon flailed with desperate opal claws and plunged, ripping himself free from our vicious grip.

I'm sorry, I'm sorry, I'm sorry! I screamed in my mind, but I knew Ido could not hear me.

"Send in the rest of the red battalion," Sethon ordered the flagmen. "We will finish this now."

Reinforcements surged around the end of the unfinished trench. The thin silver line of their progress bunched, then pushed through the ragged lines of the resistance. We streaked after the blue dragon, screaming our defiance but unable to stop the attack compelled from within. Below, the gossamer thread of power that linked Ido to his beast was under siege. A shifting circle of bright *Hua* surrounded Ido, a smaller circle within it desperately holding back the assault: resistance fighters shielding the Dragoneye, trying to repel the hunters intent on capturing him. The circle broke, then regrouped, but not fast enough. The shield had been breached by two points of *Hua*. The thread of power flickered, and snapped. The Rat Dragon shrieked.

"They have him!" Sethon exulted.

"No," I screamed. "No!"

"End your union."

I felt the compulsion close around my power and tear me from the Mirror Dragon. The vibrant, pulsing colors of the energy world slid and buckled into the solid flesh of Sethon's triumph. I lurched at him, pearl-bound hands useless, but in my mind I was clawing at his smug face. He caught me by the shoulders.

"It is just a matter of time now," he said. "Look." He forced me to face the battlefield.

Before us, the plain was no longer swirling *Hua*. It was straining bodies and screams and clashing steel. Mud made of dust and blood sprayed through the air as men whirled and lunged. But even to my untrained eye, the resistance lines were falling back. They could not hold out.

Sethon surveyed the chaos. "How does it feel to be the agent of your friends' defeat, Lady Eona?"

It felt like my heart was being ripped from my body.

It took longer for the resistance army to surrender than Sethon expected. They fought to the end of their strength and hope, finally succumbing to the greater numbers and the loss of their Dragoneye support. I watched silently as each group of valiant fighters was defeated—either killed or taken prisoner—until the narrow battlefield that Ido had carved from the earth became a picking ground for looting soldiers and the scavenger birds that hopped from body to body in black-hunched eagerness. I was long past tears, my spirit so arid I could not even dredge up enough wet to whisper a prayer to Shola for the dying and dead. My mind had withered into only one thought: I had failed them all—Kygo, Kinra, and the dragons we had enslaved.

Sethon's impatience finally took him down the steps to wait for the prisoners. He kept me by his side, his entourage of aides and attendants scrambling into positions behind us as he paced, one of Kinra's swords swinging from his hand, his other arm hooked through mine as if we strolled in a garden. The wind that Ido had created was long gone, leaving a heavy humidity that was already pulling a meaty stink from the corpses. Soldiers gathered around us to watch Sethon's final victory. Their morbid curiosity pressed on me, as hot and weighty as the air.

Another terrible thought wormed its way into my horror; was Kygo still alive? Was Ido? Sethon had ordered their capture, but things went awry in battle.

A murmur through the waiting throng announced the arrival of the prisoners. Sethon's hold on my arm tightened as the crowd parted and a straight, proud figure slowly walked into view between two guards: Kygo, his hands clasped behind his head like a common prisoner, the Imperial Pearl on defiant display above the open gorget of his armored vest. He was alive. Behind him, two hunters dragged the limp form of Ido between them—delivered senseless, as ordered.

Kygo's head was high, but I could see the pain and regret breaking through his body with every heartbeat. The defeat had stripped his spirit bare. Everything that was left was written upon his hollowed face—desperation, despair, and the core of courage that kept him upright. As the distance closed between us, his dark eyes sought mine, and I saw what else was left within his spirit. Me.

Sethon stopped Kygo's guards with a raised hand. They pushed him to his knees, a length from us. The hunters released their hold on Ido, and he collapsed onto the ground, his eyelashes and brows the only color in his pale face. I found Ryko, Dela, and Tozay, too; bloodied but alive and kneeling behind Kygo, among the weary ranks of resistance prisoners. There was no sign of Vida. I prayed that she was safe back at the camp with my mother, and Rilla and Chart.

Kygo's eyes fixed on the blood caking the front of my tunic. "Eona, what has he done to you?" he rasped. "Are you all right?"

I nodded, although I was not. "I'm so sorry," I managed. "He's compelling me." I tried to raise my hands, but they would not move. "The folio."

"You have less honor than a piece of shit," Kygo spat at his uncle.

"And you have all your father's honor," Sethon countered.

Kygo's jaw clenched, the outline of each muscle ridged along the strong bone. "I hope so."

"It was not a compliment." Sethon inhaled deeply, as if savoring his next words. "Bow to your emperor."

Kygo's voice was steel. "No."

"Bow!" Sethon said.

"I will not bow before a traitor to this land," Kygo said loudly.

His words sent a wave of anticipation through the watching soldiers, as if the gates had opened on two fighting dogs.

Sethon jerked his chin at a soldier standing guard. "Bring me one of his men."

The guard dragged a kneeling prisoner in front of us. It was Caido, his body bent with exhaustion. He lifted his eyes to Kygo, his bloodless lips shifting in a prayer.

Sethon hefted Kinra's sword. "Bow, or I will kill your man."

Kygo stiffened, but before he could say anything, Caido suddenly lunged at Sethon, his thin face twisted with desperate rage. "He does not bow to you!"

The sword swung, the heavy crunch of bone coming a moment before the spray of blood through the air. Caido's body slumped to the ground. I closed my eyes, the image of the man's head half hacked from his shoulders stark against my lids.

"Yuso," Sethon snapped. "Which of these prisoners are important to my nephew?"

My eyes flew open as the captain stepped out from the small entourage behind us. I held my breath as he slowly walked the line of prisoners, keeping a wary distance from the palpable hate that rose from the kneeling men. A gob of spittle arced out from their ranks and landed near his feet.

He stopped in front of Dela.

"This is the Contraire, Your Majesty," he said.

Dela wore men's armor and had pulled her hair back into a man's high queue, yet she was all female warrior, fierce and sharp. The wound across her face had opened again, and her cheek was smeared with blood like war paint.

"I hope your death is long and painful," she said.

Ignoring her, Yuso pointed at Ryko. "And that is the islander. He has been with the prince since the start."

"Why did you do it?" Ryko said, his voice as hard and honed as a blade—yet in it, I heard the terrible pain of his captain's betrayal.

"He has my son, Ryko," Yuso said through his teeth.

For a moment the two men stared at one another. Then Yuso moved on, stopping once more. "Tozay, his general."

Master Tozay lifted his head, his lined face gaunt and gray, the strong width of his shoulders slumped. He had always been the bulwark behind Kygo. Now, all I saw was a defeated man.

"Bring them up onto the platform," Sethon ordered. "I want every man to see me claim the pearl and kill the resistance, once and for all."

CHAPTER TWENTY-FIVE

SETHON PACED IN front of me across the small central dais. He had placed me at the base of his throne again, so that everybody could see the Dragoneye at his feet. He had removed his armor and undertunic and wore only trousers and boots, his scarred, heavily muscled torso streaked with sweat from the heat and the relentless afternoon sun. From where I knelt, I could smell the stink of his anticipation.

"Strip him," he said to the waiting guards.

Kygo lifted his head at the command. I knew he did not dare make any other move. He had already struggled once against his guards—breaking one man's jaw—and his rage had earned Dela ten strokes of a cane across her back. I glanced at the Contraire on her knees behind him, shivering with pain, her pale shoulders scored with red welts. Sethon had promised that if Kygo struggled again, I would be next.

Deftly, the two guards cut the leather bindings that held Kygo's armored vest in place and pulled it from his body. Then the knife sliced through his close-fitting tunic. He fixed his eyes grimly on the horizon as the wet, clinging cloth was peeled off his skin, baring his torso. I heard Sethon's sharp intake of breath at the clear sight of his prize. Without the high collar around it, the pearl seemed even larger, its gold claw setting dug deep into Kygo's flesh. When the pearl was removed, it would take half of his throat, too.

Sethon knew the value of creating a spectacle. I had seen it at the palace when he had killed Kygo's mother and baby brother before a baying pack of soldiers. Now I saw it as he prepared to take the pearl. He had ordered the canopy removed, and sent the flagmen and his retinue below so they would not obstruct the view of the soldiers who surrounded the command post in a dizzying mosaic of color. Apart from his prisoners and their guards, the only other men on the platform were High Lord Tuy, the physician, and Yuso. I wondered why Sethon kept the captain so close; perhaps to taunt us with the source of our betrayal. Sethon did not waste any opportunity to cause pain.

With their task complete, the two guards bowed and backed away, one holding Kygo's armor, the other the shredded tunic. Dela did not look up as they passed. I gritted my teeth, remembering the hooting enjoyment of the mob as she had been beaten. Kneeling beside her, Ryko was all tense muscle and furious eyes. But what could he do? Each of them had a guard, and we were surrounded by thousands of men. Beyond Ryko, Tozay's attention was fixed on the sprawled body of Ido at the base of the dais. The Dragoneye was flanked by two watchful hunters and still in the shadow world. He was so close I could see the rise and fall of his shallow breaths and the slow beat under his jaw. Like the others, he had been stripped of his leather armor, and a bloodied tear in his tunic sleeve showed the edge of a clotted wound. Tozay glanced up at me, shrewd eyes questioning. He was looking for hope. But he would not find it in Ido. Even if the Dragoneye did wake, Sethon would make me compel him.

Resolve hardened within me. I had to break Sethon's compulsion, or Kygo and the others would be dead within a quarter bell. Kygo had once told me that the twelve stitches that had sewn the pearl into his flesh had been the worst pain he had ever endured. Surely Sethon would be overwhelmed by such pain, too. Even if it was just for a moment. That was my one chance to break his hold on me. It was a huge gamble, and it also meant waiting until Sethon had ripped the pearl from Kygo's throat. Yet I could see no other way. Twelve breaths and twelve stitches to break the compulsion and then heal Kygo. Less than a minute. Was it even possible? But I had to try.

We were all on death ground.

"Hold him down," Sethon ordered.

Although Kygo did not struggle, he did not comply, either. It took all three soldiers to force him to his knees. Two knelt beside him and locked his outstretched arms against their chests. The third knelt behind him, on his calves. I saw the agony widen his eyes as the man's full weight settled on his shinbones.

Sethon stood on the edge of the dais. He held one of Kinra's swords; the other was still in the sheath hung on the other side of the throne from where I knelt. So tantalizingly close. But until I freed my hands from the pearl rope, it might as well have been a thousand lengths away.

Sethon raised the sword he held to the soldiers below us. The sun, low in the sky behind him, cast the shadow of his exultation across his prisoners. Thousands of voices rose in jubilation, the screams and whistles so loud they startled the carrion birds into flapping, cawing protest.

Sethon smiled as the harsh duet of man and bird quieted. "The Imperial Pearl is mine!" he yelled, the deep resonance of his voice cutting through the last of the calls. He pointed the curved blade at Kygo. "The resistance is defeated once and for all."

The men cheered again. With a measured pace, Sethon stepped down from the dais and crossed the platform to Tozay.

"We have their general!" Tozay did not blanch as the sword tip stopped a finger-length from his face. Whooping excitement rose from below. Sethon waited until it subsided, then walked across to Ryko. "The islander spy." Once again, he waited until the shouts dropped away. Three steps took him to Dela. "And the travesty that is the eastern Contraire." She flinched as he turned to the crowd and raised the sword again.

The answering roar surged and formed into a chant. "*Kill! Kill! Kill!*"

"Your Majesty," one of the hunters called through the building frenzy.

Sethon swung around. "What?"

The hunter bowed over his bent knee. "Lord Ido is rousing. Do you wish me to send him back to the shadow world?"

"Silence!" Sethon bellowed at the crowd. "Silence!" The chanting died away to a few shrill calls.

I leaned forward. Ido's breathing had deepened and, under his lids, his eyes moved as if he dreamed. *Wake up*, I urged. *Wake up.*

Sethon smiled, his scar pulling at his skin. "He can join the festivities. I will show the men an emperor who can bring two Dragoneyes to their knees."

High Lord Tuy half-rose from his chair at the side of the dais. "Brother," he said. "You saw Lord Ido's destruction of the battlefield. Perhaps it would be more circumspect to keep him in the shadow world."

Sethon stared at Tuy for a moment, then motioned to Yuso with the sword. "Tell my brother about Lady Eona's control of Lord Ido."

Yuso rose from his knees on the other side of the dais and bowed. "It does not use the power of the dragons, High Lord Tuy."

Now I knew why Yuso was still here; as a guide to my power. At least, what he knew of it.

"You see, brother: no dragons, no threat," Sethon said. "I have total control of Lady Eona, and she will control Ido."

He gestured to the physician waiting near Kygo. The portly man gave a stiff bow then hurried across the platform, his red lacquered box clutched against his chest. He bent over Ido and lifted one of his eyelids, exposing a glazed amber eye.

"He is near waking, Your Majesty." The man's voice was high with nerves. "He should rouse as soon as I use the elixir of breath."

Sethon strode back toward me, his face avid at the prospect of Ido wakening under his control. "Do it."

With shaking hands, the physician removed a small porcelain bottle from the box and pulled the stopper. The edge of a harsh scent burned the back of my throat. The bottle was thrust under Ido's nostrils. Gasping a ragged breath, the Dragoneye jerked back his head. His eyes opened, each black center like a pinpoint.

"Lady Eona," Sethon said. "Compel Lord Ido's power."

I fought the command, straining to block the force that gathered my power. The physician grabbed his red box and scrambled back as Ido hauled himself onto his feet. I felt his *Hua* leap within him as he groped for the energy world. Sethon's compulsion slammed my power through him. The force beat back Ido's call to his dragon and locked his body into a crouch. His frantic heartbeat slid under mine, both rhythms trapped inside Sethon's—and my—compulsion. Beyond him, Ryko screamed and doubled over beneath the press of power.

For a moment, everything was silent.

Slowly Ido raised his eyes and took in the platform. "Not what I was hoping for," he rasped.

"Welcome back, Lord Ido," Sethon said. He kicked the

Dragoneye in the ribs. Ido slumped forward as a roar of excitement rose from the soldiers. "Make him bow to me, Lady Eona."

The command reached through me into Ido and slammed his forehead to the platform, forcing a groan from him.

Sethon pressed his booted foot on Ido's neck. He smiled at his brother. "You see, I am the master of the last two Dragoneyes." He raised his voice into a battle cry. "I will never be defeated!"

The soldiers, still caught in their bloodlust, chanted, "*Never defeated, never defeated!*"

High Lord Tuy bowed and sank back into his chair. Sethon lifted his boot and looked at me. "Get him up on his knees," he commanded.

The blood energy lifted Ido's head and chest from the platform and held him upright. He swayed, the struggle against the compulsion rippling through our link.

"I see that Lady Eona has restored you completely, Lord Ido." Sethon reached over and drew his thumb across the thin nose and smooth modeling of cheekbone and jaw. The Dragoneye's nostrils flared at his touch, but he could not pull away. Sethon closed his fist. "I am glad you are back to your former self. We can start again." The sudden crack of bone against bone jerked Ido's head to one side.

Sethon grabbed his hair and pulled his head upright again. "Is that fear in your eyes, Lord Ido?"

"It is disgust," Ido said.

Sethon laughed. "Brave words." He motioned to the two

hunters. "If Lord Ido moves, send him back to the shadow world." The two men bowed in compliance.

I felt a rise of savage hope—Sethon was not so sure he could hold us both in his power.

"Come, Lady Eona," he said. "You can watch one of your lovers die."

He yanked me to my feet and pulled me off the dais, steering me toward Kygo. We stopped in front of Ryko, still bent double and panting.

"What is wrong with him?" Sethon said.

I pushed all the hate I held for him into my silence. I was not going to offer Sethon anything, let alone information about my power.

Sethon turned to Yuso. "What do you know of this?"

Yuso bowed. "When Lady Eona compels Lord Ido, the islander can feel it. Even the most intimate of energies. I believe it goes the opposite way, too."

"Really?" Sethon smiled at me. "We will test it later." He shoved me to my knees a few lengths from Kygo and called over one of the hunters. "Watch over Lady Eona."

Although I registered the hunter's hot hand on the back of my neck, all of my being was focused on Kygo—and his on me. Sweat dripped from his forehead and temples, and every line of his face was tight with fear, but I saw the fierce hope in his eyes, and I gave a tiny nod. *I will try, I will try*, I told him with my heart.

And then Sethon stepped between us. Kygo met his scrutiny with a steady gaze.

"So, nephew, it comes to this," Sethon said. He bent and stroked the pearl with a thick forefinger, his triumph releasing in a long breath.

"The throne and the land is my right," Kygo said evenly, although he tilted his chin away from his uncle's caressing hand.

"Your right?" Sethon shook his head. "I should have had the throne long ago instead of your feeble father."

"My father nurtured this land," Kygo said. "You have already torn it apart for your own glory."

"The same could be said for you and your attempts on my throne." Sethon glanced at the physician waiting nearby. "Is everything prepared? I want this to be quick. Twelve stitches, in no more than twelve breaths. Do you understand?"

"Yes, Your Majesty." The man's grip on the needle and gold thread shook as if he had palsy. "But it is in the throat, Your Majesty. It will be painful and if you move, I may not—"

"I will not move," Sethon snapped. "Wait on the dais for me."

The physician bowed and retreated to the small stage.

Sethon motioned to the soldier behind Kygo. "Brace his head."

I felt my whole body clench. The man—an older soldier—cupped Kygo's chin and forehead and pulled his head back. Kygo tensed as Sethon raised Kinra's sword.

"*Naiso,*" he breathed.

I shuffled forward on my knees, but felt the hunter's warning hand on my shoulder.

Kygo's voice cracked. "Look after the land."

I nodded. His face blurred through my tears.

"Keep him still," Sethon ordered the man holding Kygo's head. "I do not want to damage the pearl."

The soldier pulled Kygo back more firmly against his chest. "Forgive me, prince," he whispered.

Kygo paled. "You are killing your king," he said.

Sethon rested the tip of Kinra's sword at the edge of the pearl. The steel would finally have what it craved.

"Eona." Kygo looked past the blade to find me. "It was never just the power. You know that, don't you?"

Before I could nod, the raw love in his eyes dilated into shock as Sethon pushed the tip of the blade into his throat. His sharp inhalation rasped with wet agony as he twisted against the grip of his guards. I cradled his gaze in mine, every slice into his flesh tearing through my spirit. Blood gushed over his bare chest and down the steel.

Sethon pulled the pearl free. "I have it!" He dropped Kinra's sword, blood spraying as it spun and landed next to Kygo's feet.

The men below us roared. All I could see was the gaping wound in Kygo's throat. His three guards released his arms and legs and jumped back as his body folded heavily onto the platform. Motionless. Then his chest moved, the soft wet sound of his breath the most precious sound I had ever heard.

Sethon triumphantly held up the pearl. He turned, and in a few strides was up on the dais and in the gilded chair. Everyone's attention was on him as he pressed the pearl against the hollow of his throat.

"Now," he ordered the physician. "Quick."

He pushed his body back in the chair and braced.

Twelve stitches. Twelve breaths.

I gathered my rage and my *Hua,* waiting for Sethon's pain. Waiting for the first stitch. My best chance. Sweat gathered under my arms and at the small of my back. On the dais, Sethon's hands tightened around the arms of the chair. I heard him grunt as the needle pierced his flesh. The shock of pain resonated through his clamp of control around my power. Ryko's head lifted—he had felt it, too.

With all my strength I strained against the blood force. The grip shivered, flexed, then clamped down on me again. Too strong.

Another stitch rippled into the dark energy. I threw all my *Hua* against it, my heartbeat thundering in my ears. It shifted, then closed once more. I couldn't break through.

The pool of blood was growing around Kygo's throat. How many breaths had passed? Five, six? I was running out of time and chances.

"Eona!" Ryko's call dragged my eyes from Kygo's laboring chest. "Use me. Like you did outside the palace."

His guard pushed him down and pressed a knee on his back. "Shut up."

My mind groped for his meaning.

His *Hua*! He meant his life-force funneled through our own

link. He was not caught in the folio's dark energy or dragon power. The possibility surged through my despair, bright and sharp. Yet at the palace, I had nearly killed him.

Another stitch spiked its pain through the compulsion.

"Ryko, no," Dela pleaded.

"I will not see you die, Dela," he said. "Eona, use it!"

"It will kill you," I said.

"We are all dead if you don't." His voice checked as the guard shoved his knee harder into the islander back, forcing his chest to the platform. Doggedly, he raised his head again. "My choice, Eona!"

His choice, but I was the one who would take his life. I could not do it.

"Eona, honor me."

I looked into the fierce warrior pride in his face. Honor and duty: the heart of Ryko. He was giving us his heart. I nodded. He smiled with grim satisfaction. Bracing himself, he turned his head to Dela. Her soft moan broke into a sob.

I took a deep breath, poised for Sethon's pain. It came—shuddering through the blood force, a tiny lessening of the folio's grip. With a prayer to any god who listened, I reached for Ryko's *Hua*.

His pulsing life-force roared through me with a torrent of strength that wrenched Sethon's grip wide open. With a shriek through my blood, the rope of pearls spun off my wrists, dropping the black folio into my lap. I felt my link with Ryko unravel and snap, leaving a deep tear within me that ached with loss.

I heard Ido's roar of exultation and felt the pounding return of my own power. We were free. But all I could see was Ryko's dead body slumping to the ground.

As Dela screamed, I felt Ido unite with his dragon. My skin stung with the burn of a fast rising wind, the taste of Ido's power within it.

Sethon sat up. "Stop them!" He knocked the physician aside, his hand holding the half-stitched pearl to his throat. "Hunters, stop Lady Eona! Stop Ido!"

The hunter behind me grabbed my hair and yanked my head back. I glimpsed yellowed teeth clenched in effort, then his hand reached for the pulse under my jaw. Frantically, I groped for the black folio and threw it at his face. The rope of white pearls snapped out straight then curled back, whipping him across the eyes. Screaming, he let go of me, blinded by blood. The book arced and dropped, sliding across the boards.

I launched myself at Kygo, dread propelling me into a skidding, scrambling crawl. Was I too late?

Within the drum of my heartbeat another pressure was building. Familiar and chaotic—the ten bereft dragons. They were coming, called by the released pearl. Another terror shredded my breath: all twelve dragons would soon be together, and they would make the String of Pearls. If we did not direct their power into renewal, it would rip the land apart.

The searing rise of Ido's power suddenly stopped. I looked over my shoulder, praying he had not fallen to a hunter. The Dragoneye was grappling with his guard, punching the man savagely in the ribs. The hunter broke away and drew a long knife from an ankle sheath. He lunged, but Ido caught his forearm and twisted it brutally against the elbow joint. The knife dropped.

A wail split the air, the desolation within it chilling me. Dela's heart cry. Two guards held her back from Ryko's body. Her face was a fearsome mask—all howling mouth and wild eyes. She punched and clawed, lurching toward Ryko with the berserk rage of grief. Taking advantage of the diversion, Tozay rammed into his guard's legs. The man dropped to his knees, his sword swinging upward. With ruthless precision, Tozay grabbed the sword hilt and slammed the edge of the grip into the man's chin, knocking him senseless.

"Lady Eona, do you need help?" he yelled, yanking the weapon from the man's slack grasp.

"No. Help Dela."

Raising the sword, he charged the two guards struggling to contain the Contraire.

I spread both hands on Kygo's chest, feeling for his heartbeat through the sticky wash of blood. His eyes were shut and an ominous pallor bleached his skin. *Be alive,* I prayed. *Be alive.* A slow thud flipped under my fingertips: a heartbeat.

"Brother, get the black book," Sethon yelled.

High Lord Tuy rose from his seat beside the dais. I cursed; I should have picked up the book. Without it, the dragons could not be released.

"Tozay!" I yelled. He broke away from his opponent and swung around. "Get the folio!"

He nodded, ducking a wild punch.

The flash of a blade drew my eyes back to Sethon. He had pulled Kinra's other sword from the sheath slung on the back of the throne. Pausing for a moment to find his target, he leaped off the dais, straight for Ido. The pearl flapped obscenely at his throat, only half attached.

"Ido!" I screamed. The Dragoneye rolled away from the limp hunter and scrabbled up onto his feet, the bloodied long-knife in his hand. I jabbed my finger at the oncoming danger. "Sethon!"

He backed up, tensing to meet Sethon's running attack.

It was all I could do; I had to heal Kygo. His heart was barely beating.

With a desperate breath, I plunged into the celestial plane. The platform around me convulsed into iridescent energy, the bright colors stretching and breaking in frantic, jagged patterns. Under the bright flow of *Hua* in my hands, Kygo's meridians were dark and stagnant, only a flicker of silver in each point of power. The Mirror Dragon shrieked, her massive crimson body above the platform. The golden pearl at her throat thrummed with an ancient song of renewal, its luminous surface pulsing with runs of gold flame. Higher in the sky, the blue dragon circled, his own pearl alive with blue fire. The approach of the other ten dragons pressed around us like a terrible weight, thickening the air.

I called the Mirror Dragon, and opened myself to her power, my heart's plea joining her thrumming song. *Heal him, please heal him.* She shrieked again, the sound blending into the rushing power that roared through my pathways. Cinnamon flooded my mouth. Was this the last time I would taste the glorious spice of our union? The bittersweet thought rose through me and locked in my throat like a cry. She lowered her massive head, the great dragon eyes only lengths from mine. Their ancient gaze pulled me into the neverending cycle of life and death, sun and moon, chaos and balance. So old. Time to renew. *Your pearl will be returned,* I silently promised, and felt her soaring joy. Yet the loss to come dug darkness into my spirit.

We sang together, knitting the earth's *Hua* into Kygo's slashed flesh, fanning the tiny flicker of his life-force into bright flowing energy and a strong, beating heart. Our beautiful harmony wove sweet healing into every wound and eased my own aching spirit with a gentle embrace of golden power. Under my hands, Kygo's chest jerked, the sudden fill of air erupting into a hacking, gasping cough.

A booming shock wave of hot, spicy air ripped me out of the energy world. Ten huge dragons burst onto the plain around the platform, a rainbow circle of gleaming hides, heavy muscle, and thick manes. Real flesh-and-blood bodies as big as palace temples. I gaped at the vivid orange Horse Dragon straight ahead of me, the luminous apricot pearl beneath his chin glowing and humming. Beside him, the Goat Dragon stretched his long neck, the silver scales rippling with reflections like sinuous water, his pearl singing, too. The warmth of his lemon breath scented the air. They were all on the earthly plane, visible to everyone. It was not meant to be possible, yet every man on the platform was frozen into stunned awe. Even Ido and Sethon had broken apart from their savage struggle. The only movement was Dela, rocking Ryko's body against her chest.

I spun around, trying to take in the huge circle of beasts: the green Tiger Dragon, the dawn pink Rabbit Dragon, the shimmering purple Ox Dragon. Then a gap: the domain of the Rat Dragon. And, in the east, another gap for the Mirror Dragon. They had not yet joined the circle. We still had time.

Shrill, throbbing screams from the ground broke the awed silence. I looked down as the Ox Dragon shifted the coil of his massive tail, exposing scores and scores of mangled bodies beneath it, the muscular movement catching more shrieking men in its sweep. My stomach heaved at the mess. The ten beasts had materialized on top of Sethon's army. Half of them were crushed under dragon flesh. The other half were running from the beasts. Among the fleeing figures, I saw resistance prisoners. Thank the gods, some of them had got away.

Kygo lifted his head, taking in the great beasts around us. "Eona, what's happening?"

"The String of Pearls," I whispered.

"What?" He sat up, the sudden movement draining the new color from his face.

I caught his arms, steadying him. He did not know the truth about the dragons or the pearl. Somehow, I had to make him understand. And, I hoped, help me.

"Kygo, listen," I said. "There is no bargain between us and the dragons. There never *was* a bargain. The Imperial Pearl is their egg. We stole it as ransom for their power. Now they need it back. They need to renew the land."

"No bargain? Why wasn't I told?" He twisted around again, staring up at the Ox Dragon. The beast turned his massive horned head toward us, the shimmering purple scales of his arched neck and broad forehead softening into lavender around his long muzzle. Beneath the silky flow of mauve beard, his pearl thrummed with urgency, its surface alive with violet flame. "How do you know all this?" Kygo demanded.

There was no time to explain Kinra's memories and the black folio. I tightened my grip on his arms, trying to press the truth into him. "Kygo, trust me. If you love your land as much as you say, we need to give the pearl back to the dragons."

He stared at me. "It is the symbol of my power."

"It is also the symbol of our greed," I said. "Kygo, I trusted you with the folio. Please, trust me with this!"

He searched my face, his hesitation like a tight band around my heart. Then I saw it: a wondrous leap of faith in his eyes. "What do we need to do?"

I bowed my head for a moment, overcome by relief. "We have to get the folio and the pearl before the dragon circle is closed."

His hand went to his throat. "This is the portent coming true, isn't it? The *Hua* of All Men and the dark force." His face tensed as he felt the smooth hollow between his collarbones. "You healed me!" His eyes darkened as he realized what that meant. For him. For us. "Eona, what have you done?"

"You were dying," I said. He pulled away from me but I caught his hand. "Kygo, if we give the pearl back, everything will change. I won't have any power over you. I won't have any power at all." Even just saying the words opened a dark hole of loss into my heart. No dragon. No power. I looked around at the magnificent beasts that surrounded us.

Make it right.

He cupped my cheek. "You would give up your power?"

A roar of fury broke us apart.

"Is this the String of Pearls?" Sethon yelled at Ido. "Did you do this?"

He lunged at the Dragoneye, driving him back a few steps. The thrall across the platform was at an end. Behind us, the clang of steel rang out, pulling me around to face Tozay and Tuy. The two men were trading vicious blows, fighting for an opportunity to grab the folio on the ground between them.

Two guards ran toward us, weapons raised. I snatched up Kinra's sword, its blaze of anger driving me to my feet. Kygo dived for a fallen sword near Dela. He scooped it up and rolled into a crouch, the stiff lock of his spine registering the body in Dela's arms.

He turned to me, his face stricken. "Ryko's dead?"

"He gave me all his *Hua*," I said. "To break free of Sethon."

For a brief moment, Kygo's eyes closed. But there was no time for grief; the two guards were upon us.

I swung Kinra's sword at the stocky man coming at me. Our blades met, the impact resonating through all my joints. He had brute strength on his side. I disengaged and ducked to his left, managing a quick slash across his forearm on my way through. At least I was quicker. His companion sliced his sword at Kygo's head. Caught in the crouch, Kygo smashed the blade aside, then surged to his feet, ready for the guard's return. He was easily the better-trained man, but he wore no armor, not even a shirt that could catch a sword tip and afford a precious second.

My opponent pulled his bloodied hand away from the shallow cut. His eyes narrowed, his small mouth bunching as if he'd sucked a pickled plum. I smiled: not such an easy mark, after all. He sidestepped away from the blows ringing between Kygo and his comrade. I tracked his movement, watching for a sign he was about to attack. The flicker in his eye gave him away. He lunged into a volley of high, hard cuts—classic Monkey Dragon Third. I swung my blade into Ox Dragon First, the circling blocks holding back his hammering blows. His strength and anger pushed me backward, but he couldn't break through. With a hiss of frustration, he disengaged.

At the periphery of my vision, I caught the feinting, lunging figures of Ido and Sethon. And another figure, edging toward them. I chanced a look; it was Yuso, his fist curled around the hilt of a small curved knife—a physician's tool. Before I could scream a warning to Ido, the guard in front of me swung his sword into a vicious arc. I braced, recognizing the punishing form of Third Horse. He was going to batter me into submission. Kinra's quick reaction angled my blade and deflected the heavy blow, but the weight behind it made me stagger. I was off-balance, and the soldier knew it. Desperately, I twisted around to meet him. Not fast enough. He had turned the sword, all of his momentum swinging the edge of the hilt at my head. My body tensed for the blow.

It didn't come. I stumbled back a step and saw his face frozen in surprise. His hand spasmed, the sword clattering to the ground between us. He toppled slowly forward. Behind him, Dela jerked a sword free of his falling body. The blade was half sheathed in blood.

We both looked down at the fallen man.

"What do you need me to do?" Dela said. The grief in her face had hardened into deadly focus.

"Help Kygo and Tozay get the black folio."

With a nod, she picked up the dead man's sword, and whirled to help Kygo subdue the other guard. As I caught my breath, Yuso suddenly broke into a run toward Ido and Sethon. The Dragoneye could not hold out against both of them. I pushed everything I had into a desperate sprint across the platform. Sethon and Ido had caught each other's weapon hands and stood nose to nose, each straining simultaneously to break the other's grip and plunge his own blade home.

"Ido, look out," I screamed.

Too late. With a harsh battle cry, Yuso charged into the center of the grapple. The collision knocked the two men apart. Sethon reeled backward. Ido crashed onto his hands and knees, his broad back unprotected. I forced one last spurt of speed into my burning muscles, but Yuso was already lunging into his attack.

Straight past Ido.

For a moment, it didn't make sense. Then Yuso hooked his arm around Sethon's neck and drove his blade into the man's bare chest. Yuso wasn't after Ido; he was trying to kill Sethon. With a physician's knife.

Sethon swung Yuso off balance. Both men fell to the ground, Kinra's sword flying out of Sethon's hand and sliding across the boards. Ido rolled away from their thrashing bodies and hauled himself to his feet. Straight into my path. With no time to pull up, I slammed into his chest, the impact driving out all my air. With a grunt, he staggered back a step and caught me. I doubled over and gasped for breath.

"Were you coming to help me or kill me?" he said, half-lifting half-dragging me farther away from the vicious fight on the ground.

I struggled out of his grasp. "Where's the pearl?" I managed.

"Sethon still has it."

I caught a flash of metal as Yuso plunged the tiny knife down again. It must have found its mark, because Sethon roared with pain and punched the captain in the side of the head, loosening his grip.

I finally drew in a full breath. "Can we use the lightning? Like the beach?"

"No," Ido said. Around us, the shrieking thrum of the dragons was like the song of a thousand cicadas. "I don't know what would happen if we called our beasts in the middle of this circle. And we'd risk destroying the pearl."

We would have to get the Imperial Pearl the hard way. I tightened my hand around my sword and looked for an opening in the struggle before us.

Sethon slammed his elbow into Yuso's face, then dived for his sword. Yuso slashed wildly, the too-small knife slicing across Sethon's bare back in a crimson arc. He pulled back just as Sethon flipped over and swung Kinra's sword at him, missing his chest by a hair's breadth. Both men drew up into wary crouches. Breathing hard, they stood and faced one another, my position in their sightlines. I had lost my chance.

Sethon spun Kinra's sword in his grip. "You've just killed your son," he said. "And yourself."

Yuso's hand flexed around the knife hilt. "I am already dead." He looked at me. "Lady Eona, this buys my son's safety."

I felt my whole body tense into expectation.

Yuso ran at Sethon, the short knife raised, his whole body open to attack. Sethon plunged Kinra's sword into the captain's chest. The thrust was so hard that I saw the tip emerge between Yuso's shoulder blades and heard the thump of the hilt spring back against his breastbone. Yuso dropped his knife and grabbed the grip over Sethon's hand, holding the sword and Sethon against his body. With a deep guttural groan, he swung Sethon around until the man's back faced us. Sethon jerked at the hilt, trying to withdraw the blade.

"Do it," Yuso gasped.

Ido sprang forward and drove his long knife up into Sethon's sacral point, all of his strength behind the strike. Sethon screamed, his body arching, the shock to his *Hua* locking him against the knife. Ido twisted the blade upward.

"Shall we explore that pain?" he said against Sethon's ear.

My innards froze; the words and tone were a perfect imitation of Sethon's torture.

Ido jerked the blade again, forcing a moan from Sethon. "Exhilarating, isn't it."

He wrenched Sethon's weight away from Yuso. Without the brace of the High Lord's body, Yuso slowly folded to the platform and pitched to one side. The moonstone and jade hilt in his chest hit the wood, sending a shiver of pain through him.

With ruthless efficiency, Ido lowered Sethon to the ground, then rolled him onto his back. He scooped up Yuso's fallen knife, pressed his foot across Sethon's wrist, then drove the small blade through the man's palm, staking him to the wood. I winced as Sethon broke into a long scream, his fingers spasming.

As though Sethon's yell had roused him, Yuso lifted his head toward me, the effort cording the veins in his neck.

"Maylon," he gasped. "His name is Maylon."

I kneeled beside him. "You betrayed us, Yuso. This is all your fault. Do you expect me to forgive you?"

His eyes focused blearily on Ido. The Dragoneye had pinned Sethon's free arm with one knee. Sethon strained upward, but Ido punched him in the face with the hilt of the long knife, the impact slamming his head against the boards.

"Ido thinks you are like him," Yuso said slowly. He coughed, spraying blood. "But you still have mercy in you, don't you?" His breath sighed out into stillness.

Did I still have mercy? I felt no softness within my heart, and—may the gods help me—I understood the smile of enjoyment on Ido's face. I rose and placed my foot on Yuso's rib cage, wrenching Kinra's sword from his dead body. The burn of her anger whispered its need. *Take the pearl.* I circled both swords up into readiness, the return of their full fury and strength like a homecoming.

I watched as the Dragoneye flipped the knife in his hand and leaned over Sethon. "What shall I carve into your chest?" His voice still mimicked the High Lord's caressing tone. "'Traitor'? 'Bastard'? How about 'Always a second son'?"

Sethon tried to pull away from the knife hovering above his breastbone. With an admonishing click of his tongue, Ido pressed the tip of the blade into Sethon's flesh, dragging it downward in a wash of blood. Sethon screamed again, his head thrashing with pain.

With grim resolution, I walked over to the two men. *Take the pearl.* With every shuddering heave of Sethon's chest, the gem rolled across the bloodied hollow between his collarbones, dangling from its four rough stitches. I could carve it from his throat. Feel him writhe and scream; revenge for Kygo's agony.

"Get back!" I said to Ido.

I raised my sword.

"Wait," Ido said.

He drove the long knife through Sethon's other palm, forcing a sobbing scream from the man. Ido looked up at me. His smile was vicious and cruel and held the intimacy of a lover. "Enjoy."

Sethon's pain-filled eyes met mine as he strained to rip his hands free of the knives. For a moment, I held the sword tip over his throat. His lips drew back into the snarl of a cornered animal. He deserved the slowest death possible. He deserved pain and fear. But I could not do it. Yuso was right: I still had mercy. With a roar, I plunged both blades through his mutilated chest instead, the resistance of skin and bone jarring my hands.

Sethon gasped, his body lifting into one last thrash. The pearl rolled and settled into the hollow of his throat as the foul stink of his death release filled the air. I yanked one blade free, the man's dead weight rising with the force and dropping back onto the platform. Swallowing my gorge, I sliced around the stitches and ripped the pearl free. Kinra's swords had finally fulfilled their mission.

I opened my hand. The Imperial Pearl was heavy and hot—too hot to be holding just the last of Sethon's body heat.

Ido wrenched the long knife out of Sethon's palm and wiped the wet blade on his trouser leg. "That was almost as satisfying as I thought it would be." He looked up at me, one eye squinting in censure. "Although somewhat prematurely ended." He slid the cleaned knife into the side of his boot. "So where's the folio?"

He followed my gaze across the platform. Kygo and Dela had killed or driven away the remaining guards and were now trying to scoop the black book from the ground, dodging the whip of white pearls. Dela held her ripped shirt like a net, ready to throw it over the writhing rope of gems. Behind her, Tozay sat slumped, his arm at an awkward angle. It was clear he was hurt. The dark shape of High Lord Tuy lay nearby. At least both brothers were dead.

"Kygo has the folio," I said. "We can—"

Suddenly I could not speak. My senses were lost in a shock wave of pain that blasted every pathway within me. Kinra's sword dropped from my grip. My other hand convulsed around the pearl, the gold claw setting slicing into my palm. Through a gray haze, I saw Ido strain backward, his mouth open in a scream, but I could hear only the howl of loss in my own head. The air pressed down around us, then exploded outward. Two huge dragon bodies—red and blue—boomed onto the plain, the backlash of energy knocking me to my knees.

The massive crimson body of the Mirror Dragon—twice the size of the male dragons—filled the eastern gap within the circle. She threw back her head and called, a high ululating sound that throbbed through her long throat. The gleaming fire of her red and orange scales rippled with every shift of muscle. Huge cartwheel eyes shut with effort as she closed the circle with her body and power. Beneath her chin, the gold pearl swelled and pulsed, the song within it soaring over the thrumming shriek of the eleven other dragon pearls.

"Eona," I whispered, but I knew she could no longer hear me. She was on the earthly plane, and our link was gone.

Everything had been scooped out of me. I was hollowed, powerless, and I could not move with the raw pain of it.

"No!" It was the husk of Ido's voice, cracked and devastated.

With a roar, his blue beast answered the red dragon's call, delicate wings extending as one opal claw lifted and raked the air.

I turned my head. All my bones had dried into stiff desolation. "Ido, I can't call her."

Ido's body was a knot of agony, his fists pressed into his forehead. "They've closed the circle." Panting, he slowly raised his head and scanned the dragons. "We don't have much time."

CHAPTER TWENTY-SIX

DARK CLOUDS ROILED across the sky to form a circle above the twelve beasts on the ground. The still air shifted into a warm breeze that held the scent of sweet spices and salty sweat. And underneath it all was the dank piss-and-blood smell of battlefield death.

I heard the pound of running feet. Kygo's voice penetrated my pain.

"Eona, are you hurt?" He crouched beside me. A long cut across his shoulder bled in thin streaks down his arm and chest. Dela and Tozay stood behind him, both of them bloodied. Dela held the writhing bundle of shirt and folio.

"My dragon is gone, Kygo," I rasped. "My dragon is gone."

"No, Eona, she is here before us," he said. "I can see her in the circle."

I balled my fists against my chest, rocking with pain. "She

has gone from me." My voice rose into a sob. "I have no link with her anymore. No power."

He curled his arm around me. I leaned into him, and the cold ache within me eased a little against his warmth.

"Tozay!"

Dela's cry raised my head. I saw the general sway on his feet, his weathered face paling into a sickly yellow. Dela dropped the folio bundle and caught him, his solid weight straining her arms and bared torso. There was a nasty gash across Tozay's temple that was still bleeding, and his sword arm hung useless—broken, from the look of it. But I could not heal him. I could not heal anyone ever again.

"He doesn't look good." Kygo rose to help.

"He took a bad blow to the head," Dela said as they carefully helped Tozay sit on the platform. His normally sharp eyes were unfocused, his breathing short and hard. "He should be all right. Just dazed for a while." Dela gently pressed his head between his knees.

Kygo crouched beside me again. "Did you get the pearl, Eona?"

I opened my trembling hand. The opaque surface shimmered and flicked as if tiny fish teemed beneath its surface. He picked it up between thumb and forefinger, the loss on his face echoing the ache in my own spirit. He, too, was giving up something: the sacred symbol of his sovereignty.

"How do you renew the dragons with it?" he asked.

Ido stirred. "Renew the dragons?" Slowly, he sat back on

his heels and cocked his head at me. "Am I missing something here, Eona? What about our plan?"

Kygo stiffened at the Dragoneye's tone.

"We never had a plan, Ido," I said, meeting his stare with my own. "The ancients *stole* the Imperial Pearl from the dragons. It is their egg. We have to give it back. We have to let them renew their power."

Ido looked sideways at me, the amber eyes hooded. "I know we stole it. I have always known."

I gaped at him. "What do you mean?" Indignation pulled me up onto my feet. Both Ido and Kygo stood, too, ranged on each side of me in silent antagonism.

"I've read the black folio," Ido said. "I know what the pearl is and what it does." He crossed his arms. "The theft changes nothing."

"It changes everything," I said. "How could you know all this and still ignore your dragon's need? His hope?"

"No doubt in the same way as many Dragoneyes have before me. No one willingly gives up their own power when it can be the next Dragoneye's problem."

"Not anymore, Ido. We are the last of our kind. We have to give the pearl back."

He shook his head. "You don't understand. If they renew, we will lose our power forever."

"I know." I felt a moment of bitter satisfaction. He was not the only one who knew the secrets of dragon lore. "But we still have to give the pearl back."

His gaze sharpened. "How do you know? Have you read the folio, too?"

"No." I wet my lips. "I went into my dragon. To escape Sethon's torture." Kygo's fingers brushed my arm; a fleeting touch of consolation. "I saw memories from an ancestor."

Dela shifted; no doubt she had guessed which ancestor.

Something flickered across the wary intensity in Ido's face; a moment of empathy, or maybe it was just his own pain, remembered. He smiled thinly. "I thought you vowed you would never do that to your dragon. You keep drawing your moral lines, and you keep crossing them." His eyes held mine, his voice lowering into a caress. "You and I are the same, Eona. We cross the lines that others dare not step over. Cross this last line with me."

He wanted the dragons' power. He wanted everything. And he wanted me to take it with him.

"I won't destroy the dragons."

He jabbed his forefinger against his chest. "Do you want to feel like this for the rest of your life? As if everything important has been ripped out? Do you want to be nothing again? Because that is what will happen."

"Eona will never be nothing," Kygo said. "She is my *Naiso*."

Ido snorted. "Why would she be your *Naiso* when she could be a god with me? It is still the same choice, Eona. Either we take all the power or we are left with nothing." He held out his hand. His smile drove itself into my very core. "You and I can take it all, Eona, together. It would be like the cyclone, a hundred times over. Forever."

Kygo gripped my shoulder. "If you think Eona would destroy the dragons and take my land, Ido, then you do not know her at all. We would both die a thousand times over before we would let you have anything you want."

I stared at Ido's outstretched hand. The memory of the sea cabin—our bodies entwined and the glorious rising energy—held me still. All that power between us.

Kygo glanced at me. "Eona?"

I took a deep breath, fighting my way through the wash of sensation. With so much power, there could be nothing else. It would burn everything in its path. And every minute of every hour would hold the bud of distrust, just waiting to blossom into betrayal.

"I am *not* the same as you, Ido," I said. "I will not destroy the dragons."

Ido closed his hand into a fist. "You would choose to have no power with him when you could have all the power in the world with me?"

I lifted my chin. "That is not the choice, Ido. I choose the dragons and the land. Not my own ambition. Or yours."

Beside me, Kygo smiled.

Ido gave a low, harsh laugh. "The emperor and his *Naiso*, standing united."

Around us, the pitch of the humming pearls changed, the resonance vibrating through my ear bones.

Ido spun on his heel, taking in the swaying dragons.

"What is happening?" Kygo asked.

"The dragons are preparing to lay down their pearls," Ido said.

I remembered what he had told me on the beach. Once the pearls were separated from the beasts, they could never reclaim them, and the String of Pearls could not be stopped. It was now either the dragons' renewal or the land's destruction.

Ido faced me, his eyes narrowed with fury. "Your misguided loyalty has lost us both our power. All we can do now is avoid annihilation." His eyes fixed on the white bundle in Dela's tight grip. "Give me the folio."

Dela pulled back from his reaching hand. "I do not follow your orders."

He sucked a breath in between his teeth. "Listen to me, Eona. The Mirror Dragoneye is the only one who can direct the String of Pearls' power to the dragons. Otherwise it will raze everything to the ground, including us."

"*I* have to direct it?" My voice cracked. "How?"

"With the folio and the *Righi*."

I stared at him, my memory conjuring the blistering heat and terrible power of the ancient words. "But that's the death chant."

"Isn't that what Dillon used to kill all those soldiers?" Dela asked uneasily.

"It not only destroys," Ido said, "it creates. It holds the dragons' *Hua* in the black folio so we can use their power. "

"How do you know all this?" Kygo demanded.

"I have been studying the String of Pearls for years. The

Righi ignites the Imperial Pearl to start the renewal, and it will release the dragons' *Hua* from the folio."

"The dragons' *Hua* is in the folio?" Kygo echoed.

I searched Ido's face, trying to read beyond the fury that pinched his features into a snarl. I did not trust this turnaround. He was not one to back down so easily. But what could I do? Kinra's memory had also told me the String of Pearls could not be stopped once the dragons had released their pearls into its power circle—but she had not told me that I had to invoke the *Righi* to release the dragons from the folio.

I clasped Ido's arm. He flinched under the dig of my grip. "Is that the truth? Is the *Righi* the only way for their renewal?"

"Do you think I have a death wish because I cannot have you?" he sneered.

I snatched my hand away.

"You are not the woman I thought you were," he said. "You do not have the steel to be a true queen."

"Well, *you* are exactly the man I thought *you* were," I snapped.

I hoped he could not see the bitter truth in my heart; some part of me had believed him when he'd said I had changed him. How could I have been so gullible? He was still the same ruthless, selfish Ido. I was the one who had changed, pulled into his world of power and possibility.

Kygo shoved Ido's shoulder. "Answer her! Is the *Righi* the only way to do this?"

Ido stepped back, his body tightening into defense. "Yes."

He *was* telling the truth, and it dropped a hundredweight of dread through me. I had barely controlled the *Righi* against Dillon—now it had the force of renewal in it and the power of all the dragons to draw upon. May the gods protect us. And if they could not, at least I could protect Kygo.

I dragged at his arm. "You have to get off the platform." With a glance, I gathered Dela into my plea. "You too, Dela. Help Tozay. Get off the platform. You saw what happened to Dillon."

"I am not going anywhere," Kygo said. He bent and picked up the sword I had dropped. Kinra's sword.

"Neither am I, Eona," Dela said.

"No, both of you must go. I don't know if I can protect you."

Kygo shook his head. "I will not leave you alone with Lord Ido."

The Dragoneye circled on the spot, watching the dragons, his hands raking his hair.

Kygo looked at Dela. "Take Tozay down to the lower steps. I want you both safe. That is my command."

Dela hesitated.

"*Go!*"

Dela bowed. "Yes, Your Majesty."

She passed me the bundle. The rope of pearls writhed beneath the cloth, jabbing my hands. "Eona, please be careful," she said. "I have already lost . . ." She tipped her head back, her throat jumping with the strain of grief. "Just be careful."

Together, she and Kygo hauled Tozay to his feet. He was still dazed, but he could walk. Dela took his weight and helped him limp to the edge of the platform. As she supported him down the first step, she looked back and pressed her fist against her chest. The warrior salute. I did not feel like a warrior. I felt terrified. I remembered Ryko in the palace alley telling me I had a warrior's courage. He'd had such faith in me then. And he had died for that faith.

I lifted my fist to my chest. For Ryko, and for Dela. With a nod, she turned and led Tozay down the steps.

"What do I have to do?" I asked Ido.

"Go up on the dais," he said, nodding at the small raised stage. "It is the highest point, and once the *Righi* has ignited the Imperial Pearl, the Mirror Dragon will come for it."

I looked at the red dragon. Her huge eyes watched me. Kinra's plea whispered in my mind: *Make it right.* I followed Ido across the platform to the dais, holding the squirming bundle away from my body. Kygo walked beside me.

"You've got the Imperial Pearl?" I asked.

He opened his palm. The surface of the gem swarmed with silvery leaps and flicks. "It's hot," he said.

I laid my fingers across the soft pale curve. It was now almost hot enough to burn.

We stood together for a moment, the Imperial Pearl between our hands. "You are a queen to me," Kygo said softly. He pressed his lips against my forehead.

"Very touching," Ido drawled. "Eona, get on the dais."

I gave him a sour look and stepped up on to the small

stage. Kygo stationed himself nearby, sword angled at Ido.

Beyond the circle of swaying dragons, the ragged remains of the two armies watched from a wary distance. The dark clouds above us had swamped the bright day, casting an early gloom over the plain. The air still swirled with the spicy scent of the dragons surrounding us, the heat as much from their earthly presence as from the hot wind that whipped my hair back.

I took a deep breath and unwrapped the black folio, dropping the torn remnants of the shirt. The white pearls snapped straight up, as if they were testing the air, then planed across my hand and along my arm, dragging the folio behind them. Two quick, rattling coils and the book was bound to my arm. The folio's acid words rose into my mind, burning my pathways, whispering their ancient power. Ido stood hunched before the dais, his arms wrapped around his body. No doubt he remembered the pain of the *Righi* too.

"It is in my head," I said. My mouth tasted like it was full of blood and ash.

"Chant it," Ido said.

The words were waiting. Their bitter keen held the bound *Hua* of all twelve dragons, and the last cold echoes of Kinra. The chant quickened on my tongue and reached out to the beasts in the circle. It pulled the thrumming energy from their pearls and wove it into the blistering song that hissed from me with the fire of life and death.

The dragons answered the chant with a shrieking chorus of their own. Through the terrible sound, the Rat Dragon bellowed urgently, the blue iridescent pearl beneath his chin pulsing with azure-tipped flame. His call silenced the other beasts. They all turned to watch as he lowered his huge wedge head and gently placed his barrel-sized gem on the ground between his opal claws. The separation of dragon and pearl shuddered through the folio and my chant; an ache of loss and hope that brought a sting of tears to my eyes. With a soft cry, the Rat Dragon nudged the sphere with his flared muzzle, rolling the source of his power and wisdom a length from his opal claws.

I glanced across at Ido. He crouched in defeat as he watched his dragon give up the pearl that held their twelve-year bond.

Next to the Rat Dragon, the purple Ox Dragon threw back his horned head and howled his own song of pain and hope. The soft lavender scales under his chin and around his pearl shimmered with violet flames. He lowered his head and gently dropped the pearl onto the ground, tapping it forward with a careful amethyst claw until it lightly touched the Rat Dragon's blue pearl. As soon as it rocked into place, the green Tiger Dragon lifted his head and sang his own loss. One by one, the male dragons called to their bound spirits in the folio and placed their pearls on the ground.

I felt every longing cry resonate through the folio until eleven enormous dragon pearls—alive with flicks of colored flame—lay side by side in a circle on the trampled earth around the platform.

Only one pearl was missing.

The final call came from the Mirror Dragon. She lifted her

majestic head, the glossy crimson scales of throat and chest reflecting the blaze of gold flame from her pearl. Her throbbing call rose up like a heartbeat through my chant. She extended her huge scaled muzzle over the platform, the horselike nostrils flaring, the soft wind of her breath scented with her cinnamon power. Under the curve of heavy horns, her dark, ancient gaze held me inside the endless cycle of life and death—and the dragons' long wait for release.

Make it right.

"Give Eona the Imperial Pearl," Ido ordered Kygo. "Now!"

Kygo reached up, and the gem's smooth heat rolled into my palm. The chant in my head and on my tongue stoked the fire within the heart of their egg. Its silver energy leaped into incandescence.

"Eona, you have to give the pearl to the Mirror Dragon," Ido said.

But I already knew the ancient path to renewal: it sang in my blood and bones.

First quicken the spark of life within the luminous egg, then press its power into the gold flames of the red dragon's pearl. Once that was done, I could release the dragon *Hua* caught in the black folio and send it back to the beasts so that they could die and be reborn.

But the acid words whispered another pathway, too: a way that held all the power of the world. *Take the twelve dragon spirits into yourself*, it hissed. *Take the power waiting to create the new, and leave the old to wither and die. Take everything.*

Ido's words. The black folio's words.

The Mirror Dragon lifted her huge chin, offering her golden wisdom to me as she had once offered it to me in the arena. The *Righi*'s words seared into the Imperial Pearl, igniting its silver *Hua* into a ball of white fire that stung my hands with sharp flicks of power. This was the start of it. And the end of it.

"Good-bye," I whispered to my dragon.

Reaching up, I pressed the white flames against the gold at her throat. The two surfaces flared and melded together, the force thrusting my hands away. With a soft cinnamon sigh, the Mirror Dragon swung her head down, the huge glowing pearl dropping to the ground. She nosed it into place. As the circle of pearls closed, gold flame leapt from dragon pearl to dragon pearl, igniting each sphere into bright gold heat.

The Necklace of the Gods.

I felt the chant change within me, the hissing command shifting into a lilting call. The *Righi* was opening the way for the twelve bound spirits.

Kygo turned to me, his smile full of wonder.

I saw the blur of movement from the corner of my eye, but there was no time to cry out. Kygo's reflexes swung his sword up, but Ido was already at the end of his leap. All of his body weight drove the long knife into Kygo's back. Ido's mouth was a bared snarl of effort as he twisted the blade, arching Kygo against his body into gasping shock. The chant froze in my throat. Kygo staggered sideways and landed heavily on the dais, Kinra's sword still locked in his hand. The white pearls around my arm heaved and shivered as the Mirror Dragon screamed, her protest soaring above the roar of the male dragons.

"*No!*" I fell to my knees beside him. "*Kygo!*"

He gulped for breath, the agonized gasp bubbling with blood. I touched his cheek. Already cold with shock. Or was it my own icy horror? My other hand hovered over the knife hilt embedded in his back.

"I wouldn't pull that out if I were you," Ido said. "I aimed for the same place where the arrow hit me. He's got a few minutes."

"What are you doing?" I cried.

Ido walked up to the dais, observing Kygo's struggle for breath.

"Hurts, doesn't it?" he said.

Weakly, Kygo gripped the hilt of the sword and tried to lift it, but it dropped from his grasp and clattered off the dais, landing at Ido's feet. The Dragoneye kicked the blade away, then looked down at me.

"I'm going to give you a real choice now, Eona," he said. "If you take all the power with me, you can heal him. Stop his pain and save his life. Or, if you insist on releasing the dragons, you can watch him drown in his own blood."

"You bastard!" I went for him, my hands tensed into claws. My knees hit the edge of the dais as Ido jumped back out of range.

"I'm just making it easy for you to have what you really want," he said.

Kygo's fingers caught my sleeve. "Don't do it." Blood flecked his lips. "Don't give it to him."

"So much *honor*, just like his father," Ido said sarcastically. "I'd say between the dragons and the amount of blood he's spitting up, you haven't got long to make up your mind."

He was right. Kygo's skin had a bluish tinge around his nose and mouth, and the *Righi* was building within me again, pushing past my shock to call the bound *Hua* of the dragons. I could not move, paralyzed by the impossibility of the choice. Kygo or the dragons. My heart or my duty. All the reasons to save the dragons raged through me: Kinra, atonement, the land, the people, the future. And only one reason to save Kygo, tolling through me over and over again.

I loved him.

"Take what you want, Eona," Ido said. "You have done it all along, so why stop now?"

A slight smile curved his lips. He was so confident that I would agree. I had turned my back and he had struck like a snake.

"You'll have everything, Eona. Including him." Ido nudged Kygo's foot with his own. "It is not so bad to have her control your will, boy." Ido's smile turned sly. "I look forward to sharing your compulsion power, Eona. And I think you will enjoy sharing my knowledge. It's what you've wanted all along."

"I just wanted to be a Dragoneye!"

"You wanted power," he said. "This way you get it. And you get to save Kygo."

The Mirror Dragon screeched. Her huge red head swayed from left to right above her blazing pearl. The clouds above us flickered with the light of the flames, reflecting the intense heat.

"All right," I clenched my fists. "All right."

"Eona, no!" Kygo lifted his head, the effort forcing a bright trickle of blood from the corner of his mouth. His cold fingers touched my hand, drawing me closer until my forehead rested against his own. I felt his labored breath on my cheek, the metallic smell of his blood in every soft warm gasp. "Do what is right," he whispered, the words costing him precious air.

I pressed my lips against his cold skin. "I don't know what is right."

"Yes, you do, *Naiso*." He fell back, panting.

I stood, legs trembling. He wanted me to release the dragons. Yet, if I did, I would lose him and I would lose the Mirror Dragon. I would lose everything. If I took all the power with Ido, I would destroy the dragons and take Kygo's throne and will from him. He would hate me. I would be left with only power. I would be Ido. A wave of rage swept over me. There was no way to win this battle.

"You must do it now, Eona," Ido said.

For one despair-ridden moment, I wanted the dragons' power to explode through the land—to destroy everything in its path, and take away this terrible choice. But I had to choose, and I could not let Kygo die.

I stepped down from the dais, every harsh clicking breath from my beloved pushing me toward the Dragoneye. Ido picked up Kinra's sword and drew its blade along his hand, inhaling with pleasure as it sliced into his flesh.

"Your turn." He caught my free hand and turned it over. My palm was already cut from the gold-clawed setting of the Imperial Pearl. My eyes fixed on the moonstone and jade hilt as Ido dragged the sword tip along the same wound. A faint echo of Kinra's rage shivered through me. Was her *Hua* still in the folio too? My fingers curled around the stinging draw of fresh blood.

Ido sent the weapon spinning across the boards. "Dragoneye blood to break an ancient Dragoneye binding," he said. "When the *Righi* releases the dragons, we must hold on to the folio to take their power."

He grabbed my hand and pressed it across the white pearls that clamped the folio to my arm, then slapped his own blood-sticky palm over my knuckles. I felt the pearl rope shift and shiver.

"All right. Now we take what is ours. This is our destiny, Eona." The triumph in his eyes made them as gold as the ring of flames around us. "Call the dragons out of the folio."

"This is not destiny," I spat. "This is ambition made from betrayal and murder. Do not dress your atrocities in the garb of the gods."

He tilted his head, the harsh angle showing the ruthless set of his jaw and the deep lines of brutality from nose to mouth. How could I ever have thought him handsome? His core was rotten and hollow.

"Call it what you will," he said "But you are standing here with me in the midst of the String of Pearls, and we are about to take all the power in the world. It feels like destiny to me." He closed his hand over mine, grinding my bones together. "Call the dragons."

Kinra, help me, I prayed. *If you are still within the folio, help me.*

On a deep breath, I let the *Righi* rise again. The words boiled into my mind, a seething summons that rushed through my pathways. Beside me, Ido flinched as he felt the blistering force reach through our bodies to the dragon *Hua* caught within the folio. It was a torrent of fire through every vein and muscle, bubbling up behind my eyes and drying my mouth into a silent scream. The agony of it pressed me against the brace of Ido's body. I felt the bindings around the dragons' *Hua* blaze and burn, opening their human-made prison of blood and greed.

And I felt another spirit: the faint cool echo of an ancient warrior woman, my ancestress. Kinra.

They are free! I am free! Her joyful voice soared over the disintegrating bonds of the folio.

Free. One simple word and all of my pain crystallized into a terrible certainty. I could not take the renewal power. I could not destroy the hope of rebirth for land and dragon. This was the last chance to right a terrible wrong. The chant stopped in my throat. Time hung still in a silent, bodiless, breathless moment of truth. I had to release the dragons' *Hua.* I had to give it back. And it was going to kill Kygo.

The chant burst out of me again, my scream of anguish swept up into the howling rhythm of release.

Kinra, help me, I prayed. *Help me make it right.*

The rope of white pearls heaved against my hand. Kinra's cool presence rushed into me, the liberated dragon *Hua* following like a tornado made of fire and power. Every one of my nerves was stretched to the breaking point, my mind unraveling into the maelstrom of raw energy, throat shredding with the acid chant that pulled their *Hua* into the conduit that was my body. It slammed through me and into Ido, the force making us both stagger.

"Eona, hold the power," he yelled.

"No!"

He thrust his face into mine. "What are you doing?"

The hissing song of chaos poured through me. I bared my teeth into a smile, and in my mind I saw Dillon's death's-head grin. The *Righi* was life and death. And so was I.

Ido closed his hand around my throat, trying to choke off the words, but the *Hua* still came. Twelve spirit tethers gathering within us with the force of a cyclone. Ido wrenched at my hand, bending my fingers away from the pearls. A thin bone snapped, but I felt no pain. Everything was subsumed by the whirling, blazing power.

Against the backdrop of gold flames and plunging dragons, I saw men scrambling onto the platform, cringing away from the inferno rising from the circle of pearls. The familiar shapes of Dela and Tozay crouched among wild-eyed soldiers and resistance fighters, everyone cowering together against the intense heat and the huge thrashing, screaming beasts.

Ido dug his fingers under the white pearls. "I will not lose my power!" The spittle spray of his rage was cool against my scorching skin. *"I am the Rat Dragoneye!"*

I heaved against his weight. "I am the Mirror Dragoneye—*and I give the power back.*"

I felt the Mirror Dragon's howl shift into a cry of joy.

Ido slammed his fist into my jaw, the sound of bone against bone loud in my head. I felt no pain, although the heavy impact knocked me backward. We both staggered, tied together by Ido's iron grip on the pearls. Out of the corner of my eye, I saw Kygo pulling himself along the dais, every tiny shift forward shuddering through his determined face.

Ido yanked at the folio. *"Give it to me!"*

The end of the pearl rope curled and snapped across his hand. He forced his fingers beneath it again and ripped at the tight coils, his desperate strength sliding the folio down my arm to my wrist. With a grunt of victory he wrenched the folio free, the power unraveling out of me and pouring into his body.

I reeled from the sudden loss and crashed to the ground. The pearls swung out in a snapping circle, then wrapped around Ido's hands.

He looked down at me, his eyes black pits of *Gan Hua*. "I do not need you anymore. I can hold this power by myself."

I scrabbled backward. His body was silhouetted against the flames. Energy bathed his skin, casting him into shimmering silver light. The power of the ages, the power of all twelve dragons. And Ido believed he could hold it by himself.

I drew in a deep breath, hot air scorching the cavities of my chest, and found the pathway to the energy world. The platform around me warped and shuddered into the celestial plane. I flinched under the assault of blinding light and the writhing spectrum of color that leaped from the gold flames around the dragon pearls. Ido's energy body swarmed with silver and black *Hua*. His seven points of power from sacrum to crown circled at a speed that blurred them into solid spheres of bright color: red, orange, yellow—and then the stunted green heart point. Never truly changed.

A wedge of darkness in all the bright fury drew my eyes to the purple sphere in his crown, the center of enlightenment. The black gap was still there like a deep wound within its spinning purple vigor. And it was getting bigger. The silver energy in his body pulsed and swelled, again and again. Every throbbing influx of power forced the gap wider and wider. Suddenly it split apart, a white-hot bolt of dragon *Hua* bursting from its spinning center.

"Ido, you cannot hold it," I screamed. "Give it back to them. Let it go!"

His silvered eyes found mine. "I have it all, Eona! I am a god!"

"Let it go, now!"

His heart point exploded first. The green sphere burst under the pressure of the dragon power, a bright emerald flare that died into a dark hole in his chest. The orange sacral point was next, its flash cascading into his yellow delta, tiny exploding suns that left darkness in their wake. He writhed in agony as the blue and indigo points heaved and vaporized.

For a long moment, the split purple sphere in his crown spun with all the power of the world. Then it erupted into a blazing torrent of *Hua*, streaming into the waiting dragons. The roaring power engulfed Ido's body in gold and silver flames. I saw him reach out toward me. Then he was gone, incinerated into a glowing spiral of ash and dust, our link severed into searing loss. The black folio dropped onto the platform, the white pearls rattling around its leather binding like dry bones.

The celestial plane snapped back into the earthly platform. I stared at the charred space on the wooden boards.

Lord Ido was dead, consumed by the dragon power he had craved. All that ambition and drive, gone. I took a breath, a strangled half-sob within it. We had been bound together through power and pain. And pleasure. But he had betrayed and tortured and murdered: he did not deserve my grief. Yet there was a part of me that mourned him—the part that had smiled at his sly humor, felt the slow touch of his hand and the thrill of his power. The part of me that had once thought he could change.

Lord Ido was dead, and even in death the man divided me.

I hauled myself on to my hands and knees and crawled to the dais. My true grief was waiting for me, sprawled on his side, breath so shallow that it hardly moved his chest. His eyelids flickered as I stroked his face, cold and clammy although his skin was reddened by the heat. He licked parched lips and opened his eyes. They were already dulled and unfocused.

"Ido?" His voice was just a wisp of wet breath.

"Dead."

"Good."

I cupped his cheek, the pain of my broken bones and scorched skin suddenly sharp and full. "I have no power to heal."

He tried to lift his hand, but got no farther than a shift of his wrist. "Did right," he whispered. I slid my hand under his curled fingers, the slack weight bringing a sob into my throat. He swallowed, gathering moisture to make the words. "The dragons?"

"They have their power. They are renewing."

The corners of his beautiful mouth lifted. "Let me see."

Around us, the flames from the circle of pearls were like a curtain of leaping gold and red, the shapes of the dragons glimpsed behind it. Carefully, I settled Kygo's head onto my lap, the pain of the shift shivering through his body. The knife hilt still protruded from his back. Dark blood seeped from the sucking wound, the gloss of it catching the flicker of the gold fire. I carefully pressed my thumb and finger around the wound, trying to stop the leak of his precious breath.

The Mirror Dragon lifted her head and sang—a long rising scale that called beyond the earthly plane. The sound was like kindling to the gold flames. Every pearl flared up into high, bright heat. One by one, the male dragons moved forward and stepped into the fire of their pearls. A scorching wind rolled off the fierce combustion, the intense blaze snapping and roaring around the old beasts. The charred smell of dragon death was thick and harsh in my aching throat as each one of their huge bodies was reduced to ash. Finally, only the Mirror Dragon stood behind her pearl. She turned her head toward me, her gold and bronze flecked mane already ablaze as she stepped into the fire of her rebirth. I moaned as the flames overwhelmed her, drying the tears in my eyes into stinging salt.

The circle of fire exploded upward into bright embers that swirled and danced in multicolored streams. The huge dragon pearls cracked and split.

My breath caught as shapes emerged within the flames: curled horns, long, elegant muzzles and muscled legs, talons that sparked with the hard color of precious stones. The new Horse Dragon emerged first from his flaming pearl—bigger than the old beast, his magnificent orange scales steaming with heat, pale watersilk wings flicking out into a tentative stretch. He shook himself, his soft ocher beard shifting to show the gleam of the apricot pearl beneath his chin. The neverending cycle. As he launched himself up into the dark clouds, the flames of his pearl guttered and died. I craned my head back to watch his flight; a wide circle around the plain, his big body sleek and supple in the air. With a loud, triumphant call, he disappeared into the celestial plane.

"The land will be well," Kygo whispered.

We watched as, one by one, the male dragons were reborn.

New wings stretching, tongues tasting the air, the huff and blow of spicy breath, and the first flights that circled above us, ending in the long call of triumph and return to the celestial plane.

Only one flaming pearl remained. I held my breath as it split and fell apart, the leap of gold flames around it tinged with crimson.

Her horns emerged first, curled and tapered over her broad forehead, the fall of gold mane shifting in the fire-wind of rebirth. She rose out of the dying flames of her egg, her massive body gleaming with red scales that graduated from rose-blush around her eyes to a deep crimson across her muscular shoulders and legs. She lifted her flared muzzle and sniffed the air, the new pearl nestled under her chin a paler gold than the one before. Silk-thin wings spread and flapped once, then folded back against the long sinuous curve of her scarlet spine. She opened a curl of ruby claws, and I saw a tiny, luminous orb cupped within; the Imperial Pearl, reborn with the dragons. The ruby talons closed over it. Lowering her head, she looked directly at me. I leaned forward, hoping to see recognition in her great spirit eyes. Their dark endlessness held the wisdom of the world, but they did not hold me.

She was not my Mirror Dragon.

The harsh truth hit me: I had lost my dragon. Without even realizing it, I had expected that our union would cross the bridge of her rebirth. But it had not.

I felt Kygo's body tense against mine, the wheeze of his breath hardening into a harsh rasp. I knew that sound: the death rattle. His agonized eyes were fixed on my face. No, I could not bear it. I could not lose him, too. I cradled his head in my arms, trying to anchor him to the earthly plane. Perhaps if I held him close enough, he would not walk the path to his ancestors.

"Kygo, do not go, " I pleaded. "Do not go."

Sudden screams lifted my head. The men who had taken refuge on the top steps were diving out of the way as the new Mirror Dragon's huge muzzle planed across the platform and stopped a length or so above my head, the heat of her breath carrying the unfamiliar spice of nutmeg. I stared past the razored fangs and looked up into her dark eyes, my heart pounding. Within the wise depths of her gaze, I saw something shift. An echo of an old bond. Slowly, she lowered her great chin and delicately nuzzled Kygo's chest. She drew in a breath and on its sweet nutmeg exhale, golden *Hua* flowed into his body.

She was healing him.

I remembered Caido's wisdom and grabbed the knife hilt, yanking the blade from Kygo's body. The wound closed as the steel slid from his flesh, his cold skin warming under my touch. With a stuttering gasp, his breath settled into a deep, regular rhythm. Then I felt the soft touch of her muzzle brush against my head. Her power flowed into me: a glorious rush of joy and gratitude. The golden *Hua* pulled the bone of my snapped finger together, knitting it back into unity, and soothed my scorched skin into smooth ease. My own breath broke into a long hard sob.

I stretched up and stroked the ridged silk scales, hoping she understood my joy and gratitude, too. She crooned and pulled her head away. As she launched herself into the sky, Kygo's eyes opened. He spread his hand against his chest, pushing himself up onto an elbow.

"I can breathe," he said. He reached over his shoulder, his fingertips sweeping the flat, unmarked muscle of his back. "I thought you could not heal?"

"I can't." I pushed through the pang of loss. Kygo was alive and the dragons were free. It would be enough. "The Mirror Dragon healed you."

He sat up. "But you held me here. I was so close to the garden of the gods, I could hear my father's voice." He pressed his forehead to mine, dark eyes somber. "Then I heard your voice." His head tilted until his mouth was only a warm breath from my own. "My *Naiso*." The title softened against my lips into a kiss.

The triumphant call of the Mirror Dragon broke into the sweet moment. She was returning to the celestial plane. Kygo took my hand, and together we stood as the great dragon circled above the platform, her cries echoing around us. She arrowed her body upward, the dark ring of clouds breaking apart as her huge crimson body cut through them. With one last spiraling plunge she disappeared from the brightening sky.

Silence settled across the platform. Slowly, soldiers and resistance fighters clambered to their feet, their awe gathering them into a loose semicircle before us. Farther back, Dela helped Tozay to stand. Both alive. I sent a small prayer of thanks. And another prayer for Ryko—*May he walk in the garden of the gods.*

The semicircle parted as Dela led Tozay to us. Although the general's face was pale and drawn with pain, shrewd sense was back in his eyes.

"His Majesty is truly blessed by the gods and beloved of the dragons," he said loudly as he and Dela limped through the ragged collection of men. "He and his *Naiso* have returned the Imperial Pearl to the spirit beasts and brought renewal and peace to our land." Slowly he turned, eyeing the reverent men. "Bow before your true emperor. And bow before the last Dragoneye."

One by one, the men on the platform knelt before us in low obeisance. With Dela's help, Tozay slowly lowered himself to his knees, his keen glance meeting Kygo's in silent strategy. The Contraire gracefully bowed beside him, a fleeting smile answering mine. She had lost so much, yet she still had the strength to smile.

Kygo straightened, his hand tightening around mine. "Rise," he ordered the bowing men. "Balance has been restored to the heavens and earth, but we have work ahead of us to restore order to the empire."

Balance in the heavens. Could I still see the dragons? On a deep breath I sought the pathways of my mind-sight, shifting into the familiar streaming colors and swirling *Hua* of the energy world. High above us, the Circle of Twelve was complete, all the dragons in their celestial domains. As if she recognized my presence, the new Mirror Dragon turned her huge crimson head toward me. I felt her curious spirit brush against mine, and within it was the soft cinnamon joy of a remembered bond.

Author's Note

The Empire of the Celestial Dragons is not a real country or culture. It is a fantasy world that was at first inspired by the history and cultures of China and Japan, but rapidly became a land of imagination with no claim to historical or cultural authenticity. Nevertheless, I did research many aspects of ancient and modern cultures, which I used as a springboard to create the empire and the dragons. If you are interested in the research road I traveled, I have detailed some of my favorite findings and listed some of the books I used on my Web site at **www.alisongoodman.com.au**.

Acknowledgments

My sincere thanks to:

The fabulous four: my husband, Ron; my best friend and writing soul sister, Karen McKenzie; and Charmaine and Doug Goodman, my parents.

My wonderful agent, Jill Grinberg, and her associates.

The brilliant team at Penguin: Sharyn November, editorial director/senior editor extraordinaire; Tony Sahara, senior art director, who drew and designed both the beautiful *Eona* hardcover and *Eon* paperback cover; Jim Hoover, associate art director, who designed the very stylish interior; Janet Pascal, keen-eyed executive production editor; Abigail Powers, production editor; Gerard Mancini, associate publisher; Kim Wiley Luna, associate managing editor; Laurence Tucci, production director; and Andrea Crimi, assistant production manager.

The Young and Jackson's Writing Group: Karen, Judy, Jane, Steven, Christine, Janet, Paul, and Glynis.

The madcap and ever supportive Clan Destine group.

Antoni Jach and the Masterclass, and in particular Dr. Leah Kaminsky for her medical expertise.

Simon Higgins for his sword training, battle and weaponry knowledge, and unfailing support.

Morgan Grant Buchanan for his tai chi expertise.

Pam Horsey, for waiting to read, and for her warm friendship and enthusiasm.

And of course, the sweet hound from hell, Xander.

In addition to *Eon* and *Eona*, ALISON GOODMAN is also the author of the acclaimed *Singing the Dogstar Blues*, which received the Aurealis Award and was named an ALA Best Book for Young Adults, and the adult crime thriller *Killing the Rabbit*.

Alison lives in Melbourne, Australia, with her husband, Ron, and their Machiavellian Jack Russell terrier, Xander. She was a D. J. O'Hearn Memorial Fellow at Melbourne University, holds a Master of Arts, and has taught creative writing at the postgraduate level.

Visit her Web site at **www.alisongoodman.com.au**.

Turn the page for the first chapter of Alison Goodman's debut novel, featuring a heroine every bit as strong as Eona!

My Mother and Other Aliens

I saw the assassin before she saw me. She was eating noodles at one of the hawker bars, watching the university gates. I knew she was a killer because old Lenny Porchino had pointed her out to me at the Buzz Bar two nights ago.

"Hey, take a look at that skinny kid with the frizzy hair," he'd said, nodding his head towards the doors behind me.

We were sitting in Lenny's private booth, hidden from general view. I shifted in my seat until I could see her. Skinny, frizzy, and mean.

"What about her?" I said, banging my harmonica against the flat of my hand. I had just finished jamming with the band and my harp was full of slag.

"That's Tori Suka. She's a culler for the hyphen families. If she's in town, someone's gonna die."

Tori Suka didn't fit my idea of someone who would work for the big-money families. Too rough. She was wearing the same kind of student gear as I was: black long-wear jeans, matching jacket. Standard stuff you can get from any machine.

One of Lenny's waiters came up to the table. He was all nerves.

"Mr. Porchino, there's a guy in the crapper done too much smack. Looks like he's croaking it."

Lenny shook his head.

"Don't know why they still go for that antique screte," he said. He looked over at me. "Joss, don't ever do any of that old-fashioned powder. Does you in and wrecks your looks." He turned to the waiter. "Get Cross and Lee to dump him outside St. Vinnies."

The waiter weaved through the crowd towards two bouncers lounging against the wall. Lenny watched until he saw Cross and Lee move towards the toilets.

"Suka's not the best gun around, but she gets the job done," he said. "I wonder who the mark is? And who's hiring?" He was pulling at the ends of his mustache. Lenny always made it his business to know who was putting out a contract.

I looked at the kid again. She was leaning against the bar, throwing nut meats into her mouth. She chewed with her mouth open. How did she become an assassin? Did Careers tell her she was suited to murder?

Lenny's son, Porchi, strutted over from the bar and slid next to me in the booth. He pressed his thigh against mine. I moved away from him. Porchi's been trying to snork me since we met after I pulled his dad out of the river a year ago. Old Lenny had "fallen in" the Yarra with a bit of help from some DeathHeads on a grand-final rampage. I happened to be cruising the area and grabbed Lenny out of the river before he was mulched by the cleaning system.

Later Porchi told me that half the DeathHeads were wiped out when their hangout was bio-bombed. Very ugly. Lenny believes in paying his debts: I saved his life, so now he looks out for me. I've even got a permanent bedroom upstairs at the Buzz Bar. I think Lenny's got some fantasy about me and Porchi breeding little Porchinos and living happily ever after. Like I said, Porchi would be happy to get stuck into the breeding part of that scheme.

Lenny is the closest thing I've had to family this past year. I haven't actually seen my mother for about eighteen months. She's always in production or in a meeting. I end up talking to Lewis, her secretary, via CommNet. Reverse charges, of course.

"I'm sorry, Joss, Ingrid is unavailable right now," he always says with his ferret smile.

"Well, tell her I called. She does remember who I am, doesn't she?"

"I'm sure she has a vague memory. I'll pass on the message."

Then he signs off before I bash my head through the screen.

Let's fact it, Ingrid Aaronson is not going to win the Mother of the Year award. Not that she needs it. She's won nearly every other award that a news presenter and VR star can win. She's even won the Thinking Man's Lust-Beast award, which is funny when you know she didn't even snork anyone to make me. I'm a comp-kid. Straight from the petri dish to you. Lust factor: nil. Ease factor: ten.

Sometimes I wonder if the petri dishes got mixed up and I should be living in the mall-highrises with Mamasan and Papasan. You see, my mother is all gold hair, big blue eyes, maximum curves, and honey skin (rejuvenated twice now, but who's counting?). I'm all black straight hair, brown cat's eyes, and pale, pale skin.

Once I asked Ingrid how many people were used to make me. A comp-kid like me can have up to ten gene donors. The bioengineers just split different genes and stick them together using viruses. It's like being glued together by the common cold. Ingrid swore she only used one male donor. Name unknown, of course. If that's the case, Ingrid's Nordic heritage has been bashed into submission by my father's genes. She's positive I also inherited my attitude problem from him. She says being chucked out of twelve schools must be genetic. Sometimes I imagine he knows I'm his daughter and is keeping tabs on me, waiting for the right moment to show himself. Yeah, sure.

I swung my pack onto my shoulder and walked past the noodle bar towards the university gates. The assassin eyeballed me as I passed her. She was smiling. I was tempted to stop and ask her about career opportunities, but Tonio Bel Hussar-Rigdon suddenly grabbed me on the shoulder. He was in dress uniform.

"You're late," he said. "Camden-Stone's so mad he's ready to expel you on the spot."

Professor Camden-Stone was always threatening to expel me. You'd have thought the Acting Director of the

Centre for Neo-Historical Studies would have better things to do than pick on a lowly student. Wrong again. Old Stony Face was building a career out of making my life miserable. Tonio thinks Camden-Stone has the hots for me. If he has, I'd hate him to really love me. He'd probably put a laser through my head. Even Lenny has dropped a word of warning about the dear professor. He told me Camden-Stone beat the screte out of a girl a couple of years ago and had to pay a lot of money to keep it quiet. You've got to wonder how a creep like Camden-Stone wound up in charge of the world's only time-travel training center.

Tonio was shifting from foot to foot, eager to get back to the ceremony. According to the campus bookies, he was going to be my time-jumping partner.

Every year, the top fifty first-year students at the university can apply to study at the Centre. If you're interested, you have to take extra classes with Camden-Stone and go through tons of tests. There's only twelve first-year places at the Centre, so it's ultra competitive. I just scraped in: number eleven. Tonio Bel Hussar-Rigdon was number eight.

Tonio wasn't bad for a hyphen kid, but he was so nervy it made me want to scream. At least he wasn't a wankman like all the other hyphens. Then again, it wouldn't have mattered if he was Mr. Nice Guy of the universe. The last thing I wanted was a partner. Especially a partner who lived, studied, and worked with me. Talk about cramp your style. There was no way I was going to survive six years living in the same quarters as Tonio. Or anyone, for that matter.

"Come on," Tonio urged. "You've got to get changed and down to the Donut. Partnering is about to start."

I looked through the gates at the Donut. The huge circular hall was buzzing with vid-crews. There was even a small group of protesters standing behind a banner. Something was up. The ceremony to partner time-jumping students didn't normally rate channel time or demonstrators.

"I thought partnering was supposed to be tomorrow," I said.

"No one could find you to tell you what's happened. How come you don't carry a screen?" He leaned closer, shifting into gossip mode. "Listen to this. They've moved the ceremony for diplomatic reasons. A flaphead is coming into our time-jump class."

Tonio stepped back, a smug grin all over his pointy little face. This was big news and he knew it. The university had finally accepted one of the Chorian aliens as a student. Not only had they accepted one, but they had shoved it in the middle of our time-jumping class.

"But, that makes thirteen in our group," I said. "It won't have a partner."

"Robbie's been dropped," Tonio said softly. "He was number twelve on the list. I don't think he's been sober since Stony told him."

Poor Robbie. He must be burning. I was lucky they weren't letting two Chorians into the course. I would have been skidding on my cheeks, too.

"Come on," Tonio said, pulling me towards the gates.

I let him pull me because I was in memory overdrive. Ever since I first saw the Chorians on the vid-news, I've been obsessed with them. I was ten and expected to see some kind of giant insect. Talk about chronic disappointment. Two arms, two legs, and a head with two eyes, just like us. Then again not many humans have two noses, two mouths, and two huge double-jointed ears that flap around.

The Chorians are really into this Noah deal: everything in twos. They even have two sexes in one, like slugs. When the anti-alien lobby got wind of that, they started calling the Chorians "sluggos." The government PR people knocked themselves out trying to stop that one. The campaign posters were a scream; a big slug with a red cross through it. Really subtle. I suppose it worked. Now everyone calls them flapheads.

When I first heard the Chorians were hermaphrodites, I thought they could snork themselves. You know, the ultimate wank. That sounded too good to be true, so I did some fancy detective work on the Net. I found out that self-snorking was out. Instead, two adults fertilize each other then each of them produces one child to form a birth pair. So every Chorian is a kind of twin. I've always thought it would be great to have a twin. Instant best friend.

A few years ago Ingrid made a documentary about the Chorians. She called it "Our New Friends from the Dog Star," which is a bad name for a bad documentary. The Chorians aren't even from Sirius A, the Dog Star. They're from a planet that has Sirius A as its sun and Sirius B as its white dwarf partner. Like everything else that has been written or made on the Chorians, Ingrid's doco was pretty short on information. At least it showed the original recording of the first contact. It's the funniest history vid I've ever seen.

Six or so years ago, the first delegation of Chorians appeared in Mall 26, just before it was joined to the Mall Network. The Chorians thought 26 was a center of government and the concert stage was parliament. A traditional Disney pantomime was playing, and it scared the hell out of them. Let's face it, an enormous mouse jumping around to tinny music isn't really the height of human culture. Of course, the panto audience went into panic mode and cleared out in about ten seconds. The only one left was poor old Mickey. So the Chorians were left standing alone in front of a stage with a big mouse cowering in the corner.

It took the government people exactly five and a half minutes to arrive, shunt Mickey off into the arms of a therapist, and set up their probe equipment. Meanwhile the Chorians were trying to say hi, mind to mind. They quickly worked out we're not telepathic, so they scanned the brain of one of the feds to learn our lingo. Now Chorians speak by harmonizing words using their two mouths. Imagine being confronted by a group of aliens who all dipped imaginary hats then sang, "Howdy pilgrims, sure is nice to meet you."

The fed was a John Wayne fan.

Later the PR people made "howdy y'all" the most irritating phrase in the world. Whoever thought of setting it to lullaby music for the "Don't Be Afraid" campaign should've been shot.

About a year ago I bought an underground code from one of Porchi's contacts. It's supposed to only access RAVE-REVIVAL boards for free, but with a bit of jiggling, it also got into the government's news-boards. I found out why the Chorians were here. They've got some kind of time/space warp gizmo that lets them jump around the universe without a ship. Now they want to swap that technology for our time travel know-how. They need to learn how to manipulate time accurately. We want to learn how to get off Earth without expensive ships and space stations. So far none of these negotiations have appeared on the public vid-news channels. The PR people have been quiet, too. Although today, as Tonio pulled me past "official" vid-crews, it was obvious the government's policy of silence was about to change.

"This'll do," Tonio said, stopping in front of a reactor access hut. I opened the door. The faint thrumming of the reactor's cooling system buzzed through my feet. Tonio let go of my arm.

"I'd say you've got about thirty seconds to get changed and get back to the Donut. I'll see you there." He ran towards the crowd.

Tonio was right. I had to change into my dress uniform. Too bad it was still hanging in Lenny's office at the Buzz Bar. Turning out for a ceremony in jeans and a T-shirt, even if they were regulation, was not going to go down well. I was heading towards expulsion number thirteen, but this time I wasn't happy about it. And Ingrid would really crack the kuso. She'd spent a lot of money buying me a place in the university. She'd even bought mega shares in the Centre. The half-finished admin building is already being called the Aaronson Administration Complex.

I dumped my pack on the floor of the hut. All I could do was clean up a bit and hope Camden-Stone was in a good mood. I pulled on a new T-shirt and used the chrome handrail as an emergency mirror. What had I forgotten? My harp! I slipped it into my jeans pocket for luck and shoved my pack under some piping. Joss Aaronson was ready to meet her fate.

Go back to where the story began . . .

"Absolutely stunning . . . Full of palace intrigue and political maneuvering, soul-searching and tragic loss, trust and betrayal, and swashbuckling adventure of the first order . . . [*Eon*] deserves to be a smashing success."
—Orson Scott Card

★ "Goodman's characters hold built-in appeal for fans of Tamora Pierce . . . the plotting is elaborate, smart and capable of taking the audience by surprise."
—*Publishers Weekly*, starred review

"This intelligent, vividly written tale grips from the first page."
—*London Times*

★ "Mesmerizing . . . A world so richly imagined that it feels real."
—*Booklist*, starred review